Scorched

Siren Prophecy 2

by

Tricia Barr, Jesse Booth, Joanna Reeder,
Alessandra Jay & Angel Leya

Printed in the United States of America

First Printing, 2019

Cover image by Kim Cunningham

Published by Tricia Barr
First printed edition 2019

www.theshifteracademy.com

Chapter 1

Myreen

Moonlight glinted off razor-sharp fangs as a vampire materialized from the darkness of the alley and dove at her.

Myreen swerved to the right, dodging his attempted bite. Gripping the dagger in her hand, she rammed it at the vampire's back, aiming for his heart. But the vampire was ten times faster than she was and escaped out of sight before her blade could even get close.

She stumbled sideways, rushing to stabilize her footing so she could look around for her attacker. By the time she had squared her stance, the vampire had once again cloaked itself in shadow. She hated that trick. It had been the reason the vampire leader Draven and his followers had been able to surround her and her friends the other night.

Kol's battered body flashed in her mind, and suddenly the memory of that attack consumed her. The look on Draven's face as he appraised her from the sidelines while his gang assaulted her friends. The blast of the cannon that had shot Kol down. The heat of Juliet's flames that ultimately saved them. The feel of Kol's lips against hers when he surprised all of them and kissed her...

Reality hit her like a freight train as her assailant dove at her from behind, knocking the wind out of her as they both toppled to the ground. She rolled over as she coughed for breath, scrambling to get hold of the dagger once more to pierce the heart of the vampire that was now on top of her.

Again, she wasn't fast enough, and the vampire clutched her neck and wrenched her off the alley floor, pinning her against the brick wall with her feet dangling.

"Dear old Daddy won't mind if I take a bite," he hissed, then opened his mouth wide to plunge his teeth into her neck.

She screamed, then the vampire and the alley disappeared, and she fell like a ragdoll to the bright white floor of the simulation room.

The only door in the room opened, and Oberon walked in, offering his large hand. "What happened? You were doing so well, and then you just froze."

She took his hand and pulled herself up, gritting her teeth. "I just... got distracted."

A knowing look softened Oberon's stern countenance. "Thinking about Kol again?"

Myreen gave a solemn nod. "I never stopped. And this sim isn't helping. You designed it too similar to the alley we were in that night. It brings me back to it every time. Why can't I fight a vampire in the forest or something?"

"Because we don't live in the forest," Oberon answered.

"We live in the city. Chances are if you're attacked again, it will be in an alley just like before. You need to be ready."

She sighed and nodded again.

Oberon gave her a long look. "Let's call it a night," he said. "We've been at this all afternoon, and I think you've earned a break. A transition, rather. Get yourself cleaned up and report to the infirmary. Now that we know you're also part harpy, we need to begin your training in that area as well. Ms. Heather is waiting to give you your first lesson."

Exhaustion caught up to her, making her bones feel heavy. When he'd said they should stop, she hoped she could crash in her new bed in the avian wing. But no, only more training awaited her.

"And you'll be able to check on young Kol as well," Oberon added.

Myreen's ears perked at that. Darn Oberon, he knew exactly how to turn more work into its own reward. *That's what makes him the perfect teacher*, she thought. As tired as she felt, she would do whatever was needed if it meant she could see Kol.

After a quick shower in the locker room, she rushed over to the Nurse's Station. It felt odd to approach the door and find the hallway surrounding it empty. So many times she'd tried to come here to see Alessandra and the area had been swarming with mermaids who wouldn't let her pass. Her archenemy, Trish, had been convinced—and tried to convince everyone else—that Myreen had somehow been behind the vampire attack on Alessandra. Even after Alessandra woke up a few days ago and told everyone the truth, Trish's hatred for Myreen was still quite evident. In her eyes, though Myreen hadn't consciously directed the attack, Alessandra getting hurt was still her fault because the vampires had been after Myreen when they happened upon Alessandra.

Myreen was quite glad to no longer be staying in the oceanid wing. Trish had kicked her out after Alessandra had first been assaulted, and Myreen had run broken-hearted to her best friend and phoenix, Juliet. Juliet had welcomed Myreen with open arms and shared her room in the avian wing, but after Myreen was discovered to be a harpy, she was given her own room a few doors down from Juliet.

Getting to talk with Juliet late into the night, and even fall asleep in the same bed on occasion, was amazing! Myreen had never had close friends growing up, and she had never in her life been to a sleepover—the late nights with her best non-shifter friend Kenzie didn't really count. That went against one of her mother's three rules: No going out after dark. That, along with the other rules—no going into large bodies of water and no social media—had never made sense to Myreen. She had thought her mom was just overly paranoid. But the events of the last few months revealed that the rules were in place for one reason: the most dangerous vampire in the world was after Myreen, and he would stop at nothing to get his hands on her.

Myreen blinked away her reminiscent thoughts and opened the door to the infirmary.

Maya Heather, the school's lead harpy instructor and expert healer, was sitting in a chair beside the hospital bed on which Kol lay sleeping. It was rumored that angel sightings throughout history were truly harpies. Looking at Ms. Heather now, Myreen could believe it. She had frizzy, pale blond hair that seemed to absorb any light that touched it, giving the illusion of a glow around her head. Her heart-shaped face was softly pretty, with petite features surrounding eyes the color of a clear blue sky, even if they were hidden behind a pair of librarian-style glasses. Everything about her was welcoming and peaceful. Myreen was very grateful that Kol was in her care.

"Hello, Myreen," Ms. Heather welcomed, fluttering her dainty hands in a come-hither gesture. "Come."

Myreen walked forward, her eyes practically glued to Kol the whole time. Ms. Heather patted the seat on the chair next to hers, and Myreen sat.

"I'll bet you were quite surprised to learn that you are also a harpy," the woman said in her soft voice.

Myreen nodded. "Yes. But then again, I was surprised to learn that I'm a mermaid. Surprises keep happening. I've just learned to accept them as a part of my life, I guess." She shrugged.

Ms. Heather smiled. "You are very wise for your years."

Myreen didn't agree with that one bit.

"What do you know of harpies?" Ms. Heather asked.

"Well, I know that harpies are largely female because males are usually born human with no powers. I know that you can harness light and use it for several purposes, one of them being to heal." Myreen didn't know if there was more she should know, but at this moment, that was all she could come up with.

"Very good," Ms. Heather said. "The other day, you harnessed light to use it as a weapon. Am I correct in assuming this was your first time accessing the power of light?"

Myreen nodded.

"Using light as a weapon is a next level harpy skill," Ms. Heather said. "I'm quite impressed that you were able to do it on your very first try. Healing is the skill that comes most easily to harpies, so I would like for us to practice that."

"Okay," Myreen said, her voice wavering. She already knew where this was going, and she was afraid to fail at this like she had at being a mermaid.

"Your friend Kol looks bad, but he's much better off than he was when he was brought in three days ago. The lead pellets embedded in his skin prevented his body from healing naturally, and it was quite a difficult task to remove them without further damaging his internal organs. But as of early this morning, they have all been removed. His fractured ribs have been mended, and all his puncture wounds have been sealed. The only damage he still retains is bruising to his kidney."

Everything Ms. Heather said turned Myreen's stomach. She knew that Kol had been in bad condition after the attack, but she didn't know just how bad. It was all her fault. She was a weak, no-talent mermaid who needed protection.

"Would you like to help me heal his kidneys?" Ms. Heather looked at her with only kindness. Like this exercise was not an obligation but an invitation to which Myreen could object. How could she object? This was her fault, and she would do whatever she could to help Kol, to make it up to him.

"Yes," she replied. "But...how do I do that? I don't know anything about healing. How do you heal something you can't see?"

"I'll walk you through it," Ms. Heather said. "And as for your other concern, we'll be able to see it perfectly." She tapped some buttons on the screen of the black tablet on her lap, and a hologram of Kol's organs lit up in the open air inches above him, parallel to his body.

Myreen gasped as her eyes roamed the red-light diagram of

organs. This hologram was live, not just a static image, but current, and with moving parts. She could see the lungs expanding and contracting, his heart pumping with each beat. She had never seen technology like this before. She knew that the kitsunes at the school had invented some cool things, but this was beyond her imaginings.

"Do you see here?" Ms. Heather pointed to the one organ that was a deeper, maroon-ish color, whereas the others were red. Myreen recognized it as a kidney. "This is the bruising he sustained. If he were to walk out of here with it untended to, he'd still be functioning, but he would be in pain for weeks before it healed fully. And he may suffer long term urinary difficulty, as well as blood clots later in life. This is why we do our best to heal every wound fully, to avoid any and all complications for our patients, whether they be imminent, or in the distant future."

Myreen gulped. "So... what do I do?"

"Give me your hand," Ms. Heather said. "I'll help you with this first try. We'll do it together."

Myreen put her hand into Ms. Heather's, who then placed it over the spot on Kol's side, above his bruised kidney, and placed her own hand over Myreen's.

"Now close your eyes and clear your mind," Ms. Heather instructed.

Easier said than done, Myreen thought. Still she closed her eyes and tried her best to silence her noisy thoughts.

"Take a deep breath in." Ms. Heather inhaled deeply. "And then out." She pushed her breath out.

Myreen followed her example, and to her surprise, she felt calmer after doing so.

"Now focus only on your feelings toward the one you are hoping to help," Ms. Heather continued. "Focus on the way his pain makes you feel, on your desire to make him whole again."

That wasn't difficult at all. Myreen's desire to fix Kol was constantly at the forefront of her mind. She gave that her full attention, opening herself to it and letting it consume her. Sorrow and yearning washed over her like a rogue wave, and tears sprang, pushing themselves out of her closed eyelids.

A warmth kindled in her palm, mild at first, then growing in potency. When she opened her eyes, she saw a glow emanating between her fingers, radiating over the skin of Kol's side. Her breathing escalated as she realized what she was doing. Her eyes flickered toward the hologram. The bruising was slowly waning.

It was only when the glow beneath her hand faded that she noticed the light of the bedside lamp had dimmed, because it suddenly grew brighter.

They had done it! They had healed Kol's kidney! She knew that it had been mostly Ms. Heather's doing, but still, seeing the magic in action—and knowing that she was partly responsible—felt like an anchor lifting off her shoulders. No, more like a hot air balloon in her chest, raising her up!

Kol stirred, calling her attention to his face. His complexion, which had previously held a yellowish tint, now retained a healthy pink hue.

"Well done, Myreen," Ms. Heather said, removing her hand from the top of Myreen's. "Kol's health is now fully restored."

Myreen wanted to jump up and squeal.

"Thank you!" she gushed. "When will he be able to go back to classes?"

Ms. Heather laughed and sat back in her seat. "Tomorrow.

We'll let him sleep here overnight, just so we can monitor him and make sure no lead is hiding anywhere in his bloodstream. However, there's something I must tell you."

Myreen held her breath, waiting for the bad news.

Ms. Heather leaned forward and said, "The truth is, I did nothing here tonight. All I did was hold my hand over yours for comfort. Everything else was you. You healed Kol completely on your own."

Myreen wanted to snort in disbelief. Ms. Heather had to be saying that just to boost her confidence.

But Ms. Heather's crystal clear eyes held her gaze for a long moment, instilling the truth of her statement. Myreen got the sense that this woman was no liar. She was every bit the angel she appeared to be.

Which meant that Myreen really had healed Kol. All by herself.

Overjoyed, Myreen threw her arms around the petite harpy teacher. "Thank you," she whispered.

Ms. Heather returned the embrace. "For what, dear?"

"For giving me the chance to fix what I'd done," Myreen wept.

"What you did?" Ms. Heather pulled away from Myreen, holding her shoulders. "You were not at fault for what happened to him."

"Yes, I am," Myreen argued. "The vampires were looking for me. Kol wouldn't have gotten hurt if it wasn't for me."

Ms. Heather frowned. "Guilt is a useless emotion. It keeps us from seeing the truth, and from seeing potential solutions to problems around us. The attack on you and your friends was beyond your control. You can choose to feel about it however you wish, but allowing self-blame to darken you will only bring you down and hinder your potential. Don't sink into that pit. Rise above it and do what you can to make things better."

Myreen was taken aback by this sage advice. In a sense, what she had said was right. If Myreen allowed her guilt to weigh on her, she'd never accomplish anything. She needed to stop focusing on the negatives and start looking up. She needed to make sure no one ever got hurt because of her again. And exploring this new part of herself was exactly the way to do it.

Then something occurred to her as adrenaline flooded her veins. This wasn't the first time she had healed someone. The night Kol got attacked, he'd had a scratch on his face, and it disappeared under her hand. She'd thought she was just seeing things, distraught over Kol's condition as she was. But it must have been real. She'd healed him—twice now—and she was going to make sure to always be there to save him, not the other way around.

"When can we start combat training?" she asked, suddenly invigorated.

Ms. Heather smiled. "Tomorrow. After Defense class. Now go to bed. Get some rest. You've earned it."

With new excitement, Myreen left the infirmary and headed to the avian wing. This was the beginning of something promising.

This was the beginning of hope.

Kol

Kol couldn't avoid the stares. If he'd drawn attention and parted crowds before, now he felt like a recovered plague victim who might still be contagious. He'd nearly died in that alleyway—riddled with lead pellets from a crazy high-tech vampire cannon—trying to protect his friends. And though he'd been completely healed of all injuries, he could still feel the individual holes each pellet created when they blasted into his skin.

Or at least the memory of them.

With his heightened dragon senses, he had felt every single one.

"Malkolm?" Oberon snapped him from his thoughts. Every eye in Shifter History was on him, *again,* and he hated it. He hated that everyone was always staring at him like he'd risen from the dead. Like that guy in the human Bible. Lazarus? Was that his name? Why was Oberon allowing it in class, of all places?

Because apparently everyone was so focused on staring at the miraculously still-alive dragon that they couldn't bother to focus on his lecture? Is that why Oberon called him out? Like it was somehow his fault?

Sure, Kol had just woken up in the hospital wing that morning and been allowed back to his regular routine now that he was completely healed, but it wasn't like being healed by a harpy was so strange in the shifter world.

Get over it, people.

And now Kol was being blamed for his mere presence being a distraction.

He stared back at Oberon, waiting for him to say whatever it was that made him call Kol out.

"Do you know the answer?" Oberon asked.

"Hmm?" Question? Had he been asked a question?

Oberon smiled. He was gracious enough not to reprimand him for not paying attention, or bringing up the fact that Kol had never been caught unprepared to answer a question in all his time at the Dome. He'd gotten maybe one question wrong when called on, but at least he'd always paid enough attention to answer.

Kol shifted in his seat. "C– could you repeat the question?" he asked, trying to hide his injured pride.

"February. 1899. What major event happened in the continental United States?"

Kol looked down at his desk as if the answer was written there, but his laptop wasn't even open.

"Let's look it up," Oberon said to the rest of the class, moving his focus away from Kol.

Returning to his usual student behavior, Kol opened his

laptop and pulled up a search tab in the digital Shifter History textbook.

"Yes, Siobahn," Oberon said.

"There were record-breaking cold temperatures," she said. "Every state in the nation reached temperatures as low as zero degrees Fahrenheit."

"Thank you, Siobahn," Oberon said, walking around the classroom as he spoke. "And what was it called? Randall?"

"The Great Arctic Outbreak of 1899," Randall said, reading the screen of his laptop.

"Thank you, Randall. What else do we know about The Great Arctic Outbreak?"

Kol raised his hand, determined to regain his status as a student who not only cared about his studies and his grades, but actually cared about learning shifter history.

"Yes, Malkolm," Oberon said, stopping in the middle of the aisle of desks, two rows over.

But the director's expression was slightly different from the way he'd looked at all the other students. It was a minuscule flick of his muscles, but Kol caught it even from where he sat and was thrown right back into that alley, laying bleeding and dying as Oberon stood over him with an intensified version of that same look. The look that said he didn't know if Kol would make it. The look that filled his chest with dread, because the look advertised the seriousness of the attack.

The look he'd also seen on Myreen that night.

Once again, the memory of that kiss as he lay half-conscious flooded his thoughts. He couldn't stop thinking about it. Whenever he'd been conscious the past few days, it was all he could think about. Even when the lead in his system threw him into delusions and hallucinations, it replayed in his memory. Part of him wondered if he'd dreamed the kiss, if it had actually happened or if it was just something his brain had conjured up. But it had to be real. The clarity of that moment was real. And the way Myreen looked at him when she didn't know he was watching proved that it happened.

He should talk to her about it. He'd told himself a hundred times that he should talk to her about it. When she visited him in the hospital wing, he'd pretended to be sleeping to avoid that conversation, but he needed to bring it up. They had gone on that date as friends and he'd kissed her. Kol was grateful that they'd survived the attack, which is probably what prompted it. But still... he kissed her.

But with the school on lockdown and the fact that he should've been able to protect Myreen from the vampires—and failed—he couldn't bring himself to do it. He couldn't bring himself to put that kind of pressure on her. He couldn't have a conversation that might demand answers, not when he couldn't even own up to it himself.

"Kol?" Oberon asked, snapping him to attention again. This time Oberon's tone held a note of worry. "Did your screen freeze?" he asked, covering for him.

Kol didn't answer the last comment and let his classmates believe his computer was to blame and not his daydreaming about kissing a certain girl. "In some states that winter still holds the record for lowest temperature, even after over a hundred years," he said.

Oberon held his chin with one hand. "Anything else?" he asked, then turned to the rest of the class, inviting anyone to answer.

Kol continued to skim, but couldn't find anything out of the ordinary about the very cold weather. But then his analytic brain finally kicked in. "This is *Shifter History*," Kol said, turning the entire class's attention back to him—this time in a way he didn't mind. "Was it caused by a shifter?"

Oberon smiled in that way he always did whenever he realized one of his students—usually Kol—was doing some critical thinking and not reciting from the text. He held his hands up as if to illustrate. "Why would we be discussing the weather of 1899 in *Shifter History* unless it had something to do with..." he paused for effect, "*Shifter History*?"

The entire class recited the last part with him in clumsy unison.

"Exactly!" Oberon walked back to the front of the room and projected some black-and-white images that were probably taken that winter. Next to them, an image of the united states was projected in blue. "The human meteorologists say it began in Canada," Oberon said, pointing above the map. "And it swept from the northwest here in Oregon and Washington and spread across the rest of the country." He looked back at the class. "But it was not a natural event. What type of shifter could cause such drastic weather change?"

Kol racked his brain, forcing him to focus on the task at hand and not on the way Myreen's hair fell around him in a dark curtain the moment before he pulled her down toward him in a kiss. But the only shifters he could think of who had any control over temperature were the ones who could manipulate fire. Dragons like himself, and phoenixes. Juliet's fire-bird, racing after the vampires and screeching as she flew to rescue Myreen, invaded his thoughts.

"Alicorn?" A small mao in the back ventured. Kol couldn't remember her name and was no longer invested in the history lesson, so he stared at his screen and hoped he wouldn't be called on again.

After class, Kol was the first one out of the room. He needed to find Myreen. He needed to see her and speak with her. Without being too obvious, he scanned every hallway he walked into, hoping to catch sight of her and stage a *run-in* so he'd have an excuse to talk to her. But he couldn't find her in any of the usual places. He begrudgingly attended the rest of his classes—giving them as much attention as he'd given Shifter History—and finally caught the rumors from some passing mers that Myreen was busy with new training. Since finding out she was a chimera, she had a lot to learn about her new abilities and was kept busy with lessons to harness them.

Even as a dragon prince, the fact that she had more than one shifter nature was intimidating. How could he possibly measure up? But he shook it off.

Finally, he found her at the end of the day after dinner. She was with Juliet and Nik, but he easily pulled her away and offered to walk her back to the common room.

But the words left him. He'd mulled over what he wanted to say throughout the day, but the weight of everything that had transpired between them since the night of the attack made it so he couldn't even form a sentence.

So they walked in awkward silence. He kept waiting for her to break the ice. But since he'd been the one to seek her out, since he'd been the one to pull her away from Nik and Juliet, she probably assumed—as she should—that he wanted to talk to her about something specific.

And now he wasn't even speaking.

Kol silently growled at the floor in front of him, like it was the smooth polished blackness beneath his feet that left him so tongue-tied.

"I'm glad you're feeling better," she finally said when they reached the avian common room. He couldn't tell if he heard a hint of annoyance in her voice or if it was in his imagination.

They walked into an unusually empty common room.

"Wanna watch a movie?" he asked. Finally his mouth was working.

Almost like she'd planned for it, she yawned. "I'm actually very tired," she said. "All of my new training—"

"Of course," Kol cut her off and turned to walk back out.

"Actually, I have a room here now," she said. "Since I'm part harpy, Oberon said it was okay. And since the mers kicked me out anyway..."

He stared at her. When she'd been in another wing of the Dome, things had been different. He could avoid her if he wished, he could compartmentalize his life. But with her room this close?

He didn't know how he felt about things. More specifically, how he felt about that kiss. Not that it mattered much if it was unwanted on her part.

"So... I'm going to go to bed," she said, snapping him from his stare and turning to walk down the hallway.

"Myreen," he said, reaching out and grabbing her arm. She jerked back at the burn. "Sorry." He muttered, embarrassed that his powers were a bit out of whack. Most likely from his recent trauma. Why it had to happen while Myreen was near was infuriating, though.

She looked at him expectantly.

"Look," he said, his eyes finding the floor again. "About the night of the attack..." From his peripheral, he saw that she stared at the ground, too. He snuck a glance at her and noticed a pink tint to her cheeks. He didn't know what he was trying to say or what would come out of his mouth next, so he just unleashed the words like a floodgate. "I know that we went on that date as just friends, and then the vampires attacked and they took you—" his voice caught. He cleared his throat and looked above her head, still not meeting her eyes. "And I should've been able to save you, I should've broken away and gone after you—"

"Stop," Myreen said, silencing him. "It wasn't your fault, Kol. There wasn't anything you could've done. And you were the one..." Now she was the one trailing off.

"I just..." he said, taking a step forward and reaching up with his hand as if to brush the hair away from her face. But he dropped it without touching her.

Then her hand twitched toward his ever so slightly, like she wanted to grab it, but maybe she didn't want to get burned again and swung it back by her side. "Goodnight, Kol," she said, her eyes finally meeting his.

He frowned. "Goodnight, Myreen."

And she walked into her room.

Juliet

Everything was unbalanced.

Even with so many things to celebrate, there were just as many causing strain. Juliet never could have guessed how many students would actually like and accept her now. She liked to feel recognized in a non-jinx way, but it was overwhelming. Malachai was on cloud nine, relishing in the heroism of his daughter by overworking her.

She preferred the silence and comfort of her one friend. But now that Myreen was who she was, she was always busy with extra training. Kol was still on the mend, which continuously put Nik in a bad mood.

But Juliet and Nik were exclusive. Aside from the curfew that kept them from spending more time with each other, there wasn't a downside to that aspect of her life, which she appreciated.

Except for her father. He strongly disliked how distracted

and weak it made Juliet. Anytime she spoke Nik's name, he made her do an exhaustingly long wall-sit while balancing her fireballs in her hands. And yet, saying his name was still worth the pain. She knew she was bordering on obsession, but she'd never had the chance to feel that kind of emotion before. Sure, there was a crush here and there, but she was never given the chance to savor in the sensation of actual love. Every moment she was able to spend with him, she felt closer to that feeling. It was intoxicating. And she wanted everyone to know.

"Bye Dad. Nik should be here." Juliet wiped the sweat off her neck with the small hand towel she had. She smirked as his nostrils flared.

"Juliet, wall-sit. Ten minutes." With a stern look, Malachai set the timer on his watch, but Juliet rushed to the door.

"No, thanks. I'm meeting *Nik*." She flashed him a cheeky smile and raced out before he could stop her.

And ran right into Nik.

As he caught her, she was grateful to be held up, because she was sure to get weak in the knees just from the way his eyes shined when he smiled at her.

"Lucky I was here." His smile turned into a cocky smirk, and Juliet scrambled to get back on her feet. She nudged him then leaned in to give him a soft and delicate kiss. With perfect timing, Malachai opened the door. He loudly cleared his throat, causing Nik to take a step away from Juliet.

"Sir... Mr. Q... How are you, today?"

Juliet giggled at Nik's uneasiness.

"I'm just fine, Nikolai. I see you're keeping busy." Malachi looked down at Nik like he was going to eat him for lunch.

"Alright, *Mr. Q*, bye now." She squinted her eyes at her

father as she led Nik away from the training room. "Well, that went... terrific," Juliet teased when they turned the corner.

"Very funny. I have a feeling it would be exactly the same if you met my father. You're lucky it's my mom that you get to know." She could tell Nik was serious, so she didn't provoke him anymore. Whenever his dad came up in conversation, Nik got scarily serious.

They had just stepped into the common room when his cell phone rang.

"Speak of the devil." Nik kissed Juliet on her forehead and turned away to answer the call.

Juliet rushed through her shower, because she was meeting him again after. But when he knocked on her door early, she could feel something was off.

She opened her door while she used a towel to dry her hair. There was a somber look in his eyes as he waited at her door frame. "Are you okay, Nik?"

He looked down at his feet and spoke so low it was hard for her to hear him. "Come with me."

He was avoiding eye contact. Juliet's heart sped up.

She slipped her shoes on and threw her hair up in a wet, messy bun. As soon as she closed her door, he gently took her hand in his and led her straight to the library where they had their own secret place.

She remembered the first time he brought her there. He was so excited and nervous as he pulled her into the library. He kept looking back at her and wiggling his eyebrows. He took her to the darkest and dustiest corner, completely out of sight. Juliet never even knew it was there.

"This is my favorite spot in the entire Dome. Not one

person knows about it. Not even the guys. But I guess we could tell Kol and Myreen in case they ever need to find us. Anyway, isn't it cool?" He looked at her expectantly.

"I can see the appeal. It's... nice." She looked around hesitantly, but it quickly grew on her. She liked how cozy it was, how quiet it was—and how hidden it was.

"I found it one day when I was studying. I come here to read my books. I love it here. It's so quiet. And now I get to share it with you." He wrapped his hands around her waist and fell back against the large and surprisingly comfortable lounge chair that exploded into another massive cloud of dust. They laughed together as they coughed.

Now he gently sat her on the lounge chair and paced the small area. Juliet could feel her heart race faster and faster as he grew more and more nervous. Dust particles danced behind him as he walked back and forth.

"Nik!" Her nerves couldn't take it anymore.

Nik stopped his pacing and reluctantly sat next to Juliet. He took her hand and she felt how clammy his were. Something was wrong.

"So, you know it was my dad that called before. He had what he thought was good news. And normally it would be... But now?" Nik looked down at their entwined fingers and shook his head.

"I'm sure whatever it is, we can get through it. Together." She tried to softly push his head up. But when she did, she regretted it instantly. Dread was pasted all over his face. "What is it?"

"Kol's dad, Lord Dracul, has an opening for an assistant intern. My dad thought I was the perfect candidate. I mean, it's the direction I wanted to go when I graduated, and I've got the grades for it... so he volunteered me." It sounded like it was physically hurting Nik to relay the conversation he had with his father. "He's withdrawing me from the school. I leave within the next week. I'm so sorry, Juliet. We just got together..." Nik looked as heartbroken as Juliet felt.

But she wouldn't let something like distance come between them.

"That really sucks. But I don't want this to be over... I really like you. And I think we could make it work." She hoped he didn't catch the uncertainty in her voice.

But with the tight smile he gave her, she knew he could tell how much she was hurting. Nik raised his hand to lightly tuck the wet, curly hair falling in front of her face. This time, it was him that wanted her to look into his eyes.

"You're right. We can make this work. Because I really like you, too." Nik placed his soft lips on Juliet's. It took her breath away, to where she almost forgot to keep breathing.

"So... when do you leave?" she asked when they parted. She didn't want to cry in front of him. She wouldn't let herself.

"I don't leave now. That's what matters. But I do have to go in an hour to meet with my dad and the General for specifics. I'll be back by tomorrow morning, though." His tone became sour, but also reassuring at the same time.

"Wow. Well, I'll let you get to it. I know you have a lot of people to tell. I'll meet you at the platform doors in an hour." Juliet did what she did best: she ran. She ran before he could see her eyes swell with tears, before she would dramatically think the world would end, and before he saw the doubt in her eyes.

"Juliet!" Nik sounded just as devastated as she did. It was unfair to leave him that way, but he was going through enough. She didn't want to add pity to his list.

It felt as if the world around her moved at a faster speed.

Everything zoomed by as she numbly raced back to her bedroom. She ignored the students who now made sure to say hello to her, and she was sure she saw Mrs. Candida give her an aching look of understanding, which made her feel worse. She didn't want to stop to talk to anyone. What she needed was her bed.

Juliet slammed her door closed as she threw her shoes off. She ran for her bed and reached for her headphones, pressed play on her 90s rock playlist, set her alarm for an hour, and hid under the sheets.

She needed to ground herself before she had to say goodbye. She needed to do it the way she knew best—alone.

When there was a knock on her door after only thirty minutes of peace, she wasn't quite as distressed as before.

"Come in." With sadness, Juliet slid her headphones off.

To her surprise, it was Malachai who entered.

Juliet fell back into the bed with a loud and annoyed grunt. "I thought you were Myreen. What can I do for you? Because I am not in the mood. It is literally the worst day ever." She knew she was being dramatic, but she didn't care. And when he laughed at her theatrics, she thought her eyes would roll themselves out of their sockets. "*Dad!*" Her warning only made him more amused.

"Juliet, please. Get ahold of yourself. Quinns don't act like this." His goal might have been to make her laugh, but instead she was annoyed.

"Don't start. The last thing I need right now is another story of our lineage." Juliet sat up with her shoulders slouched. Again, he chuckled.

"Alright, alright. I came here to see if you wanted to join me for dinner tonight. You've been so busy with the mermaid and the dragon that it hasn't given us a chance to bond."

A look of unamused shock was pasted on Juliet's face. "Bond? Really? Just... whatever. Yes. I will have dinner with you. And you won't have to worry about *the dragon* anymore because his father is making him take on the job as General Dracul's assistant. He's leaving, and I don't even know when I'll be able to see him again. So unfair." Juliet threw herself back and rolled over to face the other direction.

Malachai took a deep breath and awkwardly patted Juliet on her back. "Well, that will look good on his resumé."

Juliet swung her head around to give him her most intense glare. With a small laugh, he took a deep breath and placed his hands on his legs. "I know anything I say will just upset you more, so I'll keep it short. *You* are stronger than this. The vampire ambush is enough proof of that. I mean, the way you shifted and kicked ass—"

"Dad!" He never failed to bring that up now, and it drove Juliet crazy.

"What I'm trying to say is, whatever comes your way, I'm confident you can overcome it. You can conquer the world if only you'll believe it." With his large muscles, he reached around Juliet and pulled her in for a quick—and awkward—hug.

"Um, thanks Dad. That helped."

Malachai stood. "I know. I'm a Quinn." With a smug smile and his back straight, he saluted her and left.

Juliet got off her bed and straightened her back as tight as her father's just was. She looked at herself in the mirror while she repeated all the positive things in this situation. Nik didn't break up with her. They just had to deal with getting through the separation of distance. With her dad's words of wisdom echoing in the back of her mind, she knew she could get through it. She knew *they* could get through it.

With a new certainty, she composed herself and waited for the right time to leave. Nik was usually punctual, so she knew he would already be there. She ran down the halls, eager to get to him. When she saw him pacing in front of the platform doors, she knew it was her that he was waiting for.

The moment their eyes locked, they raced toward each other for a tight and devoted embrace. Nik pulled away first to take Juliet's face into his warm hands. And even with the audience of his mother and her father, he stole a kiss.

"I will see you tomorrow. I swear I'll come back." Nik wiped away at the tears that left Juliet's eyes.

"Nothing has to change." Juliet felt her emotions getting the best of her. As her hands began to heat up, she subtly hid them behind her back.

"I miss you already, Juliet." His words soothed her hands back to normal. Mrs. Candida appeared behind Nik and gently tapped on his shoulder. "I have to go. This is not goodbye. I'll see you soon." With another soft kiss on her cheek, Juliet ran to her father's side, where they waved Nik off.

She tried not to explode from the yearning that had already planted itself in her heart. But the moment the doors closed behind him, Juliet took out her phone to send him a message.

Miss you already.

She knew it would bring a smile to his face. Malachai patted her on the shoulder while they walked back to the avian common room. "You're going to be alright, kid."

With a small smile and some determination, she nodded, because she knew he was right.

Myreen

Myreen could hardly contain her excitement as she made her way to the avian training room after defense class on Tuesday afternoon. She felt like this was the first day of class at a new school, but in a whole different way than she'd ever experienced after years of moving from town to town. She was actually going to learn something new, and she couldn't wait to explore this new part of herself.

The avian training room was a world apart from the Mer training room. There were still hoops hanging from the ceiling, all varying sizes and heights, but no oversized pool. To one corner, there was what could only be described as a miniature mountain, rocky and perfect for climbing. In the opposite corner sat a huge earthy hearth with a blazing fire. Myreen understood the need for the fire when it came to dragons and phoenixes, but she didn't see how it was relevant to harpies.

Ms. Heather stood next to the hearth, the glow of the fire shining in her fluffy yellow hair. She wasn't in her white nurse's scrubs as Myreen was used to seeing her. Today she was wearing a snug t-shirt of the same smart material as Myreen's swim top, the avian symbol over her right breast. Myreen couldn't help but notice that her feet were bare, and she tried not to stare as she came closer.

"I have always loved the warmth of a fire," Ms. Heather said, gazing fondly at the blaze as if it were an old friend. "Man-made heat just doesn't compare. Don't you think?"

Myreen made a non-committal shrug-nod. She hadn't spent much time around fires in her life. Growing up, there were no campfires for her and her mom, not even in the backyard. The no-going-out-after-dark rule was very firm, and none of the houses they'd ever occupied had a fireplace.

"I think it's funny that our prime is called avian," Ms. Heather went on. "Because you know what I think? Even though flying is something that dragons, phoenixes and harpies have in common, it's not the shared trait that binds us as a family. No, it's the connection to fire."

"Fire?" Myreen asked, confused. "But harpies don't wield fire."

"On the contrary," Ms. Heather corrected. "In the days before man-made light, fire was our only easy access to light. Even now, it remains the most potent form for us to use, save for the light of the direct sun. But we don't get that down here." She laughed. "So fire is the source we will be using to practice."

Now that Ms. Heather had spelled it out, Myreen was surprised she hadn't realized it before. She had only ever seen dragon and phoenix shifters use fire directly, so she hadn't made the connection that fire also made light and didn't just burn things.

Ms. Heather turned toward the flames and reached her hands out to warm them. "Do you mind if I get a little more comfortable?"

Myreen didn't know what she meant by that but said, "Um, sure."

With Ms. Heather's back in view, she could now see two long slits in the fabric of her shirt right over her shoulder blades. Myreen could only cock her head at that for a moment before Ms. Heather made their purpose apparent.

"Thank you." Tiny white feathers sprouted through the slits, growing and lengthening, and soon it looked like strange deformed arms were reaching out from her back.

Myreen jumped backward, a sick feeling in her chest as she watched what was surely a gruesomely painful mutation. But in seconds, the little arms filled out with the prettiest, shiniest pearl white feathers, turning into a breath-taking pair of angelic wings.

"Whoa," Myreen gasped, openly fawning over the majesty of Ms. Heather's wings as they unfurled and settled.

"Much better," Ms. Heather said. She turned around to face Myreen.

It was only then that Myreen saw the change in Ms. Heather's feet. Where Ms. Heather's dainty pale feet had been a moment ago, there were now two eagle-like claws, with talons at the end of each phalange that resembled pointed, oblong black pearls.

This time, Myreen had to forcibly pull her eyes away from the harpy teacher's feet. She had never seen a transformed harpy before. Though she had known from biology that they had clawed feet in their shifter form, she wasn't prepared for it. She had also never quite connected the dots as to why many of the students in avian shirts wore open-toed sandals. Now she got it.

She looked over her shoulder at the empty space there. "Will I be able to do that too?" Just because she could use harpy powers didn't necessarily mean she could sprout wings. After all, Juliet had been able to use her powers for a long time without shifting, and had only shifted for the first time when it was a life-or-death situation.

"I'm sure you will," Ms. Heather said. "In time. But we'll start with the basics of using your powers first. Transforming doesn't come easy for everyone, no matter their species."

Myreen knew that all too well. Mermaids were supposed to be born in their shifter form, and even after months of practice, she still didn't quite have it down. Would she be as awful at harpy shifting as she was at mermaid shifting? Would she be a horrible harpy in general? She was unquestionably a horrible mermaid, maybe the worst in the world.

She clenched her jaw. Ms. Heather's words from the other night echoed in her head. *Allowing self-blame to darken you will only weigh you down.* Myreen didn't want to be weighed down anymore. She needed to rise above and learn to fly.

"Let's get started," Ms. Heather said. "When you're more practiced, you'll be able to harness light at will. But when you're first starting out, it's best to concentrate on a particularly powerful emotion in order to connect with the light. It can be anything. The first time you did it, the emotion was anger—a powerful emotion for sure, but the most powerful is joy."

Myreen remembered the first time she harnessed light. She'd been in her first spar in Defense class, paired against her number one enemy at the school, Trish. She'd been so angry Trish was getting the best of her, that she was losing to her in yet another facet of life at the Dome. That anger had been the strongest Myreen had ever felt. She wasn't sure she could feel anything that compared, let alone happiness.

"I know joy is in short supply around here lately, but I want you to try to focus on something truly good that has happened to you, and let that joy fill you up. Can you think of something that you can be really happy about?"

Myreen thought for a moment. There were definitely things she was happy about in her life. She had great friends, even if they were few. There was Kenzie, who had remained a true friend even with the distance between them. There was Juliet, who opened her heart and her room to her without hesitation. There was Kol...

The answer was obvious, really. Kol had kissed her. And even if he was dying at the time, the way that kiss had made her feel was the closest thing to bliss she could imagine.

She must have been blushing, because Ms. Heather said, "Ah, so it's a boy then." She smiled knowingly, and Myreen felt her cheeks burn hotter. "Focus on whatever you're thinking about and let it fill you."

Lately, Myreen had had to constantly fight the memory of the kiss to keep from getting lost in it. But now she was being told to do just that, and she was happy to finally give in to her love-sick brain. She closed her eyes and brought herself back to the alley that had caused so much grief. She focused only on the kiss, remembering the way his lips had felt on hers, the way her heart had exploded with joy that quarreled with the panic of the situation. *Kol...*

She felt warm all over, a cozy lethargy settling into her belly and limbs.

"Very good. Now open your eyes and pull light from the flames."

Myreen slowly opened her eyes and aimed her gaze at the fire. She could feel it pulsing with its own sort of life, like a heartbeat thumping within its blazing center. She cupped her hands together toward the pyre in front of her and beckoned the light to her.

As easy as breathing, wisps of light flicked off the tips of the flames, like little fairies flying mellifluously through the air, and pooled into a ball in her open palms.

Myreen laughed almost maniacally as she watched, so overflowing with joy that her fingertips were practically bursting with it. The light was so delightfully warm on her skin. She wanted to jump, to dance until her legs fell out from under her.

"Wonderful job, Myreen!" Ms. Heather praised, clapping. "You're a natural!"

Myreen wanted to try something. She shifted the light within her hands and then separated them and tossed the ball of light from one hand to the other and back. All the while, it kept its shape.

"This is the coolest thing ever!" Myreen squealed. "I never imagined I could do this!"

"You can do so much more. This is only the beginning. Now let's try this a few times. Give the light back to the fire, and then call it back."

Myreen did, and after that first time, she didn't need to focus on the kiss anymore. The light gave her a joy that was plenty enough fuel. Each time the light came back to her, she couldn't help but giggle. She could do this all night!

But a sound intruded on their play time, an obnoxious ringing. Ms. Heather knelt to pick up the tablet that had been leaning against the wall on the floor safely away from hearth. She tapped the screen and the ringing stopped.

"Delphine?" she asked to the tablet.

"Maya, would you please send Myreen to the gym when your session is over?" Delphine's voice sounded from the tablet.

"Of course. We're about done. I'll send her over now." Ms. Heather tapped the screen and the call ended. "I think that's enough for today. You did very, very well. Next time, we'll do more with light, show you more ways to use it."

"Great. I can't wait," Myreen said, sending the light back to the fire for the last time.

Myreen rubbed her hands together as she left the training room, marveling at how naked her hands felt. She had never felt this fulfilled training with water, and she was almost sad to be returning to the shadows that were so abundant under the Dome.

* * *

Myreen headed next door to the gym, wondering why Delphine wanted to meet her there. After two hours of Defense class and an hour of light manipulation training, Myreen was beat. She understood the need to prepare for her prophesied fight against Draven, but she didn't think she could take any more physical exertion today, even with the fire's energy filling her. If anything, the warmth radiating from her core was relaxing her to a state of drowsiness, and all she wanted was a nap.

The gym was filled with older students and graduates, all

training harder than usual. She even recognized some teachers in the mix, which for some reason was disconcerting. It looked like they were preparing for war.

Delphine stood by the door to the Simulation Room, wearing a cute aerobics bra and tight sweatpants, her long red hair up in a tidy ponytail.

Oh, no, not another sim run, Myreen thought. But she obediently proceeded, gulping as she approached the fiery mermaid teacher.

"Good afternoon, Myreen," Delphine greeted in an all-business tone.

Usually the Mer leader spoke to her with a chipper voice, all smiles, so this new attitude was a striking contrast and stung a bit. Was Delphine insulted that Myreen had chosen to stay at the avian wing permanently?

"G– good afternoon," Myreen replied.

"How did your first harpy training session go?"

Myreen wasn't sure how to answer. Should she hide her excitement over the hour she had spent playing with light? "It was... very enlightening," she answered, deciding to go with vaguery.

Delphine ignored the pun and nodded.

"Good. Well, while I understand the desire to train you in your newly discovered talent, the prophecy stated that a *siren* would defeat Draven, so I believe that is the area we should focus on."

Myreen must have made an exasperated face, because Delphine added, "Don't worry, we won't start today." She giggled, which again confused Myreen as to the new state of their relationship. "I don't want to overwork you. We'll start tomorrow on the siren training. After speaking with Oberon, we've decided that you'll switch off on training sessions each day: one day with him, one day with me, and one day with Maya."

Myreen nodded slowly, puzzled. If Delphine hadn't called her here to train, then why was she here?

As if Delphine could read minds—who knew, maybe she could—she answered the question.

"As for this evening, I understand you feel underwhelmed by your mermaid abilities. When the vampires attacked your friends, I heard that you didn't put up much of a fight, and that's my fault. I failed to teach you how to use your powers offensively. So I called you here to show you how a mermaid can use their powers to fend off vampires, specifically. I will run through a sim, and I just want you to watch."

Myreen's brows jumped and her eyes widened. Delphine was giving her the chance to watch her fight!

Delphine turned on the screen on the wall for Myreen to see into the sim room, then walked in and closed the door behind her. Through the smart wall, Myreen could see Delphine tighten her ponytail as the white of the room was replaced by an urban scene. Delphine now stood on what looked like a rooftop, with a full moon illuminating the night sky and city lights sprinkling the horizon. It reminded Myreen of when she had watched Kol do his sim against the dragons.

No sooner had the scene filled in when a pale-faced vampire woman shot out of the darkness and darted for Delphine. Delphine dodged with hardly any effort at all, merely stepping aside with the grace of a sprite.

Before the vampire could turn around and lunge for another attack, Delphine had pulled a vial of water out of the pocket of her sweatpants, pulled the cork off and willed the liquid out in an elegant string.

She spun on her heel to face her attacker, who had just turned around and was preparing to dive at her again. The string of water slithered through the air with lightning speed and wrapped itself around the vampire's head.

The vampire stopped short, eyes bulging and mouth gaping as she tried in vain to breathe through the water. Her fingers clawed, digging through it in an attempt to swipe it away, but the water would not be removed.

The struggle went on for several minutes, with Delphine standing in place, staring at the vampire with unbreakable focus. Delphine hadn't broken a sweat, and already this vampire was half-dead. *Well, I guess they're already dead,* Myreen thought distantly as she watched with keen interest.

Finally, the vampire stopped her struggles and collapsed to the floor. The water continued to swirl around and around in a perfect ball for several seconds longer, then uncoiled and slithered back into the vial in Delphine's hand like an ethereal snake.

Myreen was seriously impressed. Without any physical exertion, Delphine had taken out a vampire! All with meager water manipulation, too.

Delphine looked toward the display wall, and Myreen could almost believe that the mermaid teacher could actually see her through the simulation.

"The thing about vampires is they're like cockroaches," Delphine said. "You think they're dead, and then they get back up. You see, vampires can drown over and over without actually dying."

As she spoke, the seemingly dead vampire stirred and began to rise.

"Delphine, look out!" Myreen shouted, forgetting that Delphine couldn't hear her in the sim.

But Delphine was prepared for it. The vampire shot off the ground, claws bared and ready to strike. Delphine narrowed her eyes on the vampire, and suddenly the vampire froze in mid-air, floating in place. Myreen stared in confusion. Had the sim malfunctioned somehow? Was this some kind of glitch?

"What many mers forget is that we can manipulate *all* liquid, not just water," Delphine said smoothly, not breaking her focused gaze on the immobile vampire.

Myreen looked closer, almost pressed up against the wall at this point. Upon closer inspection, she could see that the vampire's eyes were darting from side to side and were filled with fear. Suddenly she understood, and the realization was earth-shattering. Delphine was manipulating the *blood* inside the vampire's body, essentially making it impossible for the vampire to move at all!

Myreen's jaw dropped, anticipation storming in her guts.

"The only way to truly kill a vampire is to sever the heart-brain connection," Delphine said.

Happening so abruptly that Myreen jumped and squealed with surprise, the vampire's chest exploded right where the heart was, blood erupting like lava from a volcano. Then the now-hollow body fell to the rooftop with a *thud,* and Delphine walked to the door as the sim pixelated away and returned to the empty white room.

Delphine emerged from the room and turned off the display.

"Delphine, that was incredible!" Myreen gasped. "I had no idea our power could be so..." Myreen was lost for words.

Delphine smiled and patted Myreen's shoulder. "Well, now you know what you're capable of, and that's only from the mer part of you. Not all mer can do that, mind you. It takes years of training and hard work. But I believe you can achieve anything if you put your mind to it."

They shared a long look, and Myreen realized what had changed in the nature of their relationship. Delphine was regarding her not as student, but as a peer. As an equal.

"I'll see you tomorrow after Defense class?" Delphine asked, even though it wasn't a request.

"Yes," Myreen said.

Delphine nodded and gestured for Myreen to go ahead of her and leave the gym. As they walked together, Myreen still felt uneasy about something, and she felt she had to clear it up before any more time passed.

"Delphine?" she asked, hanging in the doorway.

"Yes?"

"Are you upset that I'm not staying in the Mer wing anymore?" The words came out shaky and unconfident, because she was afraid of the answer.

Delphine blinked with understanding, then gave her a warm, motherly smile. "No. I know the bullying you've endured by the mers. And though I've tried my best to put a stop to it, I can't be everywhere all the time. You've found good friends in the avian wing, and you are technically an avian. I understand why you feel you must stay with them, and I harbor no hurt feelings, other than those from my own failure as an instructor and mentor."

Myreen cocked her head. "You didn't fail. Like you said, you can't always control everything. Mean girls will go out of their way to be mean. That's not your fault."

Delphine looked down, the sad frown looking out of place on her pretty and usually confident face. "It's not just that. I failed in training you. I delegated the task to Alessandra because I didn't truly believe you were the girl from my vision. I decided to keep looking when I should have been doing my best to prepare you. Because of my failure, we almost lost you to Draven." Myreen could almost feel the guilt emanating from Delphine like an infectious fog.

"That wasn't your fault, either," Myreen insisted. "It was my fault for being out after dark. We should've been back hours before curfew. We were foolish. As for Alessandra, I'm glad you pushed us together. We bonded." Myreen smiled as she thought of her frenemy.

Delphine attempted a smile, which Myreen could clearly tell was fake. "Yes. Well, you should get to dinner. You'll need to take extra good care of your health now."

Myreen nodded, hearing the period in their conversation loud and clear. "See you tomorrow."

"Yes, tomorrow."

Myreen headed for the dining hall, deciding to ignore her up-and-down emotions over the day's events. She was going to just enjoy a laidback evening with her friends before getting a well-deserved rest.

Oberon

"And then the whole contraption exploded in Sora's face," Ren said, tears streaming from his dark eyes from laughing so much. Oberon's Japanese-American friend was sitting in his office, the two of them sharing dinner together after another long day of classes. "When the smoke cleared, that poor student was staring at *another* melted project."

Oberon couldn't help but laugh along with his oldest friend. "And you're positive Sora Ito really is a kitsune?"

"Oh yes," Ren replied, wiping at his wet cheeks with one of his long sleeves. "The boy can transform so eloquently. But when it comes to electricity manipulation? Let's just say he controls currents about as well as he controls his tongue after attempting to channel electricity."

Smiling and shaking his head, Oberon asked, "Was the boy hurt?"

"He singed his fingers a bit, but nothing he isn't used to," Ren replied. "I sent Sora to see Maya—against his will, mind you. Maya has been stern with him regarding the frequency of his visits."

"Poor kid," Oberon said. "I'm sure Maya gives him an earful." He took a bit of his buttered roll, then pointed it toward Ren. Between chewing, he said, "I'm jealous you see such action in your tinkering classes, my friend. It seems there's never a dull moment. All I get in shifter history lectures are a bunch of glazed eyes and wide yawns."

"Nothing out of the ordinary, then," Ren said with a wink, taking a mouthful of rice. "You're such a bore, Mr. Rex." The kitsune teacher tilted his head back and closed his eyes and fake-snored, then began coughing as he choked on the food he hadn't quite swallowed yet.

"Serves you right," Oberon said with a laugh "Besides, history isn't always fun and games. Especially shifter history." His mind wandered into the past, remembering the dark days he'd endured before, during, and after The Island had been destroyed. How too many loved-ones had died from vampire brutality.

Ren guzzled some water, coughed a few more times, then dabbed at his mouth with a napkin. "Try making math fun." He cleared his throat. "'Students, the quadratic formula is like a thirsty vampire.' You'd think that kind of analogy would bring excitement right into the classroom. But these kids... it's like they *know* they're being tricked into learning their 'rithmetic."

Oberon pointed his lettuce-loaded fork at Ren. "Now tell me, how exactly is a thirsty vampire like using the quadratic formula?"

"Well, if you ask the students, they'll tell you that they both suck," Ren said with a sly grin.

Rolling his eyes, Oberon slipped his leafy greens into his mouth and shook his head. "You know, I think that those with your kind of humor should have their jokes regulated. There's only so much dryness normal people can take."

Ren shrugged. "Perhaps for merfolk. But us? We *thrive* with dryness."

"Okay, Ren, you've made your point."

"Oh, I don't think I have!" Ren stabbed his stir fry with his fork. "Tell me, when was the last time you laughed at a wet joke? Hmm?"

Oberon shook his head. "That doesn't make any sense. What in the world is a wet joke?"

"Exactly my point." Ren placed his napkin on his not-quite-empty plate, as if it indicated some finality to the argument.

Three sudden knocks came at the door of his office, and not as timid little taps. Oberon could tell by the solid pounding that authority stood on the other side. Ren jumped a mile in his chair.

"Did you invite the grim reaper to dinner, too?" Ren said. "Because those knocks nearly scared me into a grave."

"I'd like to see that," Oberon chuckled.

Opening his desk drawer, he tapped at his tablet, causing the office door to open. In no time, the tall, bulky figure of Lord Eduard Dracul, general of the shifter military, stood stiffly in his uniform, as if his back was made of a straight, metal pole.

"Ah, Eduard, I wasn't expecting you," Oberon said as he got to his feet. He wasn't as tall as the general, but he liked to think he held the respect of the intimidating dragon shifter.

"Forgive my sudden appearance," Lord Dracul said. "The military has kept me particularly busy over the past few weeks with the increasing number of vampire attacks. I have only just visited my son Malkolm. Regrettably, I wasn't able to return to the Dome right after he was attacked. But I am glad to see how well he's recovered."

"Kol is a valuable asset," Oberon said, nodding his head. "His courage and bravery in the fight against the vampires has earned him respect beyond anything he's done in school."

Eduard glanced at Ren as if he was just noticing the kitsune. "Ah, the Master Tinkerer himself." The general removed a round object from his belt. Oberon recognized it as the vampire tracking device Ren had developed just a few months before. He'd almost completely forgotten about it after Delphine finally approved the finances for its mass production. "Your latest creation has been most helpful. However, it has done little to slim down the number of vampire attacks."

Oberon could see annoyance teetering on Ren's emotions. "Slim attacks down? By my ninth tail, Eduard, the purpose of the vamp tracker isn't to decrease the number of vampire attacks. In fact, last time I checked, that was *your* job."

A fire blazed in Eduard's eyes like a lit match dropped into a container of gasoline. "How dare you speak to me with such insolence," Eduard said, stomping into the office.

"Alright you two." Oberon made his way around the desk to get between them before blows began to be thrown. "You don't have to act like a couple of pubescent students."

But Ren had gotten to his feet and stepped right in front of the seething, towering Lord Dracul.

Unsurprisingly, Oberon's words went unnoticed.

"If the military could figure out how to undermine the vampires and their operations, we wouldn't have to rely on *my* tech to find them," Ren said.

"You witless worm," Eduard growled. "You sit here in the comfort of the most secure and safe facility in the entire world, playing with wires and a soldering iron. You tinker while I and hundreds of other soldiers are out there risking our lives protecting you and everyone you love. We are *dying* for that cause."

"I know precisely what it's like to be out there on the front lines," Ren said, his nostrils flaring as he tried standing as tall as he could. He barely reached Eduard's chest. "Before you decided to join our cause, it was me and Oberon doing it. So don't go throwing your scales around, acting as if you're the only one who's doing something in this war."

Eduard raised a massive hand, fingers outstretched, then swung it down to grab a hold of Ren's shoulder.

Oberon reached out to try to stop it, but stopped short as Ren's body went translucent. Eduard's hand went right through Ren's phased body.

"Nice try, *Lord Dracul*," the kitsune said as he walked straight through the dragon shifter's body, phasing back into his physical form as soon as he was out of arm's reach. Over his shoulder, Ren said, "Thanks for dinner, Oberon, but my useless projects won't tinker themselves now, will they?"

Eduard's chest rose and fell rapidly, and Oberon wondered for a moment if the general was going to go after Ren. At last, the dragon shifter turned around and looked perilously at Oberon.

"Why you continue to befriend Ren Suzuki is beyond me."

The fire in Eduard's eyes slowly smothered.

"He's a good man," Oberon said. "Ren can be a nuisance at times, but there's nobody in the world I trust more."

Eduard shook his head while pointing at the doorway. "You'd trust him with your life?"

Oberon chuckled. "I *have* trusted him with my life, Eduard. And I'd put my life in his hands without any hesitation. But something tells me you didn't come to my office to complain about Ren Suzuki. What can I do for you?"

Eduard eyed the open door. "I wish to discuss a... delicate matter with you." His hint at the need for privacy was about as subtle as a mermaid in a puddle.

Swinging around the desk, Oberon sat in his comfortable chair and opened the drawer that held his tablet. At his command, the door swung closed.

"Please, Eduard, sit down." Oberon gestured to the chair Ren had been sitting in. With a quick swipe of his arm, he knocked his friend's plate into the trash receptacle attached at the side of his desk, then dumped his own plate.

The tall military general slouched instantaneously, drawing a hand up to his face as he rubbed his temples with his thumb and middle finger.

"Does this delicate matter have anything to do with Kol?" Oberon asked.

Bringing his hand down on the armrest, Eduard shook his head. "No. I believe Malkolm is right where he needs to be. At least for now."

Oberon raised an eyebrow. "Even though you pulled his friend Nikolai Candida out of school based on his father's recommendation?"

"Look, Oberon, I know how you feel about us taking students out of the Dome before they complete their education. But Paskal Candida's son—"

"Is not ready for military assignment," Oberon interrupted.

The embers that had slipped from Eduard's eyes just moments before returned, like wind on hot coals, and he sat up straight in the chair.

"The boy fought off a group of vampires and caused them to flee," the general said, somehow managing to contain his anger.

"He *helped* stave off a vampire attack," Oberon corrected. "And it is quite possible he'd be dead were it not for your son."

Seconds ticked by as Eduard stared hard at him. "So you think I should've taken my son on as an intern?"

Oberon sighed and shook his head. "No. I believe that neither of them are prepared for the dangers of military life."

"I'm afraid it's a bit too late for that," Eduard replied. "Nikolai has already begun military training. He's no longer your responsibility, Oberon."

Shrugging, Oberon said, "You're absolutely right. He's yours now. And I hope you feel the weight of his life in your hands."

The general pondered this for a few moments, narrowing his eyes. "I assure you, Director, the Candida boy is in a much safer place now."

"A safer place?" Oberon snorted. "What other place is safer than here at the Dome?"

Eduard laughed. "From your perspective, you probably do believe that the Dome is an impenetrable safe-haven. Let me remind you that it's not. While you're down here sitting pretty, taking the military protection for granted, the vampires could choose to lay siege. How much food do you have on hand to keep the school going if they decided to bar off your entrance? What if they found out how to sever your electricity? They could crack the Dome and cause its depressurization, drowning all of you except for the mermaids, who they'd simply wait for as they eventually would come to the surface."

These were valid concerns that Oberon had heard several times over the years. And until recently, the argument had been that the vampires *didn't* know the location of the Dome. But that had changed. Kendall Green had revealed everything to Draven.

Yet, Oberon couldn't let that kind of mindset poison the school. If things ever got to the point of such danger, they would evacuate.

Eduard sighed heavily. "Look, Oberon. The Candida boy has my protection. I swear it to you, and I've sworn it to Paskal and Nadia. Now, may we move on to the topic that has brought me here?"

"Of course," Oberon conceded with a single nod, relieved that the general wasn't continuing his verbal attack of the Dome further.

"It's about Myreen and the prophecy."

Oberon's heart skipped a beat at Eduard's words, and he felt his mouth go dry. He picked up the glass of water on his desk and sipped at it. "Go on."

"It has come to my attention that the girl is indeed the siren of the prophecy," Eduard said.

Oberon blinked. "Has it now? There are some within the Dome that think such an idea is merely a projection of desire."

"That might be so," Eduard said. "But what do you think?"

Oberon considered telling the man that he didn't know yet, that all that had been revealed about Myreen was that she was *a* siren, not necessarily *the* siren. But he didn't believe that.

"I believe she's the prophesied siren," he said at last.

"Then you must also believe that her training must be fast-tracked," said Eduard.

Oberon smiled. "Great minds think alike, do they not? I'm personally seeing to her training. I've also tasked Delphine with one-on-one instruction, as well as our lead harpy, Maya Heather."

Eduard returned his smile. "I'm glad to hear that. I've come to request that I take over her training."

Oberon's smile faded. "That is absolutely out of the question."

Sighing deeply, Eduard said, "Oberon, her fate is no longer a school situation. It is military. If the only way we can defeat Draven is through her, I need to oversee her training. Yesterday. I need to know what she is capable of."

With focused discernment, Oberon pieced together what Eduard wanted to do with Myreen. He felt his eyes widen slightly. "You seek to weaponize her."

Eduard rolled his eyes. "Let's be realistic. The prophecy speaks of a siren who will overthrow Draven. That siren *is* a weapon by the prophecy's definition. And that siren *is* Myreen."

"No," Oberon countered. "The prophecy only alludes to Myreen's potential. Right now she is a vulnerable young student. We can't pluck her out of the classroom and throw her in a military uniform. We'd break her."

"We need her to be more," Eduard replied.

Oberon couldn't believe what he was hearing. While Myreen was their greatest hope, they had to walk the path of her training carefully.

"If we push her too hard, we could push her away," Oberon said. "Remember, Eduard, that Myreen—until just a few months ago—thought she was merely a human. She's in a whole new world full of concepts and abilities that seem alien to her. If she'd grown up here at the Dome, or at the very least with parents guiding her, she'd be better equipped to handle military training. But she needs time to figure out who and what she is. And until that point, I will see to her training. After that, I'll allow you to come and begin more rigorous instruction."

Eduard hunched over, placing his elbows on the desk and resting his chin on his interlocked fingers. The dragon shifter sighed with disappointment. "I do not feel this is the right path, Oberon. I'm in charge of an army that is fighting a war that can't be won without the girl. Every day our numbers decrease. How many lives must be spent until you feel Myreen is ready?"

It tore Oberon up inside hearing about more death. All his life had been surrounded by it. He—more than anyone—wanted to see the downfall of Draven and the vampires. The image of his beloved Serilda laying in a pool of her own blood flashed through his mind, and his throat thickened. Yes, Draven would pay for his crimes. But sending in Myreen when she wasn't prepared? Such an action could result in the death of all shifters. And that was something he couldn't risk.

"You and the shifter military must buy us as much time as you can," he said at last.

Lord Dracul studied him for a long while, then got to his feet. "We will buy you time. But you must prepare the girl—

accelerate her training."

"I'll work as hard as I dare to with her," Oberon promised.

Eduard nodded. "One more thing. You've been director of the Dome for a long time. We could use your strength and abilities in the military. Have you given any thought to passing the torch on to somebody else?"

The question struck Oberon like lightning, freezing him in place. He'd invested so much time into directing the Dome. It was the closest thing to what he could call *home* ever since the incident on Framboise Island. And to leave it all behind to join the military and help in the fight against the vampires? Perhaps if he were younger...

"My place is here," he replied. He thought of Leif's words—that Draven knew the location of the Dome, and that a vampire attack could happen at any time. If they got past the defenses and safeguards that had been put into place over the years... "But in the near future, it might well be that we all must join the fight—students, teachers, *all* shifters."

Eduard gazed at him as if he expected further explanation. Oberon didn't give anymore, but instead opened the door with a tap of his tablet.

"Farewell, General."

Eduard bowed slightly. "Goodbye, Director."

Kenzie

Kenzie listened quietly to her phone as Myreen recounted everything that had happened to her in the past few days. Some of it was cool, like her finding out she was part harpy—what was the term? Chimera. Yeah, so cool.

But the attack by Draven—*Lord of the Undead* or whatever—was what had Kenzie's mind locked in a spin cycle. That was Saturday. The day she'd been in Chicago. The day Leif had told her to go home, and quick. Did he know what was going to happen to her friends? Was he involved?

"So now I'm staying in the avian prime—"

"Wait, what?" Kenzie said, her mind catching up to Myreen's current drama. She sprang from where she sat on her bed, not sure she could take more news sitting down.

Myreen sighed. "I forgot I haven't told you. The mer kicked me out of my room, so I bunked with Juliet. But now that I know I'm part harpy, they're letting me stay in the avian wing permanently."

"Oh." Kenzie paced the room, then sunk back onto her bed. She looked at the rose she'd revived, sitting on the nightstand. It was in front of the only window in the room, still in the plastic bag she'd brought it home in. Yeah, mom hadn't been too thrilled when she saw that. She gave Kenzie a bowl to set the bag in, but that's as far as she'd gotten with the thing.

"Are you okay?" Myreen asked.

Kenzie snorted. "I should be asking *you* that." Kenzie let out a long breath, flopping onto her back. "I'm fine. I just hate that I haven't been there for you. I should've been there."

"You couldn't have known. And it's not your fault they're not letting you into the school."

"I know, but it still sucks." Kenzie pulled on a strand of her hair, staring at the ends. If she'd tried harder, maybe Myreen wouldn't be in such a miserable situation. Maybe. But they'd never know now.

"So that's about it. What's been going on with you?"

Kenzie chuckled. "Not a dang thing." Okay, so that wasn't entirely true. But she wasn't ready to divulge her dealings with Leif yet. Especially now. She didn't want Myreen thinking she was siding with the enemy. Heck, she didn't even know if he *was* the enemy or not. Her instincts told her he was one of the good guys, wolf's clothing and all, but what if she was wrong?

"Well, I should probably get going," Myreen said.

Kenzie's sat back up, and her knee began bouncing. "Yeah, me too. But we need to plan a day together. ASAP."

"That would be nice," Myreen said, though her voice lacked enthusiasm. Kenzie couldn't blame her. Her new schedule sounded brutal, and Myreen had been through so much.

When they'd said goodbye and hung up, Kenzie threw her phone onto the bed. "Claoigha," she said, low enough not to carry, but not a whisper. She was in her own room, after all, and the door was shut. She needed to talk to Leif about getting into the school. Now.

"Hello?" came Leif's uncertain voice. "Kenzie?"

"Yeah. It's me. We need to talk."

"Actually, you contacted me at a good time. Can I meet you in your hometown?"

Kenzie bit her bottom lip. It always made her nervous, knowing he knew where she lived. She didn't know if he'd go all crazy vampire on the town, though she doubted it, but there was another reason not to meet him here. "Let's make it the next town over. This is a small town. People talk."

"And where would you like to meet?"

"They have a coffee house over there. *Incredible Brew*, I think."

"Great. See you in twenty minutes?"

"Maybe. It might take me a little longer than that." Kenzie didn't have Leif's super speed. Or a car. But the buses that came into town were fairly regular. She almost asked if the bit of daylight left would be a problem, but then remembered she'd seen him during the day on Saturday. She'd have to ask him about that.

"That's fine. See you soon." She could practically hear the smile in that man's voice, and it made her knees feel a little wobbly.

"Yeah," Kenzie said, though the connection was already severed.

Had Leif done that? She thought she had to stop things, seeing how it was her magic that connected them, but maybe that wasn't quite it. She wished she had someone to talk to about all this, but for now, she was on her own.

Kenzie raced out of the room and grabbed her coat.

"Where are you going?" Mom asked from where she sat on the couch. She had a blanket draped over her lap, a sitcom playing on the small tv that sat in the corner.

"To meet a friend." At mom's raised brow, Kenzie added, "I won't be long. Promise."

"Is your homework done?"

"Yep!" Kenzie swung the coat on.

Mom sat up a little straighter. "And is this friend a girl or a boy?"

Kenzie smirked. "Boy, but it's not like that."

"And how exactly is it?"

Kenzie's face reddened. "Do you want me home before dark or what?"

"Fine. We'll talk later."

Kenzie gave a noncommittal grunt.

"Hey Kenz?"

"Yeah."

"I'm glad you're making new friends."

Kenzie smiled at her mom as she rushed out the door. Yeah, mom wouldn't be saying that if she knew who Kenzie was meeting. Which was exactly why it would never come up.

She pulled her zipper on her coat all the way up to her chin and withdrew the hat and gloves she kept in the pockets. She didn't mind the brisk air, but with the approaching nightfall, it was going to get a heck of a lot colder, and soon.

Kenzie beamed at the Christmas decorations peppering the block. Wreaths twinkled, trees glistened and glowed, and even the most mundane festively designed wires were transformed into pure magic with the tiny bulbs and tinsel.

This was her favorite time of year. She loved everything about Christmas, from putting up the tree to picking out and wrapping presents to the festive music that blared from every station.

But even with the magic that seemed to embody her every hope and dream, this year she was having a difficult time getting into the spirit. She'd find a way, though. Despite everything looming over their heads, she'd make Christmas magical again.

And now she had actual magic to help make that happen.

She got to the stop just before the next bus was about to take off. Kenzie thanked her lucky stars. If she'd been a moment later, she would've had to wait another fifteen minutes.

The ride trundled slowly to their destination, and her leg bounced as she silently urged the driver to speed up. She wished she had the grimoire with her so she could see if there was a spell for that. At least she knew the book wouldn't be found without her there. She'd discovered a spell to hide the thing. Of course, the tricky part was the revealing spell, since she couldn't read directly from the book. She didn't even want to carry a piece of paper with the spell on it, just in case it accidentally fell out of her pocket. So she'd memorized it. She silently thanked her mom for passing on her sharp mind, because remembering all these spells was proving to be quite the brain teaser.

When the bus arrived in downtown, Kenzie hopped off as fast as she could and sprinted to the coffee shop. She took a moment to catch her breath before entering, then scanned the room. No sign of Leif.

Kenzie sighed, deflating a little. It figured he wouldn't be on time. Unless he'd already been and couldn't wait any longer. But he'd said it was a good time. Kenzie scowled.

She found an out-of-the-way spot and started studying the menu. Coffee wasn't really her thing, but they had a few sweets that looked good. Kenzie decided to get a cookie while she waited.

Chocolate chip cookie in hand, she turned to find a table, only to find Leif sitting there, smiling like he owned the place.

Kenzie rolled her eyes as she sat with him. "You're late."

"Sorry. I needed a drink before I came."

Kenzie nearly gagged on the cookie she had in her mouth. She swallowed her bite quickly, hardly tasting the chocolatey goodness, and put it on the wrapper she placed on the table.

Leif wore a half-smile that nearly wiped away Kenzie's discomfort. Nearly.

"Okay, if you want me to help you, you've got to stop mentioning your..." Kenzie leaned forward and whispered, "diet."

"Why? Does it bother you? Knowing what I eat?" Leif's gaze trailed to the door as the bell chimed to announce another customer, then rested back on Kenzie.

Kenzie's knee started bouncing. "No. Yes? I just don't want to talk about it."

Leif nodded once, still wearing that infernally adorable half-smile. Was he teasing her?

Kenzie could hardly remember why she'd demanded this meeting. "*Any*way. Saturday."

"What about it?"

"You told me to go home. Said there were vampires around. Did you know they were going to attack my friends? Were you there when it happened?"

Leif looked away, his already pale complexion looking a little paler. "I'm afraid it's better if we don't speak of it."

Kenzie took a deep breath. "Okay. Fine. But I need to know you're one of the good guys."

Leif looked Kenzie dead in the eyes, his expression solemn. "I am."

Kenzie studied him for a long moment, waiting for him to crack, some emotion to betray him. Or maybe he'd pull the compulsion card. Not all vampires could compel others, but older ones sometimes could. And despite his youthful appearance, Leif had a bearing about him that seemed stuck in another century. Yeah, he was probably ancient.

Still, she felt no different, neither swayed for or against her initial impression, just her gut saying he was telling the truth.

Kenzie let out a long breath. "You said you could get me into the school."

"Ah, that." Leif leaned back in his chair, his fingers dancing along the tabletop like it was a piano. Kenzie bit her bottom lip. Yep, from the looks of it, he was a pro at the instrument. She wanted to see that, hear him play for her, get lost in his sad and haunting melody. Kenzie mentally slapped herself for her Twilight fantasy. *You're not a fangirl,* she reminded herself.

"I'm afraid the timing isn't right," Leif said, shattering Kenzie's romantic thoughts.

"Not the right time?" Kenzie said, her voice rising in pitch. "My friend was attacked, and I couldn't do anything to help her." She noticed the wide-eyed stares from around the room, and smiled as she eased back in her seat. Yeah, it was a good thing they hadn't met in her hometown. Her mom would be calling right about now, wondering what had happened.

"And what would you have done?" Leif asked, his expression still somber. "Pin one to a wall with your magic?"

Kenzie's mouth hung open. Sure, she was inexperienced with magic, but that didn't mean she was useless. But even as the argument formed on her lips, it died again. He was right. She was too green.

"Then get me into the school. I can only learn so fast at home."

"I'm sorry. Things are too volatile right now. You'll just have to be patient." The corner of his mouth pulled into a smile that was laced with challenge. "Or find the spell, and I'll do *everything* in my power to get you in."

"At this rate, it'll take me ages to get through that book, and that's not counting the locks and wards that keep the more powerful spells hidden. How long are you willing to wait?" Kenzie crossed her arms, pursing her lips into an equally smug expression.

"I've got all of eternity." Leif got up, flipping the collar of his jacket up like he was some black-and-white movie private eye.

"Well I don't," Kenzie muttered. "Wait. You're just going to leave?"

"I want to get back before dark." Leif looked around, a haunted look in his eyes. "You should, too."

Kenzie raised a brow and pressed her folded arms tighter.

Leif rested his hand on Kenzie's shoulder, giving it a gentle squeeze. "Don't worry. We'll get this worked out. And until then, you can use my apartment on the weekends for your experiments."

His fingers began to lift off her shoulder, but Kenzie caught his wrist. "Wait." She pulled a pen from her purse and wrote her number on Leif's palm. "In case you need to get ahold of me. Way quicker than a letter. Besides, you shouldn't make the girl do all the work in the relationship. I'm progressive, but not *that* progressive."

Leif smirked. "Until next time."

Kenzie didn't let go. "One more thing. How come you can walk in the sunlight?"

Leif eased his wrist out of Kenzie's grip and slid his hand into his pocket. He squinted at the large storefront windows, though his gaze seemed focused on something much further away in time and space.

"Dig deep enough in that book I gave you, and you'll find the answer."

Kenzie startled as a key clinked on the table, a silver seal charm hanging from the keychain.

"So you don't have to break in anymore." Leif winked.

Kenzie exhaled a forgotten breath as Leif breezed out of the cafe. She put the key in her pocket, a soft smile on her lips as her fingers brushed against the charm. It was an unexpected gesture, one that she was trying desperately not to read anything into.

She picked up her cookie and took another bite, but gagged as she remembered why she'd put it down in the first place. With a sigh, she wrapped it up and threw it in the trash. Total waste of a good cookie.

As she exited the cafe, her mind still brewing over the conversation she'd had with Leif, she nearly ran into a guy who looked to be about her age. Brown eyes with flecks of amber met her gaze from beneath dark hair, the long front draped partially over his face. And was he wearing eyeliner? Kenzie didn't run into many goths in Shallow Grave, but she kinda liked the look.

He smiled at her, and her heart skip a beat. "Sorry," he said.

"Yeah, likewise." Kenzie made to go around him, but he stopped her.

"I'm Adam, by the way."

Kenzie cocked a brow. "You make a habit of introducing yourself to everyone you run into?"

"Only the pretty ones."

Kenzie gave an amused huff, heat rushing to her face. *Yeah, I've gotta get out more.* "Kenzie. But that's all you're getting from me."

"Well, Kenzie but-that's-all-you're-getting-from-me, I hope we meet again."

Kenzie shook her head. She spoke over her shoulder as she walked away, "One can always dream." And feeling his eyes still on her, she decided to make a show of it, swaying her hips just a little bit more than usual, smiling to herself.

Yeah, she really needed to get out more.

Juliet

Juliet roamed around her classes and the halls with a sullen face, as if there was a black cloud over her head. Trying to be strong when her heart was breaking apart was a lot easier said than done. The only music she listened to were slow songs about love and loss. Losing Nik so soon had obviously overthrown her life and she didn't care who knew it—even if she hadn't really lost him yet.

As if she cared what everyone thought.

But the whispers were back full force. Only this time they weren't about her; the whispers were about how they understood why she was so upset, and that annoyed Juliet.

She found herself spending most of her free time in their secret place in the library. It was cozy and it was theirs.

Juliet threw her headphones on the empty spot on the chair next to her. It bounced off and fell against a tall pile of books, knocking down a few from the top. She rushed over to the pile to place the books back where they were. Glancing at them as she stacked them back up, she swallowed through the lump in her throat. She could vividly remember the day that Nik brought them there.

With a look of pure excitement, he dropped a heavy box at his feet. He didn't explain a thing, he just emptied the books and stacked them up into two piles. When the box was empty, he stood and stared at her expectantly. So Juliet walked over and picked up the book at the very top, but Nik playfully pushed the book out of her hand.

"Not that one. That's the pile of books I want us to read together. This stack over here is for you to read on your own. They're my favorites and I know you'll love them. The top one is my all-time favorite." He was so thrilled that his dimples were out in full force—Juliet's weakness.

"Well I'm not much of a reader, but for you I'll give it a shot." Juliet reached for the top book—his favorite—and stuffed it in her bag. With a wide grin, Nik lifted her off her feet and squeezed her until she couldn't breathe.

She wiggled out of his embrace and picked up her phone to send Nik a few links. "My turn. The first playlist is of my favorite songs ever. The second is of songs I think you'd like. And the last is the list I listen to when I need to calm down."

"I look forward to hearing them all. Especially what it takes to calm that fiery beast of yours." Juliet felt her cheeks warm and brought her hands up to cover them. But when he pulled her hands away, he placed a kiss on each cheek and then one on her lips. She felt faint from the warmth of his lips. Her heart pounded rapidly as she melted into another tight embrace. She took a deep breath to savor every detail.

Now, as Juliet placed the fallen books back where they belonged, she wiped a tear that fell to the tip of her nose. She yearned for his closeness and his smile. She felt disoriented without him there with her. She wanted nothing more than to be near him.

And she couldn't.

All she had were his books. She hugged one of them close to her chest and sluggishly went to the lonely chair. She opened to the first page and read it like he wanted her to. She relished in the silence and got lost in a world Nik liked most.

No one besides Myreen and Kol knew about their secret library spot. Myreen wasn't a fan of it. She said the dust made her feel like she was choking and it wasn't bright enough to actually read anything. So when she heard shuffling from the other side of the large bookshelf, she knew who—and what—to expect.

"Seriously, J. You couldn't do this in your room? What are you even doing in here?" Myreen coughed to show just how serious she was. Juliet thought she was just being dramatic.

"It's a library, so I'm reading." Juliet didn't mean to sound like such a grump but reading the book had made her more annoyed because Nik wasn't there to read it with her. With him leaving, there were tests that he wanted to take in his classes to get the credits. So instead of spending every moment he had left with her, he took most of the time to make up for the school work he'd be missing out on.

"Okay then. Someone's not happy. Again. I mean come on, you've got to get over this. You're acting like your life is over, and he hasn't even left yet." Myreen reluctantly took the dusty seat next to

Juliet and placed her hand on her shoulder. "I miss you and you haven't even gone anywhere. Doesn't that tell you something?"

"I know. I miss him so much." Juliet put her face in her hands and shook it.

"Then call your boyfriend and tell him that. Nikolai doesn't seem like the type to push you aside when you're this... vulnerable."

"I guess you're right."

Myreen took Juliet's shoulders in her hands and shook them with playful force. "See, a step back to happiness! I'll leave you to this... grimy hideout. Call him, then come find me!" Myreen comically blew a kiss to Juliet, then choked on the thick dust particles that floated in the air as she left the small space.

Juliet decided now was the perfect time to call Nik. When he answered on the first ring, her heart swelled with adoration.

"Hey, you." His low-toned voice immediately brought comfort.

"Hey, Nik. Sorry to bother you. I know you're busy."

"Busy is not even close. But I'm never too busy for you."

Juliet smiled and blushed as she played with the open book in her lap. "I just started this book in your pile and it's pretty good. It made me miss you already, though."

Nik sighed. "Trust me, I know what you mean. But I can't let my parents down."

"I know. You don't have to explain that again. Just wanted to hear your voice before my next class."

"I have to go. But let's get out of the school later. I'd hate to spend the rest of our time together in the Dome. Would you like to meet me at the diner for a shake? After your class is over?" He rushed the questions out quickly.

"Of course I would. See you there."

Juliet didn't know how she felt about their conversation. It sounded like he missed her and wanted to see her. He was also distant and distracted.

At the moment, though, it didn't matter. She was elated that she could be with him, even if it was quick. The second they hung up she raced out of the library and to her class. Time couldn't go by fast enough.

***

Juliet played with a string on her oversized cardigan as she waited inside the diner for Nik to get off the phone with his dad. It felt like it was their first date all over again. Or maybe she was just anxious to spend time with him. She waited in the booth that they always sat in and she couldn't help but think of the times they had there.

Sliding out of the booth, she headed for the jukebox and found a slow holiday song. She took a deep breath and spun around—and bumped right into Nik's chest.

"Must we always meet this way?" He pulled her in for a long hug and gave her his trademark smirk. But he didn't make much eye contact, which sunk Juliet's stomach.

"Is everything okay? With your dad?" Maybe his odd behavior had something to do with the phone conversation he just had with his father.

Nik took Juliet's hand in his large, warm ones and finally looked into her eyes. "Juliet, nothing kills me more than to be the cause of your sorrow. I thought this could work, but it isn't fair to you. You shouldn't have to go through this, and I'm sorry for dragging you along with me."

He looked like she felt, sick to her stomach.

"Why are you talking like this? What did I do?"

"No one sees you around the Dome anymore. My mom says you lost your spark in class. And you spend all your time in the library. That isn't healthy for you. And it's my fault. I adore you and I appreciate every minute we spent together..."

"But...?" Juliet knew what was coming.

"But I think it'll be better for you if we took a break. Until I can come back to the Dome..." Juliet felt like her world would crash and burn at any moment.

"*If* you come back. You don't even know if you will. Don't make me any promises. If you want this to be over, then it's over." She didn't want it to end on such a bad note, but her temper clouded her reasoning.

"Please don't. I really care about you and I don't want this to end. I only think it's better for you. Just for now." Nik had a nervous look in his eyes as he tried to reach for Juliet's hand.

But she stood briskly before he could. She had to escape before she blew up the diner. She shook her head and angrily wiped away the tears that fell.

"Forget it. Don't worry about me. Goodbye, Nik." She raced out of the diner, no longer one of her favorite places—Nik ruined that for her by dumping her there.

Once the fresh air smacked her in the face, she pressed her back against the cold brick wall. She tried to steady her breath, but it didn't work. She tried to calm herself by getting lost in the Christmas lights that hung all over the street, but they just made her dizzy. Her hands went from clammy to warm to hot. As she tried to get control of her emotions, Nik raced out of the diner after her.

"Don't leave like this, please." She could sense the desperation in his tone, which gave her mixed feelings. The cold air was the only thing that cooled her enough to speak.

"You're the one pushing me away. I'm leaving because *you* want me to. I thought we were stronger than that. I thought we weren't going to give up on each other. We can get through this, Nik. I know we can. Don't do this." She hated the way she sounded. She never begged for anything.

"If you're already this broken without me leaving, then I can only imagine the damage it'll do when I'm actually gone. This is the only way. And it's not forever. I told you I *don't* want this. But I care about you too much to let you live like this. Jules, please."

And that was the last push of fuel on the fire. He used his pet name for her, the one that she loved. The first time he said it flashed in her mind as tears fell. They'd walked hand-in-hand, window shopping along the cold and slippery sidewalk. When they came across a vintage jewelry shop, he clumsily spun her around then held her close as he whispered in her ear *"I already have the rarest and most beautiful gem of them all. My very own firestone, Jules."* Jules. It once sounded so pleasing. Now it only made her angrier.

The flames grew within the palms of her hands. She wasn't crazy enough to stay there. If she did, the diner was sure to burn down. Instead, she spiraled around and raced in the direction of the Dome.

She ran the whole way there. It was the only thing that seemed to keep her fire within her body. She needed to get to the Dome and she needed to get there fast.

She couldn't believe how easy it was for him. He didn't even want to try to give their relationship a chance.

All she wanted was to go to the sim room to shift and brawl.

Kol

Kol watched as Nik stomped into the avian common room with smoke seeping from his ears. Three fireballs orbited him quickly like a protective shield. He was clearly in a sour mood.

"Off to pack?" Kol asked, causing Nik to shoot him a glare and one of the fireballs fired in his direction. Realizing that it was Kol, the fireball extinguished before Kol had time to react. Clearly Nik hadn't seen him studying in the corner of the couch when he walked in. Nik's face instantly smoothed from fury to guilt and then tempered frustration. It was a look Kol had seen on Nik more often than he liked ever since the vampire attack. He knew the frustration was directed at him, because Nik never acted that way toward Brett or anyone else.

Nik's remaining fireballs extinguished and the smoke disappeared. Kol shut his textbook slowly. He could still feel the anger roll off his friend in thick, hot waves.

"Yes," he practically spat. "I'm off to pack." Nik turned and walked down the hall toward his room.

"Hold on," Kol said, jumping up from his seat.

Nik turned and looked at him expectantly. Thin tendrils of black smoke began rising above his nearly bare head.

But then Kol didn't know what to say. He wasn't used to discussing feelings with Nik or Brett. They usually just gave each other a wide berth if one of them needed some space. It usually righted itself after a day or so without over-discussion, like how the girls handled their problems. But they didn't have a day or so. If Kol remembered right, Nik was leaving soon. Like an *hour* soon. And it was unknown when he'd see his friend again. Kol didn't want whatever was going on to hang over his head.

"Look, Kol, if you've got something to say, just say it."

"It's messed up that they're making you leave," Kol said.

Nik shrugged, then ran a hand over the carved hair alongside his head. Kol noticed it was in the shape of a phoenix and he knew it was probably in honor of a certain girl. "The timing just sucks." Nik cleared his throat. "But it's a great opportunity, so... *whatever.*"

"Hey, and I'm sorry you have to hang out with my father," Kol said. "I wouldn't wish that upon anyone."

"*Eh...* the General isn't that bad," was all he had to say.

The space between them thickened with sudden awkwardness. Kol didn't understand how that happened, but scrambled to remedy it. "Look—"

"Why'd you have to go and do that?" Nik interrupted.

"Go and do—?" Kol realized a second too late what Nik was referring to.

"Go and run in front of that vamp bomb-thing!" He shouted. "What the *hell,* Kol? I'm not some damsel in distress. I am a very capable dragon—"

Kol held his hands up. "I know, I—"

"In fact, I'm a better dragon than *you* in some ways!" Nik turned and hit the wall with his fist hard enough to draw the notice of anyone in the avian wing, but fortunately not hard enough to leave a mark. Nik shook his hand rapidly, but Kol could still see the angry red marks on his knuckles. Nik muttered a curse under his breath.

Kol glanced down the hall, waiting for heads to pop out of doors. Either no one was in the wing, or they were, but knew who was arguing and were staying in their rooms. Cowards.

"And then you had to go and almost get yourself killed," Nik said, still angry, but the energy of his anger was gone. "All to save me."

Kol respected his friend enough to remain quiet.

"Do you have *any* idea what it would have done to me if you'd died?" he asked. "That my best friend not only took lead shrapnel for me, but died doing it?"

"I couldn't have lived with myself if I hadn't stepped in." Kol admitted.

"What if the situation had been reversed, huh?" Nik asked. "What if I'd been the one to throw myself in front of a bomb to save you? I would have said the exact same thing."

"But it wouldn't—"

"Don't deny it, Kol," Nik interrupted again. "You would've been furious. You would've called it *stupid and illogical.*"

Kol hated to admit it, and so he didn't, but that sounded a lot like something he'd say. "What's in the past is past," he said instead. "And no permanent damage was done." He held a hand up as if it proved that he was fully healed.

"That's not entirely true," Nik said in a low tone, like he didn't want Kol to hear.

"Look," Kol snapped. "Quit making me feel guilty for saving you, okay? It was a split-second decision."

"Yes. But if you could—"

"If I could do it again, I'd do the exact same thing. Get. Over. It."

Nik growled. "The prince isn't supposed to sacrifice himself, okay?" he said, then conjured a flaming red ball that he chucked right at Kol's face. Kol extinguished it before it could do any damage, of course.

But it was the comment more than the fireball that caught Kol off-guard. "I thought..." he started, but didn't finish. "I would've done it for the girls, too, you know. And not just Myreen. I would've taken the hit for Juliet, too." Kol's chest heaved with each breath. His chest hurt somehow, but it wasn't exactly a physical pain. It bothered him that of all people, Nik was using the prince card and throwing it in his face.

And he was still angry. Nik threw his hands in the air and looked like he was about to attack the wall again. "Of course you would," he said, his tone thick with ever-building frustration and anger. "As far as we knew, they were both inexperienced and essentially defenseless—until Juliet became a major badass and finally shifted."

"How are things, by the way?" Kol asked, suddenly wanting the subject to change. Pretend like Nik hadn't used Kol's family and perceived position against him. He was getting weary of the fight. And since Nik was leaving soon... "With Juliet, that is."

It struck a nerve because Nik visibly flinched at her name, his face contorting for a brief second... in pain.

“I broke things off.”

Kol hadn’t expected that. “What? Why?” he asked. “I thought you were into her.”

“I *am* into her.” He rubbed his hand over his head again. “Like *really* into her. It’s just...”

“Because you’re leaving?” Kol asked.

“Sorta. She’s not taking it well and...” Nik leaned against the wall with his arms crossed over his chest. “And I don’t want to be the one holding her back from being... happy.”

“That’s stupid.”

Nik’s eyes shot to Kol’s.

“She probably thinks so too,” Kol added.

Nik pushed off from the wall, his defenses up again, and stalked toward his room. “Whatever. It’s not like the General is forcing you from school,” he called back. “You have no idea...” He didn’t finish his thought and waved a hand. “I’ve gotta pack.”

“Is that what you did to Juliet?” Kol asked. He knew he was pushing Nik’s buttons, but couldn’t help himself. “You broke up with her, walked away because you didn’t like what she said or something?”

Nik whipped around. “Look,” he said, stomping toward Kol with a finger in his face. “You have *no* idea what you’re talking about. She’s...” he paused, his fire faltering a quick second. “She’s not like any girl I’ve ever dated.”

Nik didn’t have to say another word. His tone and expression told Kol everything. “She’s got you whipped.”

Nik’s shoulders dropped. “Yeah, she really has.” His brief vulnerability erased from his face and the familiar angry, frustrated one returned. “Don’t ever try to save me again,

Malkolm Dracul."

The usage of his full name smarted. Eduard was generally the only one who used it. Well, and his mom. But she never used a tone like that when she said it.

Kol didn't say another word as Nik disappeared into his room, even though he knew that was the closest thing to a goodbye he was going to get.

***

In defense class, Kol threw himself completely into training. The exertion helped clear his head from the run-in he'd had with Nik—who was probably already gone at that point, but Kol tried not to think about that.

They were practicing hand-to-hand combat, no shifting allowed. There were rumors that vampires were working on some biological weapon that would prevent shifters from being able to shift, or even use their powers, so they had to rely solely on their human abilities.

Most of the time Kol—as well as the majority of his classmates—thought it was dumb. They'd never encountered such a weapon, nor heard of one being used *anywhere* in the world. But Oberon insisted that they be ready anyway, and so required one training session each month.

But for once Kol was glad for it. Although it would have been easier to sink into his dragon self and shut off his thoughts in the sim, he'd been avoiding another simulation session since the incident with the invisible dragon. Concentrating on only using human abilities also took quite a bit of brain-space, but he still found that he had to put his full force and attention on it to keep the replay of his fight with Nik from continuing on a constant loop.

Kol swung his leg around, attempting to sweep Shawn's legs out from underneath him, but Shawn was quick and leapt like a schoolgirl jumping a rope. The image made Kol chuckle and he missed the undercut punch that landed square in his gut. Suddenly breathless, he took a staggering few steps backward to give his lungs time to recuperate, but Shawn took advantage and spun behind Kol, quickly hooking an elbow around his neck. It surprised Kol that he'd been trapped so quickly and effectively, especially given their height distances. The surprise only lasted a moment because Kol only had to arch his back to lift Shawn off the ground. He hooked an arm around Shawn's middle, catapulting him around his body, and slamming him onto the mat.

Shawn lay there stunned, contemplating his next move. Kol knelt to pin him with his arms so that they could be tapped out, but Shawn used Kol's momentary lack of absolute concentration to whip his head up and strike it against Kol's, sending stars flashing across Kol's eyesight and disorienting him.

While his vision was momentarily hindered, Kol used his other senses to locate Shawn, who was on his right, moving to make his signature final blow of shoving him to the ground with the force of his elbow and knee at once. Students often underestimated Shawn because of his smaller size, but in human—and even in dragon—form, Shawn was a worthy opponent.

Kol paused for a moment, pretending like the disorientation of his vision and explosion in his head was too much. He reached his leg out to catch the back of Shawn's knee in order to collapse his leg.

But he miscalculated.

Shawn was inches too far back and Kol missed it altogether, stretching his calf—freshly healed from three of the lead pellets that had embedded themselves into the muscle—until he felt a snap. New pain radiated up and down his leg. He could do nothing but lay on the mat while Shawn declared himself the victor.

Kol breathed deeply, lying on his back while his classmates cheered. Their celebration was always louder and more exuberant whenever someone beat Kol, but he acted like he didn't care. As soon as he thought he could handle the pain and finally stand, he limped off in a hurry, muttering something about finding Ms. Heather.

What a stupid, hellish day it's turned out to be, Kol thought as he inched down the hall, leaning heavily against the wall. First the fight with Nik and now that foolish miscalculation in defense class that earned him a fresh injury.

Fortunately, the entire school was still in their defense classes, so he had the hallway to himself. He could nurse his wounded pride in peace as he headed to the Nurse's Station.

It wasn't far, but it took quite a bit of effort getting there. The closer he got, the more the thought of Ms. Heather's face when she saw Kol return with an injury she'd recently spent so much time healing haunted him.

But what else could he do? Heal naturally? The thought was ridiculous.

When he rounded the corner to the Nurse's Station, though, his heart leapt at seeing who had just exited.

Myreen.

She must've had an extra training session with Ms. Heather.

And just like that, his common sense fled and a new plan formed.

"Hey!" he called. "Myreen." He said it loud enough that he hoped she'd hear and turn, which she did. He also hoped Ms. Heather wouldn't hear or feel the need to come out and see how he was doing.

Myreen looked everywhere but at Kol as she slowly approached.

He leaned heavily against the wall, hiding the fact that he was in significant pain. After what he'd been through, though, it wasn't too hard to keep a straight face.

"Hello, Kol," she said softly, then looked confused. "Aren't you supposed to be in defense?" She pointed in the direction of the defense hall.

"I uh..." he stared at the ground, then shifted when the pain was too much. The wince was enough for her to react with a tiny gasp.

"You're hurt," she said, her voice firmer. More confident.

Kol felt his face and neck flame with embarrassment. He reached a hand up to grip the side of his neck, looking at the ground in front of him. "It's just a sprain, I'm sure," he lied. The *snap* was probably not just a sprain.

Immediately she took his arm. "Here, let's get you to Maya."

"No!" he shouted, then stopped himself. "No," he said quieter. Then an idiotic thought occurred to him and he jumped on the impulse. "Maybe you could...?" He let the question hang in the air.

She looked at him with confusion for only a second before the realization hit her and an eyebrow rose. "You want *me* to...?"

She pointed at herself.

He lowered his eyes to hers, and nodded slowly, feeling—and probably looking—very sheepish for asking. "Would you?" he asked. "It's just..." he paused. "She just got through healing me and I don't want to go in there..."

She watched him for another fraction of a second before her shoulders relaxed and she nodded, gripping his arm. "Of course, I'm sure I can manage." Her voice didn't sound as sure, but he had confidence in her abilities. Plus, she needed the practice, right?

Myreen looked around, as if a gurney might magically appear in the hallway.

"Let's go over here," he pointed in the direction of the greenhouses. "Defense classes will be out soon and we won't be bothered."

She hesitated for a moment, like the mention of *greenhouses* disgusted or bothered her in some way. He couldn't remember why that might be, though, and she quickly nodded.

Kol tried not to lean too heavily on her as they limped toward the greenhouses. Though his calf sent shooting pains up and down his leg with each movement, he set his jaw firmly to hold back any cries of pain. It was just a muscle, after all, he needn't be such a hatchling about it.

"How can we get in?" she asked. "Aren't they locked. Wouldn't we need a teacher to let us in?"

"Not right now," he said, gesturing for her to push open the door to the nearest greenhouse. "They leave it open during school hours. Mrs. Coltar is supposed to supervise any students who come in, but I know for a fact she's in a parent-teacher meeting with that cocky hound. I think Jesse's his name?"

He also knew that Mrs. Coltar kept a few folding chairs

near the entrance so at least he could sit. He and Trish might've knocked over a stack of them while they'd been... *that's probably why Myreen had looked that way.* She'd heard about his little tryst with Trish. It seemed like forever ago. Myreen had to know that was *long* before she even arrived at the Dome.

If she knew about it, or was thinking about it, it didn't show on her face.

"So, you hurt your leg?" she asked.

He wanted to correct her on it, but was reminded that Brett and Nik often told him it was rude to point things out like that, because if she'd pointed out the obvious, then something was either on her mind or she was... nervous.

He snapped from his brief lapse of brain-to-mouth connection and nodded. "Yes, it's on the back of my leg," he said. "I felt it snap in a spar."

She winced as if she were the one who'd injured herself. "*Ouch,*" she said. The way she said it drew his eyes to her mouth. The way it formed an *O* and her eyebrows furrowed at the same time weirdly reminded him of the way she'd looked that night. When he'd lay barely conscious with shooting daggers of pain all over his body from the shrapnel made of lead. She was so worried that he was dying, her expression advertised that much—and he was sure her worry had not been unfounded.

Thinking about that night led his thoughts to the succession of events and what had happened next. He'd been delirious and sometimes wondered if he'd dreamt it, but more than any of his memories, that one was the clearest. When he'd kissed her.

Her lips soft and tasting of peaches. She'd kissed him back, too.

"Kol?" she asked, ripping him from his thoughts. Her voice had a nervous edge. Maybe she was thinking of that night, too? It wasn't his preferred way of kissing a girl—of kissing *this* girl—and he needed to remedy it.

Kol took one limping step forward, watching her reaction. She didn't step back, she didn't avert her gaze or frown. She looked almost... expectant? Hopeful? Confidence rose in his chest, warm and glowing like his fire.

Another half-step forward and with one swift movement, he wrapped one arm around her waist, putting the other hand just behind her neck. Fingers entwined in her thick, silky hair, he pulled her into a kiss.

This time it wasn't interrupted by that damned pain that was sucking away his life. No. Now his only injury—his stupid, brilliant injury that brought her back into his arms—had faded into the background. Their kiss deepened, and he felt her fingers reach up into his hair.

Slowly, he moved her toward the wall of the greenhouse until his calf smarted and he broke the kiss for only a moment to search for a seat. Quickly sitting, he pulled her hand forward, silently asking permission. Her small smile and bright eyes met his and she allowed herself to be pulled forward and sideways on his lap.

With both hands, he brushed the hair away from her shoulders, watching every miniscule movement of her beautiful face that mirrored the swirling emotions he felt. This time, she leaned into him and pressed her lips against his.

Kol's hellish day melted away.

Myreen

Hot! Myreen was so deliciously hot all over!

The last thing she expected to happen this evening—or *ever*—was to end up making out with Kol. Sure, she'd fantasized about it hundreds of times, especially after he kissed her in the alley. She'd excused it as an action of near-death deliria. He'd been so distant before that, so hot and cold, and they'd agreed to be friends right before.

But *this!* This was so far from being just friends. Kol was fully conscious, and his fingers were tangled in the thick hair at the back of her neck just as surely as his tongue was tangled with hers. Oh, and how delicious he tasted! Warm and heady, kind of like cinnamon.

Is this what fire tastes like?

All she knew was that she wanted more of it. More of his large, warm hands pulling her closer as she sat on his lap. More of his fingers caressing her ears and jawline as they combed through her hair. More of his lips opening and closing over hers in a perfect rhythm that made her head spin and her insides explode like fireworks.

Even in the haze of euphoria, nagging thoughts trickled through.

Kol was in this very spot with Trish, doing the same thing...

She shook it off, telling herself that this was different. She wasn't just some fling to him. She could feel it. They had a deeper connection. What she felt for Kol was inescapable; she'd tried time and again and still ended up pining for him. She only hoped that he felt the same. Why else would he push her away only to pull her back in? He must have been fighting these feelings for her, too. Though she couldn't imagine why. No, she wasn't just another mermaid to him.

As if to assert her position in his heart, she squeezed the muscles of his shoulders and leaned closer, reveling in how solid and strong he felt. Sometimes he acted like such a boy, but right now he felt like a man, and it thrilled her.

But he's not strong enough to fend against vampires and their weapons...

That one stung. She was brought right back to the moment the cannon went off and Kol fell, the memory so real for an instant that it disoriented her.

"What's wrong?" Kol asked against her slowing lips, his voice breathless and soft.

"Nothing," she said, looking into his heavy-lidded amber eyes. They held each other's gaze for a long moment, both getting lost in each other, both seeing more than just black pupils inside glossy irises.

"Myreen," he whispered right before pulling her back against him and pressing his lips to hers.

The way he said her name made her melt in his arms, and she was helpless to resist his kisses.

What about Kendall...? her brain whispered, taunting.

Kendall. She hadn't seen or heard from him since the night he tried to force her out of the school and take her to Draven. Where had he gone? Had he really betrayed them to join the vampires? If he had, was he even still alive? She'd seen first-hand what vampires did to shifters. Would his shifted allegiance matter to them? *He could be dead right now.*

Her heart sank. As betrayed as she felt, she still hated the thought of him being hurt. Yes, he'd manipulated her into trusting him from the very beginning, but he'd only done it because he was following visions he completely believed in. Could she really fault him for that?

But it wasn't just her he had betrayed. He'd planned to hand the entire school over to Draven. In fact, maybe he'd already done that. *That* she could blame him for. Turning his back on his own people—his friends and family—was inexcusable.

She'd been too blinded by his charms to see any of it. She'd let her hormones be in the lead ever since she got to the Dome, all so she wouldn't have to face the sadness of her reality. And reality had bitten her in the butt. Maybe now just wasn't the right time for this...

She slid her hands to Kol's chest—loving how it was both firm and soft at the same time—and pushed away from him.

"Myreen?" he panted, a question in his eyes as he searched hers.

Her eyes fell to his lips, and it took an amazing amount of willpower not to fall back onto them once more.

She gently climbed off his lap and stood in front of him, the distance between them leaving her feeling cold and awkward.

She cleared her throat. "You, uh, you said you wanted me to heal you."

A circus of emotions played on his face: confusion, disappointment, frustration. In an instant, Kol's expression went emotionless, reverting to his default, robotic setting. The change crushed her.

"Yeah," he said with a dry voice. He swallowed. "I'd really appreciate not having to bother Ms. Heather again."

Myreen nodded and knelt in front of his injured leg. He rolled up his pants to expose his calf and twisted his leg so she could see. A strange paint-splatter-shaped purple bruise stained the skin.

At the sight of it, she grimaced and sucked in a breath between her teeth, making a hissing sound. "Ouch! That looks awful." Empathy for the pain he must be feeling warmed her heart even further, and she resisted the urge to hug him.

"Eh, it's not so bad," he shrugged. Kol, the robot who feels no pain.

She frowned sideways at him.

Under her dubious gaze, his shoulders slumped. "But it could be worse."

"Let's be glad it isn't," she said, silently enjoying catching him in a fib.

She pulled her tablet out of her laptop bag. "Ms. Heather updated my tablet with the x-ray app the harpies use. I haven't had the chance to test it out yet." She tapped the icon that looked like a ribcage, and the app opened.

TAP TO SCAN AFFLICTED REGION, read the message on the screen.

Myreen held the tablet so that the camera was aimed at Kol's bruise and tapped the screen. A faint red glow slowly blanketed across the screen, and after it had crossed a few seconds later, a high definition x-ray image of Kol's calf appeared. His bones were outlined in yellow, his veins and arteries in branch-like red lines, and the outline of his skin was a faint white. Dark red globs congealed toward the base of the bone, where there was a small fracture, tiny splinters of yellow peppering the surrounding area.

"You've got a fracture," she said. "I've only practiced healing once, so... just don't expect a miracle."

"I have faith in you," he said, making her breath hitch.

They caught each other's eyes for a moment. Kol's face was blank, but his eyes were a storm of emotions. She looked away while she still had the willpower to do so and tried to focus on the task at hand—or leg, rather.

She set the tablet aside and looked around. It was so dark in this corner of the greenhouse. If she was going to heal him, she needed light. Suddenly, she remembered her first lesson with Ms. Heather. *Fire.*

"This is going to sound strange, but would you conjure up a fireball for me?" she asked.

He squinted. "A fireball? In a greenhouse?"

"I need the light," she explained. "And fire is the purest form of light. Just hold it in your hand so I can access it."

He shrugged and stretched out the syllables as he said, "Okay." Then he held up his right hand, palm open, and a spark ignited, growing and swirling into a bright orange ball of fire.

As she looked at the bright orb, she cleared her mind and focused on her connection to it. Thanks to Kol, she had plenty of emotional ammo to access the light. She allowed the thrill of kissing Kol to fill her up, and tendrils of light slithered out of the ball of flame and tapered into her waiting hands. She placed them over Kol's calf and willed the light to heal him.

After a few seconds, the glow that had illuminated between her hands and his leg evaporated, and she withdrew her hands.

"How do you feel?" she asked.

Kol stretched his leg forward and rotated his ankle twice. "Perfect." He looked at her, and she couldn't help but blush. "That was amazing, Myreen. You're a natural."

She snorted a laugh. "I'm a better harpy than I am a mermaid."

"I think you're a pretty great mermaid, too," he said. "The best I've ever met."

She blushed even deeper. Not wanting him to notice, she lowered her head and brushed her hair behind her ear, then stood up. "We'd better get going before we get caught in here. Someone might think we were..."

Kol gently grabbed her wrist.

"But we were," he said. His expression seemed to ask *What happened?*

Her shoulders dropped and her brows pinched together. "Kol, I really, really want to. I just... I just need some time to figure things out right now. That's all."

The shadow that had darkened his face since they stopped kissing vanished completely, and though his expression was still robotic, his face seemed brighter, happier. "Okay." His smile was small, but it was there. "Can we at least eat dinner together in the dining hall?"

Her face lit up and her lips sprang into a wide smile. "Definitely."

They exited the greenhouse and headed for the main building.

Not only was Kol no longer limping, but was that a spring in his step?

Leif

Leif's fingers ran swiftly across the ivory keys of the antique piano while he sat in his quarters. Mozart's *Turkish March* filled the air in perfect time, and he didn't miss a single note. The acoustics in his quarters weren't the greatest: the builders of the vampire fortress hadn't built the rooms with music in mind. But his eyes remained closed as he lost himself in harmonic serenity.

As he approached the final run of the song, a knock sounded at his door, causing his fingers to stop and his eyes to open. The enveloping peacefulness he'd felt shattered into dread.

"What do they want now?" he mumbled under his breath as he stood from the piano bench and made his way to the door. Before reaching it, hurried knocks came from it again.

"I'm coming," he said with irritation. Leif grabbed the handle and pulled a little too hard, catching the thin edge of the door before it could slam into the wall. Standing in the doorway was his assigned Initiate, Piper Adams. Her sandy blonde hair was tied back in a tight ponytail, and her gold-framed glasses made her light-brown eyes appear slightly bigger than they actually were. The strangest thing for Leif was having to look up at her. He was tall by most standards, but she was at least two inches taller. He couldn't help but stare at her with annoyance.

"You play the piano beautifully, sir," she said, flashing him a smile.

Leif ignored her compliment. "I didn't summon you. Why are you here?"

His harshness didn't faze her. Like all Initiates, Piper was used to being mistreated, believing that any attention was better than none. And Leif took no pleasure in mistreating anybody, but Piper had interrupted his piano playing. Nothing irked him more than being stopped mid-song. Except for being stuck in Draven's trophy room, perhaps.

"I was sent by Draven to retrieve you," she replied.

Leif doubted that. Draven would never speak directly to an Initiate unless it was about a genetic or technological discovery he needed to understand the science of. But choosing one to be a messenger? He held too high a station for such a trivial task. More than likely, Draven asked another vampire to send for him, and that vampire had asked Piper to do the job.

"He's returned from his mission in Alberta?" Leif asked. He didn't know what business the vampire leader had in Canada. Probably more recruitment. "What is it he wants?"

She shrugged her gangly shoulders. "Beyond meeting with you, I don't know."

Of course she wouldn't. Piper's role in Draven's plans was to help him in his quest to create vampire-shifters. She was a talented Harvard-taught molecular biologist. She was no geneticist, but apparently her knowledge about macromolecules and how to get them to sustain hybrid vampire-shifters was extremely important. Most of it went over Leif's head.

"But he did say he wanted to see you immediately," she added.

Leif sighed. "Well, I best not keep him waiting." He stepped out of his quarters, shut the door behind him, and turned to walk down the LED-lit hallway.

Piper ran to keep up with him. "May I ask you a question?"

"You just did," Leif pointed out. "But yes, you may ask another."

"Is my blood...?" she stammered, but those three words already revealed to Leif what she was going to ask. "Are you afraid of how it will taste?"

Leif had yet to drink from her in the time they'd been assigned together.

"I'm sure your blood tastes just fine," he answered as they approached the stairway.

"Then why do you avoid me when you're thirsty?" she asked in a whiny pitch that reminded Leif of a beginner violinist trying to play high notes.

He was already down several steps when he stopped and looked her directly in the eyes.

"I don't trust myself with Initiates," Leif said. "Believe me, I'm doing you a favor by not drinking from you."

Piper gave him a confused look, moving a few stray hairs behind her ear. "But all other assigned Initiates are taking care of their vampires' needs. Don't you understand how that makes me feel?"

Leif's eyes widened with surprise. Her words reminded him

of a married couple's quarrel. And he definitely did *not* have that kind of relationship with Piper.

"Piper, I'm going to be straight with you," he said. "The last Initiate I drank from ended up dead. Completely sucked dry."

This time, Piper's eyes widened. "How? Is it something you... can't control?"

"I can control it. What happened to that last Initiate—what I did to her—that was twenty years ago. I had a moment of distraction. I *have* quenched my thirst from humans since then, but I don't want to risk relapsing. What I'm trying to say is that I value your life, and it wouldn't be fair if you died for the sake of filling my belly."

Leif watched as awe and gratitude filled her countenance, like a crescendo of music, starting softly, then steadily growing in volume.

"You... value me?" Piper stammered. "You care?"

"I care about all life," Leif said, not liking where she was pushing the conversation. He knew Piper was looking for acceptance. "Look, I don't know you all that well. I know you're a brilliant student who has achieved much in academics, and I know you want to become a vampire. That's about it. I don't know your family life. I don't know what your other interests are. I don't know *who* Piper Adams is." Leif glanced up the staircase to see if anybody was within earshot. He drew close to her, placing his lips next to her ear and brought his voice down to a whisper. "But what I do know is that you will never be valued like that by anyone else here. You're seen as a resource. And like in the human world, resources *always* have a limit on their value."

Leif was taking a huge risk saying this to her. He knew it. But her need to feel accepted and valued… she needed to know the truth.

"But if I become a vampire, my value will increase," Piper said. "Won't it?"

"Your status will," Leif replied. "But don't confuse status with value. They are not synonymous."

He turned around and took a few more steps.

"You wish you weren't a vampire," she mumbled in realization. It was strange hearing it come from her, and it caused him to stop again.

"I used to think there had to be others like me," he said distantly, recalling his first time at Heritage Prep. He'd hoped back then to find other like-minded vampires. But if they existed, they never revealed themselves. His mind returned to the present and he realized how dangerous his words were. If any of his words got back to Draven, he'd be in trouble. Turning around he looked up at her. "Listen, all of this…"

She shook her head quickly. "Don't worry, I won't say anything. You've actually given me a lot to think about."

Leif was shocked. Most Initiates would have jumped at the opportunity to climb the ranks, even if it meant stomping all over others to get there. And he didn't entirely trust Piper not to—she could simply be giving him false hope. But it was hope. And that was something Leif lacked a lot of over the years. It felt good to consider that out of all the vampires and potential-vampires, he may have influenced one in a proper way.

"You'd better hurry to the trophy room," she said.

He nodded, staring at her for a moment longer, then bounded down the stairs.

Increasing his speed, he passed floor after floor, feeling the air parting around him. It brought a sense of freedom amidst the confines of the vampire fortress.

That freedom soon dissipated as he slowed down to a walk on the main floor of Heritage Prep. Draven's trophy room loomed across the Great Hall, and it seemed like an invisible rope was tied around his waist, drawing him in.

Draven was across the way, just outside the door to his trophy room, but what shocked Leif was the person standing in front of him. A boy—no older than nine or ten—gave the vampire leader a hug at his waist, then quickly ran toward the stairs that led to the lower levels.

Leif felt a sweltering anger burn within him. Draven had his hooks inside an innocent little boy? What was he playing at?

"Who kept you?" the vampire leader called across the room, breaking Leif free from his spell of anger.

A jab of fear went through him like a copper dagger, causing him to freeze in place. Had Draven somehow heard his conversation in the hallway and the stairs? Leif cursed himself for being stupid enough to confide in Piper out in the open.

Draven's arms unraveled and his hands came forward, fingers outstretched and palms up. "Joplin? Bach? Tchaikovsky?"

Relief pulled the stabbing fear away and Leif grinned. "Mozart today. The *Turkish March*, to be specific." No longer frozen, Leif moved toward the doorway.

"An excellent piece, to be sure," Draven said, nodding his approval. "It has a bouncing pace that makes one want to go out and change the world."

"Indeed it does."

As he made it to the arched doorway, Draven placed an arm

around Leif's shoulder and walked into the trophy room as if they were best of friends.

"Leif, it's good to see you again," Draven said. "Here, take a seat. We need to talk."

They both made their way to Draven's desk. Hanging on the walls surrounding them were body parts of different shifters from throughout time, mounted as Draven's prizes—trophies from countless fights he'd won.

Draven sat, and Leif followed.

"How was Alberta?" Leif asked, at least somewhat interested as to how it involved Draven's grand plans.

"This time of year?" Draven laughed. "Cold and snowy. But I didn't request your presence to discuss how my trip went. I want to hear about yours."

An unsettling panic crept like a spider crawling under his skin. Leif had purposely gone back to Chicago while Draven was busy in Canada with the intent of getting away from Heritage Prep for a time. He'd even had the chance to see Kenzie briefly. But what frightened him so was that Draven had just returned and had already heard about Leif's absence. Maybe Draven *had* asked Piper to retrieve him from his quarters, and inquired about Leif's dealings then.

"Your recent trip to Chicago," Draven clarified. Leif kicked himself for not immediately answering, but the fact that Draven knew he'd been in Chicago made that spider-like feeling in his body increase exponentially. Leif hadn't told Piper where he was going, so how did Draven know where he'd gone?

"Cold and snowy," Leif replied, attempting to mask the panic flooding his chest. "Much like Alberta."

Draven threw him an insincere smile. "Would you mind

explaining to me why you went back to your home?"

Leif sighed heavily, his mind coming up with several coverups—most of them not very convincing. "Things did not sit well with me after our attack at that alley near the Chicago subway station."

Draven nodded, and Leif hoped his on-the-spot story was good enough. "Yes, you have always needed to satisfy your memories, haven't you? Always living in the past."

"It's a habit that's helped with strategic planning," said Leif.

"And it's also been known to be a complete waste of time," countered Draven. "But do tell, please, was your trip a successfully strategic move for our cause?"

Leif stared at him for a few moments, determining which web of lies he should weave for himself. He decided on the most plausible. "It was the dragon shifters we encountered that drew me back to Chicago."

"The dragons?" Draven asked, cocking his head to the side. "What about the dragons."

"One of the boys..." Leif started, dipping into his memories from over one hundred years ago. "The dark-haired one. He resembled a certain enemy of mine from my past."

Leif held Draven's penetrating gaze, and he felt as if the vampire leader was seeing straight into his mind.

"You believe the dragon we shot down was of Dracul lineage?"

Hearing the name on Draven's tongue filled Leif with rage, his mind forming the image of Aline Dracul. He'd blamed a lot of people for ruining his life over the years, but Aline was one person he'd never be able to forgive.

"If what you say is true," Draven said, rubbing at his chin

in thought, "then that shows that the Draculs are involved with the shifter school." He laughed loudly, casting his eyes about as if Leif's words were the best news in the world. That the Dracul name could bring such happiness to anybody only enraged Leif further. "If word gets out that we killed a Dracul, we could very well rally more of the older vampire lines to our cause. After all, Leif, you are not the only vampire with a cause for hatred against the Draculs."

Leif held no malice for any Dracul other than Aline. The sin of an ancestor didn't trickle down through the generations. At least, not to Leif.

"Are we sure we killed that boy?" Leif asked. "The shifters have been notoriously good at staying alive, even when we think it's impossible."

Draven snorted. "We riddled that dragon with enough lead to kill him ten times over. But I do suppose there is always the chance he was saved in time. Even if that's the case, the branch of vampires still holding a grudge against the Draculs will be running at the chance to ensnare them."

Leif nodded slowly, resigning himself to the fact that he might have just made matters worse for Oberon and the shifter school. He shouldn't have brought up the possibility that the dragon shifter they'd encountered in the alley had been a Dracul.

"It sounds like our attempt to capture Myreen wasn't a complete failure, then," Leif pointed out.

"We'll see," Draven said. "But on the subject of Myreen, I have a new mission for you."

Leif couldn't stop his eyes from widening, causing Draven to grin again.

"I see that sparked your interest." The vampire leader

leaned forward and interlocked his fingers, resting his elbows on the desk. "I want you to personally see to the capture of my daughter."

"Wh– what?" Leif stammered.

"As a daywalker, you're the best option for the job," Draven explained. "We know where the shifters enter and exit their school. Eventually, Myreen will come out. And when she does, you'll grab her and bring her to me."

"This task is being assigned to me alone?" Leif asked.

"You are fully reinstated here at Heritage Prep," Draven replied. His eyes narrowed ever so slightly. "Just as I trusted you before your desertion fifteen years ago, I trust you again now. And you're the only one who can survive in sunlight. So yes, you'll be on your own."

Leif could hardly believe what he was hearing. He'd expected to be trapped at Draven's fortress—or at the very least sent out on missions where other vampires could keep an eye on him.

"Nobody else that I trust is as familiar with Chicago as much as you," Draven continued. "Plus, you already know what my daughter looks like. You are the obvious candidate for the mission."

"I am honored, Draven," Leif replied, bowing slightly, attempting to bury the excited emotions that threatened to burst from him. He looked into the vampire leader's sky-blue eyes. "I will take on this responsibility."

Draven's face grew serious. "If you succeed and bring Myreen to me, you will be rewarded beyond measure. Your status will elevate higher than any other vampire's—excluding me, that is—and you will have made your mark on vampire history."

Leif nodded, having no intention at all to follow through with Draven's plan. And if history forgot Leif, he'd be entirely fine with that.

Draven whipped his hand up and pointed his index finger in the air. "If you fail me, it'll be back to the Madness Chamber for you."

A memory surfaced briefly in Leif's mind—one not from his distant past. He'd been forced into a tank of water in the dungeons of Heritage Prep recently. For twenty-four hours, he'd drowned over and over in that water, but that hadn't even been the worst of the experience. The Madness Chamber's waters had been mixed with hallucinogens that threw him into memories from long ago. But the memories were muddled by his own mind. It had taken three days for the drugs to wear off.

"Last time, you drowned for a whole day, right?"

Leif nodded slowly as he tried to force the memory from his mind.

"That was punishment for abandoning me fifteen years ago," Draven reminded. "Failure in this mission is not acceptable. If you do not succeed in bringing me Myreen, I will see that you stay in the Madness Chamber for three whole years."

Setting his jaw, Leif looked back up at Draven and said, "Understood."

Draven hunched over his desk and put his face right in front of Leif's, slowly looking back and forth between his eyes. "Bring me my daughter, Leif. Bring me Myreen."

Juliet

Juliet felt like the walls were caving in on her whenever she left the comfort of her own bedroom. She was so broken that she it seemed like her world was crashing and burning around her as she slummed it around the Dome. She only made it a few hours attending classes before she decided she wouldn't go to the others. They weren't as important as her broken heart.

She felt alone and distressed, like she did when she was first brought to the Dome. Selfishness distorted her true reality. She knew she wasn't alone. She had Myreen. Other students tried to befriend her, but there was too much sadness in her to even want to make new friends. She also knew she was being crappy to the one friend she had.

When Juliet told Myreen about the breakup, the way her mouth froze in an open O proved how unexpected it was. Myreen was there for her in any way she could be. While Juliet cried, Myreen passed her the tissues. While Juliet cursed Nik's name, Myreen bad-mouthed him with her.

The first day, everyone understood that what Juliet needed was to mourn the end of her first relationship. But now? By the way everyone rolled their eyes at her, she could tell she'd held on too long. And yet, she didn't care. She still wanted to walk around numb and dispirited.

Malachai had had enough almost immediately. Her privacy came off the table the minute she skipped her classes. While she hid under her covers, he barged into her bedroom to yank them off. She thought if she locked the door, it would stop him for entering.

She was wrong.

He burned the knob with his fire until the metal melted, hissed, and dripped down on the door. Juliet watched with annoyance as he effortlessly pushed it open and crossed his arms.

"Until you get back to class, I will do this every day."

"I'll just replace that door knob, Dad. That won't stop me!" she growled.

She dramatically jumped out of her bed with flames dancing in the palms of her hands. Malachai's arms fell to his sides while his nostrils flared and his eyes widened. He straightened his back, standing at his full—and intimidating—height while he stared at her.

When flames appeared in his own hands, Juliet knew she'd gone too far.

The hair on her arms stood up when she returned her fire back into her body. With a loud grunt, Juliet threw herself onto her bed and pulled her covers over her.

Malachai tore the covers off and threw them in a ball next

to her feet, then stomped out of her room with a triumphant glare.

Even with the unfortunate promise from her father that he'd return, there was nothing that felt important enough to leave her room.

The only thing that brought Juliet pleasure was the Christmas movie marathon on the Hallmark Channel, which made her feel like a masochist. She watched it on her tablet, ignoring the glances from the repairman who replaced her doorknob.

What she really yearned for was a single phone call from Nik—to hear his voice say her name, to hear his laugh... or for him to ask her to get back together.

She held onto her phone like it was her lifeline, clutching it between her palms while she watched a movie about how a dog brought a couple together in time for Christmas. Their story felt like the only thing keeping her faith in love alive—since Nik crumbled it up.

Juliet's new doorknob rattled, which made her heart skip a beat. Deep down, she hoped it was Nik on the other side of the door. But she knew it wasn't.

She slammed her hands down on the bed as she prepared herself for another visit from her father, vowing to use every ounce of her strength to hold down the covers so he couldn't rip them off.

But when the door flew open, it wasn't Malachai who stormed in—it was Myreen. The door slammed shut and Myreen stood with her arms crossed, exactly the way Juliet's father had. Juliet took a deep breath, then melted back into her bed.

"Thought you were my dad. He's being crazy." Juliet rolled her eyes and paused the movie on her tablet.

"*He's* crazy?" Myreen's look of annoyance caught Juliet's attention. Her stomach turned as she recognized the same look of disappointment.

"What, you agree with what he's been doing to me?"

"I mean, J, this isn't healthy."

She knew Myreen was right. She knew her father was right. But the pain in her heart overruled the sense in her brain.

Juliet didn't want her sourness to ruin the one good friendship she had. She sluggishly rose from the bed and walked to a basket on her desk. She rummaged through the contents, not caring about the mess she was making. Empty candy wrappers and half-eaten chocolates spilled around her desk, and Myreen groaned.

Finally, Juliet found the unopened package of popcorn that she was searching for. She walked back to her bed and ripped it out of its plastic sleeve, then unfolded the popcorn bag into the palm of her left hand. As the bag began to grow, Juliet felt the popcorn kernels pop and tickle her palm.

She knew to keep her fire within her hand or the bag would catch fire. All she needed was a nice simmer. When the room filled with the buttery aroma and she felt the last few kernels pop, Juliet tore the bag open and patted the empty spot on the bed next to her.

Myreen finally untangled her arms from her chest and tentatively sat on the bed. "Just because that was an awesome trick doesn't mean you're off the hook." Juliet knew Myreen was serious because her lips were stuck in a pout.

"I know. I figured this could break the tension. If you stay and eat this *and* watch this next movie with me, then I promise to listen to what you have to say without dismissing it." Juliet gave Myreen her most innocent smile. Even if it was forced, she looked forward to Myreen's company.

Myreen gave Juliet the side-eye. "Fine. But I want you to swear." As she grabbed a handful of popcorn, Juliet gave in.

"I swear."

Halfway through the movie, the pain started to hit Juliet hard again. The woman in the movie was dumped by her fiancé a week before her sister's wedding, and to avoid embarrassment, she bought a date from a magazine ad. Soon after, she clearly began to fall for the fake-date guy.

Myreen paused the movie and swung her head toward Juliet. "That's what you need. A rebound!" Her eyes lit up as she pointed to the woman on the tablet like she'd just solved everything.

"A rebound? Do you not remember that Nik was my first boyfriend? It's not like I have experience pulling guys in. Getting Nik to acknowledge me was hard in itself. And honestly, I'm not ready for that. How can I be open to another guy when my heart still belongs to Nik?" Juliet already doubted herself, which made her want to snatch the tablet out of Myreen's hand and press play.

Myreen rolled her eyes and hid the tablet behind her. "That was before everyone knew you were such a badass. If you come with me to eat in the dining hall tonight, I could point out three guys who would gladly take the title of your new boyfriend."

The way Myreen spoke so confidently gave Juliet a glimmer of hope. But Nik breaking up with her flashed in her mind, and she only wanted to hide under her sheets again.

"You're wrong, Myreen. No one wants me. Nik didn't."

"You swore you wouldn't dismiss what I had to say!" Myreen's lips begin to pout again.

"I said after. The movie isn't over yet!" Juliet was backpedaling, but it wasn't like she could just glue her broken heart back together.

"Oh, please. That's just an excuse. Who cares about Nik? Forget about him. It's his loss, not yours. And you can't keep doing this to yourself. I miss my friend!"

Now, it looked like Myreen was on the verge of tears, and that was when it finally hit Juliet.

Before Juliet could say a word, Myreen stood. "It is not okay for you to hole yourself up in your room like an ursa in hibernation. No guy is worth all this grief! *You* are better than that. There are plenty of other guys in this school, let alone *in the world.* This has to stop! Before it completely consumes you, you have to snap out of this!" She paced in front of Juliet's bed.

"*This* is not what you want Nik to hear about," Myreen said. "What do you think Kol or Brett are telling him when he's asking about you? Which you know he is. You have to show everyone you're stronger than this. You have to show *Nik* you're stronger than this. Just like the woman in the movie. She was just as broken as you are, but she realized that her turd of an ex-fiancé was not the only fish in the sea. You are a *phoenix.* Act like it!"

"You're right."

"I mean, even your dad... Wait, what?"

"I said, you're right," Juliet said. "You, my dad, the movie, you're all right." Juliet felt a heaviness lift from her shoulders as she realized how silly she'd been. She was hiding from the world over one guy. She couldn't let that define who she was.

"Of course I am!"

They giggled for the first time in a while. Juliet didn't realize how much she'd missed this.

"I'm proud of you, J. Now, go take a shower and meet me

for dinner."

Before Juliet could argue, Myreen was out of the room.

"But the movie isn't over!" Juliet shouted.

She didn't think Myreen heard her, but the door reopened and Myreen stuck her head in. "We all know how it ends: she lives happily ever after. Life isn't like Hallmark movies, Juliet. You're the writer of your own story." With a wink, Myreen left.

Surprisingly, Juliet understood exactly what she meant.

Chapter 12

Oberon

Once again, Oberon was in his classroom after-hours. His last defense class had gotten out an hour and a half before, and he'd planned to sit and grade that day's shifter history homework assignments. But he hadn't been able to concentrate—not on grading homework, at least. Instead, the glow of his tablet's screen illuminated his face with pictures of his beloved Serilda.

The picture he'd stopped on was of her at the top of one of the mountains in South Dakota. She was wrapped in a blanket, her porcelain-white face illuminated by a spectacular sunrise. Her eyes almost looked manipulated by computer software, but it was the light of the sun that had brought out the true blue in them. Her blonde hair was pulled back in a loose bun. Her thin lips held a slight smile, but it captured the magic of the moment so perfectly.

"My dear Seri," he said, running his finger along the screen, longing to touch her face again, to escape to the mountains and sit with her and watch the sunrise drawing in another day. It was gryphon custom to mate for life. He was supposed to grow old with Seri. Together, they were supposed to have as many children as possible to increase their numbers. But Draven had ended all of that. Draven had ensured that Oberon was the last of his kind, killing his wife and unborn child in the process.

The screen faded to an opaque charcoal, the image of his wife only slightly viewable. *Incoming call from EMERGENCY* filled the top of the screen.

There was only one person on his contacts list codenamed *Emergency.*

"Leif," he whispered.

At the same time, he felt his phone vibrate in his pocket, and he decided to use it instead of the tablet to answer the call. Withdrawing it from his pocket, he held it up to his ear.

"Hello?" he said, backing out of his photo library on his tablet and issuing the controls to close his classroom door.

"Oberon, it's me, Leif." The vampire's voice seemed almost cheerful—a stark contrast from the ominous, panicked way Leif had spoken during his last call. "Is this a good time?"

"Yes," Oberon said, rubbing at his eyes and discovering that tears had pooled up while he'd been viewing pictures. "Classes are out for the day. I was about to start into grading some homework."

"Listen, I'm in town for the next little while," Leif said. "Can you meet me in an hour? We need to talk."

Oberon looked down at his watch. "Yeah, that should be fine. Let's make it Neville's again."

"Fine. See you then," Leif said. Then the line went dead.

Oberon realized just how stupid it was that he'd labeled Leif as *Emergency* in his contact list. If anybody ever saw his phone flashing with that, it would bring up some difficult questions.

Shoving the phone into his pocket, he tapped the tablet to open the door, then put it in sleep mode.

He stepped between the empty desks, shutting the lights off before he exited and tapping his watch to close the door behind him. Walking down the hallway was Vauna Vex, the Were Transformation teacher. She'd been one of the students at the former school on Framboise Island. Oberon had been the one to save her and her father, Matías, from the terrible attack. She was a mao of Colombian descent, and most of the male students were entranced by her beauty. And she knew it, too.

"Good afternoon, Miss Vex," he said, nodding to her as he passed.

"Director," she replied with a nod of her own, grinning with full lips that framed perfect, white teeth.

Had Ren been around, he would have mumbled some comment about her beauty, and Oberon would have been quick to rebuke him, reminding him just how much older he was than Vauna.

Oberon got lost in his thoughts as he speed-walked back to his quarters, smiling at students and saying *hello* as he passed them.

But seeing Vauna triggered his memories of the day Draven and his vampires had torn down The Island. The school's nickname hadn't protected them. Oberon recalled the younger version of Vauna staring at him with frightened green eyes. Matías held the same look on his face. They'd seen the carnage surrounding them. They'd witnessed their home being destroyed. And their hopeless, harrowed faces were etched in

Oberon's mind. Not even the dazzling, hypnotizing smile of Vauna Vex twenty years later could replace that image.

He found himself in his office, surprised that he'd made it there at all. He couldn't remember the walk.

It was so hard shaking off the past. He didn't want to forget it—not completely—because it was what had given him purpose all those years ago. It was what was still giving him purpose. But he had a job to do.

Grabbing his tan overcoat from the rack in the corner of his office, he put it on, pulling on the collar to straighten it over his shoulders. After buttoning it up, Oberon took his dark brown scarf—also hanging on the rack—and folded it up, placing it neatly in his pocket. He'd need it as soon as he left the comfortable warmth the Dome provided.

"And where do you think you're off to?"

Oberon jumped at Ren's voice, but as he turned around, he couldn't see his heart attack-inducing friend.

"Very funny, Ren," Oberon grumbled. "Where are you hiding?"

The kitsune stepped out of the wall next him, causing Oberon to jump once more.

"Ren!" Oberon swung a fist at his friend's shoulder, but Ren phased just at the right moment, forcing him to miss.

"It never gets old," Ren said, grinning broadly.

"I'm glad you're so easily amused," Oberon said, frowning. "But I'm in a hurry. Do you need something?"

"I just saw you storming down the hallway and thought I'd come and check on you. Are you doing okay?"

Oberon sighed. "Yes. I've just got a lot on my mind."

Ren nodded. "You have a lot of weight to carry, and I'm

not talking about the recent poundage you've been putting on." Oberon's stomach was jabbed by one of Ren's fingers, which he immediately swatted away.

"Ren!" Oberon growled. "Look, I just need to get away from the Dome for a little while. I'll be back soon enough."

The playful look on Ren's face melted as fast as an ice cream cone in the Mojave Desert. "You look about ready to pay some vampires a visit."

Oberon's heart skipped a beat. He was about to pay a visit to one particular vampire, but not in the way Ren was alluding to.

Sighing, Ren said, "You are, aren't you? You're going to go blow off steam by finding some vampires to kill. Just like the old days."

Shaking his head, Oberon said, "No. But I could, right about now. What I'm going to do is go to a human restaurant, order myself a slice of pumpkin pie, eat it, order another slice and eat that, too, then maybe stretch my wings out in the sky and sort out how to best protect this school."

Ren angled his head to the side, appearing to be having some sort of internal struggle. At last he nodded, his lips drawing into a straight line. "You know, I've always been more of an apple pie guy."

In frustration, Oberon moved past his antagonizing friend without saying a word and exited his office.

"Remember what I said about the weight you're carrying," Ren called after him. "One slice is more than enough."

With long strides, Oberon walked away and made for the retinal-scanning door that would let him escape the confines of the Dome.

Leif, you better have something good to say, he thought.

***

Oberon almost wished he *would* cross paths with a group of vampires as he walked the streets of Chicago. It had been years since he'd got caught up in a fight.

His anger slightly dampened as he considered the irony of his thoughts. He was about to go talk with a vampire, while at the same time he wanted to rip another one's head off.

He considered Ubering to *Neville's*, but Oberon wasn't running late. And even if it delayed him a bit, walking in the cold allowed him more time and space to blow off steam.

As he walked, he considered some of the more difficult tasks he still needed to take care of. Kendall Green, for one, presented multiple problems. The mer had defected to the vampires, and Oberon hadn't found it in himself to notify the parents of their son's betrayal. Kendall had done the unthinkable—he'd broken promises regarding secret information about the Dome and the shifters. He'd given Draven crucial information about Myreen. As director of the school, Oberon couldn't lay a finger on the boy for his actions, but he sure wanted to tear the fish's tail off for what he'd done.

A light snow fell all around, and he welcomed it with pleasure. Snow couldn't exist within the Dome—except for the simulation room, but that didn't count because it wasn't real—so Oberon took the time to enjoy Mother Nature's offering.

The roads were wet and slushy, and cars kicked up the mucky moisture off the ground and flung it close to his boots.

Store windows flashed their silver and gold decorations, and white pillars were wrapped in red ribbon to make them look like giant candy canes. There were lit Christmas trees with shiny ornaments on display within each one, and they seemed to all be trying to outdo each other in elegance and beauty.

Oberon felt calm and peaceful, and he realized how much simpler life seemed out in the city. Deep down, he knew the city was just as crazy as life in the Dome. But for the moment, it felt like a quiet night in a recliner, a mug of hot chocolate in one hand and a book in the other.

Even though it was freezing cold in downtown Chicago.

He walked by a man in a red suit and hat wearing a ridiculously huge, fake white beard. Santa Claus grinned ear-to-ear as he rang a bell, shouting "*Ho, ho, ho,*" and prompting passersby to donate loose change for a good cause.

A few more blocks and he saw the giant neon sign shining *Neville's* proudly. As far as Oberon knew, it had never changed for as long as he'd lived at the Dome, and it had become his favorite eatery so close by.

Oberon could smell the fresh, roasted coffee as he approached the welcoming double-door. Hanging on one of the windows was another neon sign that had a design that looked like a coffee cup with the word OPEN underneath.

The door opened and the bell attached to the crash bar jingled, adding its little voice to the spirit of Christmas. A gentleman bundled up for the cold walked out, holding the door open for Oberon.

"Thank you," he said.

"Merry Christmas," the man replied as he let go and walked away.

"The same to you," Oberon replied before the door shut.

"Welcome to Neville's," the hostess said with a smile. She wore a navy blue suit coat that matched her skirt, a white collared shirt underneath. On her head sat a Santa hat. "Would you like a seat at the bar, or are you waiting for your party to show up?"

Oberon scanned the open area—the restaurant wasn't busy, but it was late afternoon still—and saw Leif off in one of the corners, waving at him as inconspicuously as he could.

Smiling, Oberon pointed toward the vampire. "It seems my party is already here."

She nodded. "Wonderful. Go ahead and take a seat. Your waiter will be right with you."

He looked at the hostess's name tag. "Thank you, Janice."

Passing several empty tables, Oberon made his way to where Leif was stewing in the corner.

Leif stuck a single finger up in the air as Oberon approached, causing him to stop and look up at the open ceiling.

"The music," the vampire said with disgust.

Oberon hadn't even noticed it. A contemporary pop version of Jingle Bells was playing softly.

"What about it?" Oberon pulled out the chair opposite of Leif and sat.

"It's like watered-down blood. Whatever happened to music that actually *sounds* like Christmas?" Leif flicked the full glass of water sitting on the table in front of him.

Leif's grouchiness seemed to subside as he looked around with a worried look, most likely afraid he'd spoken just a little too loudly about blood and its possible consumption. Fortunately, no other customers were nearby, and their server hadn't come their way yet.

Oberon didn't quite know how to reply to the analogy, but he smiled all the same. "I'm afraid my experience with the taste-quality of blood limits my understanding of what you just said, but I get it. In my book, the classics are the best."

Light footsteps sounded behind him, and he turned to see Vicky—the same server who'd helped him the last time he'd come—approaching. It was as if her auburn hair held the same intricate braid it had months ago. Her uniform dress was light yellow, and her apron white. In her hand was a steaming pot of coffee, but what was most noticeable were her brightly colored fingernails, alternating green and red. Just like Janice, Vicky was wearing a Santa hat, but hers was green.

"Welcome back to Neville's," she said with a smile. Her lips matched the color of her red fingernails.

"Thanks, Vicky," Oberon said as she poured him a cup of coffee. She handed him a few single packages of creamer and a container of sugar.

"My pleasure," she replied. "I hope you're planning on getting something, because your friend is once again adamant about coming to a restaurant with the purpose of *not* eating."

Oberon glanced at Leif and found him frowning, his head tilted down as he stared daggers at the table.

"Luckily for you," Leif said to the waitress, "I ate before I came."

An awkward moment surrounded the table, and Oberon worried Leif would actually pounce on Vicky.

Oberon cleared his throat. "You know, Vicky, what I really could use right now is a big slice of pumpkin pie."

His words broke the spell—at least for their server.

"Going for dessert first today, are we?" she asked, pulling out her pad of paper and pencil.

"And second, I'm afraid," Oberon replied with a chuckle.

"More than likely I'll be getting two slices. But let's start with one."

"I'll go get that right now," she said as she jotted it down with quick scribbles. With one last scowl at Leif, she turned and walked away.

"You know," Oberon said, opening a package of creamer and dumping it into his coffee, "you could try a little harder to be a bit more civil. Especially around the holidays."

"That waitress is relentless," Leif said, pointing a pale finger toward the back area of the restaurant where Vicky had disappeared. "And trust me, I don't use that term lightly. In my lifetime, I've known a *lot* of relentless people."

"Perhaps we need a new meeting place," Oberon suggested, dumping a packet of sugar into his cup and stirring it. "One that doesn't involve food."

"Food doesn't bother me," Leif said, looking out the window next to them. "Persistent waitresses do."

Leif mumbled his last words as Vicky approached with a piece of pumpkin pie that had to be at least a quarter of a whole one. She placed the plate in front of Oberon, then handed him a rolled-up napkin that had the prongs of a fork sticking out of the top.

"Can I get anything else for you?" Vicky asked.

"You've already brought me perfection," Oberon replied, staring at the massive piece in front of him. A large dollop of whipped cream had been placed on top. "To ask for more would be way too selfish."

"Overindulgent," Leif corrected.

Vicky snorted. "At least he ordered something." She looked back at Oberon and smiled. "Just let me know if you need anything else, okay?"

Oberon nodded. "I will. Thanks, Vicky."

She left them alone, returning to the back area once again.

"I'm glad to see you, Leif," Oberon said. "You went silent for quite some time, and I was beginning to think Draven had done you in."

Leif chuckled, running a hand through his long black hair. "Not yet. But I'm still walking on dangerous ground."

Again, Oberon nodded, then pulled his fork out of the napkin wrapping. The prongs sunk easily through the cream and pie.

"I thought we should meet to update each other on what's been going on," Leif continued.

"And Draven's okay with this meetup?" Oberon raised the first bite of pumpkin pie to his mouth. The spices made for a taste explosion, and he closed his eyes and savored the flavor.

As his eyelids opened, he found Leif looking at him with a bored annoyance.

"Of course Draven's not okay with this," Leif replied. "I've been assigned a solo mission here in Chicago, which explains why I can meet with you without him knowing."

Oberon gave him an impressed look. "A solo mission? You must be moving up Draven's ranks at break-neck speed." He took another glorious bite.

"He's simply using me for my ability to walk in daylight," Leif replied. "But let me start at the beginning. Heaven knows, I have all the time in the world to speak while you satisfy your satiation."

Oberon smiled between bites. "You know me so well."

The vampire explained what he'd gone through to be reinitiated into Draven's legion. The torment sounded horrendous, and Oberon had to swallow down a gulp of hot coffee to stop himself from choking on pie when he heard Leif tell his story.

"And I've been on a few missions," Leif said. "I was there during the attack on Myreen and her friends."

The fork Oberon was holding clattered on the table, and he dabbed at his mouth with his napkin. "You were there? And you didn't warn me?"

Leif tilted his head and narrowed his eyes. "And that wouldn't have been obvious, right? I was with Draven the entire way. He had me on a tight leash and wanted to make sure I really was serious about joining him again."

"You must have done your job," Oberon growled. "That attack nearly killed one of my students."

Leif studied him with his azure eyes. "I actually didn't participate in the fight. Draven wasn't happy with me."

"And yet he sends you here on a solo mission?" Oberon questioned.

Leif sighed. "I already told you, I'm here because of my abilities. No doubt it's another test to prove myself, though."

"And what is your mission?" Oberon noticed that he'd consumed most of his delicious slice.

Leif cleared his throat and hunched over the table. "Draven wants me to bring Myreen back to him."

Oberon polished off the last crusty bite and sat back, analyzing the vampire. "That's it? A simple grab and run?"

Leif nodded.

"She's a siren," Oberon said softly. "She'd stop you in a heartbeat if she didn't want you to take her."

Leif chuckled lightly. "If I were planning to kidnap the girl,

I'd make sure I'd keep her mouth shut. But I have no intention of taking her."

Oberon smiled. "I'm glad to hear that. Because this conversation would be heading in a very different direction if you were making such plans."

Leif blinked. "I'm still on your side, Oberon. But this is a test I will ultimately fail, and Draven has already informed me of the punishment I will suffer for returning empty-handed."

Oberon sipped his coffee, then placed the cup back on the table. "What do you propose we do?"

"Well, if she is the prophesied siren you think she is, I say we storm Heritage Prep Academy with everything you've got and get Myreen to end Draven and his reign."

A bombardment of feelings struck Oberon, but mostly shock. "A full-on assault on the vampire fortress?"

Leif shrugged. "Why prolong it? If the prophecy is true, why would you want to wait? To let Draven become even more powerful?"

"The girl needs training," Oberon said. "And we're working on that."

"You said it yourself," Leif replied. "Myreen's a siren. She can command anybody she wants to at any time. That includes Draven. Drill a hole in that accosted place and force Draven out, then let Myreen do her thing."

Oberon shook his head. "You make it sound so simple. But it's not. At this point she can't even protect herself. We're building her confidence. We're strengthening her. But we aren't prepared to attack Heritage Prep."

"Oberon," Leif said heavily, "Draven will not wait to assault your school. The longer you wait, the grander his plans will grow and the more likely your people will fall."

Setting his jaw, Oberon stirred his coffee. His mind felt like the swirling brown liquid, a vortex of unknowns spinning round and round.

"I should get back to the school," he mumbled.

"And I should return home," Leif replied. "But I have one more request for you."

Oberon returned his attention to the vampire.

"I have come in contact with a particular person who desires admittance into your shifter school," Leif said. "She's attempting to help me bring Gemma back to life."

A sting of guilt stabbed at Oberon. He'd promised Leif that if he rejoined Draven as a spy, he'd set the goal to bring Gemma back. Was Leif giving up on him?

"You have a debt to me, Oberon," Leif said firmly. "If Kenzie—the selkie helping me—succeeds in bringing back Gemma, you will grant her admittance into your school. Is that clear?"

"A selkie?" Oberon said with surprise. Her name was Kenzie... The night he brought Myreen to the school, her friend had announced that she was a selkie. And her name was Kenzie. A few days later, Delphine had discovered her sneaking into the school and promptly kicked her out. "Their species are not allowed within our shifter school. They aren't true shifters."

"You owe me, Oberon," Leif said darkly.

Oberon sighed and looked out the window at the snowflakes falling on the other side of the glass. "I will do what I can to allow her in," he finally said.

Leif shook his head. "*You're* the Director. You have the authority to make it happen."

Oberon looked back at Leif and met his gaze. "After the

vampire threat is taken care of, I will see to it that she's allowed in. Although, I don't know how much of a favor it'll be for her."

He wasn't entirely sure how he'd get the other teachers on board with bringing in a selkie, and didn't even know what type of curriculum should be assigned to one. But he'd figure that out later.

Leif looked past him, a scowl forming.

"Ready for round two?" Vicky said sweetly as she approached.

Oberon looked at her and smiled. "You know, the slice you brought me hit the spot." He slipped his credit card out of his pocket and handed it to her. "Charge away."

"It was a pretty big piece," she said as she took his card, then turned on her toes and made her way to the register at the front of the restaurant.

"How long are you going to be in Chicago?" Oberon asked Leif.

"As long as I can," Leif replied. "Draven asked me to wait for the right moment to kidnap Myreen. As far as I'm concerned, that opportunity won't present itself for a while. In fact, could you mandate that she can't leave the school? That would make my job easier."

Oberon shook his head. "We're a school, not a prison. But I can reinforce with her just how dangerous it is to be out, even in daylight."

Leif noticeably stiffened at his words, and Oberon couldn't help but smirk.

"Your daywalking abilities will remain a secret," he said, hoping to ease the vampire's discomfort. "But it sounds like Draven has no issues in finding human allies."

Leif relaxed ever so slightly and nodded. "That he does."

Vicky returned with his card and receipt. "Thanks for coming in," she said. "You'll come back for more another day, right? We have a lot of pie that needs to be eaten."

Chuckling, Oberon said, "Oh, I'll be back. Don't worry about that."

She gave Leif a glare before walking off.

Oberon got to his feet and reached out to the vampire. "Thanks for the meeting, Leif. We'll figure this out."

The cold flesh of Leif's hand nearly froze Oberon's hand as they shook. "I'll be in touch," the vampire said.

Together, they walked out of the restaurant, and Leif followed the snowy northern street after saying goodbye.

"Oberon?"

He whirled about to find Delphine walking toward him. She was bundled up in a fluffy purple overcoat with a sparkling white scarf wrapped around her neck. A matching purple beanie covered the top of her head down to her earlobes, and her red locks flowed out like angel wings.

"What are you doing here?" she asked, her warm breath steaming the cool air as she walked to him.

"I... needed pumpkin pie," he said awkwardly, throwing a thumb toward the door of *Neville's* restaurant.

She put her white-gloved hands on her hips. "We have pumpkin pie at the school."

He grinned. "Not *Neville's* pumpkin pie. But that's enough about me. What are you doing in downtown Chicago all by yourself?"

"Last-minute Christmas shopping," Delphine said. "With everything going on at the school, I haven't had time to do any this season."

Oberon looked to the side sheepishly. "I should probably get to shopping soon, too."

Looking back at the mermaid, he found her biting her lip.

"Are you okay, Delphine?" he asked.

She sighed, her breath steaming once again in the winter air. "I'm more concerned about you, Oberon."

Oberon stood a little straighter, trying to exude confidence. "Why is that?"

"Well, with everything going on and the threat we're facing, I'm worried about how it's affecting you. You've been through the destruction of one school at the hands of..." she looked around to make sure they were by themselves. "...you know."

"I will not let it happen again," he replied through gritted teeth.

"I just want you to be careful how you handle this situation," she said.

Her sincerity touched him, but he didn't want to seem vulnerable. "I'll be fine. And I'll make sure that we're all fine."

She nodded, resting a hand on his chest.

"I should get back to the school," he said, stepping away from her.

"Of course," she replied. "I'll see you back there before sundown."

Oberon gave her a smile, then swiftly walked down the snowy sidewalk.

Had she seen him with Leif? If she discovered he'd been speaking with a vampire, what would that mean?

Those thoughts invaded his mind as he made his way back to the subway, the hopeful spirit of Christmas fizzling away like his breath in the wintry air.

Chapter 13

Juliet

A million scenarios ran dizzily through Juliet's head. Breaking down in front of everyone was at the top of her list. Embarrassing herself in front of everyone wasn't rare, but this was over a guy. It made her angry how weak she looked.

She wanted to hide—hide from the judgment that she was sure she would get from the professors, hide from having to answer questions, and hide from anything that reminded her of Nik, but that was everything.

Before Nik broke up with her, students were actually trying to get to know her. They asked her questions about her past the most—something she wasn't completely comfortable with.

The last time she left her room, everyone looked at her like she was a lost and injured puppy. At the time, she didn't care. Now it turned her stomach.

Worst of all, her dad's disappointment practically pulsed

through the thick walls of the dome. She needed to regain the badass reputation she'd earned after the vampire ambush.

So, instead of walking around sulking, she told herself she would keep her head high and her headphones off. Which was huge. Still, they were in her bag, just in case.

Juliet placed her palm on the cool metal of her doorknob and took a deep breath, straightening her back. *I've got this.*

She opened the door to reveal an empty common room, which is what she hoped for. She'd had two choices: One, walk through the busy halls while everyone stared, or two, walk in late to class with only a handful of students staring. She opted for option two. With only a few stragglers in the halls—who did stare in shock—it was easier for Juliet to prepare herself.

Her first class was Phoenix Mastery, which was taught by her father. He wouldn't penalize her for being late, because her showing up at all was more important. She just hoped that he wouldn't make a big deal about it in front of the class. Especially when Brett was in that class with her. She didn't want him reporting everything back to Nik.

An ache began in her temples, and she massaged the sides of her head as she took her time getting to class. She wanted to stall more, but she knew that if she didn't get it over with now, she would only sink back into the lonely silence of her room.

At last, the doors came within eyesight and the pounding in her head intensified. And yet, she still held her head high when she walked through the classroom door. Her father's voice echoed through the large, quiet room.

"Well, what do you know? Welcome back, Sunshine!" Malachai comically threw his hand over his chest and all Juliet could do was stare in shock. Her father raised his eyebrows and crossed his large arms.

"Do you need assistance finding your seat, Juliet?"

Her eyes closed to a squint. She kept her gaze locked on his until the moment that she sat down in her chair. The other students snickered as they watched the stare-off.

"We were just discussing how to accustom yourself to the abilities of a phoenix. If you can answer a question correctly, I'll excuse your tardiness."

Juliet couldn't believe how much attention he was putting on her. She thought he would be happy to see her. But she wasn't giving in to his pressure.

With a curt nod, she agreed to his game.

Malachai walked slowly to her side of the room. "What is the most lethal ability a phoenix can possess?" He placed his hands on her desk and leaned down to stare at her.

Juliet smirked. He probably thought she would be stumped, but she wasn't.

"That's a trick question, *Mr. Q.* Every phoenix is different. And every phoenix comes into their own abilities at their own time and strength. So there isn't specifically one ability that tops all the others. It varies with every phoenix." Juliet leaned back in her chair with one eyebrow raised.

With his lips in a tight line, Malachai removed himself from her desk and walked backward toward the center of the room.

"That is correct. Part two of your pop quiz: Since you're the only phoenix in the class to use your ability in a real and dangerous situation, which one called out to you most?"

Now she knew he was putting the spotlight on her, and thought different of his attitude. He seemed amused.

"Well, that's another trick question. Since that was the first time I shifted, I didn't have much to go off of. So I don't know which one is most lethal for me. But I do know that my fire cry was highly effective." Juliet sat up straight in her chair, her chin raised.

"Anything else?" Malachai leaned against his desk.

"Um, I feel that I excelled in my fire manipulation that day. I used it in several formations. I turned it into pellets, a rope, and expanded it while it was in rope form."

Now completely distracted from the Nik drama, Juliet gave her full attention to the class. This was just what she needed.

"*That* is what our lesson is going to be about for the day. You're all familiar with the different forms you can turn your fire into, but to extend it to another shape from a distance is something different."

It felt like the eyes of everyone in the class were still on Juliet.

"First, you'll form a regular fireball. Nothing massive. Your maximum size is a basketball. Second, we'll focus on changing its shape into something effective to use in battle—throwing stars, daggers, ammo. You get the picture. Push your desks to the side of the room and find an open area to practice."

The students followed his orders, then spread out.

Juliet was thankful for the assignment, because it required all her focus. Just like that, Nik was blocked from her mind completely. Even the close proximity to Brett didn't distract her.

Juliet sat in the corner with her back turned to the students. She crossed her legs and placed her hands, palms up, on her knees. With a few deep breaths, she felt calm enough to summon her fire. The comforting burn started in her stomach, and she split it in two. Juliet moved the heat to her shoulders, down her arms, and into her palms.

A hiss came first, and she had to concentrate on the size and shape of her flames. When she was ready, she closed her eyes and thought of freeing the blaze from her body. Like sparks of electricity, the fire popped and grew in her hands. They started as small as two baseballs, but as she joined her hands together, they melded and grew.

The whispers would have distracted her before, but now that the connection she had with her fire was so strong, she couldn't care less. She stared into the hypnotizing orange flames and remembered how effective it was in rope shape. With one hand still elevated before her, she lifted the other to the top of the fire. Juliet moved her hands to the side while pulling the tips of her fingers together.

In a trance, she twisted and turned her fingers until she had a long and thick pile of flaming rope in front of her. She stared at the end of the rope and opened her hand to form a thicker piece. Squeezing her hand lightly around it, indents of her knuckles formed in the hilt. She lifted it up in front of her and smiled, proud of her work.

"Is that a whip?"

Malachai surprised her, which was no good when she was so focused. Her hand tightened around the grip as she spun around and sprang to her feet. The loud smack that the whip made against the wall shut the entire class up.

But what surprised her even more was the slow clap her father started. If it weren't for the heavy look of pride in Malachai's eyes, she would have been embarrassed.

With a shy smile, Juliet turned back around to sit quietly by herself. She was so into the lesson she barely realized how fast the time was going.

Malachai announced that there was only five minutes left, and Juliet's anxiety rushed back. The fireball in her hands sparked with her unbalanced emotions.

Quickly, she let the fire die in the palms of her hands, like a candle wick coming to the very end of its string. With thoughts of entering the busy hallways, panic filled her mind. She scrambled to get her bag and almost tripped over the line of desks against the wall.

Malachai dismissed the class, but asked for Juliet to stay behind.

"Are you alright, Juliet?" He sat her down and handed her a water bottle he pulled from his desk.

"I'm fine. Just the thought of leaving this class to get to my other classes was tough to accept. I liked yours so much today that I forgot I have the others to get to. It was just the right amount of distraction. I don't think I'll be so lucky the rest of the day."

"You did so well in today's lesson. I'm proud of you for making it to class today. I know it's hard, but it'll get easier. With time. You just have to be brave enough to get through the obstacles." His tone was a lot lower and smoother when he spoke to her, not like class, when he sounded fierce and intimidating.

She threw her arms around him in a tight hug. "Thanks dad."

As she let go, Malachai reached behind him and signed a small piece of paper. "Take this pass to your next class so you don't get marked for being late. Focus on the work in front of you and everything else that's clouding your mind will float away."

Juliet hoped with all her might that he was right.

***

Juliet was disappointed that her dad's advice didn't go exactly as planned. While she tried to throw herself into the school work, it wasn't thrilling enough to block her brain from returning to Nik. She was glad when the day was over. All she wanted was her bed and her Hallmark movies. She had all weekend to do just that.

Juliet opened her bedroom door and threw herself onto her bed. She didn't move for minutes, relishing in her comfortable and quiet space.

Just when she thought she would fall asleep from the warmth, knocking sounded on the other side of her door. And whoever it was let themselves in.

"So, how was your first day back?" Myreen asked. "See any guys good enough to be your rebound?" She lay onto Juliet's bed, letting her feet hang off the edge.

"That's the last thing I was looking for, Myreen. Aside from my dad's class, the rest of the day was just as painful as I thought it would be. I just can't get Nik out of my head." Juliet didn't care that she sounded like a broken record.

Myreen's eyes almost rolled right out of her head. "J, you have got to give it a rest! If class didn't help and a rebound guy is out of the question, then there's only one more thing left to do." Myreen sat up, breaking out into a wide grin.

Juliet followed suit. "I'm afraid. I'm very afraid."

Myreen gently shoved her elbow into Juliet's arm. "What you need, is a girl's day out!" She jumped off the bed with a clap and went straight for Juliet's closet. It took her only a minute to find an outfit. "Wear this tomorrow, let your hair down, and put on that dark lipstick that I love on you. We'll leave first thing tomorrow morning. At least, first thing after sleeping in. Now get some rest. We're gonna have fu-un!" Myreen sing-songed, then left with a squeal.

As soon as Myreen was gone, Juliet messaged her father to inform him of her new plans. To her surprise, he didn't object.

Malachai: I'm confident you'll be safe. Your first shift proved you can handle yourself.

As she thought about tomorrow, Juliet reached for her dark burgundy lipstick. It wasn't only Myreen's favorite, it was Nik's, too. But in that moment, she decided she needed to end the connection that Nik had over so many things in her life.

If it had to start with lipstick, it would.

Kenzie

Kenzie bit her lip as she stared out the window of the L, the city rushing by in a blur. These trips were becoming pretty regular. Not that she minded. The big city called to her, reaching out with promises of life and activity like she'd never have in Shallow Grave. It didn't hurt that her best friend went to school here. Of course, in this instance, that was only her alibi.

Kenzie hugged her book bag tighter, glancing around at the other passengers. No one paid her any mind. Which suited Kenzie just fine.

She pulled her hat off, the warmth of the car finally becoming too much for the layers she'd worn. Chicago in the winter was nothing to mess around with, and Kenzie had stopped just shy of a snowsuit when gearing up for this outing. Now she was roasting.

She could feel her hair sticking up as the static electricity made stray strands weightless. *Whatever.*

The train hissed to a stop at Conservatory and Central Park Drive, and Kenzie stood, bag and hat in hand. She hurried out with the crowd, taking one gulp of the cold air, and began fumbling with gloved hands to put the hat on without losing grip of the bag.

"Hey!" A shoulder had bumped into hers, and Kenzie turned to give the person a glare. Her mouth dropped open instead.

"Kenzie?"

"*L Police*?" Kenzie gave Wes a lopsided grin as he guffawed. She glanced at the train behind him. "Might want to hurry."

Wes glanced back, but shook his head, his breath coming out in puffs. "I can wait for the next one." The doors hissed closed, as if prompted by his dismissal. "I didn't think I'd see you again."

Kenzie snorted. "Seriously. What are the chances?" And then she remembered her hair, probably still floating in the air. She jammed her hat onto her head, her body warming until she almost wanted to take it back off again. Almost.

Wes had the decency to hide his smile with a fist. "Maybe the chances are pretty good. You haven't been going up and down the Green Line looking for me, have you?"

Kenzie rolled her eyes. "You wish. Tell me, does that line actually work?"

"I'm not sure. It's the first time I tried it. Why don't *you* tell me?"

Kenzie pursed her lips, then started walking. Yeah, it was kinda working, but she had a date to catch. Sort of.

"Hey, wait up." Wes jogged a few steps, then fell into step

with Kenzie. "So, this might sound a little creepy, but I haven't been able to get you out of my mind."

Kenzie smiled. "You're a regular Hallmark channel movie, aren't you?"

Wes laughed. "Hey, knock it if you like, but I hear the girls go nuts over that stuff."

"So, what does that make you?"

"Lonely."

Kenzie laughed, like full-out, drawing-the-wide-eyed-stares-of-everyone-around-her laughing. She kinda liked watching this dude squirm. It looked good on him.

"Where are you going?" Wes asked after she'd finished.

"I'm meeting someone at the conservatory." Kenzie could just see the gleaming panes of the conservatory through the bare branches of winter-ready trees. Even from here, it looked impressive.

Wes smiled. "Garfield Park? Love that place."

"It's my first time."

"Does this someone you're meeting happen to be a boyfriend?"

Kenzie shook her head, a wry grin on her face. "No. And *no*, I don't have a boyfriend."

She thought she saw Wes stifle a fist pump, though he immediately flipped back to a placid expression. "So I wouldn't be upsetting anyone if I asked for your phone number? Or a date?"

Kenzie's grin widened. "And you don't think that would upset me?"

"You're smiling."

"Yup."

"So?"

"Hmmm." Kenzie tapped on her chin, as if lost in thought. Wes's eyebrows shot up.

But they'd come past the trees, and Kenzie's gaze roved over the empty fountain on one side and the large glass-and-brick building on the other side. The graceful curves and glittering panes of the conservatory were so much prettier in real life.

"So?" Wes asked again, and Kenzie realized she'd stopped.

"Hm? Oh, we're here."

Wes shook his head, chuckling. "I meant about the date. Or at least a phone number. I figure if second chances are rare, third chances are near impossible. And I'd hate to waste my chance."

Kenzie bit the outside edge of her lower lip, weighing the pros and cons. Finally, she held out her hand. "Give me your phone."

Wes fished it out of his back pocket and handed it to her.

Pulling off one glove with her teeth, Kenzie found the camera, took a quick selfie—wishing she'd worn a cuter hat—then set the pic up with her phone number. No last name, though. She liked him, just not enough to be completely stupid with her information. Then she sent herself a text.

She handed his phone back and put her glove back on. "There. Phone number. Happy?" Kenzie took a quick pic of Wes's shy grin with her own cell and saved it with the number his text had provided.

"Does this mean I get a date?"

"Maybe. It's a long way from Shallow Grave to Chicago."

Wes lifted a brow. "Shallow Grave?"

Kenzie smirked, hitching her thumb over her shoulder. "I should probably get in there."

"I could come with you. You know, until your friend gets there."

Kenzie shook her head. "I've got things to do. *You* probably have things to do." *And I'm meeting a vampire to talk about magic.* Yeah, not exactly something she wanted to involve a human in.

Wes swore under his breath. "Yeah, thanks for the reminder. I should get this delivered," he said, nodding toward the bulging pocket of his jacket. He hopped on one foot, then broke into a sprint as he headed back the way they'd come. "I'll text you!" he called over his shoulder.

Kenzie chuckled, shaking her head.

The warmth of the conservatory wrapped around her like a blanket as she walked through the doors. The lobby was modest, and Kenzie found an out-of-the-way spot to get situated. She pulled her winter gear off and stuffed them into the book bag, which she wedged between her feet.

Then she remembered her hair. Sighing, she grabbed a hairband from her backpack—which she kept for just such an emergency—and pulled her unruly hair into a ponytail. When she finished, she pulled the bag back into her arms.

The greenery just past the doors looked lush and welcoming, and Kenzie briefly wondered if Leif had wandered in while he waited. Not that she was *that* late. She pulled her phone out again, checking the time. Yep. Only a few minutes past two. Not enough to bore the vampire. Did eternal creatures get bored? He certainly didn't have much by way of entertainment in his place, so Kenzie assumed the answer was no.

With her phone in hand, she decided to pull up Wes's pic. The mischievous glint in his eyes drew her in. He wasn't exactly vampire-level good looking, but he was cute. In an earthy, normal kind of way. Brown eyes, brown hair, brown jacket. And hopefully a nice distraction from her almost obsessive fascination with Leif.

Which was the reason she had called this meeting. Well, part of the reason.

Her phone dinged, and a text wiped away Wes's handsome smile.

Wes: What's ur fav color?

Kenzie snorted.

Me: Black. Like my soul. :)

Wes: O-O Checks roses. No black. Note to self: get spray paint.

Kenzie clapped a hand over her mouth to keep her laugh from echoing around the lobby.

"What's so funny?"

The sudden presence behind her made Kenzie startle. She shrieked as she whirled around. "Leif!" She punched his arm, which was hard as rock. Huffing, she shook her hand to try to get rid of the prickling sensation. She blacked out the screen and stuffed the cell into her bag. "What took you so long?"

"Believe it or not, I've got other projects I'm working on."

Kenzie cocked a grin at him. "More important than mine?"

Leif met Kenzie's gaze, and the look on his face wiped away her mirth. "No. Not more important, but certainly more dangerous."

"Oh. Like what?"

Leif nodded toward the interior of the conservatory. "Let's talk in there."

Kenzie nodded and followed him in.

The air grew humid as they passed through the doors,

emerald palms towering above them. Kenzie could almost imagine herself on some forgotten island. A pond reflected the greenery, filling the space even as it created room.

They followed the sound of pattering water around a bend, revealing a waterfall that looked like it was ripped straight from nature. The way it fell on and over the moss- and fern-covered rocks was almost musical. Yeah, she'd have to come back here.

Leif eyed the bag Kenzie clutched. "That looks heavy. May I?"

He held out his hand, and Kenzie gave it to him. "Thanks." He picked it up like it weighed nothing. *And after I've been lugging it around like a kettle bell all day.*

"Come on. I'll show you my favorite room."

With the bag over his shoulder, Leif navigated left and into a narrower portion of the conservatory. The smell hit her first, reminding Kenzie of a hair salon with all its fruity, tropical scents. The heat was almost oppressive with her sweater on, and Kenzie pushed her sleeves up.

"It's great," Kenzie said, though she wasn't sure there was much difference from the last room. They were all green to her.

Leif ran his fingers along one of the leaves. "I used to work in an orchard. These trees and plants aren't quite the same, but I get the same feeling when I'm around them." His fingers curled back again, as if he'd been burned.

"What was it like?"

Leif let out an amused huff, his eyes focused on the distant past. "Tending an orchard? Hard work. Quiet. I worked for good people. I met Gemma there."

"Oh, wow. Was she, like...?"

"My fiancé."

Kenzie put her hand on the back of her neck as she angled

her face away from Leif. "Oh. I was gonna say girlfriend. You barely look legal."

Leif chuckled. "Very legal, I assure you. So, what is it you wanted to show me?"

Kenzie looked around, but there weren't many people at the conservatory today, and what few were there were far enough away not to be a problem. "You remember the plant spell?"

Leif nodded.

"Well, I figured out what the words mean. Kinda."

Leif lifted a brow. "How does that help?"

"If you understand the arcane language, you can make your own spells." Kenzie bit her lip as she watched Leif's face light up.

"You understand the language, then?"

Kenzie snorted. He must be crazy. "Nooo. Not the whole language. But I kinda understand *that* spell, which gave me an idea for changing it so it works on living things."

"Humans?"

Kenzie sucked a breath through her teeth. She'd been trying the spell out on every dead creature she could find—flies, squirrels, even a dead bird she'd found on the side of the road. But humans? She was sooo not ready for that yet. Not that she'd admit it. Not to him. "I don't know. Maybe? Magic can be a little... finicky. I need to try it out on something first. Like a squirrel or a—"

"A cat?"

"Yeah. Sure, I guess. As long as it's a small one." She went back to chewing on her lip. In truth, she worried a cat of any size might be too big, but she didn't want to tell Leif that. Not much had come of her first attempts, and she had to keep tweaking her tweaks. But she'd had a breakthrough just this morning. At least, she thought so.

"Okay. Well, let's test it out."

"It's not that simple. We have to use—" Kenzie's eyes traced some people wandering through their section of the conservatory. "—something that isn't alive," she hissed.

"No problem. There's this creature that's been caterwauling down the street for the past week. I'm sure I can find the cat behind it."

Kenzie blinked. "Oh. Okay." It would be today, then. She didn't know why that surprised her. It was the reason she'd come, but she didn't expect to be able to find a test subject so soon. If she were being completely honest, she'd kinda hoped this would be more of a get-to-know-you session. The conservatory was certainly romantic and intimate enough. But now she'd be performing magic. And in front of *him.*

She pushed up her sleeves again as her pulse kicked into high gear.

Leif looked her over, a frown pulling at those pouty lips. "Unless you're not ready."

"Pfft. Nah. I'm just a little nervous is all. I mean, there's always the chance it doesn't work." *Or, you know, I die or something.* The attempt she made at resurrecting the bird had landed her in bed for two days with flu-like symptoms. And it hadn't even worked. Altering spells could be a tricky thing, which was why selkies had taken to writing everything down in grimoires. That, and it made it easier to recall and pass on working magic spells. Kenzie sniffed. *I can do this.* There was one more tweak she wanted to try, anyway, and maybe a recently deceased subject would be easier to work with. "Okay, how do you want this thing to go down?"

"I'll go find the cat while you head to the apartment?"

"Sure." Kenzie pulled down her sleeves hoping to trap some of the heat. Cooling off would feel good once she got in the wintry Chicago air, but after that?

Leif nodded. "Then let's go."

He turned to leave, but Kenzie's hand shot out to stop him. "My bag?"

"Of course."

He handed it back over. Kenzie put it on the floor as she retrieved her coat, stuffing the hat and gloves in the pockets. She'd wait until she was outside to finish up. "Thanks. See you soon!"

But when she looked up, Leif was already gone.

Kenzie sighed. "That's gonna take some getting used to."

***

Ten minutes later and Kenzie was back at Leif's apartment. And she didn't even need to use magic to get in this time, thanks to the key he'd given her. The one with the cute selkie charm attached to it. *My key.* The thought made her feel warm and rosy all over.

Her coat, hat and gloves lay on the counter, while the book was resting on the blanket she'd left on the floor. He didn't move it. Was that because he wasn't there, or because he wanted to keep that spot for her? Kenzie liked the idea of the latter one, no matter how far-fetched it might be.

She'd checked her text messages on the ride over. Wes had said goodbye, but nothing more. She decided there was no need to respond. Maybe she'd text him when she was on her way home. Maybe. It might be good to let him squirm a bit first.

The door banged open and Leif stepped in. A large gray shorthair with a white stripe running from snout down to his nether-regions was in Leif's hand, gripped by the scruff of his neck. The cat was growling, a low, dark sound coming from its throat. Kenzie gulped as she took in the sheer size of the feline. She'd told Leif she wanted a small one, right?

Leif hissed back, the motion more animal than human, and Kenzie felt her first real spark of fear since their encounter in the alley. In that moment, the vampire was all predator, and on an instinctual level, she knew she was the prey. The cat probably felt a similar discomfort with the situation, as his eyes darted in every direction.

Leif closed the door with his foot, bringing the cat further in. "Sorry. It's a rather annoying creature."

"Are you really one to talk?" Kenzie asked, folding her arms to steady herself.

Leif laughed, the hearty, good-natured sound scattering the last vapors of her fears. "I suppose not. Come on. Let's get started." He twisted the cat's neck so fast, Kenzie didn't have time to think.

She gagged, then turned away from the creature, unable to look at the odd angle of its neck without freaking out. "A little warning next time." Kenzie gagged again. She pulled her arm over her nose and began breathing from her mouth.

"But look, no blood."

Kenzie gagged a third time, and she ran for the bathroom, making it to the toilet just before the bile hit her mouth. She groaned when she'd finished, then ran some water in the bathroom sink to wipe her mouth. "Hot fudgesicles, you are so gross sometimes."

Leif was leaning against the doorframe, smirking. "You do realize I'm a vampire, right?"

"Yeah, but you don't have to go all 'I vant to suck your—'" Kenzie stared at the water and took a deep breath to keep from gagging again. "You know."

Leif chuckled. "Okay, fine. I'll try to be a little more sensitive to your—"

Kenzie cut a glare at Leif, and he held up his hands.

"I was just going to say 'sensitivities.'"

Kenzie rolled her eyes. "Fine. Just... go put something over that thing so I don't have to look at it again."

Leif nodded, then left. She heard him open the closet by the front door, and in a flash, he was back at the bathroom. "Okay. It's safe to come out now."

Kenzie took a deep breath, flicked her hair over her shoulder, and straightened her spine. She marched out of the bathroom with every air of confidence she could muster, but hesitated when she neared visual range of the blanket and book and... *soft little pillow.* Sure, the mental diversion probably wouldn't work, but it was worth a shot.

She peered around the corner, her eyes widening as they landed on the mass that was the cat. Because Leif had used the kitten shirt she'd gotten him to cover up the... *pillow.* Kenzie groaned. "Really? That's the only thing you had?"

Leif spread out his arms. "You've seen how little I keep here."

Kenzie's face reddened, and she wondered if he knew she'd been snooping. Not that there was anything to snoop, really. "You have like, five of the exact same black shirt, and you want to throw the shirt *I* gave you on top of... it?"

Leif shrugged. "I'm not much of a cat person."

"Yeah. I figured. Whatever."

She plopped down in front of the book, not allowing her gaze to wander to the lumpy shirt as she opened to the plant spell page. A loose leaf of bright white notebook paper stood stark against the time-worn pages, and she plucked it out, reading back over her notes.

The wording had to be tweaked a little to affect a life with a soul. It had taken several tries, but she thought she finally had it. Maybe.

There was just one problem.

"So, I found out that the original spell drew from my life force. I'm not keen on the idea of giving up my life for your lady love, or whatever."

Leif nodded once. "Nor would I ask you to do so."

"And I was thinking to myself, you know, Kenz? You've got a vampire on your team. He's a pile of limitless life force."

"You want to draw from me for the spell? Would that even work? I'm not entirely sure I qualify as *alive.*"

Kenzie's shoulders sagged. "I don't know. It's all just theory until I try it out. And even then, experimental spells can have... unforeseen consequences." Kenzie pulled her lips inward and clamped down on them as she waited for Leif's reaction.

"If you're talking about death, I have nothing to lose."

Kenzie nodded. *Sure. The undead guy has a death wish. Figures.* "Okay. Then you're ready?"

Leif nodded.

"I'll need you to sit beside me." Kenzie smiled, patting the spot on the blanket to her right.

Leif sat, all traces of humor gone. Kenzie bit the side of her lip, wondering if she was doing the right thing. But the vampire was willing. And if the spell didn't go right, maybe luck would hold out and nothing would happen—rather than something horrible.

Kenzie closed her eyes and took a deep breath. She couldn't think about the consequences. Not now. She'd deal with that later—*if* there were any.

Focusing once more on the page she'd created, she began intoning the words of the spell. "Croileathra, kruthitheoirha, goraih maigh agaht."

The first tingles of magic danced in the tips of her fingers, gathering strength from the blood pumping through her veins. Kenzie took a moment to savor the feeling.

Picking up Leif's hand, she placed it on top of the shirt, then covered it with her own. His frigid skin sent a shiver through her, and she snuck a glance at the vampire that had so consumed her life. Did he know how she felt? She wasn't entirely sure she knew.

"A guinle chashaid a guin, a bhron antas druíl," Kenzie said, and the atmosphere in the apartment changed, the light dimming. "Dághéin i croígh aghus spioradah!" Energy bubbled under her hand, and she focused on moving it downward. Leif sucked in a breath, and Kenzie hesitated a moment, but she couldn't stop it now. A half-cast spell was as bad as a mis-cast one. Besides, it was basically done.

"Croileathra, kruthitheoirha, goraih maigh agaht," she ended, letting out a long breath with the final syllable.

She closed her eyes and pressed her hands to her face. "So?" she asked Leif after several moments, hoping he was in a good enough condition to answer her. She had a flash of morbidity, envisioning leaning over the vampire's corpse, reviving him with true love's kiss. *Idiot.*

Leif let out a whisper of a breath, and a moment later Kenzie heard fabric moving.

"Leif?" Kenzie asked, sliding a finger aside so she could peek through.

The cat was curled up in Leif's lap, looking as cozy and happy as could be. And he was alive.

Kenzie pulled her hands away, her eyes widening. She blinked a few times, wondering if the scene would change. It didn't. A smile began to grow. "We did it." She turned her smile to Leif, who wore an adorable half-smile of his own, a hand resting on the cat's back. "We did it!"

"*You* did it."

"Yeah, I guess I did." But something felt weird. Maybe it was just because it was so surreal, or maybe she just wanted to play it cool in front of the vampire, but the excitement quickly fizzled. It didn't feel quite the same as when she'd revived the plant.

Kenzie stared at the cat, wondering what she was sensing. "Hey, look! He likes you now." She reached out a hand to pet the cat, but he hissed, swatting at her.

Leif caught the offending paw before it could do any damage and hissed at the cat, who settled back down, though it continued to look at Kenzie through narrowed eyes.

Kenzie stuck her tongue out at the creature. "Ungrateful mange. Ugh. The thanks I get." She looked back at Leif, who was petting the cat now, a curious expression on his face. The gray-and-white fur looked like it belonged, perfectly meshing with Leif's admittedly boring choice in wardrobe. Her vampire looked so adorable, and she briefly considered giving him a celebratory peck on the cheek—or the lips—but he had that menace in his lap, and she didn't fancy feeling the bite of his claws.

Kenzie put her hands on her cheeks. She wasn't dying with fatigue. Maybe that was the difference? "How do you feel?"

"Thirsty."

Kenzie frowned. "Right. Like, Kenzie's-life-is-in-danger kind of thirsty or just I-really-need-a-moment-with-my-fridge thirsty?"

Leif smirked. "The latter. Do you mind?"

Kenzie waved a hand in the air. "Sure. Just... don't slurp or anything. Got it?"

Leif nodded, taking the cat with him. Kenzie was grateful for that. Maybe he'd put it away or something while he was up. When she heard the fridge open, she started talking. "You know, you're still going to have to wear that shirt I got you."

Leif laughed. "I don't think so."

There was a plastic crinkling sound, so Kenzie continued. "Seriously. You owe me one. Unless you've gotten me into that school."

"Yeah. About that. Oberon's working on it."

"Seriously?" Kenzie held her breath and leaned forward. Was this it? Was she getting in the shifter school?

"Yes. But it might take a while." The fridge door closed, and Kenzie exhaled. "There are some threats they're having to deal with, so bringing in a new student—especially one who probably won't be very well received—isn't the best idea." He gave Kenzie a pointed look, but she shrugged it off.

"You said there are threats. Does it involve the vampires? Or Myreen?"

Leif focused on the cat purring in his arms. "I'm not at

liberty to discuss any of that. Just know your friend is being looked after."

Kenzie sighed. She knew. It didn't make things any better, but Kenzie was certain her friend was in good hands. *Just not* my *hands.*

"I can handle the haters, you know," she said, picking at a burr on her sweater.

"I don't doubt it."

Kenzie's stomach growled. Her face reddened and she started gathering her things up. "I should go." It was stupid, being so incredibly embarrassed at being so understandably human, but she couldn't help herself.

"I'm sorry. I should've gotten you something to eat."

Kenzie waved his concern away. "No worries. I'll grab something quick on the way back." *And pick apart every moment of our entire time together.*

"At least let me pay for it." Leif slipped a bill into her hand.

Kenzie didn't bother to look at it as she stuffed it into her pants pocket. "Thanks. But you still owe me. Wear the shirt. And I need proof."

Leif laughed. "We'll see."

"What're you gonna do about the cat?"

Leif shrugged, looking at the thing resting in his arms, it's eyes half-closed and a mighty purr rumbling from its throat. "I suppose I should keep an eye on it for a bit, just to make sure the spell worked as intended."

"Good idea." Kenzie eyed the cat. "Do you think anyone'll miss him?"

Leif shook his head. "I'm certain he's feral."

Kenzie shouldered her backpack, ready once more to brave the winter weather. "Until next time, I guess."

"Until next time."

"Make sure you take good care of Rainbow!" Kenzie called over her shoulder as she slipped out of the apartment. Leif's laughter carried through the door.

She wasn't quite ready to leave Chicago yet, despite what she'd told Leif. It seemed every time she came to the city, it got a little harder to let go again. She planned on spending the rest of the available afternoon doing a little exploring—after grabbing something to eat, of course—by herself. The whole cat thing had sent her mood plummeting for some reason, which obviously had nothing to do with the amount of affection Leif had thrown at that crazy little cat once she'd brought it back to life. Despite the fact that he "wasn't a cat person". Whatever.

But no matter what she decided to do, she'd have to make it home before dark. Apparently, Mom and Gram had heard about the increased vampire activity, and they weren't taking any chances. *Good thing* my *vampire can handle the daylight.*

The brisk air chilled her as she exited the lobby and headed toward the L. Her emotions tumbled as she replayed the last ten minutes or so in her mind, though they were definitely tipping in favor of elation.

Seeing Leif always put her in a tailspin, like a twisted game of he-likes-me, he-likes-me-not. Only there was no end to the petals she could rip off. Not even the new texts from Wes could cheer her up. In fact, they were sort of starting to get on her nerves.

"Hey, Kenzie?" came a voice, and Kenzie stopped and turned toward it.

She squinted at the guy, then her eyes widened. It was the dude from the café, the one she'd run into after her last meeting with Leif. "Hey." She couldn't remember his name. Aaron or

Regan or something?

"I thought I recognized you," Café Dude huffed as he jogged toward her.

"Yeah. Strange seeing you here. What brings you to Chicago?"

Café Dude pointed back over his shoulder. "I'm actually staying nearby. Last time we met I was visiting a cousin."

"Oh." Kenzie guessed that could happen. Maybe. "So weird. But I should be going. I actually live out that way, and my mom will be expecting me home soon." Definitely *not* a lie. She briefly considered inviting him on her little spree through town, but decided against it. She already had Wes in her back pocket—literally sending her another text now, as her phone was buzzing again—and then there was Leif.

The guy gave her a strange look, but all Kenzie could think about was how much time it must have taken him to put that guyliner on. It made his eyes mesmerizing, in a kinda-cool, kinda-creepy way. Okay, so she was staring, but he didn't seem to mind.

He pivoted away from Kenzie for a moment, then pivoted back, sucking in a quick breath. "Can I have your number?" he asked, the words coming out in a rush.

Kenzie blinked. "What? No quirky pickup lines?"

He shook his head. "Nah. I like the direct approach."

Kenzie smirked. "Okay. Fine. 555-2341."

The guy raised his brows at Kenzie, a stunned look on his face.

"What can I say? I like the direct approach, too." She shrugged and walked away, giving him the benefit of another hip sway. She had no idea why he brought out the witch in her, but she was going to roll with it.

I must be on fire! Two guys in one day.

But not the one she really wanted.

Kenzie sighed. She'd sort this mess out later.

Maybe.

Kenzie

It didn't take long for Café Dude to send her a text. Adam—apparently—had a very good memory. Kenzie almost regretted not inviting him along for her little side trip. She had a feeling he'd be a lot of fun.

But the texting was becoming too much. Mostly Wes. She couldn't decide if that was a good or bad thing. At the moment, it kinda made her want to block his number. Instead, she powered her phone off. That way she didn't have to listen to another stupid chime from another stupid text that wasn't from Leif.

Kenzie sighed.

"Kenzie!" came a voice from behind her.

Kenzie paused mid-stride, her mind flashing with recognition. She whirled around just as warm arms and blue-streaked raven-colored hair crashed into her.

"Oh my crap! Myreen! What are you doing here?"

"Me and Juliet needed some girl time." Myreen stepped back, revealing Kenzie's favorite ginger.

Kenzie wrapped her arms around Juliet for a brief hug and then gave her a smug smile. "My, don't we look extra nice today." Juliet wore dark lipstick, which made her yellow-green eyes glitter, and black, furry earmuffs tamed her red curls—a warmer alternative to her usual headphones.

Juliet rolled her eyes, her tanned skin reddening. "Thanks. Myreen said just because I don't have a boyfriend, doesn't mean I shouldn't dress up."

Kenzie pouted her lower lip. "Aw, I hadn't heard. I'm sorry."

Juliet shrugged and waved Kenzie's concern away.

"Enough about he-who-shall-not-be-named. What are *you* doing here?" Myreen asked, her face shining with excitement.

Kenzie shrugged, looking off to the side as if something needed her attention. "Oh, nothing much. Trying to dig my way out of Shallow Grave, I guess."

"Anything we can do to help?" Myreen asked, her face so sweet, so trusting.

"Nah." Kenzie felt like the biggest jerk of all time, keeping her whatever-it-was with Leif a secret. She should've brought it up weeks ago. But she hadn't, and she couldn't bring herself to fix it now. Not with Juliet upset. The girl looked like she was about ready to swap out her earmuffs for headphones.

"Oooh, I know! You can come with us," Juliet said, beaming at Kenzie.

Kenzie shrugged. "Sure, if that's cool with you two. Where you girls headed?"

Myreen giggled. "We decided to just be spontaneous. You

know, wherever the wind takes us."

"At this rate, the wind might just pick you two lightweights up and take you home." Kenzie pulled her coat a little tighter against a gust as they began walking. A sly grin spread across her face. "There is *one* place I've always wanted to go."

Juliet clapped her hands together. "Where?"

Kenzie shook her head. "Not telling. Just let nor'easter Kenzie blow you away." She winked, then grabbed each girl's hand and took off for the L.

***

Ten minutes later and they were standing in front of the Bean, heads craned back to take in the enormity of it.

"Whoa," Juliet said.

"You got that right." Kenzie pulled out her phone, internally kicking herself when she saw the dark screen. She wasn't entirely sure she wanted to turn it on, but this was a selfie moment she just couldn't pass up. The phone lit up, playing its little jingle as the power came on. "Okay, girls, huddle up for pics."

They spent several minutes posing, both in front of and reflected in the Bean. The way the curved surface stretched and squished their bodies and faces—along with the city skyline—was enough to dissolve them all into giggles.

Kenzie's stomach growled again, and Myreen started laughing. "You need to feed that wild beast before it eats you alive."

Kenzie chuckled. "Yassss. Now, where's a good place to eat around here?"

Juliet pointed. "There's something over there that smells good. Let's give that a try."

Kenzie bit her lower lip. "Better watch it or I'll be calling you Toucan Sam." At Juliet's confused look she added, "Follow your no-Oooose."

Myreen rolled her eyes, though she was still smiling. "She gets punnier when she's hungry. Come on."

They made their way down to The Grill, just on the other side of the Bean. People swarmed in and out of the establishment, laughing and chattering, while ice skaters wove around the outdoor rink to a Michael Bublé Christmas tune.

Warm air greeted them inside, along with an elegant interior and a perky hostess. "How many in your party?" the blond asked, a big smile on her face and a Santa hat on her head.

"Just the three of us," Kenzie said.

"Alright. Right this way." She jotted down a note at her station and then led them through the restaurant.

"Wow! This is way nicer than I thought it was going to be," Juliet said, her eyes taking in every inch of the place.

Kenzie had to agree. Dark and light woods stood against sleek black iron and leather, canned lighting and wall sconces standing like jewels, even with the full light of day pouring through the floor-to-ceiling windows.

She slipped her hand into her pants pocket and discreetly pulled out the bill Leif had given her. She gaped as she saw the one hundred printed in the corner. *Rich old vampire, check.* Good. That meant she could cover everyone's expenses. *Thank you, Leif.*

The hostess sat them at a large table by one window, handing everyone menus before she excused herself.

Kenzie tried to study the menu, but her eyes kept wandering to the skaters. Most followed the edges of the rink, but a few of the more daring ones cut tricks at the center.

"We should go skating," Myreen said, bouncing a little in her seat.

Juliet scrunched her nose. "Uh, have you seen my two left feet? There's no way I'm putting blades on those things. I'd be lethal."

"They're not sharpened," Myreen said, playing with the napkin in front of her. "Not for this kind of thing."

"I'm with Red on this one," Kenzie said, pointing her thumb at Juliet. Besides, the cold, pale ice reminded her of Leif, and she just wanted to forget him. Like the way she'd felt as he sat next to her, her hand over his, his life essence pulsing beneath her fingertips...

"Hey, I'm Eric and I'll be your waiter today" said an attractive, young man. Kenzie blinked and smiled. "What would you ladies like to start with?"

Kenzie glanced down at her menu. "Cheese curds. We're sharing. And a Dr. Pepper for me."

Myreen ordered a water, and Juliet got a Coke.

When the waiter walked away, giving them time to look over their menus, Kenzie leaned forward. "Was it just me, or did Waiter Guy give Juliet his *full* attention?"

Myreen gasped. "I think you're right. Juliet!" She nudged her friend with her elbow.

Juliet blushed, sinking in her seat. "I don't think so."

Kenzie shook her head, wearing a knowing smile. "Aw, come on. You're like bronzed perfection over there."

Juliet shrugged. "I mean, I don't know. The only person who's ever acted like I might be even a little attractive was—"

Myreen shook her head. "Uh, uh. We're not talking about

he-who-must-not-be-named today."

Kenzie shrugged one shoulder. "Besides, you don't have to be dating Waiter Guy to bask in his admiration for an hour or two. You're fierce and fun and dang cute. Own it."

Juliet sat up a little straighter. "You really think so?"

"Uh, duh!" Kenzie said, while Myreen nodded and smiled.

"Thanks," Juliet said, her shoulders hunching forward just a little as she played with a curl.

"Here are your drinks," Waiter Guy said, serving Juliet's drink first. Kenzie held her hand over her mouth, trying to stifle her snickers as she waggled her brows at Juliet behind the waiter's back. "Are you girls ready to order?"

The girls placed their order, Waiter Guy beaming a little brighter as he took Juliet's.

As Waiter Guy scurried back to the kitchen, Kenzie broke out in laughter. "I *told* you!"

Juliet blushed, a shy smile on her face. "So, what are we doing next?"

"Hmmm." Kenzie tapped her chin. "Hold on." After digging her phone out of her bag, she did a search for local events, and found one nearby. Her face split into a grin. "Perfect." She slid her phone back into her bag.

"So?" Myreen asked, her brows raised.

Kenzie shook her head. "Nope. It's a surprise."

Juliet sat back, folding her arms. "How about you give us a hint."

Kenzie leveled a mischievous smirk at Juliet. "You like music, right?"

Juliet nodded. "Yeah. What about it?"

Kenzie raised her brows twice, then sat back with a self-satisfied smirk.

"That's it?" Myreen asked, stirring her water with her straw.

A chime from her bag made Kenzie pause. It was Adam again. She hadn't responded to his first text, and he was wondering if he had the right number. Kenzie laughed.

"What's so funny?" Myreen asked as Kenzie typed out a reply.

Kenzie glanced up at Myreen. "Oh, nothing." Juliet snatched the phone out of Kenzie's hand. "Hey!"

"This one's from *Adam*," Juliet said, smirking at Kenzie. "He's trying to find out if he has the right number." Another chime sounded and Kenzie's cheeks reddened. "Ooh, and it looks like this one is from Wes—cute pic, by the way—and *he's* wondering if black licorice would appease your black heart."

Kenzie snatched her phone back, smiling even as she groaned.

"What's all this?" Myreen asked, folding her hands on the table. "Have you been holding out on us?"

Kenzie shook her head, sliding her phone back into her bag. "New development. I've run into both of these guys by chance—today, for the second time—and they both asked me for my number."

"Aaaand?" Myreen asked, a single brow raised.

Juliet leaned forward.

Kenzie shrugged. "I'm just taking things one text at a time."

Myreen and Juliet squealed.

"It's just like a Hallmark movie," Juliet said with a sigh.

Kenzie snorted. "Hardly. Okay, well, maybe Wes." At the renewed excitement, Kenzie added, "But the verdict's still out. They might all be losers." Leif's handsome features swam in her mind, and Kenzie shook her head.

"I guess we know who's owning it," Juliet said, smirking. She wadded her discarded straw cover and threw it at Kenzie.

"Hey!" Kenzie said, grabbing Myreen's straw and flicking some water at Juliet.

"We're in a *restaurant,*" Myreen hissed through a barely-contained grin.

"What about you, Myreen?" Kenzie asked. She'd been notably quiet about her own love life, and her cheeks colored when Kenzie asked.

She shrugged. "Not much to talk about."

"The rumor mill has her with Kol again."

"We're just friends!" Myreen said, but her cheeks turned an ever deeper shade of crimson.

Kenzie rolled her eyes. "Okay. No more guy talk. This is *supposed* to be a girl's day out, right?"

"So what's in the bag?" Myreen asked, visibly relaxing. She retrieved her straw and stirred her water again, the ice clinking delicately against the glass.

"Nothing much."

"Nothing, like the texts you got earlier?" Juliet guessed.

Yes. Exactly like that. "Haha. No. Just boring school books. I forgot to empty them out before I ran out the door." Kenzie adjusted in her seat, taking a sip of her pop, hoping her poker face held.

The waiter came over then, balancing a full tray. He handed out the cheese curds first, placing steaming hot plates in front of everyone—shrimp and lobster ballerine for Myreen, Manny's deli combo for Kenzie, and a green chili cheeseburger for Juliet. "Let me know if you need anything else," he said, his gaze lingering just a moment longer on Juliet than on anyone else.

They burst into giggles again as soon as he left.

"I'm sorry," Kenzie wheezed between giggles, "but the dude

is totally crushing on Juliet."

Juliet scoffed. "Whatever, two-texter."

Kenzie put up her hands. "I know. I know. I said I'm sorry." She popped a cheese curd into her mouth, feeling that satisfying crunch as the melted cheese oozed through her mouth. Heaven. On. Earth. She lifted one side of the basket, angling it at her friends. "Peace offering?"

The girls tucked in, the chatter calming. Kenzie took a bite of her sandwich, groaning as some of the Russian dressing trickled down the side of her mouth. *Best corned beef and pastrami ever.* She looked over at her happy companions, chowing down on their own meals, and couldn't help but smile. This was why she wanted in that school so bad. These girls got her, in a way that no one else really could.

Another chime interrupted her meal. Kenzie slid her phone out to silence it, but paused as she saw the latest text from Wes. Sure, he seemed fun now, but what happened when she started going to the shifter school? *It's only one date. It's not like I'm planning on marrying the guy.*

She'd cross that bridge when she got there. As she slid her silenced phone back into her bag, she smiled again at her friends, trying to give them a nonchalant shrug as she filled her mouth with another bite of sandwich. The guys could wait. Right now, she was getting some much-needed girl time.

***

The girls stood in a spacious room at the Chicago Cultural Center, the elegant walls punctuated on each side with arches supported by thick columns. A small band wearing blue uniforms with a rainbow across the top tuned their instruments in one corner. The large expanse of cleared floor was peppered with children, some dressed in leotards and tutus, others in seasonal attire. And some looked as unprepared for the event as Kenzie and her friends were.

"Are you sure we're supposed to be here?" Juliet whispered at a volume that wasn't quite private.

Kenzie nodded. "They said everyone's welcome." Sure, they were about ten years older than the average participant—all the adults sat in chairs placed around the edges or at the back of the dance floor—but Kenzie wasn't going to let that stop them.

Myreen's smile was as wide as it was nervous. "I love the Nutcracker. And ballet."

Kenzie snorted. "You would."

"I did mention that I have two left feet, right?" Juliet added as a young lady in an elegant, pale pink ballerina outfit—complete with ballet slippers and a glittering crown atop her perfectly bunned hair—came to the front.

"You and me both," Kenzie assured her in a hushed tone. "Don't worry. We'll both look like idiots."

Juliet shook her head and rolled her eyes. "Yeah, that makes me feel a *lot* better."

"Alright everyone, thanks for coming!" the ballerina said, her elven features pulled into a warm smile. "I'm Avery and I'll be teaching you some ballet. I want you all to relax and have fun, and when we're done, it's going to be a free dance to music from the Nutcracker, played by these beautiful people." Avery motioned toward the band, who smiled and waved as the room quietly applauded. "Okay everyone, let's try first position."

Kenzie and Juliet giggled together as they wobbled and flailed through the different moves the instructor taught. Myreen fared much better, and even got an appreciative nod from the instructor. The band pitched in whenever the ballerina asked, giving the group a beat to practice to. Myreen ended up surrounded by the more experienced children, while Kenzie and Juliet ended up in the back, but having just as much fun.

When it came time for the free dance, Kenzie and Juliet stepped aside to watch Myreen and her little munchkins dance their little hearts out. When the choreography ran out, Myreen stepped off the dance floor, huffing and puffing. The munchkins carried on merrily without her.

Juliet and Kenzie clapped and cheered for Myreen.

"Thanks!" Myreen said between breaths. "I always wanted to be a ballerina."

Juliet shook her head. "I think I've always known I didn't have a prayer, but this was fun." She shot Kenzie a smile.

"So, where to next?" Myreen asked.

Kenzie shrugged. "Let's just head south and see where it takes us."

Myreen and Juliet agreed.

So the girls made their way south, taking in the sights, riding the L, and generally just enjoying themselves.

Kenzie pulled out her phone, scanning for anything interesting. "Oooh, it says there's a house by Frank Lloyd Wright around here." She looked up, finding only blank stares from the other two. "Frank Lloyd Wright. The architect?"

"Well, yeah, but why?" Myreen said, her brows still pinched.

Kenzie shrugged, looking at the ground. "I don't know. If nothing else pans out, architecture might be cool. Girls' gotta have hobbies, right?"

"You? Architecture?" Myreen asked, looking dubious.

Kenzie shrugged again. “Sure. Why not?”

“You don’t exactly seem like the type,” Juliet volunteered, rushing to add, “But I bet you’d be great at it.”

Kenzie smiled, her shoulders around her ears. “We don’t have to go.”

“No, we can go.” Myreen threaded her arm through Kenzie’s, giving her a sideways grin, and Juliet looped her arm around Myreen’s other arm. “I’m just surprised I’m only now finding out about this. Come on. Let’s see what the place has to offer.”

“Okay. Cool.” Kenzie tapped on her screen a few more times, bringing up the directions. She pointed at an opening between some buildings. “Let’s cut through here.”

The girls were halfway through the alley when Myreen and Juliet stopped dead in their tracks, yanking Kenzie to a stop in the process.

“What’s up?” Kenzie asked.

Juliet and Myreen stood, slack-jawed, their little chain broken. Kenzie looked around, but she didn’t see anything weird.

“This is the place, isn’t it?” Myreen finally said.

Juliet nodded.

“The place?” But even as she said it, Kenzie realized what they were talking about. Myreen was particularly pale, and Juliet was glancing around the alley, her body poised to strike, the first whispers of flames at her fingertips. It was *the* alley. The one where they’d been attacked.

“Oh, crap. I’m sorry. I had no idea,” Kenzie said.

Myreen shook her head. “It’s not your fault. You didn’t know.”

“Yeah,” Juliet echoed, putting down her fists. “We should probably get back to the Dome. It’s getting kind of late.”

“Right,” Kenzie said. “I should get home, too.” She threw a

worried glance at Myreen and Juliet, who were cautiously backing out of the alley. She followed them, muttering a quick sweeping spell under her breath. "I'm really sorry, guys."

Myreen managed to conjure a smile, though it didn't quite reach her eyes. "It's fine. It was good seeing you, though."

"Yeah, we'll have to do this again, sometime," Juliet said, visibly relaxing as they eased out of the alley. "You know, the girl's day out and fun and stuff. Minus the creepy alley trip down memory lane."

"Right. Yeah." Kenzie accompanied the girls back to the subway, where they split, Myreen and Juliet going back to the Dome while Kenzie headed for home.

One day she wouldn't have to part with her friends. She just needed to find a way to hurry Oberon's promise along.

A text came in, and Kenzie pulled out her phone. It was Wes. Again.

Wes: Hey, I know this might be too soon, but when should we have our date?

Kenzie tapped the side of her phone with her fingernail. She didn't have any plans. Not really. Though she kinda hoped to see Leif again next week.

"You know what? Screw it," she muttered. She was tired of the slump. Wes would be the perfect distraction from her self-defeating, obsessive ruminations on Leif and the shifter world.

Me: See u this Saturday?

Kenzie's finger hovered above the button a moment before she got the nerve to hit send.

Wes: It's a date, came his almost immediate reply.

Kenzie smirked. Yeah, Wes would do nicely.

Kol

With Kol's height, he easily found the book he was looking for high on the top shelf: *Frost Boarding House - The Original Shifter School: A History.* It was thick, which was both good and really daunting. At least the massive size meant the answer he was looking for was likely to be in it.

After what happened in the greenhouse with Myreen, he wanted to know more about the damned Dracul curse and if there was a way to lift it. He shook the image from his mind, determined to *not* think about it as much as possible. He knew he wasn't in love with her, but his feelings were definitely getting increasingly more complicated.

He walked to his study spot in the center of the school library and sat among his notes, pushing them aside to make room for the large book. The edges were decorated with flowery, silver leaf borders and reminded him of the old shifter fairy tale book his mother used to read from. It took a lot of years, but he was finally beginning to understand why his mother's favorite was the tragic romance of *Dante and Calliope*, the immortal mer and harpy who fell in love and were forbidden to be together. It must've reminded Victoria of her own tragic romance with Eduard.

Kol ran his fingers through his hair, tugging at a handful of it. That was another image he wanted to rid from his mind. The sorrowful smile was a permanent fixture on his mother's face.

Another reason to break the curse.

Carefully, he lifted the cover and flipped through the pictures and text that depicted the history of the boarding house. Located in Washington state, the house became a haven for shifters, and then a makeshift school before it was destroyed by vampires. He wasn't interested in the founding of the boarding house, since it housed only humans for the first several decades, but he flipped through the beginning photos anyway.

He stopped at a picture, an old black-and-white that must've been taken in front of the house. Four people were in the picture—all simply dressed and looking like they ran the place. A middle-aged couple stood in the center; the man had a smiling sort of face, but the woman's looked forced. A young girl, a teenager probably close in age to Kol and most likely the daughter of the couple, stood next to the man. She smiled, but Kol could tell she was the skeptical type. The sort of person who would require a person to prove their worth before she gave them her loyalty. It was funny that he could tell that about her in a picture. On the other side of the couple was a young man, maybe in his twenties. His hair was dark and was pulled back at the nape of his neck. His expression was a lot like the man's: easy going, happy, and kind.

Kol wondered what type of shifters they were and glanced at their names listed at the bottom. The young girl, the skeptical one, was Camilla Frost. Next to her were James and Jane Frost. Definitely her parents. The man in his twenties was named Leif Villers. None of the names were familiar shifter names, or otherwise known, so he continued to flip through the book.

He was looking for a specific name: *Aline Dracul.* He didn't know if he was a direct descendant of Aline or a distant relative, but she was the supposed reason for the Dracul curse. Kol called his older sister, Tatiana, to verify Aline's name—claiming it was for a school paper because he didn't want her knowing the real reason for his interest—and according to her, Aline committed some inexplicable crime. As retaliation for her misdeed, a curse—*the curse*—was placed on the entire family line.

The curse stipulated that if ever a Dracul fell in love—and by association even someone who married a Dracul—the love would be forever unrequited. Kol's mother loved his father deeply, but he'd seen his father's flippant attitude toward her since Kol was a young child. Kol suspected that his father was still in love with his former mistress—his half-brother's, Adam and Alex's, mother—but she had refused to even see Eduard for years.

They both loved but were not loved in return.

Kol stopped on a page picturing a young woman. Her clothing wasn't simple like the people in the first, and even in black and white he could tell her dress was probably expensive. She wore a traditional head wrap, much like the ones his Romanian ancestors probably wore, and her features were familiar. In fact, her nose looked almost identical to Tatiana's.

Scanning her name, his suspicions were confirmed: *Aline Elana Dracul.*

He'd found her.

The book slammed shut, pinching two of his fingers.

"Studying on a Saturday?" Brett asked, sitting across from him at the table. "I've been looking everywhere for you, *man*! And I swear half the student population has escaped to Christmas shop, so it wasn't like I've had crowds to search through."

"They're letting students go topside?" Kol asked. *Surely Myreen wouldn't be stupid enough to leave the safety of the school,* he thought.

"Yes." Brett let out an exasperated breath and spun the book to read the title. Fortunately it held no interest for him and he turned it back with a raised eyebrow. "I'm bored. Wanna hit the sim?"

Kol almost asked Brett if he knew which students left the Dome, hoping he wouldn't say Myreen's name, but his friend wasn't that observant. "Who's still around?" Kol asked instead, attempting to sound only slightly curious.

Brett balked with an annoyed smile. "I didn't take roll call, Kol," he said. "But Nik's not here."

Now Kol flashed an annoyed smile. "Yeah, I knew that, *ya dumb bird*."

Brett flipped him off. "C'mon," he said. "You're a straight A student. I need to blow off some steam. Let's go fight computer vamps!"

Kol packed up his books and notes like that was exactly what he intended to do. And he would, he just needed to know that Myreen was still at the Dome first. "You know, that Juliet girl shifted for the first time that night we were attacked," he said. "She might wanna practice on the sim. Should we go find her and Myreen? See if they wanna join?" Okay, so he knew he was being obvious, but part of him didn't care.

"Umm... sure," Brett said, while Kol carefully stashed the Boarding House book in his bag. "I haven't seen either of them, but we can go find them."

Kol shouldered his bag—he'd definitely need to take a closer look at the book later, now that he knew Aline was in it—and followed Brett out, trying to hide the building dread that Myreen and Juliet were some of the students who left the school. On the other hand, Brett might've walked right past the two of them on his way to the library without noticing. Kol doubted he'd pay attention to either of them, even though Juliet was a phoenix.

"That Juliet girl is pretty badass," Brett said as they exited the library. "She really made Mr. Q earn his keep yesterday in class. And he's her *dad!"*

So maybe Brett *did* pay attention to her.

They made a quick stop at the dorm room so Kol could drop his bags and books before they went searching. Kol asked a couple of harpies in the common room if they had seen either of them recently.

"Sure, this morning," one with long white hair said. Kol couldn't remember her name. "I remember the dark lipstick Juliet was wearing." She let out a low whistle. "It looked like she might be heading out for a hot date."

Kol and Brett looked at each other, but Kol was certain they weren't thinking the same thing.

"What about Myreen?" Kol asked. "Dark hair with blue

streaks."

"Yeah, yeah, we know who *Myreen* is," the other one with more yellow hair said, rolling her eyes. He didn't remember her name, either. "And no, we haven't seen her today."

Kol nodded a quick thanks, then shoved Brett out the door with more force than he meant to.

"Whoa, what's up?" Brett asked, hands raised in mock surrender.

"N– nothing, I just..." he trailed off. He wasn't in the mood to be mocked for caring.

But Brett surprised him by sobering. "You're worried they left."

"Yeah," Kol said, taking long steps toward the stairs.

"Alright," Brett said. "We'll find them. They're probably just off watching one of those cheesy Christmas chick flicks somewhere. I'm sure they didn't leave. They know it's dangerous."

Kol stopped to look at his friend. Brett was acting the way Nik would in the same situation, even though he didn't have dating history with Juliet. Brett was worried because Kol was worried.

"I'll check the dining hall," Brett said, shrugging off the grateful expression on Kol's face. "You check the training room?"

Kol nodded and rushed off. He checked the training room and pool, catching a few mer stares while he was there. He plastered his go-to stoic expression when asking if any of them had seen Myreen, then stalked away like it didn't matter that none of them had since the day before.

As soon as he was out of the building, he practically sprinted to the greenhouses, but all of them were locked so she couldn't be inside.

His heart began to beat furiously with the exertion, coupled with his rising panic.

Myreen had left the Dome.

Kol was almost certain of it, and the memory of the attack in the alley forced itself to the forefront of his mind. Juliet had been capable in that fight, but if she and Myreen faced something similar, just the two of them, they wouldn't survive.

Kol sped to the main part of the school. He'd find Brett and they'd figure out a way to sneak out, even though the sun would set soon. He calculated it would be dark in about an hour.

An hour. He walked faster.

When Kol entered the grand hall, his fear instantly extinguished but his anger ignited. He was almost surprised actual sparks didn't shoot from his hands. Myreen and Juliet walked in from the subway platform, laughing and joking, their heads huddled and arms locked together.

Kol stomped toward them.

"What the hell?" he shouted. Several heads looked at them, then quickly away.

"Can we help you, Kol?" Juliet asked, her voice calm but with an edge of a tease. She thought he'd overreacted.

"You two *left?"*

"Girl's day out," Myreen answered, lifting her chin slightly. "We needed a girl's day."

Kol gripped two fistfuls of his hair. "Are you two complete idiots?" he shouted. They both flinched. "Don't you remember our little incident with the vamps?"

"We're back!" Myreen said, taking a step toward him. "The

sun hasn't even set. There are no vamps out during the day. We made sure to be back long before it got dark."

"And they're not the only danger," Kol lowered his voice. "And *you,* Myreen, more than *anyone* should be more careful."

"The Dome isn't a prison, Kol," Juliet chimed in.

Kol unleashed the full force of his anger into his stare at the fiery-haired girl.

"And... that's my cue to leave," she said, backing away. "See ya later, Myreen," Juliet said, shooting Myreen a cowardly look of sympathy.

Myreen didn't seem to notice. "She's right," she said when her friend exited. "This is not a prison. I'm free to leave if I want." Her expression was confident, but faltered slightly. "*During the day,* of course," she added, a little *less* confident.

He glowered at her for several seconds. Enough to make her squirm. "You could've been killed, or worse—"

"What's worse than being killed?" she interrupted with her own shout.

"You could've been taken," he said, crossing his arms over his chest. "And if you don't think that's worse..."

"Whatever. You're not my *parent,* Kol," she said, but winced at the word. "And you're not Oberon, either. He didn't forbid me from leaving."

He stared again. This girl—this beautiful, wonderful girl—was asking for trouble. She had no idea the sort of danger she'd put herself in by leaving the Dome. It was infuriating. And he hated how much he cared.

"Whatever!" he threw his hands in the air. "Go and get yourself killed."

And he stalked off.

Chapter 17

Myreen

"What's *his* problem?" Juliet asked, glancing at Kol over Myreen's shoulder a few tables away.

Myreen didn't turn her head. She knew she would see that brimstone glower on Kol's face aimed at her, and she wasn't in the mood. She just remained hunched over the tuna sandwich she wasn't eating.

"I can't believe he's *that* mad at you for leaving campus for a few hours, and me for being the one to take you out," Juliet continued.

Myreen shrugged. "I mean, I guess I get it. He's afraid that something bad is going to happen to me out there. But yeah, this is a bit much. What does he expect me to do, stay in this fish bowl for the rest of my life?"

Juliet sighed. "I wish he would get over himself, already. He obviously has it bad for you, but rather than confess his feelings for you and make *whatever this thing is*"—she waved her hands in the air in front of Myreen—"between you two official, he's being a butt and treating you like a caged bird."

Myreen pursed her lips. She still hadn't told Juliet about the make out session in the greenhouse from a few days ago. Juliet was struggling enough with her breakup with Nik, and sharing that seemed like it would be shoving her own happiness in her friend's face. Also, the kissing hadn't made anything official. She and Kol hadn't talked about it since it happened, but that was probably because she'd told him she needed time. He had probably been waiting for her to make first contact. Well, until now. Now he looked like he hated her.

"How's that going, by the way?"

"Huh?" Myreen blinked out of her ruminations and cocked her head at Juliet.

"The harpy training, I mean," Juliet clarified. "I know this is off-topic, but it's kinda fun being able to refer to you as both a fish and a bird. It reminds me of the story of Dante and Calliope." She laughed, and Myreen attempted a laugh to humor her.

"Actually, it's going great. I feel so much more confident with the harpy stuff than my mermaid powers. It just seems to come so much easier." She frowned. "Sometimes I think maybe I'm not really a mermaid at all...but I don't feel more at home anywhere but in the water. It's... weird."

"You never know. You might feel differently when you get to fly as a harpy," Juliet suggested with a shrug. "When are you going to try shifting?"

Myreen snorted. "I'm so not ready for that. As a mermaid, I

don't really have a choice. Saltwater gets on my skin and shifting is automatic. I wouldn't know the first thing about trying to shift into something totally new at will. Especially something that's so completely opposite of a mermaid."

"I know better than anyone else at this school what that feels like. I tried so many times to shift and failed. Little did I know all I had to do was die first." Juliet laughed, but it didn't reach her eyes. "But it's what we are. It'll happen for you eventually. After all, you're the prophesied one." She winked.

"Ugh, don't remind me." Myreen hung her head. "I have my first siren lesson after this. Yet another thing that I have no clue how to do."

"Again, welcome to the club." Juliet raised her soda can in a mock toast. "As an ex-member, I have faith in you." She offered an encouraging smile.

"Thanks." Myreen picked up her sandwich. She'd just eat it quickly, so she wouldn't have to feel the heat of Kol's scowl on the back of her neck.

***

Myreen's legs wobbled with uncertainty as she entered the music classroom for her first siren lesson with Delphine. The room was empty, of course, but she still felt strange about training for a skill that would assumedly bring about the end of a centuries-old war in the same place where she and her classmates created lovely melodies. *Shouldn't this have been done in the gym? Or the mer training room?*

Delphine was perched at the base of the theatre-style steps, and when Myreen looked her way, she patted the spot beside her. Myreen swallowed nervously and walked toward her, taking a seat.

"Have you been drinking plenty of water today?" Delphine asked.

"Umm, yes?" Myreen answered, unsure as to what that had to do with this lesson. She always drank a ton throughout the day, more than what was considered normal for non-mer.

"Good, that should help." Delphine braided her fingers and placed her hands in her lap. "Now, before we start, let's talk about what happened in the alley, when you used your siren voice in front of Draven. Can you tell me how it happened? What were you feeling?"

Myreen let out a shaky breath and replayed the incident in her mind. "Well, one of the vampires had gotten hold of Juliet and was going to hurt her. I felt so useless, being the only one of my friends who didn't know how to fight, and when I thought she was going to get hurt, I... I refused to let that happen. So I yelled at the vampire to let her go. And he did."

Delphine nodded. "I see. And were there any other times in your past that you might have used your siren voice without knowing it? Any time that you voiced what you wanted and the person did exactly what you said?"

Delphine's question was one she'd been debating for several nights. There had been one other time in her life that she'd heard that voice come out of her mouth, that she'd felt that strange vibration throughout her core. It was the same day she tried quite hard *not* to think about.

"Well, there may have been," she answered. "The night that my mom..." She couldn't finish the sentence, her throat tightened and closed, silencing her. She swallowed and skipped past it. "There was a party with the kids at my school. I had never been to a real party and I wanted more than anything to go, but my mom with her silly rules, she refused to listen to me, to budge at all. I was so tired of being held back from normal things kids are supposed to do. So I told her to let me go to the party, in a voice that wasn't mine, and she did." She looked down at her lap, self-hatred churning like storm clouds inside her gut. "It all seems so stupid now."

Delphine put her hand on Myreen's shoulder. "I'm so sorry your last moments with your mother were so tremulous. I had no idea. No wonder you carry such sorrow. But you must learn to forgive yourself someday. Your mother wouldn't want you suffering over it forever. Don't you think?"

Myreen nodded, knowing that forgiving herself wasn't something that would happen any time soon. Shoving it into a box deep inside herself and ignoring it? That was something she could do, and she was getting quite good at it.

"I've never met a siren," Delphine continued. "In fact, I haven't heard of one in our history for centuries, so little is known about them. About you. But from what you've told me, it seems that your powers stem from your will. The two times you've used your siren voice, you truly wanted the things you asked for. So I think if we want to harness this power of yours, we need to focus on exercising your will."

"Forgive my ignorance, Delphine, but what can my powers even do?" Myreen asked. "So far, all I've seen them do is control people, make them do things against their will. I don't know if that's something I really want to practice on other people."

"I'm sorry to say that I know little more than you," Delphine admitted with a shrug, forcing her brilliant red locks to spill over her shoulders. "Yes, they can be used to control people, and that is what they are most known for. But it is said that, at least in the ocean, the siren call can be used to beckon sea creatures and even change tides. There are some legends that say a siren's voice can even bring back the dead." Delphine snickered at the sight of Myreen's eyes bulging. "But we won't bother with such dark magic, I promise you." She smiled at Myreen.

"So… How exactly are we going to practice using my siren voice?" Myreen asked, biting her lip. She didn't want to make Delphine do anything against her will.

Delphine's smile widened, and Myreen saw a mischievous twinkle in her emerald eyes. Delphine turned toward the storage closet door and called, "Trish. We're ready for you now."

Trish? What the heck?

The door opened and Trish entered the room with her arms crossed under her chest and a scowl on her face. Myreen's heart raced as Trish came closer, worrying what was expected to happen. Was Delphine going to pit them against each other again? As much as Myreen hated Trish, she didn't want to hurt her, especially after she almost obliterated her with light the last time.

"Trish is still serving detention for kicking you out of your room in the Mer wing," Delphine explained, waving her delicate pale hand toward Trish. "As one of her sessions, I thought she'd be the perfect person to help you unlock your siren abilities."

"Wait, what?" Genuine surprise loosened Trish's default nasty expression, and she dropped her arms to her sides.

"I– I don't know about this, Delphine," Myreen stuttered, shaking her head.

"But I do. I foresaw this exchange, and it works out perfectly." Delphine winked at her, ignoring Trish's resistant comments and obvious growing apprehension. "There's something you want from Trish, very much I should think. Something she owes you."

"I owe her nothing," Trish sneered even as fear darkened her mascaraed eyes.

As Myreen looked back and forth between the two of them, understanding dawned on her. Yes, there was something she wanted from Trish, something she wanted very deeply. Trish had been the root of every social problem Myreen had since she arrived at the Dome, and what Myreen wanted most was for all her hazing to stop. Delphine was giving her the opportunity, and *permission,* to make that happen.

But if Trish only accepted her, maybe even liked her, because Myreen forced her to... would it be worth anything if it wasn't real?

The idea of having the whispers stop, of no longer seeing malice on the faces of her fellow mer, was so incredibly tempting. Yes, she did want this more than she ever realized. It was second to wanting her mom back...

Having made her decision, Myreen rose from the step and approached Trish, concentrating on what it was she wanted. With each step she took closer, Trish tripped backwards, shrinking little by little in fear, until she was backed up against a wall. Now they were face-to-face, and the desire was so great, Myreen could feel the power welling up inside her.

"Apologize to me for the awful way you've treated me," Myreen intoned, her siren voice vibrating through her body as it flowed mellifluously past her lips.

Trish's beautiful doll face went blank as the command worked its magic. Then her brows puckered, and she said with full sincerity, "I'm sorry, Myreen. I've said so many horrible things about you. I kicked you out of your room, I've turned as many people as I could against you. I even tried to get you severely injured by locking you in the sim room. I blamed you for Alessandra getting hurt, and even after she woke up and said you were innocent, I still hated you. You didn't deserve any of it. I'm so sorry."

Hearing those words were more satisfying, more healing than she could have ever imagined. Just hearing Trish admit all her wrong-doings toward her and that she didn't deserve it somehow made it all better. That was enough for Myreen.

"Thank you," Myreen said, then tapped into her siren powers once more. "Forget this apology and return to life as you know it, but the next time you try to hurt or spread rumors about someone, imagine those same things are happening to you."

Trish's eyes remained blank for a few seconds after Myreen stopped talking, then she came back to her senses. "Please don't hurt me," she begged, wincing, having forgotten the whole ordeal just as Myreen ordered.

"I'm not going to hurt you," Myreen said. "You can go."

Trish's eyes widened, and she looked over Myreen's shoulder at Delphine, who nodded. That was all she needed to scramble out from under Myreen's shadow and scurry out of the room.

Delphine stood and looked at Myreen. "You surprised me. You could have ended her hazing once and for all."

"I wanted to," Myreen confessed. "But I knew I wouldn't feel right about it. I'd never know if her being nice to me was real or just because I forced her to change. I realized it wouldn't mean anything if it wasn't real. And... an apology was enough. That's all anyone wants from their bully, isn't it? And with the last little stipulation I added, maybe she'll think twice the next time she bullies anyone, not just me."

Delphine beamed at Myreen and put her hands on either of Myreen's shoulders. "You are exactly the right person to have the powers of a siren, and I am so proud of you for making a choice even I would've been too selfish to make."

Myreen's heart swelled. Delphine was the only mother figure she had left. That the head mer would say such a thing to her... Myreen almost wanted to cry with joy.

"For our next lesson, we'll try using your siren voice in the lake, I think, see if we can't have some fun with our aquatic neighbors," Delphine said with a girlish excitement.

"I can't wait," Myreen said honestly. Now that she knew she could use this voice for good and not just for self-gain, she couldn't wait to see what else it could do.

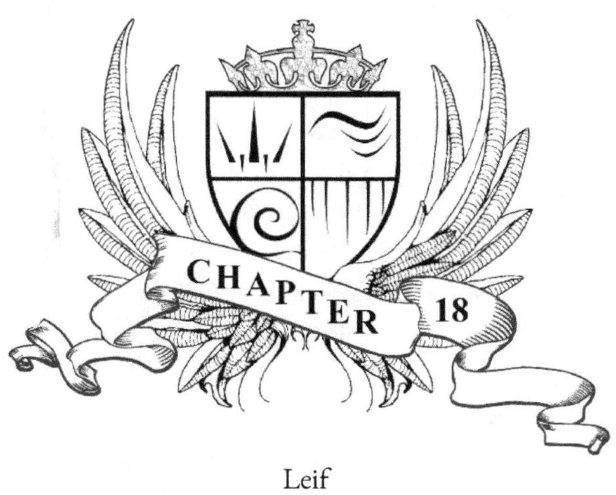

Leif

It was late and it was cold, but neither bothered Leif. Time was just as irrelevant as the weather. A snowstorm had passed earlier in the day, but a bitter wind had carried it away from Chicago, leaving the city even colder and the sky open.

Leif played the part, wearing a puffy gray coat and jeans, although his body needed no insulation. His flesh was as cold as the air, anyway.

As ordered by Draven, Leif was within close proximity to the subway station that led to the shifter school. He sat on a park bench with a good vantage point of the staircase that led down to the station. The park was far enough away that Leif felt confident he wouldn't look too obviously camped out and stalker-ish. Over the past week, he'd seen police officers go by, their sights not dwelling on him for too long. It was Chicago—there was a lot going on to keep them busy.

As it was late and the city was mostly quiet, Leif doubted that any shifter would come crawling out of the subway station. Every night had been the same: nobody resembling the daughter of Draven had come out.

Leif turned another page of the book he was reading. For all the music he'd memorized from his favorite composer, Leif had relatively no idea who Ludwig van Beethoven was. For the past few evenings, he'd read about the prodigy's abusive childhood, and how he'd been scorned by his father for his "playing by ear" methods with the violin, telling him that he'd never amount to anything. Leif's own childhood was remarkably similar. His father had been abusive, both physically and verbally, and while Leif hadn't spent any time with music as a child, he'd been told enough times that the trees in the orchards would produce just fine without him.

The camaraderie he felt with Beethoven increased, and Leif knew that the sonatas and marches he'd studied over the years would only have more meaning for him now.

Being so enveloped with the composer's history, Leif hardly noticed the soft footsteps in the snow behind him. Snapping the book shut, he whirled around to mark whoever it was daring to sneak up on him.

It was Piper. Leif barely recognized her underneath all the layers she wore. Her hands were shoved into the side pockets of a padded dark royal purple overcoat that hung down to her shins. She wore tan boots that somehow looked fashionably feminine, and her blonde hair was scrunched under a lavender beanie. A green scarf wrapped around her neck and trailed down her front.

Piper stopped as soon as their eyes met.

"What are you doing here?" Leif stated, getting to his feet.

He immediately regretted it. Piper had never shown any ill-will toward him. Sure, she had her quirky moments, but she'd always been kind.

She pulled her white-gloved hands out of her pockets and shrugged awkwardly. "Draven sent me."

He stepped toward her. "Draven sent you? At this time of night? Piper, you're going to freeze to death." Leif could see her teeth chattering.

"I guess you'd have to turn me into a vampire to save me if that were to happen," she said, a small smile creeping across her face.

Leif didn't see the humor and set his jaw. She knew how he felt about her desire to be turned.

Her grin disappeared. "Draven's waiting in your apartment. He sent me to gather you."

"Draven's here?" Leif said with disbelief.

Piper nodded.

"Why in the world did he come? I've only been away from Heritage Prep for one week."

Piper shrugged, then wiped at her nose with her sleeve. She was shaking uncontrollably.

Her condition pushed away Leif's frustration momentarily. He couldn't let her stay out in the cold like this.

"Let's get back to my apartment and get you warmed up," he said. "I'm afraid I don't have fixings for coffee or tea, but you can at the very least take a warm bath."

Piper nodded ever so slightly, little puffs of air releasing from her mouth as she breathed quickly. "That sounds perfect."

He put his arm around her shoulder, knowing that his own lack of body heat would do little for her, but he hoped she'd at least take some comfort in the gesture.

Leif never thought he'd see the day he'd be walking a vampire Initiate back to his apartment, but that was precisely what he was doing.

***

Leif opened the door for Piper, and they walked into the apartment complex.

"Thank you," she said through chattering teeth as she quickly entered the warmth of the lobby. He watched as Piper eyed the large gas fireplace with several couches and chairs surrounding it.

"I've got a smaller fireplace in my apartment," he said. "You can warm up there."

She nodded, and together they walked through the lobby and past the restaurant that was closed for the evening.

Leif took long strides as he passed his neighbors' doors. He didn't know them—he generally kept to himself. Getting to know humans was dangerous. All it took was one of them finding out that he was a vampire, then suddenly a group of hunters would be forcing their way through his door. Because he was a *threat to the community.* Yes, it had happened, but before he'd made his way to Chicago.

They finally arrived at his place. Judging by how intact the door was, it was obvious that Draven hadn't forced entry.

"Should I be concerned that Draven so easily entered my apartment?" he muttered as he tested the doorknob. The door was unlocked, and he threw Piper a hesitant glance.

She shrugged. "Draven's the most powerful vampire in the world. I'm not sure there's any place in the world that could keep him out."

Leif snorted. "Except for the shifter school."

"For now."

Pushing the door open, the dim lamp in the far corner of Leif's apartment shone through, revealing a woman with black hair styled in a pixie cut lying unconscious on his authentic Kashan rug. Leif recognized her immediately as one of his neighbors. He'd never spoken with her before and didn't even know her name. Her head was tilted to the side, revealing a vampire bite in the softness of her pale neck.

Stepping past her, Leif found Draven sitting in the only heirloom he'd salvaged from the Frost Boarding House a hundred years before.

It bothered Leif to see him sitting smugly in the chair that had survived the destruction of vampires. Draven was staring at him with disinterest.

"There's our Winter Watcher," Draven said softly.

"You left a mess on my rug," Leif replied.

"Her name is Jolene," Draven said, crossing one leg over the other as he sat up straight. "And it appears your pet is doing a fine job cleaning things up."

Leif shooed Rainbow away, and the cat meowed in frustration as it hid behind the curtains. It was one thing to see a vampire guzzling blood, but it was unsettling seeing a cat lick the bloody remnants as if they were the spills from a bowl of milk. Was Rainbow showing vampiric tendencies? After all, the thing had died, and Leif had noticed the small creature pawing at the blood bags he'd been drinking the past few days.

He made a mental note to talk to Kenzie about it.

Draven chuckled. "She sacrificed a date with a doctor to

spend the evening with me."

Disgust bubbled in Leif's throat. "You hypnotized her to gain entrance into the apartment complex, didn't you?"

Draven nodded, his eyes flashing back down to the sleeping form on the rug. Tapping his head, he said, "She wasn't endowed with much up here. Really, it was far too easy to control her mind. But her blood was remarkably sweet. I'd highly recommend drinking from her at some point, if you get the chance."

Leif didn't even entertain the idea. "Why are you here?"

Draven smiled as he leaned forward. "I came for an update, of course."

Leif blinked a couple of times. "An update? On what?"

"You've been silent since you started your mission a week ago," Draven replied. "I thought I'd visit you personally to discover your progress."

"About finding your daughter?" Leif snorted. "You don't think I'd contact you the minute I capture her?"

Draven chuckled, then snapped his fingers. "Oh, I know you would. But it would be difficult to catch Myreen if you weren't around the subway station when she emerged from her underwater home, wouldn't it?"

Leif wondered at the vampire leader's irony. Hadn't he just been pulled away from his post to have this conversation? Still, alarms were going off in his mind. Draven suspected something. He was trying to catch Leif in his words.

"I haven't seen Myreen appear, and I've kept my eyes on those stairs nearly the entire time I've been back in Chicago."

Raising a finger, Draven said, "'Nearly' being the keyword, right?"

Leif shrugged. "I'm a vampire. Even I must step away for a drink from time to time."

"And how long does it take you to gain your fill of blood?" Draven questioned.

Leif was falling deeper into the vampire leader's snares. To be honest, he'd been running particularly low on his stash of blood bags in his refrigerator. After his visit with Kenzie, he'd headed for the nearest blood bank. The place had been busy, and Leif's attempt at stealing a box of blood bags had very nearly failed because of the amount of staff there. In the end, he'd been successful, but it had taken a lot longer to obtain his precious blood bags than he'd anticipated.

He tried not to let his increasing anxiety show. "I suppose that depends on how thirsty I am."

Draven rose from the chair, keeping his untrusting eyes on Leif. "Let me change the question to something a little more direct, then. What were you doing on Saturday afternoon?"

Leif shifted his gaze to Piper, who was standing close to his unconscious neighbor, stuck in an awkward posture as she was forced to listen to the tense conversation. Looking back at Draven, he said, "I was keeping watch over the subway station, just as you've asked."

Draven sighed as he slipped a hand into his left pocket and withdrew a small tablet. "Leif, Leif, Leif. You should know me better than this." The vampire leader handed Leif the device. "Go ahead and hit play whenever you're ready."

Leif looked down and saw the *Play* sign hovering over a still of the stairs leading down to the subway station, with him in the foreground on his favorite park bench.

"You've been watching me?" he asked, feeling a surge of

fear and anger. Most of all, he felt stupid. Of course Draven would be keeping an eye on him. This task to kidnap his daughter was extremely important. He wouldn't just let things fall by the wayside. The question was, how? Maybe there'd been a drone or another piece of tech in the air—something Leif had completely missed. Or perhaps a hidden camera in a tree.

"I merely tapped into the city security camera system," Draven said, spinning a finger in the air. "Surely it doesn't hurt to have multiple eyes on the subway station. You know, just in case one of us misses something."

Leif hit the *Play* icon with a mildly shaking finger, and the camera footage showed 11:55 a.m. as the recording time.

"As you can see," Draven said, "you're on the phone. After verifying with Piper, it is confirmed that you were not talking to her. Beatrice also verified that you weren't speaking to her. And you were definitely not on the phone with me."

Kenzie, Leif thought with a grimace. How well would that revelation go over with Draven? *Yeah, I was on the phone with a selkie who was eager to show me some of her magic...*

He was a terrible liar, but he blurted out the first thing that came to his mind. "I was following up on a lead about a certain dragon shifter line."

Draven's eyes widened. "You've located the Draculs?"

Leif bobbed his head. "I have a source that has seen one known as Eduard here in the city."

Draven rubbed at his permanent five o'clock shadow. "That's fascinating. Especially when you see what happens after you leave the premises."

Looking back at the screen, he saw himself quickly walk out of the camera frame. At the 1:01 pm marker, several people climbed the steps out of the subway station, including two teenage girls. One was clearly Myreen, and Leif's heart plummeted.

Draven tapped the screen, pausing the video. "In case you couldn't tell, one of those disembarking passengers is my daughter. The other one—according to Kendall Green—is the same phoenix shifter we fought against in the alleyway. Her name is Juliet Quinn."

Quinn, Leif thought. The face of another phoenix with the same last name surfaced in his mind—Evandrus. It had been over a hundred years since he'd seen Evandrus Quinn. But back then, Camilla Frost—whom Leif loved like a sister—had begun a relationship with him. Could this Juliet have any relation to Evandrus?

"Don't you find it at all coincidental," Draven continued, tearing Leif from his thoughts, "that not long after you left your watch, my daughter appeared from the subway station?"

"I had no idea," Leif sputtered.

"Indeed," Draven replied. "What's even more convenient is that if you skip ahead to 3:55, you'll see that Myreen and her friend return to the subway station, and ten minutes later, you return to your watch."

A spike of panic shot from Leif's stomach, and he fast-forwarded the video to that point in time to validate Draven's claim.

To his horror, the vampire leader was correct. But what was even more shocking was that there was a third girl walking back to the station, and he recognized her immediately. What in the world was Kenzie doing with Myreen and Juliet?

"It makes me wonder, Leif, just how many times could you

have missed my daughter coming out of her hiding place over the past week? How many times could you have missed snatching Myreen?"

Shrugging, Leif said, "You're the one with a video feed. Have you seen her come out before or after that time?"

Draven gave him a serious look. "I don't have time to monitor video surveillance, Leif. That's why you're here." Draven sat up again, relaxing a bit. "But upon a fast-forward viewing, no, she *hasn't* stepped out of the subway station besides this one time.

Leif shook his head, completely shocked at what this footage meant. "I can't believe it. I can understand your distrust, Draven. But believe me when I say that I had no idea your daughter would come and go during that one window of time."

"I want my daughter," Draven stated, pointing a finger right under Leif's nose. "You've missed at least two chances. Your lack of productivity is grinding away my patience."

"She's bound to make another appearance during Winter Break," Leif said quickly. "Chances are Myreen will surface again then."

Draven shook his head. "That's not good enough. If you're incapable of capturing Myreen, you'll have to be on the lookout for her friends. If you can successfully kidnap one of them, we can use them as bait."

Friends? Now that Leif knew that Kenzie was friends with Myreen, did that put her in jeopardy? He'd have to talk to her after Draven left.

"That could upset the entire school if students start going missing," Leif warned.

"Why should we be concerned about upsetting a school of

shifters?"

This was one of the things that had pushed Leif away from Draven fifteen years ago—his complete lack of empathy for other living beings was so abrasive. The vampire leader was so focused on his goals, he didn't care who he stampeded over to get to them.

Draven snatched the tablet from Leif and made a few quick motions on the screen, then handed it back.

"Thanks to our mer friend Kendall, here are a bunch of snapshots of Myreen's friends, with their names." Draven placed his hands on his hips and smiled broadly.

Leif looked down to see a close-up of the girl, Juliet Quinn. She had fiery orange hair, tan skin, and yellow-green eyes. Her name was bolded at the top, and once again, Leif wondered if she had any relation to Evandrus Quinn from the boarding house long ago.

"The next picture will be of particular interest to you," Draven said, smiling slyly.

Leif swiped his finger to show the next friend. The picture was of a young man with thick, dark hair and serious amber eyes. Leif could tell right away which family this boy came from without even looking at the bolded name.

"Malkolm Dracul," continued Draven. "If you were to catch him, you'd be able to satisfy your own personal vendetta as well as help me. You know, the whole 'kill two birds with one stone' concept."

Leif held no angst toward the boy with sharp features staring at him from the tablet. He'd done nothing wrong. Malkolm had nothing to do with Gemma's murder.

But Leif played the part, gritting his teeth and flaring his nostrils. He pretended he was looking at the face of Aline Dracul, which wasn't too difficult. The boy resembled her in so many ways.

"Before you break my tablet," Draven said, still grinning at Leif's reaction, "move on to see the other two boys that could potentially draw Myreen out."

Doing as Draven said, Leif swiped to find the next boy, named Nikolai Candida, his short, dark hair shaved with unique patterns. Like the Dracul boy, this one was labeled as a dragon shifter.

Swiping one more time, Leif found a boy with longer, blond hair, as well as blue eyes. His appearance screamed *California Surfer*, but the young man was labeled as a phoenix shifter, so Leif doubted the boy spent much time in the water.

"Most of these students happen to be the same shifters who fought us in the alley near the subway station," Draven said. "Kendall says that Myreen is closest to Juliet Quinn and Malkolm Dracul, so our best chances are kidnapping one of them to draw Myreen out."

Leif nodded, swiping back to Juliet and then to Malkolm. "I'll start looking for them."

"Good," Draven said, clapping Leif on the shoulder. "You'll notice that the other girl who was accompanying Myreen was not in the group of individual photos. I have an agent attempting to learn more about her as we speak."

A stab of panic struck Leif like a knife to the back. *Kenzie, you're on his radar now.*

"But if any of the others come out, you're to grab them. To make sure that you do, your Initiate, Piper, will be by your side from now on."

Leif did his best to hide his disappointment. Now he'd not only have to worry about security cameras watching him, Piper would be keeping an eye on him, too. But maybe that wasn't so bad. In the last conversation they'd had, Leif told her about some of the not-so-great things about being a vampire, and they seemed to have an effect on her. Perhaps he could pursue that some more?

"I'll be glad to have her help." Leif nodded toward his Initiate, who was still standing awkwardly, looking out of place.

Draven kept his hand firmly on Leif's shoulder and looked at him for a long moment.

"I need my daughter, Leif," he said with a cold seriousness that sent chills down Leif's back. "She's the key to a locked door full of answers."

Leif nodded. "We'll get her."

"Keep my tablet," Draven said, glancing down at the screen, then brought his light blue eyes back up to meet Leif's. "I'll be watching."

The vampire leader moved away, stepping past Leif's still unconscious neighbor, and headed for the door.

"What about my neighbor?" Leif said, stopping Draven as he was reaching for the doorknob.

Draven threw him a cold look. "She's your problem." With that, Draven swung the door open and stepped out. The door closed, and Leif found himself alone with Piper and his inert neighbor.

Sighing heavily, Leif stared at the unconscious woman, shaking his head. "He leaves messes everywhere he goes."

Juliet

After their epic girl's day out, a weight lifted off Juliet's shoulders. She wasn't one hundred percent back to herself, but she was close. The reassurance of happiness after heartbreak was much needed, especially when it came from Myreen and Kenzie. They reminded her that even if it felt like life was over, there was more to look forward to.

Of course, if someone mentioned Nik's name, her heart still tore into pieces; she was just better at hiding it now.

There was progress, though. She no longer had any tears left to cry, and whenever she passed the library, she didn't want to bury herself inside. Secluding herself became suffocating, so she spent most of her time in the defense room or with Myreen—though those moments were accompanied by endless eye rolls and near-constant subject changes. It was like it was Myreen's new super power. But she was the only friend that Juliet wanted to confide in. Even if it was ten times in one day.

As they walked into the dining hall for breakfast, they saw Kol walk toward his table. Juliet's stomach sank. Her mind spun in circles as she wondered if Kol or Brett ever updated Nik on how she was. Just then, Kol looked over at Myreen and gave a curt nod.

Juliet focused on how Myreen returned the gesture, then acted like nothing had happened. But Myreen's eyebrows scrunched together when she turned away. Without another word, Myreen led the way through the buffet, then to an empty table in the dining hall—as far away from Kol as possible.

A small part of Juliet envied Myreen. She at least got to see Kol every day. But Juliet was sure that if Nik was still there, they'd still be together. She tried to erase that last thought by focusing on Myreen.

"So, when are you two going to kiss and make up?" Juliet meant for it to sound like a joke, but Myreen's eyes grew wide.

"What's that supposed to mean?" Myreen lowered her voice to a whisper.

Juliet shrugged her shoulders. "Uh, nothing? It was a joke. But now I'm wondering why you just got so defensive. Like you're in loooove"—she sing-songed the word to emphasize she was still playing—"with the Dracul prince or something. Which I would totally ship." She laughed at her own, dry humor.

"Juliet, please. That's not even funny."

"Okay, okay. Deep breaths. I didn't mean to get you so upset. I just wondered if you two were ever going to speak again." Juliet knew she was treading in deep water, but she didn't get why they were being so stubborn.

"I don't know the answer to that, so please just drop it."

Myreen focused on her tray and nudged a piece of cantaloupe with her fork.

"Fine. But first, I just wanna remind you that you're lucky that you get to see him every day."

"It doesn't even matter. We're fighting right now." Myreen's face turned a light shade of red.

"Yeah, but how much longer are you guys going to avoid each other?" Juliet knew she wouldn't be able to push much further, but it didn't stop her from trying. "If Nik were here—"

"J, stop. Nik's not here! Get over it, already!" Myreen spoke through her teeth, and Juliet's heart sped up, all joviality gone.

"Gee, thanks. I had no idea! It was just a joke. Teach me to talk about Kol."

"No! It's because I'm sick of hearing about Nik. It happened. Move on!"

"What great advice! Let me do that for you right now!" The ball of emotion building in Juliet's throat stopped her from saying more. The burn began in her eyes, and she stood. As if losing her boyfriend wasn't enough, adding her best friend to the list made everything worse.

The last thing she wanted was for Myreen or anyone else to see her cry—and clearly she'd done it for too long. She grabbed her tray and chucked the food into the trash, then slammed it down and sprinted for the exit. Without looking back, Juliet raced to her room so she could sulk in private.

It was thirty minutes until Mastery Class, but Juliet decided she'd skip it. If her father saw her eyes blotchy and red, he'd think it was about Nik again. Malachai had shown a lot of pride on her progress, and she didn't want to disappoint him. She figured if she waited to see him at their one-on-one session, he'd be more understanding and open. Besides, she didn't want to show up to class, in front of her fellow phoenix students, with tear streaks on her cheeks—Brett especially.

Rumors floated through the school faster than lightning, so Juliet knew it was only a matter of time before everyone knew that she and Myreen were fighting. Her plan was to avoid the situation for as long as possible; she'd practically become a professional at hiding.

What she didn't have any practice in was arguing with a friend. She didn't know if she should apologize or wait for Myreen to apologize first. She didn't know if avoiding Myreen would make things worse, or if space was exactly what they needed. What she did know was that their fight hurt her just as much as breaking up with Nik.

She didn't want to fall behind in class, so she pulled her personalized eReader from her bag and searched for the *Phoenix Mastery Level 1* class book. She looked through the table of contents until she saw a chapter that looked interesting and tapped it. *Globe of Life.* A mini picture of a globe of fire came up, and she leaned the eBook on her lap. She straightened her back and took a few calming breaths as she wiped her eyes dry.

"Okay, enough. No more tears. Focus." She heard her voice quiver. Hopefully, with enough concentration, she'd be okay.

It took Juliet twenty minutes to get through the chapter. She wanted to be sure that she could master the Globe of Life without her father instructing her. It sounded easy enough, but she knew that with one wrong step, her days of lighting rooms on fire would be back. Not something she wanted to add to her plate. The eReader was in front of her, acting as a guide—just in case—but she felt confident that if she kept her mind clear of the drama, she would succeed.

Juliet rubbed her hands together and closed her eyes. She didn't want to think of the fire within her until she had a completely clear mind, which took longer to do than she would have liked. But once focused and calm, she was ready to proceed. The warmth of her power came to her with ease, starting in her stomach. She took a deep breath to savor the euphoric heat and ran it through her veins.

The book instructed to form a ball the size of a snow globe, so while Juliet embraced her power, she also thought of the shape and size she wanted it to be. When the electric sensation simmered down, she willed the flames to escape her fingertips.

With one hand above the other, she watched her flames connect in a pretty, web-like form, coming together in a perfect sphere. It felt heavy in her hand, which is what the book said would happen. Pleased with herself, she glanced at the book for the next step.

Now that the globe was formed, she had to hollow it out. With the tip of her pinky, she gently touched the top part of the globe. Very lightly, she twirled her finger, allowing the flames to escape. They followed her finger, which she rolled round and round until the globe in her hand was hollowed out.

Now she had one empty ball of fire in her left hand and what resembled a blazing ball of yarn in her right one. What she had to do next was the most complicated step, according to the instructions. And this was the part that made her nervous.

With the fire in her right hand, she had to concentrate on an image—a moving image. She could pick anything, but she knew that if she let herself think for too long, it would be nothing but chaos. So she picked the first thing that popped into her mind: a Christmas tree.

It seemed easy enough. She was supposed to think of the object while closing the fire in her hand into a fist, turning it into ash. When she was satisfied, her fist closed tightly until the flames turned to weightless ash.

Juliet lifted her hand and poured the dark dust into the tiny hole on top of the globe. With the same hand, she used her finger to seal the hole shut, and the globe became heavy again. She glanced at the eReader. Now all she had to do was shake her globe and watch her image come to life.

Juliet smiled as she shook the globe and awaited her Christmas tree.

Like a sand storm, the ash swirled and spun in dizzying circles, forming into strings of fire. They patched together, starting at the tree stump and growing until the top of the tree touched the top of the globe. Branches and needles shot out, turning the trunk into a full and beautifully formed pine. It glowed and sparkled a bright orange in the translucent globe, which made it look like it was on fire. It was the most magnificent image Juliet had ever seen.

Just when she thought it was over, the image morphed into something completely different. The tree broke into pieces twisting into a heart. As she watched, confused and disappointed that she'd done something wrong, the heart split in half and fell to the bottom of the globe, turning once more into dark dust.

"A broken heart. What a surprise." Now that Juliet was upset all over again, she wanted to put the globe down. She wondered what the other students had worked on, and if they'd been successful. Maybe if she brought her Globe of Life to her one-on-one session with her dad, it would excuse her absence from the class. Though, there was always the chance it would disappoint him as much as it did her.

But Juliet didn't want to make a hazard of the globe—the instructions stated to crush the entire thing when complete—so she decided to bring it with her. Class wouldn't be over for another fifteen minutes, so she grabbed her bag and raced as gently as she could to her dad's office before students began filling the hallways. Thanks to skipping class, she made it without running into anyone.

She probably shook the globe fifty times, watching the tree turn into her broken heart over and over, before Malachai finally walked in. The minute he saw, his eyebrows shot up.

"There'd better be a good reason for you missing class today." He didn't look at her as he took his seat behind his desk.

"Well, Myreen and I got into a fight and my emotions were all over the place. I figured it was safer for everyone if I skipped."

Now, he raised his eyes to Juliet's face. "I see. Friends come and go, Juliet. You'll find a way to make it easier for yourself. It took me an entire year after I had to leave you and your mother. I hit the sim room hard." He gestured to the globe. "What do you have there?"

Juliet stood and brought it over. "I didn't want my time to be wasted, so I looked in the mastery book and found this cool chapter about the *Globe of Life*. It was really fun to make. And it works. I think it's just defective... like me." She didn't want pity, but she couldn't keep the sorrow out of her tone.

She shook the globe so her dad could watch her unique picture. His eyes grew wider and wider until the heart split and fell to ash.

"Wow. For one, I'm truly impressed. Half of the students in

the class wouldn't have gotten this far without my help. Second, there isn't anything to be disappointed about. This only reflects what you felt in your core when you made this. My only piece of advice is to try this when you're not feeling broken inside. No amount of meditation will erase what emotions you truly feel in the moment of creation. Work like this would deserve an A plus, though. Very well done."

Malachai's eyes glowed with pride as he took the globe out of her hand. She needed to hear that more than she realized.

Her father stood and recovered a small cylinder glass vase and stand from a closet hidden in the corner. He placed her globe on the stand and covered it with the vase. Like a trophy, Malachai displayed her globe directly in the front center of his desk.

"There. It's perfect. Now when you're a pro at all this power stuff, seeing this will remind you that you can do anything. With or without anyone by your side." His large hand came around her shoulder and he squeezed her gently into his side.

"Now, let's get this one-on-one started. By the looks of it, I say we go change and meet in the defense room. I think blowing off some steam could help that broken heart of yours. Maybe if you feel up for it, you could even try the sim when we're done." He wiggled his eyebrows, which brought a smile to Juliet's face—something she thought she couldn't do after fighting with her best friend.

"Thanks, Dad. I'll meet you there in ten."

And with that, she was again reminded that she was never alone.

Not anymore.

Oberon

"Watch and be amazed!" Ren touted.

It was their lunch hour, between classes, and Oberon had been pulled into the glass-partitioned research lab in the section where the heart of tinkering took place for the school. There were all sorts of machines and devices of every size and shape pushed to the sides. Only a handful of them were out, as a few dedicated students were working on projects for Ren's class.

"Please hurry," Oberon said, covering his eyes as if he were being blinded. "Having to see you in your smart clothing isn't exactly what I'd had in mind when you expressed your desire for me to witness what you've been working on."

Ren gave him a sly grin. Snapping his fingers, he said, "You'd rather see me in no clothing, then?"

Oberon rolled his eyes. "Ren, that is hardly—"

"Trust me, that's precisely what you're saying," Ren said, cutting Oberon off.

Ren brought the hand he'd held behind his back forward. Clasped between his fingers and palm was a skinny, tubular object that had a cable sticking out at the top.

Oberon glanced from the device, then back at Ren. "It looks like a stick of dynamite."

Ren's sly grin broadened. "In a way, it is. You know why? Because it's going to blow your mind."

Before Oberon could complain, Ren slid the cable into one of the inputs on his smart clothing. In an instant, the parts of the kitsune covered by his clothing completely disappeared, leaving only Ren's head and neck, his arms from his biceps to his fingers, and his legs from just above the knees down to his toes, visible.

"Whoa!" Oberon said.

Ren looked down at his missing body parts, then made eye contact with Oberon again. "Mind blown?"

"Very much so," Oberon mumbled.

"Can you imagine what we could have done back in our glory days with this kind of tech?" Ren held the device in front of him. "Jade would still be alive. Same with Seri..."

Oberon stiffened as Ren said his wife's name, the awe he'd felt just moments before melting away into a bitter sadness. It was useless thinking about such things—the what-could've-been's. It only tore open the age-old scars he'd acquired as a newlywed and a father-to-be.

Ren cleared his throat. "Remember our infiltration of the theater in Pierre? Draven wouldn't have even known what hit him. We could've stopped him in his tracks back then."

"Well, we didn't," grumbled Oberon.

Ren's face fell and his shoulders dropped. "Look, I'm sorry. It's hard for me not to think about these kinds of things when

I'm tinkering."

"It's all right," Oberon said. "Forget about it. The invisibility tech is a masterpiece, and will be extremely helpful. The military will be particularly overjoyed to put it to use."

"What new useless trinket will we be overjoyed to use?" a skeptical voice sounded from behind.

Oberon closed his eyes and sighed. *Now, of all times?* Opening his eyes once more, he gave Ren an annoyed look, then turned around. Eduard Dracul was approaching, Nikolai Candida awkwardly trailing him, looking like a mer out of water.

"General Dracul, what a pleasant surprise," he said as nicely as he could without sounding too fake. He gave Nikolai a warmer expression. "Welcome back to the Dome, Intern Candida."

Nik sent him a grateful smile while Eduard nodded his head in acknowledgement, looking past Oberon, and observing the various parts of Ren that were visible.

"Is this some phasing technology?" he said with exasperation. "Don't tell me you're in two places at the same time. I'm not quite sure how useful it is to have your body in one place and your head, arms, and legs in another."

Ren snorted. "If I've made the brilliant Eduard Dracul believe that this *trinket* is a phase-inducer, then I'd say the invention is quite a success. Wouldn't you, Oberon?"

A scowl formed on the general's face. "It must be a sad life, trapped in this prison you helped form, unable to fight the real battles that are waging in the real world every day."

Ren opened his mouth to give a retort, but Oberon stepped in.

"Is this how the military trains their recruits and interns?"

he asked. "To be belligerent and disrespectful?"

Eduard's scowl darkened as he shifted his eyes to Oberon. "We train our recruits and interns to show respect to rank—something I hold, and the lowly tinkerer does not."

Electricity crackled behind Oberon, and he knew Ren was about to make a grave mistake. In front of Oberon, Eduard held a dancing flame above an outstretched hand.

"That's enough!" shouted Oberon. "We already have enough enemies—we don't need to start attacking each other."

The static behind him slowly fizzled out, and the flame before him extinguished.

"That's better," Oberon said, feeling like he was dealing with a couple of juveniles. "Now then, what Ren has invented is a device that integrates with smart clothing that has cloaking capabilities."

Ren patted his stomach, and for a moment, what seemed to be a ripple hung in the air, then went back to the emptiness it held before.

Eduard's hard features softened as he looked Ren up and down again. At last, he straightened his stance and pulled his uniform down at the stomach, removing the bunching that had formed during his heated moment. "Forgive my harshness, Mr. Suzuki. Your latest creation is quite remarkable and useful."

Ren's scowl was replaced with proud humor. "Apology accepted." Pulling the camouflaging device free from his smart clothing, his whole form reappeared.

Eduard's eyes stared greedily at the cloaking gear. "When will it be prepared for field testing?"

Ren looked up, as if in deep thought. "Well, it's only in the prototype stage right now. And we'd have to get Delphine to clear bringing in more resources—which won't be cheap."

"I'm sure she'll be just as impressed with your research as I am," Eduard replied.

Ren raised a finger. "I should mention that the invisibility has a few limitations."

The general nodded. "Technology usually does. What sort of limitations are we talking about?"

"It works great when a shifter is in human form, but it doesn't work at all once the user has shifted."

Eduard's expression solidified like a rock. "You call that a limitation? It sounds useless! What are we supposed to do? Fight vampires while in human form?"

The dragon shifter's tone brought forth another scowl from Ren. "At this point, *Lord* Dracul, I would categorize the cloaking device as reconnaissance hardware. It's great at getting your soldiers in and out of dangerous places undetected."

No retort came from Eduard, which Oberon was quite grateful for.

"Technically," Ren added, "this isn't a limitation of the cloaking device. It's a limitation of the smart clothing. I'm not going to go into the nitty-gritty of how the smart clothing works, but it should be noted that smart clothing doesn't rip and tear like normal clothing because it essentially tricks the shifting and shifted body into believing that it doesn't exist. *It* phases until the body is returned to human form."

Oberon nodded in understanding. "So the cloaking device phases along with the smart clothing."

Ren smiled and snapped his fingers. "Harvey, we have a winner."

Pulling at his already-straightened uniform again, Eduard

said, "The military would benefit from having these. I'll inform Delphine that we have requested your latest creation."

"Outstanding," Ren replied with an unamused tone.

Oberon subdued the smile that was trying to cross his face. "Well, Eduard, I can't imagine you came all the way to the Dome just to check in on Ren's inventions. Is there something I can do for you?"

The general eyed Ren before returning his gaze to Oberon, likely debating with himself whether or not to speak in front of the kitsune.

"It's about the siren," Eduard said at last.

I should have guessed, Oberon thought. Out loud, he said, "She has a name, Eduard. I presume you've come to check on Myreen's progress?"

"On the contrary, I've come to give her one-on-one training," Eduard replied.

Oberon shouldn't have been shocked by his abruptness, but he was. Raising his eyebrows, he said, "It's been just over one week since your last visit. We've escalated her combat instruction, but Myreen is not ready for military training."

"No one ever is," Eduard said, looking over his shoulder at Nikolai. "Are they?"

The Candida boy straightened his back. "It's hard, sir, but it's worth it."

Eduard gazed back at Oberon and raised his hands to the sides, as if they were a weighing scale. "We could wait weeks, months, even *years* before you feel like the girl is ready. But you know as well as I do that time is not on our side."

"I can't deny the urgency," Oberon replied. "But at the same time, if you try to force somebody to wear shoes much too big for them, you can guarantee there will be tripping and falling. And if those shoes are even bigger than we believe them to be, Myreen might not be able to get back up."

Confusion splashed across Eduard's face.

"We might break her," Oberon clarified.

The general tilted his head. "If the girl *is* the prophesied siren, she will *not* break."

It was apparent that Eduard wasn't going to be swayed. He hadn't come to the Dome to ask permission, but he'd at least had the decency to talk to Oberon before going straight to Myreen.

Oberon set his jaw, momentarily looking at the students working hard on their projects, a few more trickling in. Thankfully, the glass walls were soundproof, and the commotion that had occurred between Ren and Eduard hadn't drawn their attention.

He wondered if he'd done Myreen a disservice, bringing her to the Dome. Her life had been in constant flux since the day she'd arrived. Throwing the military at her now would be another whiplash.

At the same time, the military general brought up a good point. When would Myreen be ready? If the vampires did decide to lay siege on the Dome, the school would be in grave danger. No training he could provide would help Myreen—or the school for that matter—if such a thing occurred.

I need an update from Leif, he told himself, making a mental note to reach out to the vampire. *See if he knows what the vampires are planning.*

Sighing, he brought his eyes back to Eduard and raised a single finger. "You can have one session with her. This afternoon. In lieu of the exercises I had planned for her. She can show you her progress."

This small victory showed on the strong features of Eduard Dracul.

"But I will be there to monitor everything," added Oberon. "As will Delphine. If I find anything to be... excessive, I'll put the session to an immediate end."

Eduard nodded. "I am amenable to those terms."

Oberon had an extreme desire for Eduard to depart from the research lab. His authoritative presence was exhausting.

He cleared his throat "In the meantime, feel free to visit the dining hall if you're hungry. If food doesn't interest you, I'm sure somebody is in the simulation room testing their abilities. You could always go and observe potential recruits."

Saying those words made Oberon sick to his stomach. The last thing he wanted to do was have more students pulled early from the school.

"Thank you, Director," Eduard said, bowing slightly. "My intern and I could use a bite to eat."

Nik anxiously shuffled his feet behind the general. Perhaps being back in the Dome was an uncomfortable experience for the young man? He hadn't been gone that long.

"Come, Intern Candida," the general said. "Show me the way." Looking one more time at Oberon, he said, "I'll see you this afternoon. And Ren? Good work on your latest creation."

Lord Dracul turned around and made for the exit of the research lab, and Oberon turned his attention back to his kitsune friend.

Ren happened to be folding his arms proudly. "You know, I think that's the first time he's ever called me by my name."

Kol

"Malkolm," a deep voice called from behind as Kol walked toward the dining hall. His first thought was that his father was at the school, but the timbre of the voice was off.

He turned, a scowl forming on his face as Nik strutted toward him with a wide grin.

"How's it going, man?" Nik asked, easily ducking from Kol's attempt to flick him on the head. It was a half-hearted attempt, anyway. Kol was glad to see his friend.

Kol rolled his eyes and stepped back to lean against the wall with one foot hitched behind. "Not practicing my *Eduard* impersonations," he said. "That's for sure."

"Well, when you spend every waking minute with the general, it's almost expected."

Kol couldn't tell if Nik still joked, or if he was merely pointing out the irony of his unhappy situation with sarcasm.

"How's that going, anyway?"

Nik shrugged. "I'd rather be here, if I'm being honest." He moved to lean against the wall next to Kol, as if the action proved his words.

"You don't have to tell me," Kol said. "I wouldn't want to spend every waking minute with the general, and he's my father."

"It's not too bad, and my mom's happy," Nik offered. "Especially when I told her that I'm basically Eduard's assistant. And since Eduard just travels around having secret meetings, I'm a glorified coat rack and coffee runner."

"Well, I'm glad it's not me," Kol said, clapping a hand on Nik's shoulder.

Nik ran a hand over his near-shaved head. Kol knew this was his way of prepping himself to ask an awkward question or say something that caused trepidation, so he waited.

"H– how's Juliet?" he asked after a moment.

The mention of her name angered Kol. "Being reckless."

Nik's head snapped to Kol. "Reckless?"

"She and Myreen snuck out to the city a few days ago."

"They left the Dome?" Nik's tone was incredulous.

Kol nodded. "They said they needed a *girl's day.* Whatever that means." He scoffed.

"It's probably my fault," Nik said quietly after a moment.

"How so?"

"Well, I broke up with Juliet before I left. Brett texted and said Juliet's been *mopey.*"

Kol clapped a hand on his friend's shoulder again in a mock-gesture before saying, "You're giving yourself too much credit. When have you ever made a girl *mopey*?"

Nik shrugged off Kol's hand and punched him in the shoulder, knocking him off balance so Kol had to plant both feet on the ground again. "Thanks, jerk!"

But they laughed it off.

"How about you? How are things with *Myreen*?" Nick sang her name.

Kol stared at the opposite wall, feeling the heat rise in his neck. "We kinda made out in one of the greenhouses."

When he eyed him in his peripheral, one of Nik's eyebrows pointed at the ceiling.

"But I haven't spoken to her since Sunday," Kol said. "And I pretty much told her she could go and get herself killed." He blew out an exasperated breath.

"I thought she was different than the others?" Nik only sounded half-surprised. It made Kol want to crawl in a hole.

He chose anger instead and gripped a fistful of his hair. "She is!" He let go and smacked the wall behind him. "But I was so angry that she could be so *stupid* and go topside, the words just came out."

"You really care about her."

"Her safety is important, yes," Kol said, not exactly answering the non-question. "But if she'd been captured..." He let the gravity of the words hover in the air in front of them. "It would be disastrous for all of us. Every shifter would be in danger." He looked wearily at his friend. "And I haven't spoken to her since."

Nik's expression returned to normal and he nodded with understanding.

"What are you doing here, anyway?" Kol asked, shoving his angry—panicked—feelings toward Myreen aside. "Is my father here?"

"Yes," Nik said, snapping to a more business-like demeanor. It was so unlike Nik. "He's asked me to fetch you. He's in Ms. Dinu's office and wants to speak with you."

Kol paused for a few seconds before answering. "Alright," he said. "Let's get this over with."

***

Eduard sent Nik to the kitchen for their lunches when he and Kol arrived, proving that Nik really was Lord Dracul's errand boy. Nik probably felt it was demeaning, but Kol was grateful, since it meant his friend was safe.

Kol had only been in Ms. Dinu's office a handful of times, and most of the space was not particularly interesting. A few feminine touches that were typical in any of the female faculty offices decorated it, such as a purple orchid on the edge of her desk, a knitted blanket hung over the chair in the corner, and a framed watercolor of what looked like a harpy woman with golden eyes and a white braid talking to a partly submerged merman with jet-black hair hanging on the wall.

What *was* interesting about Ms. Dinu's office was the framed painting on the back wall. The one Ms. Dinu could see from her chair as she graded essays and scored tests. It was an enlarged print of the oil painting Kol had once seen hidden away in one of the undisturbed, dusty rooms at home. The painting was of a fearsome dragon with iridescent, purplish-blue scales. Its wingspan filled the canvas from edge-to-edge, and the icy blue eyes reminded him of his sister Tatiana's, which led him to believe early on that it must be the portrait—the shifted portrait—of one of the Dracul line. Kol couldn't help but turn as he entered the room to gaze at the painting. It wasn't the original, but still conveyed the power of the beast.

"Isn't she magnificent?" Eduard asked. He was perched on the edge of Ms. Dinu's desk.

"Who is she?" Kol asked without turning. He hadn't missed seeing his father when he entered the room, he was just drawn to the painting, and always look at it whenever he had reason to be in his dragon mastery teacher's quarters. "Do you know her?"

Kol heard his father move toward him, stopping at his left. "She was our relative," he said. "And a famous one, at that."

Kol eyes immediately looked down at his father.

Eduard's smile was knowing. "Aline Dracul," he said, then crossed his arms and turned away from the painting. "The original is at the manor, but your mother detests it and demanded that it be moved somewhere she was less likely to see it on a daily basis."

"Aline Dracul? The one who—?"

"Yes, yes." His father cut him off, waving a hand in a gesture that demanded they get on with the topic they were meant to discuss. "The woman who brought the curse upon the Draculs. That's probably why your mother hates it," he mused. "But we don't know her story. Whatever she did to bring on that loathed curse couldn't have been as bad as the curse itself." He eyed Kol with a hint of a smirk. "Perhaps we should track down those selkies someday and make them pay for over a century of Dracul misery, *huh?*"

Kol was at a loss for words. It was the most he'd ever heard his father talk about the curse. Most of the time he acted like it was a myth, or that it didn't exist. So Kol merely nodded.

"But that's not why I wanted to speak with you."

Kol situated himself internally, if not physically. He never knew what grandiose task or chastising conversation Eduard had planned.

"Now that it's confirmed that Myreen Fairchild is indeed the siren of the prophecy, we no longer need you to acquaint yourself with her."

Kol swallowed. He wasn't sure he'd heard right.

Eduard walked toward the watercolor of the harpy and mer. "We have the information we need and now it would be best if you no longer have contact."

"Just like that?" he asked.

Eduard turned back, his arms clasped behind him. "Just like that." His eyes suggested he was not pleased with Kol's response. "You were not thrilled with the assignment in the first place. I thought you would be happy to be relieved of it."

"It's just... I..."

"Listen to me, Malkolm," Eduard said, positioning himself in front of Kol so they were only a foot apart and nearly eye-to-eye. "The girl is dangerous. You almost got yourself killed when those vampires attacked, and they weren't there to attack you. Being near her puts you in danger. I will not lose my son in such a wasteful and pointless manner."

It shocked more than warmed Kol to hear that his father cared whether he lived or died. It was obvious that he would—Eduard was not completely uncaring of his children. Kol just couldn't remember ever hearing the words spoken aloud.

"You are released from seeing the girl. You will break your ties with her immediately." His words were final. The syllables clipped to emphasize the point.

Kol felt his mouth turn dry, but nodded his ascent.

"And if things go according to plan, Myreen will be leaving the Dome shortly."

"Leaving?" Kol felt the panic burn. A white-hot fireball just beneath his ribcage. *But it's not safe for her!* he wanted to say, but didn't.

"With me," Eduard explained. "Leaving under my direction and protection."

Just like that.

Kol hated the idea, but Eduard was a force no one could reckon with. Even if Oberon or Delphine was against the plan, he was certain that his father would find a way to have them overruled. There was nothing a seventeen-year-old student of the Dome could do to stop the inevitable.

After a few more formalities, Kol inquiring after his mother but not hearing the answer, Eduard dismissed him and the two parted outside Ms. Dinu's office in under five minutes.

Just like that.

He was released from his duty to befriend, to spend time with, to *seduce* Myreen. Although the latter wasn't exactly an order, only implied, anything Kol had done to resemble it had been completely of his own free will—mixed with his warring impulse to keep things in the friend zone for his own sake. To protect himself.

Without really seeing where he was going, or having a destination in mind, Kol half-stumbled, half-jogged down the hallway. At least that's how he felt. He didn't attract any unwanted attention, so maybe his steps looked more normal on the outside.

And as if he'd conjured her from a dream, the dark haired, heart-stopping wonder of a girl manifested herself in a secluded hallway.

Kol snapped himself to clarity.

She glowered at him when their eyes met, then kept walking toward the dorms.

"Wait, Myreen," he said. His voice sounded more normal than he expected. "Could we talk?"

She stopped, but didn't turn right away. Perhaps deciding whether to actually allow the conversation?

Why had he stopped her? His father instructed him to end his relationship with her—whatever that was. Was that his goal? Was he ending things now? Was he telling her that he no longer wanted to see her, that he no longer was *allowed* to see her?

She turned. Her blue eyes lifted to his as he slowly approached, but he stopped just outside her invisible personal bubble. Giving her space.

"I'm sorry." The words flew from his mouth.

She folded her arms. Her mouth pursed and an eyebrow rose.

"I had no right to explode at you like that. You should be able to make your own choices."

Myreen's eyebrow relaxed. Her lips too.

"Even if they're stupid and reckless ones." That flew out, too.

Her glower, which was more of a scowl now, returned. "Look, Kol, whatever—"

"Just let me get this out," he said. "I shouldn't have said that. I'm sorry." He held his hands up in surrender and took two more tentative steps toward her.

Her face softened. "You have no right to try to control my life."

"Yes," he agreed. "Like you said, I'm not your par..." he stopped himself. "I'm not your guardian. I'm not Oberon."

Myreen's face softened more. She unfolded her arms. "And you're not my boyfriend." It sounded like a last-ditch effort to put her foot down, to stand up to him. But he quickly realized that he was having a pleasing effect on her.

The same effect she was having on him.

And then without a second thought, more words flew from his mouth, words he never expected to say. "I want to be your boyfriend." His eyes immediately bored into the floor. "W– will you be my girlfriend?"

Myreen

Myreen couldn't believe her ears. *Did Kol, the robot dragon with a secret heart, actually just say he wants to be my boyfriend?*

Her heart leapt into her throat, making it hard to breathe, let alone answer.

Kol just stood there, hands stuffed in his pockets, looking sheepishly at her. The silence seemed to be physically hurting him, but she couldn't make her lips open, couldn't force out the excited *YES!* that built up in her chest like a balloon ready to pop.

"Ah, Myreen, just the girl I was looking for."

Oberon's deep voice broke the staring contest she and Kol had been unwittingly playing, and they both turned to him. The expression on the Director's face was more grim than usual, and it instantly caused Myreen's anxiety to spike. *Did vampires attack again? Is someone hurt?*

"What is it?" Myreen asked, torn between not wanting to leave Kol hanging and worried about the reason for Oberon's sallow face.

"The military has taken a... special interest in you," he said, his jaw clenched as he spoke. "General Dracul is here and expects to see a demonstration of your skills this evening." The words themselves didn't sound too upsetting, but by the tone of Oberon's voice, it felt like he was delivering a death sentence.

"Wait, wh– what?" she stammered. She looked from Oberon to Kol, who's facial muscles were now tense. General Dracul was Kol's father. Did he know about this?

"We'll continue this later?" Kol asked with a hopeful lilt in his voice. Then he spun around and disappeared down the hall, his absence leaving her feeling oddly cold and vulnerable.

She watched him walk away, wishing she could go with him, then turned back to Oberon. "Why does the military want to see my so-called skills?"

"Because General Dracul knows about the prophecy, and to him, you are the key to winning the war he's been fighting his whole life."

"But... is it too much for them to give me a little warning? Or some time to practice more? I'm completely unprepared for this." Her voice had reached a high pitch and now echoed through the hall.

Oberon put his hands up in a calming gesture, and she took a long, steadying breath.

"I know," he said, his voice much softer than before. "I've tried to hold him off, tried to make him understand that you're a student, and one who's still learning. If he had his way, you'd be at his base training night and day. My hope is that if we show him your progress, that will be enough to keep his claws out of your life, at least for the time being."

Myreen's chest rose and fell in quick repetition. She hadn't even been aware that the military knew about the prophecy, or that she was the siren of which it foretold. Now, come to find out, the general had a keen interest in her. She'd heard rumors about Kol's father. Cold, heartless, brilliant in strategy. She wasn't sure if this was a good thing or a bad thing, but the vibes Oberon was throwing off hinted at the latter.

"You'll do just fine," Oberon said, all traces of his earlier tension gone. "He'll want to see you demonstrate your water and light manipulation, as well as your siren voice. But I don't want you to stress about it. Just think of it as a talent show with a very small audience. Take the rest of the afternoon to practice, and arrive at the gym at six o'clock." He smiled at her, then nodded once before going back the way he'd come.

Flustered to a disorienting degree, she stood in place for a long moment, unsure which way to go. The military wanted to see what she could do. They were about to be gravely disappointed. She had only just started manipulating light, and her water manipulation was sloppy at best. As for her siren voice, she'd only used it once on purpose. She had to do her absolute best this evening. What would it mean for her, for Oberon, for the world, if she failed?

* * *

Five-thirty.

Myreen had watched every single minute pass since the start of the hour. As Oberon advised, she spent the afternoon practicing. As Oberon specifically advised against, she had stressed about it the entire time.

Maybe she wouldn't have been so worried if Oberon hadn't seemed worried. Anything that upset Oberon didn't bode well for anyone. This was a big deal, and Myreen couldn't afford to mess it up.

But she couldn't focus. The fact that a very big issue was left unsettled between her and Kol was eating her up. Kol was such an emotionally skittish creature that she feared he'd retract his offer if she didn't accept it soon.

Sure, when they'd made out two weeks ago she'd told him she needed time, which was girl code for "not open to a relationship at this time." That was mostly because the relationship it looked like they were heading toward was primarily a physical one. As much as she enjoyed—loved, craved!—kissing him, she didn't want to be just the girl he made out with whenever the mood struck. She didn't want to be Trish.

Now he actually wanted them to be *together.* And it scared her how much she wanted that, too. Maybe it was the fact that a giant hole was left in her heart by her mom's death, or one of the million other misfortunes that had befallen her since, but she wanted to be *his,* and she wanted him to be *hers.*

As she watched the zero on the clock turn to a one, she knew that she'd never be able to focus on the upcoming presentation if she didn't give Kol his answer.

She left the mer training room and bolted for the gym, some unknown sense telling her that Kol would be there. When she entered the gym, she looked all around for him, but he was nowhere in sight. Out of the corner of her eye, she saw the display to the sim room revert to a blank wall. Sure enough, the door opened and Kol emerged, glistening with sweat and gripping a towel around the back of his neck on either side.

Her heart galloping, she practically sprinted toward him. When he looked up and saw her coming his way, that same hopeful glint she'd seen earlier returned, and a smile tugged at the corners of his lips.

She grabbed his wrist and pulled him back into the sim room, closing the door behind them.

"Yes," was all she could say.

"Yes?" he asked.

She nodded, then lifted up on her toes and pressed her lips on his. In response, he put his hand on her hips, gently but firmly pulling her closer as his lips opened to kiss her back.

Bliss. This was pure bliss! Kol was her boyfriend, and she was his girlfriend! In the midst of all the serious, life-threatening danger that surrounded them, something so trivial as a new title made her happier than she'd been in months. Maybe ever.

Her joy consumed her, filling her limbs and spreading out through her fingers. Suddenly the fluorescent lights on the ceiling shattered with an alarming *pop*. In darkness, their lips parted and they laughed heartily, still clinging to each other.

When their laughter subsided, his hand caressed her cheek, and even though she couldn't see him, she could still feel his eyes on her.

"Even in darkness, you're still so beautiful," he said softly.

She nestled her face into his hand, savoring his touch. She didn't want this moment to end, but she knew it had to.

"I, um... I have to go," she all but whispered. "I'm supposed to present my skills to your dad."

"I know," he said behind audibly gritted teeth.

"But I'll come see you after. We can do more of this." She

lingered against his broad chest for a moment longer, then pulled away and reached for the door knob. The door opened just a crack, but Kol put his hand on her upper arm, gently stopping her.

"Wait. About the presentation... Don't show him your siren voice." In the half-light the cracked door cast on his face, he looked dead serious.

She didn't ask why. Kol knew his father better than she did. If Kol was asking her to fail at that task, there must be a good reason.

She nodded. "Okay."

Relief smoothed his face and he dropped the arm that kept her in the room. "See you tonight." Then he pushed out of the room and rushed across the gym and out the door.

Her senses still tingled from kissing him. She skipped to the private training room where she was due to meet Oberon and General Dracul, her steps getting smaller and slower the closer she got, her Kol-induced high diminishing.

She opened the door. Along one wall of the small room was a row of chairs in which sat Oberon, Delphine and a man she'd never seen before but recognized instantly as Kol's father. He was a large man, not just in height like Kol, but also in girth. He looked like a tank. He had Kol's same char-black hair, the same serious set eyes, even if his were a darker shade of amber than his son's. He radiated the same sort of aura, hot and powerful, like authority and pride and smoke merged together.

Next to them stood Nik, dressed in a military uniform and standing upright and stiff like a statue. Although, he did smirk and wink at Myreen when she entered.

On the opposite wall, standing on matching pedestals, were

two steel bowls, one full of water and the other cradling blazing embers. She knew what those were for. And on the wall catty-corner stood a rubber sparring dummy. She knew what that was for, too.

Upon her entry, all three rose from their chairs. General Dracul stepped forward and offered his hand.

"Pleasure to meet you at last, Miss Fairchild." His smile was all charm, of which she'd seen whispers of in Kol. The smile was immediately disarming, but her intuition told her not to drop her guard.

She shook his hand, surprised by the strength of it. "Thank you," was all she could think to say.

"I have never met a chimera, so this is indeed a great honor," he said, laying it on thick. "It would please me beyond words to see you demonstrate your skills. After all, our future lies in your lovely hands, and the soldiers I represent need to know your education is on track to help us win this war. If you'd be so kind." He held out his hand toward the pedestals.

She nodded and stood in the space between the two. She stole a glance at Oberon and Delphine, both giving her nods of encouragement.

Light was the element she was most comfortable with, and with Kol's hot kiss still fresh on her lips, fueling it would be easy. She allowed the memory of seconds ago to fill her up, inviting the sheer jubilance of being Kol's girlfriend to overwhelm her. Then she turned to the fire and beckoned their light toward her open hand.

Just as countless times before, the light slithered out of the flames, as if being sucked through the air, and swirled into her palm. Turning toward the dummy diagonal to her, she tightened the light into a ball and hurled it. The orb shot through the air like a bullet and smashed into the dummy's rubber chest, sending it crashing to the floor.

Myreen turned to her audience to gauge their reactions. Delphine wore a pleased semi-smile, but both Oberon's and General Dracul's faces were unreadable. Her eyes flicked toward Nik to see his brows were as high as they could go and his jaw slack.

When no one spoke, she turned toward the bowl of water. She wasn't as confident with this skill, but she knew she could do simple tricks with the water, which would have to suffice. Closing her eyes, she focused on the water in the bowl and imagined that it was a part of her. Then, as if she was raising her own hand, she willed the water to lift out of the bowl. She didn't have to look at it to know that it had pulled into the air; she could feel it like a limb. She commanded it to stream like a mercurial banner, flying above their heads in a circle before returning to pool in the steel bowl.

Again, when she was finished, she looked at her audience of four. The water trick was obviously less entertaining than the light attack, but it was the best she could do, and though the faces of her superiors were masks, Nik didn't look impressed. Then again, he was a dragon, and water rarely impressed them.

The general leaned forward and looked at Nik.

"Candida, approach Miss Fairchild," he ordered.

Nik had a curious look on his face, but he did as he was told. Myreen felt as questioning as Nik looked.

"If you would, please demonstrate your siren voice on young Candida here," General Dracul requested.

Oh.

Nik's eyes nearly jumped out their sockets, but his posture betrayed none of the alarm his eyes so clearly screamed.

Now was the moment. Kol told her to fail at using her siren voice. She didn't know what repercussions would follow for doing as Kol said, but she trusted him enough to believe that the outcome would be worse if she didn't.

She stepped toward Nik, who looked as though he might soil himself if she came any closer. Nik was directly between herself and General Dracul, blocking her face from the general's view, so she thought it safe enough to wink at Nik.

Then she took a deep a breath in and out as if preparing herself and said, "Stand on one foot."

Of course, nothing happened, and Nik's brows creased in uncertainty as he stared at her.

She cleared her throat and repeated the words. Again, her tone sounded like her voice, and Nik continued to stand there with both feet planted firmly on the ground.

She coughed a few times and then stepped around Nik to face the three in chairs. "I'm sorry, I can't seem to access it right now. I'm still learning." She feigned bashfulness and looked away.

The look of disappointment was clear as red letters on General Dracul's face, but he stood and said, "That's alright, Miss Fairchild. These things take time. I trust your teachers will make certain you master these skills." He forced a fake smile, then strode past Nik. "Come along, Candida. Until we meet again, Miss Fairchild." With Nik in tow, the general marched out of the small training room.

Now alone with Oberon and Delphine, she let out a breath she didn't know she'd been holding.

"You failed on purpose," Delphine said with a coy smile. "Why?"

Myreen shrugged, thinking it best not to say she did it because a boy told her to. "I just sensed it was the smart thing to do."

"We can only hope," Oberon said, looking distantly at the floor. Then he looked up at her. "You did very well, and now you deserve some rest. Why don't you head off to dinner?"

"Okay," she said.

"And I'll see you bright and early tomorrow to work on that siren voice, as you clearly need the practice." Delphine's smile was crooked and jocular, making Myreen smile wide in return before she left the room.

She could only hope that Kol's advice was wise, and not just residue of a father-son rivalry.

Kenzie

Kenzie stood outside the rock climbing place, chewing on her bottom lip. She tugged on the strap of her bag, which felt incredibly light without the grimoire weighing it down, and took a deep breath.

To be quite honest, she'd never been on a date. Spending most of her life in loser exile meant that few guys were willing to risk their social status to even try to ask her out, while the few daring enough were gross enough that she'd declined.

So this would be a first. And though it had to be during the day to appease her mom, the lack of date-typical atmosphere didn't do much to calm her nerves. Nor did the fact that he'd told her to wear something comfortable—or *athletic*—improve things.

Here goes nothing.

She pushed through one side of the gleaming glass double-doors and found her steps faltering once more. The place was huge. Like, ginormous. Brightly colored handholds dotted the walls on either side of her, which were shaped like some strange, geodesic canyon.

Kenzie gulped.

When Wes had told her about this place, she'd thought it would just be some cute little climbing gym. Like what you'd see at an amusement park or arcade, just more of it. But this was something else.

"You came!" Wes said, bounding up to her. He'd already stripped off his winter gear, leaving him in some beige cargo pants and a brown tank. Yeah, this guy was so granola. At least he was built like a tank instead of a potato. She could definitely appreciate that.

"Course I came. How black do you think my heart is?"

Wes chuckled. "Come on. You can drop your stuff off over here."

He led her to a sofa where it looked like he'd moved in. All his gear was draped over the back and arms of the thing. *And I thought* I *wore a lot of layers during the winter.*

Wes scrambled to push all his stuff aside. "Sorry. I was trying to let it dry a little before you came."

Kenzie lifted a brow. "How long have you been here?"

Wes shrugged. "It's my usual Saturday hang-out spot. I came right after I had breakfast."

Kenzie nodded, pushing and pulling at her lips. "So, are you like, a pro climber or something?" The words sounded stupid as they came out of her mouth, but she was so out of her element right now.

Wes chuckled. "Nah. I just like climbing. It comes in handy

for my job."

"Do you regularly scale buildings to deliver your messages?" she asked, wearing a side smile.

Wes chuckled as he shook his head. "No. Not ever. But these," and at this he curled his arms into the classic muscle pose, making his biceps ball and pop, "are handy for carrying heavy things."

Kenzie's brows arched. "Well, okay then." She blushed, then busied herself with de-layering, taking off her bag and hat—and gloves and coat and scarf—and dropping them on the couch. How was it that him being dorky made her lose her head? If she were being graded on this date, she had a feeling she'd flunk out.

Wes went off, she assumed, to grab some gear for her or something. So she might have squealed when strong arms picked her up and cradled her.

Kenzie turned her breathless face toward Wes's. He was grinning like a cat.

She whapped his chest. A nice, firm chest, if she were being honest. "What'd you do that for?"

"I told you I could pick up heavy stuff."

"You're calling me fat now?"

Wes's face paled a little, a nervous laugh escaping his lips. "No. I wouldn't—"

Kenzie laughed. "Don't hurt yourself. I was just teasing. I know I've got junk in the trunk."

Relief washed over Wes's face as he put her down. "You know, I hadn't noticed. But now that you mention it..." He bent back and she swatted him again for being cheeky. Wes laughed. "Don't worry. I'll have plenty of time to verify your story once you're on the wall."

Kenzie rolled her eyes. "You know I'm going to suck at this, right?"

Wes smiled, bringing his nose nearly to hers. "I don't think that's possible."

Kenzie smirked. "Challenge. Accepted."

***

Wes took Kenzie through all the basics, talking about handholds and krabs—or carabiners—and harnesses and belays. Some of it she got, some of it she didn't, but she kept nodding anyway.

When it finally came time to climb, she surprised herself by not being quite as awful as she'd thought. She was still bad, but at least she made it halfway up the wall before she started struggling.

"There's a foothold to your left," Wes called to her from the ground.

Kenzie balanced on her right foot and gripped her hands tighter. They were shaking at this point, and she had the feeling she wasn't going to make it much higher. Sliding her left foot off its perch, she stretched her leg out, trying to feel for the foothold. She didn't think she had the strength to turn and look, not if she didn't want to fall like an idiot.

But her foot couldn't find its mark, and her arms finally gave out. *Idiot status: unlocked.* The drop stopped abruptly as the safety line locked, then began to ease her toward the ground.

"Ah, you almost had it," Wes said, guiding her back to her feet. Which was good, because if he hadn't, she would've fallen on her butt. Who knew it would be so difficult to find her feet on a slow descent?

Kenzie blushed. "Nah. I sucked."

Wes shook his head as he unclipped her harness. "No. Your arms just aren't used to being used like that. Besides, I've seen worse."

"Doesn't mean I didn't suck," she said, cocking her head.

"Well, it couldn't have been more adorable. Want to go again?"

Kenzie snorted. "Yeah, I think I'll pass."

Wes shrugged, then looked down at the watch he had strapped to his wrist, his brows crinkling. There was a tattoo on the back of his hand she'd never seen before, and she grabbed his fingers to look at it.

"What's this?"

It was a sword, five dots circling the blade. The symbol felt familiar, but she couldn't say why.

"Oh, that." Wes withdrew his hand and rubbed the tattoo. "It's like a frat thing."

"For college?"

"No, for the courier business."

"Oooo-kay." It was kinda weird how invested he was in his job. Not like, creepy-weird, but it definitely crossed the "normal" line. She hoped that wouldn't be a problem.

Wes let out a long breath. "Yeah, I think we've got time."

"For what?"

Wes smirked. "Want to see me climb?"

"Oh, sure. Show me up." She chuckled, bumping him with her shoulder. "Yeah. Go ahead. Strut your stuff. I need to see those big, burly arms in action." *Yeah. Real smooth, Kenzie.*

Wes grinned so brightly she though he might combust. "Wait here."

Kenzie shrugged as he darted away. She crossed her arms as

she waited, looking around at the other climbers. A few were on the walls, some had climbed to a gym area above, and others were gathered around someone, probably an instructor, giving a lesson that sounded a lot like what Wes had gone through with her earlier.

"Ready?" Wes asked from behind her, and Kenzie jumped.

"Yeah." She turned to see him strapped into a harness, grinning from ear to ear.

"Sorry. Didn't mean to startle you."

Kenzie gave a quick shake of her head. "No worries. So, let's see this superpower of yours."

Wes clapped his hands together and pumped his brows before choosing a spot to climb. It was one of the darker colored sections, marking the more challenging courses, and it had a section at the top where it jutted out from the wall, adding another layer of difficulty.

Kenzie bit the corner of her lip, unsure how anyone could make it to the top of that section without deviating to the easier course.

As Wes began to climb, Kenzie's mouth dropped further and further open. He was like Spiderman, scaling the easier bit in what felt like mere seconds. When he came to the slanted bit, he slowed down. He took his time, finding the right hand and footholds, keeping his feet grounded so he wasn't dangling from his arms. She could see the sheen of sweat all over him, his sinewy muscles stretching and bulging as he used everything he had. And then, he was over the lip and back on a vertical stretch and touching the top.

He stayed there a moment grinning at her before letting go and rappelling back to the floor.

"Okay. Like, holy. Freaking. Cow!"

Wes dipped his head. "Thanks."

"So, how does one become so good at climbing? Dip in a vat of radioactive waste? Scientific experimentation? Freaky parents?"

Wes laughed. "No. Just good, old-fashioned hard work. Why? You want to be my climbing buddy?"

Kenzie snorted. "Yeah, no." At Wes's faltering smile, she added, "But today was fun. Thanks."

Wes shook his head. "Fun's not over yet. Give me a minute and we'll get going."

Kenzie nodded, trying to shove her hands into the pockets of her yoga pants—and obviously failing when there were no pockets to be filled. She sighed and wrapped a hand around her other arm instead.

This should be easier, shouldn't it? Kenzie had the nerves of a first date, but not the flutter. She liked Wes. He was cute and seemed honest and kind. But she just wasn't feeling the sparks. Heck, she'd had more of a "moment" performing magic with Leif than she'd had here with Wes.

Just give it a chance.

"Okay, man stink's gone," Wes said as he started gathering his things. "You ready to go?"

Kenzie pasted on a smile, releasing her arm and grabbing her own stuff. "Yeah. Where are we going, again?"

Wes smiled.

***

For the second time that day, Kenzie hesitated outside a door, despite the bite of the cold winter air.

"A cat café?" She scrunched her nose and gave Wes a sideways look. Thoughts of Rainbow popped into her head, and the memory brought a worried thrill with it that made the idea of seeing any cat—even one she'd never resurrected—a little intimidating.

"Yeah. I thought it'd be fun."

"And what if I'm allergic?"

Wes's eyes widened. "Oh, crap. I hadn't thought of that. You're not, are you? Oh, man you are." He swore as he turned away from her, his gloved hands locking behind his neck.

"Relax. I'm just messing with you."

He turned back to her, and at seeing her smirk, relief washed over him. "I'm sorry. I'm just really nervous and I feel like I'm messing this all up."

Kenzie snickered. "Maybe that's how I like 'em."

Wes let out a breath, then opened the door. "After you?"

She inclined her head and went inside. The lobby was minimalist, the most noticeable part being the sliding glass doors behind the counter. A woman stepped out through those doors, a wide grin on her face.

"Hi, I'm Jenna and welcome to Kitty Town. Would you be Wes?" She held out her hand, and Wes took it in a firm shake.

"Yep, that's me. And this is my girlfriend, Kenzie."

Kenzie took the woman's hand next, smiling her biggest, despite the little *girlfriend* bit. There was something about this woman she liked, though she couldn't quite put her finger on it. Although the cat thing didn't hurt.

"Well, come on in and make yourselves comfortable." Jenna slid open the glass door and they followed her through.

Kenzie was impressed.

The cat room was white. Like, white walls, white carpet, white furniture—just about everything. But despite all the whiteness, it didn't feel like she was walking into some dirty, hairy, cat place. Although, there were probably about a dozen cats, lounging, climbing—eying the newest entrants with mild curiosity.

Kenzie bent down to pet a small gray one that had begun rubbing against her legs, then scooped it up and began petting its pretty little head. The warm fluffy ball of fur started purring like the playing card she'd stuck on her bicycle so the spokes would slap against it. It helped that it looked nothing like the gray-and-white one Leif had found, its soft body much smaller and its hair longer.

Kenzie only half listened as Wes worked out the details with the owner. Then Jenna left, sliding the door closed behind her.

Wes came over and began scratching the kitty in Kenzie's arms behind its ears. "I'm having food delivered to us here. I ordered for you. I hope that's okay."

"As long as it's not sushi, I think I'll be fine." She smiled at the cat, who seemed perfectly content. Other cats were making their way over, and Kenzie wondered if she'd have time to pet them all. "You're just a little star, aren't you?" she said to the gray one, nuzzling his wet, pink nose.

"I figured you were a cat lover," Wes said, scooping up his own cat. He grabbed the extended front paw of the calico in his arms and waved it at Kenzie. Using a high, cartoonish voice he said, "Hi, pretty lady. Want to take me home?"

Kenzie laughed. "My mom would probably kill me. And then my Gram would resurrect me to do it again. Literally." They had a strict, "no pets" rule. Animals didn't always take so kindly to the paranormal, and with what her mom and Gram did as side gigs, they didn't need anything messing that stuff up. Besides, Mom had enough to do without the added hassle of taking care of a pet.

"Well, if you happen to enjoy yourself, maybe we'll have to make this our place."

Kenzie blushed. She'd let the girlfriend comment slide, but this guy was talking like he was in it for keeps. She didn't know whether to be frightened or flattered. Although, looking into those syrupy chocolate eyes, she almost thought she might melt.

Almost.

She put the gray cat down and found a seat, a couple more furballs making themselves at home on her lap.

"Man, those cats really like you," Wes said, sitting on a chair beside hers.

"Yeah, I guess so."

"It's so weird. It's like you have this..." Wes pursed his lips as he waved a hand, the gesture encompassing her entire body. "I don't know, magic? There's something about you, and I want to find out what that something is."

Kenzie looked down at her occupied lap with a smile, conflicting emotions waging war. She should be swooning right now. Here was a cute guy that obviously liked her, had gone to great lengths to impress her, but she still couldn't get her mind off Leif. Sweet, lonely Leif, who was probably at home right now, by himself, with nothing better to do than to pet *his* new cat—assuming he hadn't kicked it out or killed it—and think about his long lost love. Kenzie didn't have a shot against that.

Still, she wasn't from Wes's world. Not really. She was a selkie, and she didn't know what she would do if she really fell for him. Would she tell him the truth? Would keeping her secret feel like a burden?

Kenzie looked over at Wes again, taking in his lopsided grin and hopeful eyes. She could appreciate that, couldn't she? Besides, she'd told herself she needed the distraction from the shifter world.

If anyone was deliciously distracting, it was Wes. Sweet, loyal, granola Wes. Right?

"So, what do you want to know?" Kenzie asked, bringing a hand up to pet the white cat now rubbing against her shoulder. She realized she was beginning to sweat, and she pulled off her winter gear, throwing them onto the floor. A few of the cats came over to inspect her stuff, sniffing and pawing and then walking away with their tails in the air like they hadn't just been rolling around like little kittens.

"Everything?" Wes said, his grin turning shy.

Kenzie chuckled. "Yeah, that's a little broad, lover boy. Let's start a little smaller."

"Okay. Well, I already know your favorite color is black—like your heart—and you like cats, so really, your heart can't be *that* black."

Kenzie lifted an amused brow. "Wanna bet?"

"No. I think I'll decide that for myself. How about this—what is the worst thing you've ever done?"

"The worst?"

Wes shrugged. "Yeah. Why not? Most people want to tell you all the best stuff about themselves, but what they choose as their worst? That tells a lot about a person."

Kenzie smirked. "So, you're trying to psychoanalyze me now?"

"Nope. Just trying to get to know you." He leaned back in his chair, pulling the ankle of one leg over the knee of the other. "How does that make you feel?"

Kenzie giggled. He seemed to be catching on to her particular brand of humor.

She turned to face the large window that looked out onto the street, watching the cars and people go by. What was the worst thing she'd ever done?

She thought back to the fights she'd had with her mom and sometimes Gram, the incident in kindergarten when she'd set her then-friend's skirt on fire, and all the lying she'd done since tapping into the shifter world her mom was trying so hard to keep her out of. Then there was that particularly dark phase, right after her dad had died, when the already spiraling little girl she'd been had withdrawn into her ugly little cocoon of grief before crawling out as the angsty, magic hungry, devil-may-care girl she was today.

But the thing that hit her the hardest, the thing that made her chest squeeze until she wasn't sure she'd ever be able to truly breathe again, was Myreen.

It had been Kenzie's suggestion that they go to the party that night. Heck, she'd practically pushed Myreen into it. And though she knew it had probably saved her best friend's life, she felt responsible—responsible for Myreen losing her mother, for her being alone now, for the misunderstandings afterward and the ensuing distance.

A tear trickled down her cheek, and she sniffed, wiping it away and hoping Wes hadn't seen.

"The worst thing I've ever done is not be the friend I wanted to be. It's not entirely my fault, but I'm not exactly blameless, either." She pasted on a smile as she turned to Wes. She expected any number of reactions from him, but she didn't expect for him to be staring at her like he was, his eyes searching her face in what felt like worship.

And she didn't expect him to lean closer, his full lips parting, his brown eyes closing. Kenzie was drawn like a magnet to those lips, and when they met, her heart stuttered. They were warm and soft, and reverent.

When Wes pulled away, Kenzie's eyes remained closed, savoring the flavor of spearmint he'd left behind. Okay, so there was definitely some chemistry there. She could work with that.

A lazy smile curled her lips as she slowly opened her eyes. "What was that for?"

Wes blinked, as if coming back to himself, and he blushed. "I just thought you could use a kiss."

"And why'd you stop?"

A look of surprise flashed across Wes's face, but his answer was cut off as the door opened.

"Sorry to interrupt, but your food's here," Jenna said, nodding to Wes.

Wes got up, giving Jenna a tight smile. "I'll be right back," he said to Kenzie.

Kenzie settled into her chair again, grabbing the new cat walking on the backrest and giving it a good pet. The orange tabby began to gently knead Kenzie's legs.

She gazed out the window again, letting the familiar movements of humanity soothe her, when she spotted a flash of black and chains that looked awfully familiar. Kenzie squinted at the figure, but it moved out of sight. Had that been Adam? She supposed it could be, but the figure had been far enough away that she couldn't be sure. He did say he was living in Chicago. Adam didn't seem like the needy type, anyway. They'd had a few conversations via text—apparently he had a very good memory to have caught her number as she rattled it off—but they hadn't talked about anything too serious. And there's no way he'd know she was in town today. *She* certainly hadn't told him.

When did I become so paranoid? Maybe it was all the shifter and vampire stuff. Man, she really did need a distraction.

Wes came back in, pulling her from her thoughts. The food smelled delicious.

"I got us both grilled chicken sandwiches with bacon and avocado. I hope you like it."

Kenzie's stomach growled in response. "I'm pretty sure anything you throw at me at this point will be welcomed."

They both chuckled.

Kenzie dug in, and their conversation continued to flow. And every now and then, Wes's eyes would dart back to her lips. Considering he didn't look the least bit grossed out, she assumed she wasn't eating like a total caveman and he probably wanted another kiss.

Which was good, because a few more of those would make Wes the perfect distraction.

Juliet

The Defense Room became Juliet's new favorite place. For one, it was far away from the library, and two, it was the only place where her mind could be completely clear. She replaced her sulking with workout and combat routines—all a gift from her dad.

With her headphones plastered on, she felt like herself again. Only this time she knew how to tap into her phoenix form. With enough focus, she could use her phoenix vision to hit her target. She even felt more balanced, as if her wings were always out, making her lighter on her feet.

It became addictive. She looked forward to the rush she felt every time she walked into the defense room. But most importantly, it kept her secluded. If she had her headphones on, everyone knew to leave her alone. Which was exactly what she wanted. She didn't want to make any new friends, and she definitely didn't want to see the one person that she *thought* was her friend. Avoiding Myreen was hard, but with her headphones on, Juliet could pretend she was invisible.

The upcoming weekend made Juliet both anxious and excited. She usually spent her weekends with Myreen, but now that they were fighting, she'd be alone. Just like she used to be.

She decided to start the day in the Defense Room, and she set her alarm for seven in the morning—a time when no student would be caught awake. That way she wouldn't have to worry that Myreen would be around, and she could have the defense room to herself.

As Juliet got ready, she picked up the apple on her desk and stuck it in her mouth. She planned on training until lunch, so she didn't want a heavy meal in her stomach. With the apple between her teeth, she picked up her long hair and tied it into a high ponytail. She threw her half-frozen jug of water into her towel bag and tossed it over her shoulder. Juliet made sure to be as quiet as a mouse when she left so she wouldn't wake anyone.

The walk to the Defense Room was quiet, but the empty halls also created an eerie feeling. The only noise she heard were her own footsteps, which made her uncomfortable. She picked up her pace and made it there without falling once, though. So, that was a win.

Full of relief that the space was empty—just as she thought it would be—Juliet switched on the lights. It was a beautiful sight, and she had it all to herself.

She pulled out her headphones and threw her bag onto an empty shelf by the entrance, then hit shuffle on her mix of hard rock and classical songs. It was a weird playlist, but it calmed her. The soft, familiar melody of Beethoven began its mesmerizing tune, and with that, Juliet decided to start her morning with

Yoga—another means of helping her gain control over her clumsiness.

Lucky for her, the following four songs were all classical, so she got just the right amount of relaxation.

She grabbed the jump rope as a hard rock tune started to play and did reps until the song finished. She picked up the hand weights next, doing reps until the next song ended. She stayed with the flow, matching her exercises to the music.

When sweat began to drip down her forehead, she knew she was ready for a break. Retrieving her jug from her bag, Juliet drank the ice-cold water until she couldn't breathe. The towel—cold from the water jug—felt like heaven on Juliet's flushed cheeks.

But the room was still empty, and she didn't want to stop just yet.

Refreshed and ready for something different, Juliet jogged to the target range on the other side of the exercise equipment. There were different levels to choose from, but Juliet had only gotten through one of the medium stages. She'd tried the hardest difficulty once, but found that she needed a lot more practice. So she'd made a goal: she wouldn't try her hand at testing out of the Sim until she defeated the hardest stage—more than once.

A rock song began while Juliet stared at the panel. She touched her finger to the screen to choose the type of targets she wanted—too bad the faces of certain students weren't an option. She picked the default clay pigeons, and feeling ambitious about her speed, she entered in seventy-five miles per hour. And difficulty? Medium-hard.

Juliet went to the starting spot and jogged in place as the screen counted down from ten, steadying her breathing.

She moved along to the beat of the song and cleared her mind, thinking only of her fire. The heat came to life in her stomach, and she brought it to her fingertips in record time. When the number hit three, Juliet prepared herself, holding the balls of fire like they were baseballs. The panel went blank, then a target flashed onscreen with a bullseye.

Juliet blinked to focus her phoenix vision. With it, she could easily spot her moving targets. She used it the entire time. Targets flashed by at a dizzying speed, but Juliet hit every single one. She ducked and jumped to catch her marks, adrenaline rushing through her, causing her heart to race. Usually she would be afraid of losing control, but this time she was on fire.

The panel finally blinked to inform her that the drill was over. She pulled off her headphones and was startled by the group of shifters who stood watching her. She hadn't even noticed their arrival. Her classmates awkwardly clapped, which made her want to bolt from the room. With a few nods of acknowledgment, Juliet brushed past the onlookers to grab her bag.

She didn't bother to wipe the pools of sweat off her face, and she was sure that her hair was no longer tight in her ponytail. She couldn't care less, though. She only wanted to get back to her room to shower and get ready for lunch.

The second Juliet left the Defense Room, people started whispering. She had no idea what they were saying and she didn't want to know. Word traveled fast, and she assumed this was about her target session, but she wasn't going to stick around to find out. Juliet lifted the headphones off her shoulders and placed them back on her head.

This time she selected the playlist with only classical songs.

Something about it matched her mood, and she melted inside the minute the songs started. They calmed her instantly.

Which was good, because Nik was the first thing she saw when she rounded the corner.

Her heart skipped a beat. He looked the same. His familiar short-cropped hair had a negative-image of flames shaved into the sides. But now he wore the uniform of the military. She wanted to rush into his arms, or kiss him fiercely, or punch him in the face, or run away and cry. She didn't realize just how much she'd missed him until she saw him. Seeing him back at the Dome made her feel as if everything around them disappeared, as if everything could go back to normal. Well normal, *and* in uniform. But it couldn't.

Numbly, Juliet slid her headphones off so she could hear the whispers around her.

"Do you think she'll start crying again?" one of the maos said.

"Think she'll slap him for breaking her heart?" a short naga hissed.

"Naw," one of the younger mer said. "She'll just run away."

They were so invested, she was sure there was someone collecting money for bets.

She stood there, unsure of what to do. If he showed even the slightest interest in speaking to her, she would have. But once their eyes met, he acted as if he didn't see her.

He averted his eyes, looking everywhere but at her. That made Juliet more furious than expected. The least he could do was say *hi.* But he chose to ignore her.

Juliet wanted to do what everyone expected—she wanted to cry and slap him and run away. But she wouldn't give them the satisfaction.

Instead, Juliet did something she never would have thought she'd have the guts to do. The adrenaline from her time in the Defense Room still rushed through her. She knew what to do. She'd take her cue from the girls in her Hallmark movies and play dirty.

With a quick sweep around the room, Juliet's spotted only one she found attractive. Jesse Barnes, the hound shifter with a temper—the perfect rebound. With more confidence than she actually felt, Juliet walked over to Jesse and tapped him on the shoulder.

He was tall, towering over her as he turned to look at her. "Uh, hi? What's up?" His eyebrows scrunched together as he stared at her.

"Hey, Jesse. Wanna go out with me? Get some food? Have some fun?" Again, confidence radiated off her and she had no idea where it came from.

The group of hounds behind Jesse teased him and playfully patted his back, and Juliet's cheeks got hot.

Jesse's eyes grew as wide, as did his smile. "Oh, for sure. Anytime, anywhere."

His smooth response made her stomach turn into knots. For a second she knew that what she did was wrong, but it wasn't enough to end the show for everyone—especially Nik.

"Cool. Christmas Eve?" Juliet outstretched her arm to grab Jesse's large, warm hand.

"Sure!" he said, squeezing her hand.

Juliet spun around to walk back to her room.

Finally, she'd gotten Nik's attention. And he looked broken.

His mouth froze in a frown, and his eyes took on a puppy dog look that touched Juliet's heart. She felt terrible, but he'd hurt her first. Revenge wasn't her usual path, but this time she thought he deserved it.

Now it was her turn to ignore him, and she didn't want to feel bad about it. Myreen had told her she needed to get back out there. Maybe it was good advice, even if they were still fighting.

She walked through the students, who were whispering even louder now, and spotted Myreen in the crowd. Myreen didn't look happy. If Nik wasn't there, Juliet might have tried to understand why, but she wanted to get the message across loud and clear. Everyone wanted her to move on, so she'd done just that. Right? With or without being logical, of course. But she owed it to herself, after what Nik put her through.

For once, she didn't care what Myreen or Nik thought.

Myreen

Myreen's mouth hung open as she watched Juliet saunter down the hall with a confidence she'd rarely seen in the girl. Which would have been great, if she wasn't playing such an awful game.

Juliet made to go by, her head in the air, her eyes averted. But Myreen wasn't going to just stand there while her friend ruined her life over a boy.

"What do you think you're doing?" Myreen hissed, yanking on Juliet's arm. The girl was seriously sweaty for this early on a Saturday morning, but Myreen ignored it.

"Taking your advice." Juliet crossed her arms, shrugging out of Myreen's hold.

Myreen's brows rose.

"You're the one who said I should get a rebound guy."

"I thought you weren't ready for a rebound."

"Yeah? Well, now I am."

"J, this is not at all what I meant. You did that for Nik's benefit, not yours."

Juliet's gaze narrowed on Myreen, a fire sparking in her golden eyes. "So what if I did? He nearly killed me when he broke up with me. I don't see why I can't return the favor."

Myreen shook her head. "It won't make you feel any better."

Myreen thought she saw a flash of regret in Juliet's eyes, but her chin hardened as it blinked back out. "Yeah? What do you know about it? I've only seen you get close to two guys since you've been here. One of them defected to the vampires and the other won't even talk to you!"

Myreen shrunk away from her friend as if she'd been slapped. Where was all this venom coming from? Sure, things had been rocky between them for a while now, but still. She blinked a couple of times before she could formulate a proper comeback. "For your information, Kol asked me to be his girlfriend just yesterday."

Juliet blanched, then her cheeks flared crimson. "Gee, congratulations Myreen. Thanks for rubbing your happiness in my face. It was very *mer* of you to tell me."

Again, Myreen was staggered by her friend's scathing words, and her voice rose in pitch as she sputtered in her defense. "I'm just trying to tell you that I know what I'm talking about."

"And I'm just trying to tell you to *back off.*" Juliet glared at Myreen, then donned her headphones and took off at a sprint.

Myreen watched Juliet leave, her blood boiling, her hands clenched into fists. Sure, Juliet might be hurting, but that didn't give her the right to take it out on everyone else. Besides, it had been weeks since Nik broke up with her. Why couldn't Juliet just get over him? It was beyond annoying, but this was borderline unforgivable.

Myreen folded her arms and huffed. Well, if Juliet wanted to be like that, she could do it on her own. Myreen didn't want any part of her stupidity.

***

Myreen ate breakfast by herself, pushing the food around her plate more than consuming anything. She wouldn't even be up if it weren't for the one-on-one Oberon had scheduled for her with Ms. Heather.

Her training was becoming overbearing, as the expectations began to weigh heavier and heavier, her progress never quite meeting anyone's approval. Except maybe that fireball she'd made for her demonstration with Lord Dracul, though the only ones who seemed truly impressed were Nik and Delphine.

Still she had to try. She was the prophesied siren, after all.

Myreen sighed as she dumped what remained of her breakfast and headed to the Avian Training Room, certain that the day was only headed downhill from there.

"Go ahead and put your bag in your locker, dear," Maya said from next to the fire, a warm smile on her face. "We're going to try something fun today."

Myreen raised a skeptical brow, but shuffled over to the wall of lockers anyway. She pressed her finger to the pad, and her door popped open with its usual digital greeting. She stuffed her bag in, then turned back to Ms. Heather.

"So, what are we doing today?" Myreen asked as brightly as she could.

"I thought it was time you tried to shift."

Myreen sighed. The thought of failing at another type of shifter form terrified her. Ms. Heather had brought it up a few times, but Myreen always said she didn't feel ready. She still didn't, even though it had been weeks and she was doing well with her harpy powers.

"It's okay," Ms. Heather said. "No one expects anything from you."

It wasn't true. *Everyone* expected something from her. Oberon, Draven, the shifter military—though thankfully nothing more had come of Lord Dracul's visit. Still, it was hard to shake the weight of those expectations, even in Ms. Heather's sweet presence.

Myreen nodded. She had to at least try. If she failed, maybe they'd look for someone else to fulfill their prophecy. Someone who didn't feel like they were drowning in their own ignorance.

"So, how do I do this?" Myreen asked, kicking off her shoes and peeling off her over-shirt so her smart shirt could do its job more effectively.

"Try to relax your shoulders. I always feel so tensed up when my wings are furled. And just like manipulating light, you'll want to fuel the change with an emotion." Ms. Heather gave Myreen a wink and a knowing smile, and Myreen blushed.

Myreen took a deep breath and shook out her shoulders. Finding emotion wasn't going to be a problem. Her frustration with Juliet was an obvious source, but her new *boyfriend* would work nicely, too. To be honest, she was tired of dwelling on the negatives in her life.

So Kol it was.

Closing her eyes, she rolled her shoulders and breathed in. As she exhaled, she imagined letting all the stress release from her back. She focused on Kol. His eyes, his lips, the way he made her feel every time they kissed—she got so lost in the emotions she almost didn't notice the tingly feeling tickling beneath the bones of her shoulder blades. Myreen latched on to that sensation, willing it grow and stretch.

At last, there was a pop, coming in time with a small explosion of joyous sensation in her belly, and a soft rustling in stereo. At the same time, she felt her toes fuse and lengthen, the bones sliding into place with ease. Hard talons curled out, gripping the smooth floor.

"Beautiful," Ms. Heather murmured.

Myreen opened her eyes to see, and was astonished at the soft, pearlescent white feathers framing her body. She turned her head to try to take the whole thing in, and her wings spread to their full range. Her talons clicked against the floor as she turned around, and she looked down to see gray feet with deadly black claws glinting in the firelight.

Myreen stared, dumbfounded. She'd actually done it. She'd shifted into a harpy. Her stomach did cartwheels as realization dawned, bringing a thrill that buzzed through her.

"That was excellent, Myreen," Ms. Heather said, resting her hand on Myreen's shoulder. "Would you like to test those wings?"

"A– as in f– fly?" Myreen stuttered.

Ms. Heather smiled.

Myreen floundered for a moment. Could she really fly with these wings? Would she crash?

"It's okay, dear. How about I take a moment to show you something else about your new form first."

Myreen nodded, releasing a forgotten breath. "That would

be good."

Ms. Heather nodded. "I want you to stretch out your fingers, making sure to point them away from yourself or anyone else."

Myreen did as instructed, nervous anticipation coursing through her veins.

"Now flick like you're flinging off some water, and imagine your fingers are getting longer."

Myreen did so, and razor-sharp talons extended from her fingernails. She turned her wide-eyed gaze on Ms. Heather.

"Unlike your feet talons, your finger talons come out at will. You can do one at a time, or all at once. Like this." Ms. Heather lifted her pointer finger, and a talon sliced upward. She relaxed her finger and it retracted just as quickly. Then she flung her hand as she'd instructed Myreen, and all her talons flew out. She wiggled her fingers, and Myreen could imagine how deadly those glinting blades would be in a fight.

A pang of regret hit her as she remembered her helplessness during the fight in the alley. If she'd only known... Myreen shook the thought off. She couldn't change what happened. She could only work on not being helpless going forward. And she was making some progress in that area—now she actually had a weapon at her disposal.

"That was so easy," Myreen said, looking at Ms. Heather with awe. Being a harpy was so different from being a mermaid. It felt natural, freeing. While being a mermaid made her feel more herself than she'd ever remembered before, it dimmed in comparison to finding her harpy form.

"And flying will be easy, too. Here." Ms. Heather stepped back, shaking her head as her wings unfurled in their full glory.

The angelic sight still caught Myreen by surprise.

Ms. Heather smiled as she crouched, then leapt into the air, her wings sweeping downward. With a few quick beats she was aloft, taking full advantage of the height of the room. She rolled onto her stomach and tucked her wings in, darting through one of the rings, under the second and spreading her wings to buoy upwards before diving through the third. It was elegant, effortless. Myreen doubted she could even come close. But seeing Ms. Heather fly made her want to try.

She waited for Ms. Heather to land, her heart drumming a frantic beat.

"Alright, your turn," Ms. Heather said, folding her wings but not retracting them. "I'll be right here if you need me."

Myreen nodded, then took a step back from Ms. Heather. She crouched like she'd seen her teacher do, and took a deep breath. *Here goes nothing.*

She leapt and pressed down with her wings, but the timing was off, and she ended up on her hands and knees. Standing, she brushed herself off.

"That was an excellent first try. Why don't you extend your wings first this time, so you don't have to coordinate as much for your lift-off."

Myreen nodded, then crouched again, this time lifting her wings as instructed. When she jumped, the timing was perfect. She felt a pocket of air catch under her wings, and she beat them frantically to continue to lift. Her chest tightened as her wings began to tire. But a wind ruffled her hair, and a moment later she caught the draft. She spread her wings to glide, marveling at the ingenuity the Dome was built with.

A smile spread across Myreen's face as air flowed through

feather and hair. *I'm flying!* This must be how Kol felt, and she had the sudden urge to go for a flight with him.

"Excellent job, Myreen! You're a natural." Ms. Heather crouched again and was soon in the air, gliding by Myreen. "Would you like to attempt a few tricks?"

Myreen shook her head. "I'll consider it an accomplishment if I can land without falling on my face."

Ms. Heather chuckled. "You've done exceptionally well. Why don't you take a few laps while I show you how to land?"

Myreen gave a nod. "That would be great."

She circled around the upper reaches of the transformation room as Ms. Heather tucked her wings in and fell away. At the last minute, she spread her wings wide, and her feet readied in front of her, talon and knee absorbing the impact of her landing.

Standing again, Ms. Heather retracted her wings, leaving behind the simple nurse Myreen knew so well. "Feel free to stay aloft as long as you'd like," she called to Myreen.

As much as Myreen was enjoying herself, there was one place she wanted to be more.

Myreen tucked her wings like Ms. Heather had done, and flared them again as she neared the floor. Her landing wasn't nearly as graceful, but she managed to stay on her legs, her wings helping to compensate for her stumbling talons.

Myreen beamed at her teacher. "I did it!"

"Very good! I'll have to take you on a flight in the simulation room so you can really stretch those wings."

Myreen scrunched her nose. "I'd have to fight?" It might not be so bad now that she'd accessed her harpy form, but defense training still wasn't on her list of favorite activities. If anything, it had fallen further down the list ever since they'd increasing her training.

Ms. Heather laughed. "No. I'll leave the combat sims for your defense instructors. You and I can just go for a leisurely flight."

"Thank you!" It sounded amazing, and if she didn't want to see Kol so bad, she might've suggested they go now.

"Well, Myreen, it's time for your final lesson today."

Myreen cocked her head. What more could Ms. Heather teach her?

Her patient teacher smiled. "Putting the harpy away."

***

Ten minutes later, she was back in the avian common room. She didn't expect to see Juliet there—she usually hid in her room when she was upset—but Juliet was just leaving, freshly showered, headphones on and nose in the air, acting like she didn't see Myreen. She was wearing that dark lipstick that made her eyes pop, the one Myreen always encourage her to use. Myreen rolled her eyes. If Juliet was determined to pursue this Jesse guy, that was on her.

So when she didn't see Kol, she opted to go to his room to find him. She needed to vent, and he was the only other person she could really talk to.

When she got to the door and knocked, her heart flip-flopped and she nearly turned and fled. Sure, he'd asked her to be his girlfriend, but what if he'd changed his mind? He'd done it so many times before, throwing hot and cold vibes until her head practically swam. She wanted to believe this time was different, that he'd finally come to terms with whatever dragon he'd been fighting, but that tiny bit of doubt reminded her that she wasn't sure she could handle his rejection again.

The look on his face when he opened the door melted all her fears. His eyes softened at the sight of her, drinking her in. Before she might've thought his calculating gaze was just that—analyzing her body language and thoughts and intentions. But now there was a spark of something more, something human behind those equations, and it made her giddy. Or it would have, if she wasn't so steamed about Juliet.

"What are you doing here?" he asked, peering down the hallway.

"I just thought... now that we're official and all..."

Kol's brows rose. "Oh. Do you want to come in?" he asked, hesitation lacing his words.

Myreen nodded.

Kol stepped aside, and Myreen brushed past him, her heart hammering in her chest. The last time she'd spent any time alone with a guy had been with Kendall. While she could begrudgingly admit that their time together had been enjoyable, she couldn't deny that what she felt when she was around Kol was so much stronger.

Myreen lifted a shirt off his bed so she could sit. Kol snatched it and threw it in a pile he had on the floor, wrinkling his nose as he shoved it aside.

"Sorry, I haven't had time to do laundry in a while," Kol mumbled.

To be fair, that was the only thing in his room that wasn't perfectly tidy. Her eyes skimmed along the neat row of shoes by the door, the textbook aligned with the corner of the desk it sat on, and his tablet on top of that. Myreen's brow crinkled. She hadn't seen many books since coming to the Dome. Everything here was so digital and high tech.

Kol was done cleaning, and he leaned up against the desk, blocking her view and bringing her back to the reason she'd come.

Kol pushed his hands into his pockets as he stared at the floor.

"So, what do you want to do?" Kol asked at the same time Myreen blurted out, "I can't believe Juliet."

"Wait, what?" Kol folded his arms. "What about Juliet?"

"She's being an idiot." Myreen shook her head. "We're fighting." She put her face in her hands, trying to keep her tears in check. This wasn't how she wanted to spend her time with Kol, but her frustration with Juliet had reached its boiling point.

After a moment, Kol sighed, and the bed dipped as he sat beside her.

"If she's a good friend, you two will make it through this."

Myreen dropped her hands to her sides, leaning her head back as she tried to blink back errant tears. "It's just so stupid. I mean, she was the one person I could rely on to lighten the mood in this fishbowl, but all she can do is moan about Nik breaking up with her. And now?"

Kol's hand curled around hers, and she leaned on his shoulder, closing her eyes.

"I'm... sorry?" Kol breathed into her hair.

A smile curled Myreen's lips, and she nuzzled deeper into his shoulder. Kol lifted his arm and nestled her under the crook. His movements were a little stiff, a little hesitant, but Myreen let out a contented sigh. She hadn't realized how much she needed him right now.

As the negative thoughts filling her head began to drain, her mind turned again to her lesson. She straightened and looked Kol in the eyes, a soft smile on her lips. "I flew today."

"Really?" Kol's brows lifted. "How'd it go?"

"It was incredible!"

Kol smirked. "I told you flying was better than swimming."

She tapped a fist on his arm. "I couldn't get you out of my mind when I was up there, flying around the training room. So in a way, you kind of helped me get my wings."

Her mouth quirked as she looked to Kol for a reaction. He swallowed, looking nervous, or stunned, or...

Kol stared at her from under lidded eyes that seemed to glow with a consuming fire. He leaned in, his soft lips parting ever so slightly. Myreen closed her eyes and met him. Her body went hot and cold as she got lost in that beautiful kiss. This time, no doubts clouded her mind, no hesitation pushed her away. She was Kol's girlfriend, and she wanted to enjoy every minute of it. He ran his fingers through her hair, making her skin tingle and her toes curl, and her hands clamped around his firm biceps.

Everything—her frustrations and fears and worries—melted away as she got lost in those glorious lips, which tasted like cinnamon and promises.

They broke away for air, then looked at each other and laughed.

Kol ran a hand through his hair, an errant strand tilting forward as soon as his fingers were through. "What do you do to me?" Kol asked, his husky voice filled with awe.

She hoped it was exactly what he did to her.

Kenzie

Kenzie stood outside a dingy motel, wondering where she'd gone wrong.

She was *supposed* to be meeting Leif. When he'd given her this address, she assumed he'd moved or something. But now? She glanced down the street, wondering if she'd transposed the numbers of the address.

She pressed forward anyways. He'd given her a room number, after all. No sense looking for a better place if she hadn't at least verified that this wasn't it.

She'd barely lifted her hand to knock when the door swung open and a cold hand yanked her inside.

Kenzie stood breathless in the dim light, waiting for her eyes to adjust and hoping she hadn't been pulled into a room housing some psycho. But the hand had been cold. If it was some random psycho, there was a good chance it was a vampire, in which case she should already be dead. Right? Her eyes began to adjust, and to her relief, it was definitely Leif.

Still, she jumped and yelped when something rubbed up against her legs.

"Kenzie, calm down," Leif said, though he sounded about as on edge as she felt.

"Why are all the lights off? And the curtains drawn? And why do you have a cat here?" She could just make out the outline of the cat, still weaving against her legs. "Is that Rainbow?"

Leif shrugged, flipping on the light for her. "Sorry, I didn't want to be disturbed."

Kenzie picked up the door hanger and waved it. "That's what *this* is for."

Leif grabbed the do-not-disturb hanger from her and briefly opened the door just a crack to slide the thing on. The cat gave an angry yowl, shooting Leif a warning look.

"It's okay," he reassured the cat. "That was the last time."

"What's going on?" Kenzie asked, shrugging off her backpack. She started unwinding her winter clothes and depositing them on the bed.

Okay, yeah, so this was kinda weird, but she trusted Leif. He seemed a bit cagey, but he'd never done anything that made her feel threatened. Besides the alley, but she just hadn't known him then. Or the time he'd hissed at the cat, but that was him trying to contain the creature. Unless... "You're not like... hungry, or anything. Are you?"

Leif scrunched his nose as he shook his head. "I'm good. No, actually I was hoping to talk with you about a couple things."

Kenzie let out a breath, but then her brow rose. "And it couldn't be said over the phone?" A part of her—okay, a very large part of her—was squealing like a fangirl right now. Could this be it? Was Leif going to confess his undying love for her? Oh, crap, they were in a hotel. What was going on in that gorgeous head of his?

"My apartment is no longer safe for you to visit."

"Of course." Kenzie's head bobbed up and down, as if this was exactly what she'd expected him to say. Even she almost believed her little bobblehead act. Almost. "And why not?"

"First, I need you to tell me how you know Myreen."

Myreen? "You didn't... I mean, you're not the one..." Kenzie put a hand over her mouth, a cool dread spreading over her. Had she misjudged? Is that why he'd befriended her? To get to Myreen? And if so, that likely meant... "Her mom?"

Understanding dawned on Leif's face. "No. No, I didn't kill her mom. I had nothing to do with that."

Kenzie took a deep breath, hoping to calm her thumping heart. Of course he didn't have anything to do with that. What was she thinking, jumping to the worst conclusion so fast? Sure, he was a vampire, but this was *Leif.* Dependable, controlled, witty Leif. With the deep, blueberry eyes, the cold, hard—at least she assumed so—pouty lips, and the dark, wavy romance-novel-worthy hair that she just wanted to sink her fingers into. Kenzie bit on her lower lip, hoping Leif wouldn't see the heat flooding her face.

"So, how do you know Myreen?" Leif continued. If he noticed Kenzie's sudden fluster, he didn't indicate it.

"I'm her friend. From before... well, everything, I guess. She'd just moved to town, but we were like, instant besties. I mean, you understand, right?" She gave him a meaningful gaze—she might have even batted her eyes a time or two—but Leif's mind was elsewhere.

Leif ran a hand through his hair, then absently picked up Rainbow, who had begun running figure eights across his legs. "The vampire who came after her is the leader. Draven. And he's got footage of you with her. They don't know who you are yet, but it's just a matter of time."

Kenzie plopped down on the edge of the bed, her mind reeling. Myreen was wanted by the lead vampire? She didn't even know vampires had a leader. "What does he want with Myreen?"

Leif shook his head. "Nothing good. I'm trying to prevent Draven from getting to her, but you can't hang out with her. Not now."

"But she's my best friend! And she still needs me." Her conversation with Wes just yesterday played back in her head. She couldn't let Myreen down again. Not after all her friend had been through.

"Your friend is fine. Oberon is making sure of it." Leif paused, letting the cat down. "But you can't come to my apartment. Draven has left an Initiate in my care, and she's with me most of the time."

A pang of jealousy spiked through Kenzie. "And where exactly does *she* think you are now?"

"Grabbing a bite." He flashed Kenzie a smile, and any other time it might have made her heart flutter—or her gag reflex act up—but her mind was whirring with all the new information.

Leif sat next to Kenzie, putting his hand on hers. Which abruptly ended the whirring and started up a different kind of storm.

"I need you to promise me you'll be careful. Don't visit Myreen. Stay out of Chicago."

"Why?"

"I need to know you're safe."

Kenzie stared at Leif in stunned silence, hardly breathing. Why did he need to know she was safe? Was it just her magic or something more? Was he leaning her way? Should she lean toward him?

They stayed like that, unmoving, for one second longer than was comfortable. But when Leif retracted his hand, the warm air that filled in his wake might as well have been an entire lake of distance.

He was just like the shifter school—completely out of her reach.

Kenzie pursed her lips. "I'll be as careful as I can, but I can't promise the rest." She blushed as she remembered Wes. The chemistry might not be as strong as what she and Leif had—whatever that was—but it was there. And if Wes had any shot of distracting her from... well, all this, then she didn't want to limit her time with him by staying out of Chicago.

Kenzie's brows scrunched as the cat jumped into Leif's lap and began purring again, this time an awful growling sound accompanying the gentle hum.

"What the heck is wrong with Rainbow?" Kenzie asked, flinching away from the cat. He sounded agitated, though he looked relaxed in Leif's arms.

"That's the other thing I needed to talk to you about."

Kenzie sat up straighter, cocking her head. "What about him?"

"He... He seems to have gone through a bit of a

transformation." Leif looked a bit disturbed, maybe even hesitant. "I believe he's a vampire."

"*What?*" Kenzie stood up and whirled on Leif. "What do you mean? Why would you think that?" She started running the spell through her head, trying to figure out if she'd done something wrong. Her pronunciations had been flawless, of that she was certain. Mostly. But changing things like she had... and using Leif's life force to resurrect the cat... "You think I turned him into the undead."

Now that he mentioned it, the eyes did look a little red, some fang-like teeth poking over his lower lip.

"He got sick after you left. When he showed an adverse reaction to light, I locked him in the bathroom until he could stand the artificial lighting, though that seems to be remedying on its own. In all that time, he never ate or drank, and he never had to go to the bathroom. I've found there's only one thing he *will* eat."

"Aw, crap." Kenzie let her head fall back, and she stared at the ceiling. "I can't believe— Aw, man. What are we going to do with Vamp Cat?"

"His name is Rainbow, and I'm planning on keeping him. As long as he remains in my care, I believe he'll be fine."

"Are you *serious*?"

"Yes. Why not?"

"Because he sounds like a gremlin when he purrs like that, and he's a *freaking vampire*!"

"His purr is pitch perfect," Leif said, his tone soft and low. "It's middle C."

"Excuse me?"

"Middle C. It's a musical—"

"And that makes it okay to bring him here? With *me*?" Kenzie was livid. This was a mistake. Leif had to realize that. Her magic had created a monster, and Leif wanted to keep the thing as a pet? *But he won't let* me *in.* Kenzie swatted at the air as if she could shoo away her pesky thoughts.

"I fed him before you got here. You don't have to worry."

Feeding. Kenzie slid her hand over her mouth, unable to keep out the thought of Vamp Cat licking up a bowl of blood. She held up a finger and tapped her foot, but the gag took hold, and she rushed for the bathroom, relieving herself of whatever breakfast was left.

"Sorry," she murmured as she came back out. She stopped at the sink to clean up and wash the taste of bile from her mouth. "Okay, so what if he gets out? Will he start turning people? Other animals? Crap, this is so not what I had in mind."

"I don't think so. You generally have to *want* to turn someone in order for it to happen. I imagine a cat working off instinct would have little need for such a thing, and would probably have greater control over whether he turned another or not."

"He's a cat, not a philosopher."

Leif chuckled. "Actually, he escaped already and found himself a mate. But she's been the only one he's turned, and it seemed quite intentional."

Kenzie's brows shot up again, her eyes bugging so badly she almost expected them to pop out of her head and start bouncing around.

"It'll be okay. I'll keep an eye on him."

"Like when you kept an eye on him as he turned Mrs. Kitty?"

"That was one mistake, which will not happen again, now that I know the signs."

Kenzie folded her arms. "And your *Initiate* is okay with this?"

Leif shrugged, his gaze falling to the cat still purr-growling in his lap. "She actually wants to be a vampire."

"She *wants* to be a vampire?"

Leif nodded, his expression grim. "Her and a lot of other people, actually. There's a whole Initiate program designed to lure in the best and brightest human minds to recruit into the vampire hive."

"Brilliant idiots." Kenzie sighed. What would a girl who wanted to be a vampire that much do? Kenzie had a few ideas, herself—not that she wanted to be a vampire, but the thought had crossed her mind. On more than one occasion.

"I was hoping you'd be able to find the spell that allows vampires to daywalk. You know, for Rainbow's sake. I have to put him in the bathroom during the days, as well as his lady friend who's still suffering the ill effects of the transformation."

Kenzie sat on the edge of the bed again, covering her face with her hands and throwing her head back until she hit the mattress. This was a nightmare. She'd actually turned Leif into a cat person. Except it wasn't regular cats, it was a monster cat. Or two. And she'd created those monsters.

Cool air kissed the small strip of skin on her belly where her shirt had pulled upward, and a shiver raced through Kenzie as her imagination filled in that space with Leif's cold touch.

Okay, so maybe this wasn't the worst thing in the world. She was alone with Leif—besides the cat, but hopefully he wouldn't interfere. He wanted to look for magic—she could get on board with that. And he'd brought her here because he was concerned for her safety, which meant he cared. At least, she hoped so.

She could work with this. Right?

"Do you know where she wrote the spell down?" Kenzie asked, peering through her fingers at Leif.

He smiled down at her. "No. But I'd recognize her handwriting."

She sat up, pulling her shirt back into place, though she was tempted to leave it. "Sounds like a plan. Got a few minutes?"

"Yes. I don't have a specific time frame at which I need to return."

Kenzie's mouth curled into a wicked grin. "Okay. Let's do this."

Kenzie grabbed her bookbag and pulled the book out. She tossed the grimoire onto the bed, scooting up to the headboard to sit. Leif hesitated a moment, but then sat beside her. Kenzie almost ragged him for it, but decided against it. She'd take whatever she could get from the vamp. For now.

"So the book is divided into three sections," Kenzie began, angling it so Leif could look over her shoulder. "The first is the simple spells and a little on history and techniques. Obviously, your spell wouldn't be in there."

She flipped forward a few pages, the smell of ancient oils and magic tickling her nose. "The second section is a little more advanced, and certain pages are sticky. I think it's the magic holding them together. It could be in there, but most likely it would be in one of the sticky bits."

She thumbed forward until she came to a block of pages that refused to budge. "The third section is completely inaccessible until I can figure out how to unlock it." She looked at Leif. "Have you done any research on your girl's family?" She had a feeling there was some plant-based magic in the mix, but whether it played into unlocking things was hard to tell. If she knew more about what they did or favored, she might be able to start unlocking the grimoire's secrets.

Leif shook his head. "I haven't had the time. And I don't know how she unlocked it. All I know about Gemma's family is what she told me, which didn't extend much past the general abuse she received at the hands of her sisters. Maybe let's just try the second section and hope it's in one of the non-sticky areas?"

Kenzie nodded, though she had a feeling they'd come up empty-handed. She had never heard of a selkie spell that helped vampires, so she figured that one would be buried deep.

"So, what was she like?" Kenzie asked, needing to fill the emptiness with words so her beating heart wouldn't give her away. It was the only thing she could come up with, and though she felt a pang of jealousy at the source of the topic, she wanted to know what made Leif tick. *What keeps a self-loathing vampire going?*

"She was strong and gentle. She was always helping out wherever she could, even if it about killed her to do so. She stood by me when I was turning, and worked tirelessly to find something—anything—that would help me in my altered state. She never judged me for what I became, either."

"So, why continue to search for a way to bring her back? Don't get me wrong, it's incredibly romantic, but... why not move on?"

Leif sighed. "Have you ever felt a connection with someone that transcended everything else?"

Kenzie shook her head, though she briefly considered what she felt for Leif. Wes didn't even compare, but she was just getting to know him. Maybe that was something that developed over time?

"She keeps me grounded, even now." Leif brought something out of his pocket.

It was a pin—a green leaf with glinting gold veins, tiny gems providing a frame that sparkled despite the dim hotel lighting. But it was the cameo in the middle that arrested Kenzie. Something about the profile of the woman—so stoic, so reverent—made Kenzie feel like she knew the woman. Like she could understand Leif's every emotion for his long lost love.

"Whenever I feel I'm losing my way, this reminds me I have something worth fighting for."

Kenzie nodded, turning her eyes back to the book, but she didn't even see anything on the page anymore. *I'm hopeless.* How this vampire could pull her in so completely without even trying made her head spin. Even now, her fingers itched to feel his cool skin, her lips wanted to taste his frigid kisses. And he was talking about his dead lover. The one he'd been pining over for who knew how long.

"You actually remind me of her," Leif said, a soft half-smile on his face as he put the pin back in his pocket. "The day I found you, I thought you *were* her. And then I sensed the magic in you. I should thank you, Kenzie. You've given me a hope I haven't felt in a long time."

Kenzie's gaze met Leif's, his eyes so full of heartache and promise. Was he seeing her now, or the woman he'd lost? She leaned forward ever so slightly before she realized what she was doing. Pausing, she waited, wanting to feel his affection, even if it was directed at another.

Rainbow jumped onto the book at that moment, breaking whatever spell had been cast. Leif grabbed the cat and stalked away from the bed, the cool emptiness warming beside her.

Kenzie sighed. She was in love with a man who was in love with a ghost. She wondered if she could fill that void for him. Just for a while. She could be his beloved Gemma, and she could feel that incredible connection he talked so passionately about.

There were only two ways that could end, and they were both ugly.

Kenzie shook her head, focusing once more on the book. The sticky pages—the ones where she couldn't read the spells caught between—annoyed her enough that she almost wanted to rip them out. Almost.

She slammed the book closed. "We're not going to find anything powerful without unlocking this thing."

"I'm sorry."

Kenzie snorted. "For what?"

Leif didn't elaborate. Maybe words had escaped him. Maybe he just didn't know why.

Kenzie threw the grimoire into her bag, and grabbed her winter gear to suit back up. Slinging her bag onto her shoulder, she paused at the door. "I should get home."

"Of course. You'll still...?"

Kenzie hazarded a glance over her shoulder. Leif looked so frail and vulnerable in that moment, even cradling his beloved Vamp Cat.

Kenzie nodded. "Yeah. I'll keep looking." Of course she would. If Leif was a drug, she was hooked. There was no way she could stay away from that mystery for long. *Or him.*

She left out of the room quickly, needing to put as much distance as she could between herself and the vampire before she exploded. She pulled her phone out of her bag, her heart sinking when there were no new texts from Wes. She sent him a quick one to see what he was doing, but his short response let her know he was working.

Figures.

Her phone chimed again, lighting up the screen.

Adam: What R U up 2?

Adam. Kenzie had almost forgotten about tall, dark, and mysterious.

Me: Hanging around Chicago for a little. Y?

She'd stopped moving forward as she stared at the screen, waiting for a reply. It only took a moment.

Adam: Wanna grab something 2 eat?

Okay, so she was already kinda using one guy as a distraction. Did she really want to use two of them? Kenzie bit her lip. There was something about Adam that she was drawn to, though she couldn't place her finger on it.

"Aw, heck with it."

Me: Yes.

She might have held her breath while she waited for him to respond. Lucky for her, it didn't take long. He sent her an address—one that, incredibly, wasn't too far away—and she took off.

Kenzie arrived at the café first, and she sat at a table, her leg pumping to some invisible beat.

And then Adam walked in.

Everything stopped as she watched him saunter over, his eyes especially smoky today, his lips pulled into a smirk. He was every bit as dark as she'd remembered, and her heart sped up a beat under his wolfish smile.

"Kenzie. I've got you cornered at last."

Kenzie laughed. "It would appear so."

"Can I get you anything to eat? Drink?"

Kenzie nodded. "Sure. A mocha and a BLT. Thanks."

Adam gave a single nod, then stalked to the counter to order, his trench coat sweeping behind him. Now *this* was a proper distraction.

She knew she shouldn't be here, flirting with Adam, but he had a certain allure that she found irresistible. Almost as irresistible as Leif, though with Adam, she knew she actually had a shot. Being here, with him, made her feel dangerous and reckless, and the thrill gave her a sort of high she had no desire to quit. She sat on her hands anyway, just in case. Maybe that would help keep her out of trouble. Maybe.

He came back and sat down with a table marker, leaning back in the chair like he owned the place. "It'll be a few. So. What brings you back to the city?"

Kenzie shrugged, mirroring his casual lean. "I've got some friends I like to visit."

"Yeah? What do you all like to do together?"

"Oh, sightseeing, eating good food, talking, whatever." She folded her arms, wondering where he was going with this.

Adam leaned forward, his face coming within inches of hers. "I bet a girl as pretty as you has a lot of guys fawning over her. I mean, why else travel all the way to the city weekend after weekend?"

Kenzie pursed her lips and shook her head. There were two guys in her life, but only one of them seemed interested in her.

And at the moment, Wes didn't really count. Not when he wasn't here and Adam was looking at her with those smoldering eyes, carrying a gleam she was certain she could get lost in.

They stayed that way, locked in some sort of unspoken battle she didn't quite understand. But it got her blood pumping. She might not know what was at stake, but she certainly knew how to win. Her gaze flicked to his lips, which looked as cool and dangerous as everything else about him.

Before she could think, she crossed the remaining distance and crashed into those lips. He stiffened at first, but then melted into the kiss, gently prying her mouth open, the energy between them becoming a devouring beast. His tongue teased hers, tasting like coffee with some metallic undertone popping against her taste buds. She groaned under his pressure, nearly forgetting herself, the magic inside her tingling below the surface, begging to be let loose.

"Excuse me," a woman said, blushing as she set down a tray with their food.

Kenzie and Adam broke apart, both a little wide-eyed and breathless. Kenzie pulled her lips in and bit them, looking at the waitress with what she hoped conveyed innocence. Sort of.

"Sorry to interrupt." The waitress gave a brief smile and grabbed the number from their table. "Let me know if you need anything else." Nodding, she turned to leave.

"Thanks," Adam said, rubbing his lower lip.

Aw, man. Is he trying to wipe the kiss off? Kenzie couldn't believe she'd done that. She wanted to kick herself. She barely knew this guy and she was throwing herself at him like she was desperate. *Desperate to forget someone else.* Ugh.

Adam sat back, then looked at Kenzie with brows raised.

"You surprise me."

Kenzie shrugged, pulling her BLT toward her.

"I like that," he continued, as if she was waiting for an explanation.

Kenzie blushed, staring hard at her sandwich. "Oh yeah?"

"Yeah. We might have to do this again."

Kenzie wasn't sure if he meant the kiss or the food, but she didn't seek clarification. She turned her head a little to take in Adam's face, which was once more wearing that smirk.

Point for Adam. He had a dangerous kind of beauty that she wanted to explore further. Chances were, at the end of the day, Wes would win out.

But for now? She was just glad that someone besides Leif could hold her attention.

Leif

"Ten days," Piper said through chattering teeth. She wore a hooded purple parka that made her look twice her size, and still the girl couldn't keep warm. "It's been ten days since Draven dumped me off here, and there hasn't been any sign of Myreen or her friends."

Leif held back a smile. Piper, the overzealous Initiate—the one who got excited about *everything*—was miserable. What made matters even better was that she was miserable about a vampire task that had been assigned by the vampire leader himself.

"I've warned you," he said with a shrug. "Being a vampire isn't all it's cut out to be."

"I'd do just about anything to have you turn me right here and now," she snapped. "At least then I'd stop freezing to death."

The smile slipped away from Leif's face like rubber on ice. "There are far worse things than feeling cold."

She held up a gloved finger. "Not right now." Puffs of breath steamed from her mouth. "I just don't get it. It's the Saturday before their Christmas Break, and none of Myreen's friends have come out. I mean, shouldn't students be going home to be with their families? And that's not even the craziest thing. None of them have come out since I've been here, and at least one of us has been here every day and night keeping a lookout." Piper narrowed her eyes at Leif. "Unless you've been sneaking away from here when I go back to your apartment to sleep."

Leif had bought a mattress out of pity for his Initiate, who, during the first two nights, hadn't slept well at all on his hardwood floor, next to the fireplace. Since then, she'd slept better, but being out in the cold always seemed to put her in a sour mood.

"Draven's monitoring this location," Leif said. "I wouldn't dare leave the station unmarked at this point. He'd have my head mounted to his wall of trophies."

Disgust unraveled on Piper's face. "You think he'd really do that?"

Leif shrugged. "Probably. But not until after drowning me for three years."

The sun momentarily snuck from the clouds and illuminated Piper's face. Her jaw dropped, as if a weight had been tied to her chin and suddenly released.

Raising his eyebrows and smirking ever so slightly, he said, "Are you *sure* you want to become a vampire?"

Piper swallowed with difficulty and her glasses fogged up as she let out a deep breath. Rubbing at them, her magnified-brown eyes looked at him. "Draven doesn't trust you."

Nodding, Leif said, "That's very apparent. Your very presence proves that. I'm sure he's asked you to watch my every move."

Piper's head bobbed softly. "Yes. He wants me to report anything I might perceive to be out of the ordinary."

Leif swung his arms out and twisted his hips, putting himself on display. "You've been here ten days. Have you discovered anything out of the ordinary?"

"Well, there is one thing," she replied, looking down.

A chill ran down Leif's spine. Nearly a week ago, he'd met with Kenzie to warn her about Draven's recent interest in her, as well as to inform her about his new vampire-kitty, Rainbow. Had Piper tailed him? Had she planted some device in his clothing that tapped into his conversation? What had she reported to Draven?

He hoped his anxiety didn't reveal any sign of guilt.

Piper looked him up and down with interest, and he straightened his back as she analyzed him.

"How is it that you can survive in daylight?" Piper asked.

His worry melted away like snow in the spring.

"During my Vampire History classes at Heritage Prep, I learned that there exist protective rings and bracelets that have been enchanted to shield vampires from the harmful rays of the sun, but they have mostly fallen into myth. The whereabouts of such trinkets are unknown, and you don't wear any form of jewelry."

Leif felt the weight of Gemma's brooch in the pocket of his dark slacks, and a sly grin crawled across his face.

"That, Piper Adams, is a story for another day. For now, all you have to know is that Draven selected me for this shifter-snatching job *because* of my ability to daywalk."

Movement at the stairs of the subway station pulled his attention away from his Initiate. People had been going up and down all day, but Leif couldn't help but recognize the boy emerging from the stairway. He looked the same as he had during the fight in the nearby alley. Leif was impressed the dragon shifter had survived the attack—he remembered the amount of lead the young man had been hit with. This time, he was *alone*.

He was tall, bundled up in winter gear, but his dark hair was visible, and even from this distance, he could see the young man's amber eyes.

"I've got eyes on one of Myreen's friends," he said with a nod toward the station.

She followed his hard stare. "Is that the Dracul boy?"

"That's him," Leif replied, setting his jaw. The young man was a descendant from a woman he loathed more than anything. In his opinion, the boy shouldn't be alive—Aline Dracul should never have been able to have offspring. Not after the unforgivable crime she'd committed against Gemma. He quickly corrected his thinking. This boy was not Aline, and had done him no ill-will. For all he knew, Aline never even had children, and this was some other relative. But despite the boy's heritage, Leif had no intention of snatching him. "Malkolm Dracul."

"Let's get him!" Piper said, eager to finally start moving.

Leif grabbed her arm firmly as she stepped forward.

"You haven't ever tailed somebody before, have you?" Leif whispered. "You don't dive right in the first chance you get."

"But we may never get another chance," Piper said.

To be honest, Leif would be entirely fine with that. But he had to at least pretend like he was trying to ensnare the Dracul boy.

"Look how many other people are down there," Leif pointed out. "It's far too open, and too many witnesses. If we swoop in and take him now, we'll have more than a dragon shifter to worry about."

"So what do we do?" asked Piper.

"Like I said, we tail him, but from a distance," replied Leif. "If we get too close, we risk getting discovered. And you don't want to be around the Dracul boy if he shifts into his dragon form to protect himself."

Malkolm moved northward through crowds with long strides, pausing for a moment as he looked at a nearby alley—the same alley where Draven had ensnared Myreen and her friends. The same place they'd learned that Myreen was a siren.

"What's he doing?" Piper asked.

Leif ran a hand through his hair. "He's recalling the attack we made on him and his friends just weeks ago. Come on. We can close in a bit now that he's distracted."

Side-by-side, they headed in the dragon shifter's direction. Leif was surprised to feel Piper's gloved fingers slide between his.

"Hey," he said, starting to pull his hand away.

"Hold on," she said quickly, resisting him. "We'll look less conspicuous walking together like a couple."

Leif hesitated, but let his Initiate keep her hold.

"Good point," he said. "But if you start looking at me with lover's eyes..."

Piper laughed. "Don't worry, I won't."

Together, they followed the Dracul boy, who had seemed to gather his wits and move on from the alleyway.

"What's the plan?" Piper asked.

Leif couldn't directly answer: they were surrounded by a large group of pedestrians. Talking about a kidnapping wouldn't go over too well in front of a crowd.

"You know, dear," she said nonchalantly, catching onto his unease. "I'm not entirely sure where we'll put my sisters up once they arrive. The apartment is considerably small, and poor Megan is allergic to cats."

"We'll just have to find other lodgings for them," Leif said, his terrible acting skills shining through like a candle in the dark—drawing more attention than he would have had they not said anything at all. But Leif understood what Piper was saying beneath her lines. "The cats are staying."

He looked at her out of the corner of his eye and found her struggling to conceal her irritation.

"But the cats are weird," she muttered. "Not normal."

Leif couldn't argue with that. "I can't just throw them out on the streets. Can you imagine what would happen?"

The crowd splintered, and soon, they found themselves alone again, still following Malkolm Dracul.

"Those vampire cats will be the death of me, Leif," she whispered. "Every time I go back to your apartment, they claw at the closet door. One of these days, they'll claw their way through and eat me in my sleep."

"I'll figure it out," he whispered back, looking around to make sure nobody could hear them. "Let's stay focused on our mission. We need to follow him to a more-secluded area before we can risk grabbing him."

"And once we find that secluded area, how do we go about the actual kidnapping?"

"You distract him with your expert extroverted-ness," Leif said. "I'll take him from behind."

Piper blew out a long breath. "That's a lot of pressure."

Leif arched an eyebrow. "Why? All you have to do is distract him for two seconds. That will give me plenty of time to—" He pounded his left hand with his right fist.

"That works," she replied, impressed.

Malkolm turned a corner, instantly concealed by one of the larger apartment buildings. Leif was half-tempted to say that they'd lost him, that they should turn back around and wait for him to go back to the subway station. But Piper pulled him forward, hurrying her pace.

"We're going to lose him!" she cried.

A gunshot sounded, and Leif instantly felt a tear burning at his free arm, making it go numb. That numbness did nothing for the pain. It was enough to make him cry out and wrench his hand away from Piper as he felt at his wound. As quickly as it had hurt, it healed, and Leif was relieved to discover that the bullet that hit him had merely grazed him. He'd been lucky. Judging by the pain he'd felt, he hadn't been hit by an ordinary bullet: the shooter was firing copper bullets. If one landed in just the right place, he'd be dead.

The numbness remained, though, and would for the next several minutes—perhaps the rest of the day. Copper was a vampire's greatest weakness, and Leif's past was riddled with terrible experiences with the red metal.

A stream of panic flooded his gut. Whoever was shooting at him knew he was a vampire, but the gunman also knew Leif was a daywalker. And anybody with that kind of knowledge was a serious threat.

Screams erupted all around and pedestrians ran into the nearby buildings to get out of potential danger.

"Leif!" Piper cried. "You've been shot!

Instinctually he pulled on nearby shadows to hide himself, but his abilities would only protect himself. Piper was merely human. Moving quickly, he hastily pushed Piper behind a nearby bench.

She trembled with fear. "What's going on?" she squeaked.

"Stay there," he commanded. "And keep out of sight."

Had they been baited? Was the Dracul boy part of a shifter trap that they'd just set off? Had Oberon betrayed him?

Another shot fired, and Leif felt a slight displacement in the air next to his cheek. His shadow concealment likely saved him, but it also marked him in broad daylight. He needed to get to the gunman before a successful shot was fired.

Leif's rapid senses caught sight of the next bullet's origination as it zinged through the air, striking the bench Piper was behind.

So she's been marked, too, he thought.

But now he saw the gunman, peeking his head around the corner of a nearby store decked out with Christmas decor across the street. He was just one hundred feet away, aiming a rifle their way.

The shooter was a young man, wearing a brown coat and a brown beanie with small locks of brown hair crossing his forehead. What was most noticeable was a marking on the back of his right hand—a tattoo Leif was all-too familiar with from his earlier days working for Draven. The dark mark consisted of a blade pointed downward, encircled by five dots. He'd learned years ago that each dot represented the four main shifter primes, as well as the vampire race.

"A hunter," Leif hissed. So the attack was separate from the Dracul boy's emergence.

Leif began moving to intercept the attacker, and he could tell the hunter had figured out he'd been spotted. Fear flitted over the hunter's youthful face, and he flung his rifle over his shoulder, its strap catching around his back so the muzzle pointed up in the air, then ran out of sight. The store exterior provided him excellent cover.

However, Leif was faster than any human.

Using all his speed, Leif sprinted across the street, dodging cars in the process, receiving a chorus of honks—no doubt wondering what this misty form moving through the street was—then stopped at the corner of the store. Not wanting to step out into the open and risk getting shot again, he peeked around the side and saw the young man throw his rifle through an open window in the back of a small, gray sedan. Through the back windshield, the barrels of several guns could be seen sticking up, likely mounted to a gun rack installed inside the vehicle.

The panicked brown eyes of the hunter spotted Leif, and he rushed into the front passenger seat and slammed the door. A half-second later, the car peeled away, kicking up rocks and leaving behind the smell of burnt rubber. The last thing Leif saw on the car was a black decal on the bumper that matched the hunter's tattoo.

Leif's rush of adrenaline told him to chase after the car—it would be easy to keep up—but he was in daylight, and passersby would see him. And most of all, he needed to protect Piper. She couldn't protect herself in her weak, human form.

Releasing his shadowy concealment, he waited for traffic to stop at the nearby intersection and crossed legally.

Upon reaching the bench Piper was cowering behind, Leif held his hand out. "Hey, you okay?"

His Initiate turned and looked at him with terror seeping from her eyes, only magnified by her glasses. She took his hand unsteadily, and he helped her to her feet.

"They tried to shoot me," she mumbled distantly, staring at him while the event replayed through her mind.

Leif nodded. "They wanted to kill both of us."

"Who were they, and why were they after us?" Tears streamed from her eyes, and Leif pulled her into his chest with one arm.

"Hey, it's okay now," he said, hardly believing he was providing comfort to anybody. It felt foreign to him, but at the same time, it felt right. "But we need to get off the street and to safety. We'll take the L and get away from the city for a while."

She sniffed and looked across the street, not toward where the shooter had been, but where the Dracul boy had been last seen.

"What about our mission?" she asked. "What will Draven say when he finds out we failed?"

Leif shook his head, shocked that she could even be thinking of such a thing after such a traumatic event.

"Unfortunately, we can't camp out by the station anymore," Leif said as he walked with Piper back toward the subway station, still holding her closely. "Hunters have been watching us. Coming back will be a deathtrap. We'll have to inform Draven that we need a different plan."

Piper nodded against his chest.

But the hunter attack had been the perfect distraction, giving them a good reason as to why they hadn't been able to catch Malkolm Dracul. And while it had been dangerous, Leif was grateful it happened.

Kol

Kol was excellent at compartmentalizing his thoughts and feelings. Most of the time. He was so talented at it that he was accused more than once of being wooden and unfeeling. That he was closer to something of *artificial intelligence*, a robot, rather than a living, breathing dragon.

He blamed it on his father most of the time, because his mother was the direct opposite. And Tatiana, his sister, didn't seem to have the same issues, either.

But when the image of *her*—of Myreen—entered his thoughts, he lost all control, no matter which direction he wanted his thoughts to go. Glancing at his bed, he couldn't help but picture her sitting there next to him as she had only hours ago after she surprised him by knocking. If he closed his eyes, he could almost feel her *light* still energizing the air. The way her *light* had busted those bulbs yesterday when she'd agreed to be his girlfriend.

His girlfriend.

No girl had ever owned that label. He tried not to think about the fact that no one *should* own that label. Instead, he imagined the way Myreen's eyes lit with fire as she lamented her fight with her friend, Juliet, her lips pouting.

And then they picked up where they'd left off at the greenhouse all those weeks ago.

Kol had tried and failed to write the essay for English that was due last Thursday. He'd never asked for an extension before, but with everything that had happened the past several weeks—and being that he was a *prince*—he got a pass. He'd never used the Dracul card before, and cringed a little that his grade demanded it.

What was a few more hours? He'd write the damned essay later.

This whole *girlfriend* business made him uneasy, and so he pulled out the history book about that first shifter school he borrowed from the library: *Frost Boarding House - The Original Shifter School: A History.* There had to be a way to break the curse. It pained him, more than he'd even admit to himself, that the instant he fell completely in love with Myreen, he'd lose her.

The fact she actually wanted to be with him advertised that his feeling hadn't deepened past infatuation just yet. The curse wasn't triggered. Yet.

Flipping through the first few pages, he discovered the one he'd found in the library. The picture of his relative Aline Elana Dracul. The person who caused the Dracul curse. Studying her picture, Kol was surprised at how Aline's nose—large and Roman—was near-identical to his sister's.

The book listed background on Aline. It said she fled her family in New Orleans for unknown reasons to find solitude and sanctuary in Washington state, and was taken in by a human family, *the Frosts.* It said Aline and her bodyguard, a phoenix named Evandrus Quinn, spent a year helping convert the once human-only boarding house into a safe house for shifters, and then a makeshift school where she and Mr. Quinn assisted in helping shifters control their powers and defend themselves.

Quinn. Kol wondered if this *Evandrus* was any relation to Malachai, the phoenix teacher at the Dome, and Juliet's dad.

Juliet, who was Myreen's friend.

Myreen.

And there she was again, intruding on his thoughts.

He imagined running his fingers through her silky hair, whispering secrets that made her laugh that breathy laugh that made his skin spark, feeling the press of her body against his chest...

Kol slammed the book closed and bounded from his bed. Throwing on his gray wool overcoat and the red scarf his sister had sent to him as an early Christmas present, he marched out of his bedroom. Before he realized where he was going, Kol found himself out of the Dome and on the sub heading into the city.

Might as well finish Christmas shopping, he justified as he stomped up the steps from the tunnel. The city buzzed with the activity of last-minute shoppers, and he quickly merged into the crowd. But when he walked past the alley—*the alley,* the one where he and Myreen, Nik and Juliet were attacked by those vampires—he paused. It was such a drastically different memory, but it intruded on his thoughts more often than he would like. It felt like it happened just yesterday; it felt like it happened a hundred years ago.

When the hair at the back of his neck stood on end, Kol had that very familiar, very disconcerting feeling he was being watched. He resumed walking and resisted the urge to look behind him. It was probably just PTSD, but part of him swore he saw some shadows shrink just then. Quickening his steps, he rounded a corner he hadn't intended to. Vampires couldn't come out during the day, anyway.

Kol felt every bit the hypocrite. His own words about Myreen stupidly leaving the Dome rang in his ears. *Whatever!* he'd said to her. *Go and get yourself killed!*

At least Myreen had Juliet with her when they'd left the Dome for their "girl's day out." Not that Juliet was the most reliable protection, but she had handled herself well in the alley and could've at least called for help if something happened.

Here, today, in the middle of Chicago, Kol was alone.

Then he swore he heard a gunshot, but decided it was more of his paranoid imagination. Still, without another thought, he dialed Brett, thinking he'd be the more available friend. The call went straight to voicemail.

He tried Nik next, who answered on the first ring.

"Can you get away from Eduard for a few hours?" Kol asked.

There was a pause. "I think so," Nik said. "He shut himself in Oberon's office again for phone calls or something. I've been counting ceiling tiles for the past half hour, which is code for wandering the school because Eduard doesn't seem to care what I'm actually doing."

None of that surprised Kol. He'd experienced both extremes growing up. Either Eduard had his attention focused on

Kol like a microscope, watching every minuscule movement and showing distaste if one strand of Kol's hair disobeyed—or he was too busy with other things that he didn't care whether Kol was doing his algebra homework, or practicing his fireballs in the master walk-in-closet.

"Meet me in the city?" Kol asked. "M Burger at Water Tower Place?"

"Yup," was all Nik said before hanging up.

Kol requested an Uber, then when he arrived at M Burger ahead of Nik, he ordered two Chicago doubles and two orders of jalapeno cheese fries. The loudspeaker played *Silver Bells* when Nik joined him, and they ate in near silence until they'd finished.

"Since when does Malkolm Dracul go to a mall?" Nik asked, discarding his tray.

Kol eyed his friend as he dumped his and wondered if the news of his and Myreen's relationship had spread across the Dome yet. It was only a matter of time. Nik wasn't technically a student anymore, but he'd still spent plenty of time at school as of late. Kol shoved his hands into his coat pockets and led the way toward *shopping*.

"Since I suddenly find myself with a girlfriend to buy for." Kol ducked his head, almost in embarrassment. He wasn't sure what the right emotion was in this situation. It was an awkward way to announce he had a girlfriend.

He was so completely out of his element.

Nik punched him in the arm. "Congrats man!" he said, but his enthusiasm was severely lacking.

"It's Myreen," Kol said, as if clarifying would change Nik's reaction.

Nik's eyebrows pinched, and he leaned away from Kol. "I

know."

Kol's shoulders lifted. "You don't sound thrilled."

Nik sighed. "Having a girlfriend—and one like Myreen—is a sure way to trigger a certain curse."

"*Ah.*" Kol knew it. He'd questioned himself more than once since yesterday, but hearing it from his friend still deflated his mood.

"I don't want you to get hurt." Nik's voice was off. Almost like he was sad, or *more sad* than he was even a second ago.

"Are *you* okay?" Kol asked. He was never good at reading the emotions of others, even his best friend, but he could tell something was wrong.

"It's just..." Nik paused. "I saw Juliet this morning."

"Oh?"

"Yeah. She'd been training and had her hair all up in those... *fiery* curls."

Kol suspected Nik had different adjectives in mind, but didn't mention it. "I thought you broke up with her."

"I did. I figured it was for the best, since I was leaving."

"Smart," Kol agreed. He'd probably do the same if he found himself in a similar situation. *Maybe.* It was smart, but would he break up with Myreen tomorrow if he was sent away? Eduard might take *her* away. Would she break up with him? Kol didn't like where his thoughts led, and that scared the hell out of him.

"Anyway," Nik continued, "she asked out one of the weres today."

"A *were?*" Kol was more shocked than appalled. He didn't know what girls—well, girls who weren't weres themselves—saw in the weres. They were volatile and explosive. They started fights over green beans and music subscriptions. They were slaves to the moon, but more than anything else, they weren't *born* shifters. They were bitten. They were *made.* It was probably Lord Dracul's influence on his son, but despite Kol's rationale that they were in fact, shifters, he'd always seen them as *lesser.* He hated himself for it, but it was true. He held regular humans in a higher regard than the weres. Especially the hounds.

"Yeah. Jesse is his name, I think?"

"The... dog?" Kol scoffed.

Nik nodded.

"Do you think she's moved on?"

Nik shot Kol a glare. "Brett says she's trying to get under my skin," he retorted. "You know, make me jealous?"

"*Ah,"* Kol said. But it was too late. He felt extra-blind to those emotional cues. First Myreen, and now Nik.

"But thanks for the confidence, man."

"Sorry," was all Kol could think to say.

Nik shrugged. "So what do you have in mind for Myreen's present?"

"There's this store called Pandora, I think?"

"The one with the jewelry? I think I've seen the commercials."

"Yeah. I figure I can't screw up too bad with jewelry."

Chapter 29

Kenzie

It took a lot of begging to get her mom to let her come to Chicago on Christmas Eve, but playing the my-best-friend's-spending-her-first-Christmas-alone card finally did it. It's not that Kenzie wanted to flake on her mom, she just had an obligation to be a good friend.

And a burning curiosity to know what Leif was up to.

Kenzie carried her backpack, this time filled with presents. Okay, so there were only four, but she was feeling jolly enough to imagine it was her own personal Santa pack. It was Christmas Eve, after all.

She hummed along to Christmas tunes as she made her way through the city to the shifter school entrance. She wasn't going in, really. There was no way she was trying that again until Oberon gave her the go-ahead. If Leif was being truthful, hopefully that green light would come soon. Maybe even in time for Christmas? Maybe.

Still, it couldn't hurt to try to butter up the gryphon. Right?

She made her stop at the end of the green line, letting the passengers dissipate before whispering her magic word and slipping onto the secret platform. There was a car waiting, as she'd hoped. She slid three of her gifts onto the seat—wrapped in cellophane so as not to get blown up on arrival out of suspicion—and made sure the name tags were visible beneath the bows and curls of ribbon.

For Myreen, she'd included the rose she'd resurrected, an unspoken promise that she'd do everything in her power to figure out how to bring Myreen's mom back. If she could do it for Leif, she'd do it for her best friend in a heartbeat.

For Oberon, she'd gotten a meat and cheese basket. She had no idea what the gryphon's tastes were, but she figured food was the key to every guy's heart, so it couldn't hurt. Unless he was a vegetarian, but he didn't strike her as the type. And just in case he had a sweet tooth, she'd taped a pack of Kit Kats to the front of the basket. Maybe he'd get the message and give her a break.

The final gift was for Juliet. It wasn't easy coming up with something for the phoenix, but she'd finally settled on a key and heart necklace. Besides the fact that it was cute, she hoped it encouraged her friend to remember that it was *her* heart to give and take.

Kenzie stepped off the train and headed back toward the exit. Looking around the platform for cameras, she waved and smiled. She hoped that if they didn't recognize her, they'd at least understand her little break-in bore no ill intent. She grabbed her phone out of her bag and sent Myreen a quick email. If Myreen got it in time, maybe she could be at the other end to intercept the presents. It would ruin the Christmas surprise a bit, but it was better than getting nothing at all.

Back on the public platform, the next outbound train was just arriving, and she boarded it along with a handful of other people. This one headed directly by Leif's place if she rode it far enough, and it just happened to be her next destination.

It was probably stupid, getting the vampire anything, but she couldn't help herself when she spotted the little vampire pet capes. Rainbow and his little lady friend would look adorable in them—assuming Leif could get the capes on the creatures. But that wasn't her problem.

She might have also gotten him a book of sheet music. It was all current stuff—she figured he probably had all the classics—but the thought of him banging out Bad Romance put a smile on her face.

Of course, the radio silence Leif had put on their communication since their little hotel meeting was driving her nuts. She wanted to contact him, but Leif's warning still rang fresh in her memory. It sucked, feeling so helpless while her friend was hunted by the leader of the vampires, but putting herself in harm's way wouldn't make her any more productive. So she was letting Leif call the shots. For now. Besides, she had the magic he needed to get back his love. He'd come back to her when he could. *If* he could. Right?

It was that last part that weighed the heaviest on her. If something happened to Leif, then what? She'd be alone with her magic, her secrets. Again. Not to mention she'd lose his friendship. The idea was so cold and lonely, she could almost feel the vampire beside her.

Concrete walls turned into tracks above the city as the L neared Leif's apartment. Kenzie watched the city whiz by, wondering what Wes and Adam were up to. Wes had actually gone quiet on her, which helped soothe her guilty conscience. She wasn't the kind of girl to two-time a guy, but Wes just wasn't quite what she needed at the moment. Neither was Adam, to be honest, but his allure was stronger. She could get lost in those guy-liner eyes and rough chin stubble. And he kept her guessing. Like kissing her the way he did at the cafe, and then not inviting her on a date. If he was really into her, shouldn't he have made plans for last weekend? Then again, it was Christmastime. Maybe he was just busy with family or something.

Kenzie shook him out of her head as she came to her stop. She shuffled off the relative comfort of the L and into the cold wind. It whipped at her clothes, finding every chink in her armor against the winter chill. But she smiled, as the seasonal weather completed the yuletide feeling.

She headed toward Leif's building, casting wary glances at everyone she passed. She wasn't stupid enough to go right to his apartment door, but she figured she could at least leave her gift somewhere for him to pick up. And if no one could help her, the bag she'd packed his gifts in would hang nicely from the handle—so basically she was saving her stupidity for plan B. But she'd be careful. As preparation, she'd signed the tag as K, and swept her scent away with magic so she couldn't be traced.

Leif's soul-crushing smile played in her head, and she wished she could be there when he opened everything. She'd only seen that smile a handful of times, but she was aiming to make it a permanent fixture.

The familiar building loomed ahead, and Kenzie slowed a pace or two, scanning for signs of Leif's handsome face—or anyone who might know him. Not that she knew what his Initiate looked like, but she figured the girl must be gorgeous. Right? A perfectly primped brunette sauntered past, and Kenzie marked her as a potential. Or maybe the doe-eyed blond clutching her fancy coat against the wicked chill.

Kenzie gave up as she reached the door. Really, the Initiate could be anyone. And it wasn't like she could do anything about it, even if she did know.

She pulled her knit cap down a little lower and fluffed up her scarf as she walked into the warm lobby. A peppermint scent tickled her nose, the song coming over the speakers fading away as Jingle Bells took its place. Dishes clanked in the quiet dining room, and Kenzie wondered if they were closing or getting ready for an evening crowd.

She made her way to the concierge, who looked like he was packing up for the day. "Excuse me," she said, in the sweetest voice she could muster.

The concierge turned to regard her with an annoyed expression. "Can I help you?"

"I'm sorry. I have a gift for a friend and I didn't know how to get it to him without ruining the surprise. He lives in apartment 823?" She gave him a hopeful smile, and he sighed.

"Give it to me. I'll get it to him before I leave."

"Thank you! So much. Oh, here." Kenzie dug in her bag, pulling out a Snickers bar she'd stashed in case she needed a snack on the return trip. "For your trouble. Merry Christmas?"

The concierge took the candy bar with a shrug and a nod.

Kenzie left, humming the rest of the Jingle Bells tune.

It was incredible how quiet the city seemed. Tomorrow would likely be even quieter as families gathered around Christmas trees and exchanged presents. But today's lull was a little eerie. She wondered how Leif would be celebrating, and hoped Myreen and Juliet were having a nice time. She hated that she was still on the outside of all their excitement. But it wouldn't be forever. She'd make sure of that.

The wind blew her scarf into her face, and she unzipped her coat to stuff the errant cloth in.

But she crashed into someone before she could begin, a liquid warmth seeping through her white sweater. Looking down, she saw coffee dripping off her shirt, droplets clinging to the fuzz on her scarf.

"What the heck, man? Watch where you're—" The words stuck in her throat as she met the mischievous smirk and smoldering eyes of Adam. Just as quickly as her heart had stopped, it sped up. "What are you doing here?"

"Out for a walk. What are *you* doing here?" he asked, taking a step closer.

"Ruining sweaters, apparently." Kenzie sighed, wiping at the stain on her shirt, but gave up when her efforts only served to spread the liquid further.

"Yeah, sorry about that," Adam said, sounding anything but sorry. He picked up his emptied cup and tossed it into a nearby trash can. "Let me buy you a new one."

"What?" she asked, her gaze flashing again to his mouth, which was pink from the chill.

Adam shrugged. "I ruined your sweater. It's only right I get you another one."

She bit her lip, contemplating the time. She'd told her mom

she'd be back before dark, but she'd also told her that she was going to visit Myreen. Maybe another hour or two wouldn't hurt anything, and she could still get home before dark.

"Fine," Kenzie said, lifting her chin. "But you owe me two shirts."

Adam's brows rose. "Two?"

"Yep. This one was from my mom and I really liked it." She met his gaze, challenging him to deny her.

Adam smirked. "I'd better make it three."

They wandered through the streets, trying to find a store that was open while she and Adam chatted about the coming holiday and their celebration plans. Well, at least she chatted about that. Adam seemed to be brooding a little harder today.

"So what about you?" Kenzie asked, trying to turn off the flow of words she'd accidentally let loose. She'd have to watch herself if she didn't want to let something slip. "What are you doing for Christmas?"

Adam shrugged. "This is pretty much it. I'm actually glad I ran into you. It was going to be pretty dull, otherwise."

Kenzie blinked. She thought he was staying with a cousin or something. But maybe his family life wasn't so great? So she deflected, trying to smooth over any ruffles she might have accidentally caused. "What? You don't have an endless supply of guyliner tutorials to keep you occupied?"

Adam laughed, shaking his head. "Yeah, you're surprising, alright."

The pair ran across a thrift shop that looked promising, and with a silent agreement, they headed toward it.

Before they'd reached the display windows, Adam grabbed Kenzie's arm, spinning her toward him. He pressed his hand on the brick behind her and leaned in, his eyes searching hers.

Kenzie's heart thumped in her chest, and she licked her lips. Every fiber of her being wanted to squirm under his stare, but she held herself still, not willing to concede whatever power she might hold in this relationship—or whatever it was.

He must have seen something he liked, because his lips came crashing down on hers. Kenzie met his kiss with her own fervor, melting, dying, getting lost in his ravenous darkness.

Then he was gone again, her frozen lips kissing the air. She opened her eyes, so full of questions, on the guy currently driving her wild.

Adam chuckled. "Just wanted to see if it was as magical as the first time."

Kenzie jutted out her chin. "And?"

Adam pressed his smiling lips together and nodded her toward the door.

Kenzie folded her arms. "Four shirts. And a new dress."

Adam's head bobbed in agreement, his hand sliding behind her back as he ushered her inside.

Juliet

Christmas eve was like any other day for Juliet and her mother. They didn't celebrate with gifts, and there was no other family to spend it with. So she tried not to expect anything too different with her father, since he wasn't the mushy type.

Before the fight with Myreen, Juliet had looked forward to spending that day with her, excited to celebrate and exchange gifts. Now she only wanted to do what she always did: nothing. The Hallmark channel would be blowing up with a marathon, which she wanted to indulge in, but because of the hole she'd dug herself in, she couldn't do that. Not all day, anyway.

Juliet knew from the moment she woke that her heart wasn't into the idea of going on a date with Jesse. Sure, he was cute in a rugged kind of way, but he seemed rowdy and temperamental. And more temper was not what she needed.

She kept her morning clear so she could watch two movies

before her date. And a gift arrived from Kenzie, a cute necklace that helped to cheer her just a little. But the short confrontation she'd had with Myreen played over and over in her mind, causing her mood to sour. Why did Myreen have to get in her head like that?

Obviously, she only asked Jesse out because Nik was watching. And it was clear that Jesse was not the right guy for Juliet. But her emotions had gotten the best of her, and she'd acted on impulse. Although, she was kind of proud that she'd reacted that way, rather than accidentally starting a fire.

All Nik had to do was acknowledge that she was there. Even a wave would have sufficed. Instead, he'd ignored her, and now she had to get ready for a date that she didn't want to go on. She wasn't ready for that yet. What annoyed her most was that Myreen knew just how much she wasn't ready.

For only a second, Juliet wished that she wasn't in the stupid fight with Myreen. She could really use a friend. But then, she could easily picture Kol asking Myreen to be his girlfriend, and as much as she wanted to be happy for her friend, she was more envious in the end. Myreen knew *that* as well. Juliet couldn't believe it was so easy for Myreen to tell her about Kol. As if that was going to help the situation at all.

Even still, she believed it was mostly Nik's fault. If only he hadn't broken up with her, everything could still be the way it was. Part of her knew she shouldn't blame Nik for the way things turned out, but she was cranky. She tried to center her mind on all things positive. It helped a little, but she still wished things were different.

The Hallmark movies did nothing to keep her mind off the drama in her life, and she wished she'd gone to the Defense

Room instead. She looked at the clock, but she she'd have to start getting ready for her date. The knot in her stomach grew.

Juliet still couldn't believe that Jesse was so quick to say yes. She never got the impression that he liked her or was interested in dating her. So quick an answer caused a momentary spike of confidence. She'd been sweaty, her hair wet and gross, and he'd still agreed. Maybe his rough reputation was wrong.

Still, he wasn't Nik.

The sooner she got this over with, the sooner she could hide back under her covers where it was safe. Enough students had witnessed the interaction that word of her date had likely spread like wildfire around the school. They probably all assumed she'd bomb it. She wouldn't give in to those expectations. As much as she didn't want to go, she would try to enjoy herself.

Especially since Nik would hear about it.

As Juliet got dressed and did her hair and make-up, she couldn't help but wish that Myreen was there with her. It was difficult not to talk aloud about something as serious as a date. She was nervous, a small part of her was even excited. Though she couldn't tell anyone, which made her feel lonely.

The stubborn part of her refused to admit that if she tried to talk to Myreen, they would probably be okay. But Myreen didn't have to blow up on her, and she definitely didn't have to call her out after she asked Jesse out.

She looked in the mirror and felt satisfied with what she'd chosen all on her own: a thin, lacy black turtleneck, and a tight, tan mini skirt with black tights and black boots. It gave off the perfect message of wanting to be cute but not wanting to show any skin. She grabbed the necklace heart-and-key Kenzie had sent, and clasped it around her neck. Juliet ran her fingers through her long curls, making them just a little bouncier. Lastly, she reached for her lipstick. The dark lipstick was becoming her signature look, but it only brought memories of Nik and Myreen. So Juliet put that shade back down and picked up her cherry-red gloss.

"There we go." She shrugged her shoulders as she turned away from the mirror.

Juliet's fingers brushed over her headphones as she headed for the door, wishing she could bring them with her. She grabbed her jacket and her purse and took a deep breath before exiting.

Exactly as she thought, the other students didn't even try to hide their shock. Eyes were wide, mouths open. With her head high, Juliet walked through the common room, listening to all the whispers directed her way.

"She looks so good. Go girl!" Leya—a harpy—said under her breath.

"I can't believe she's actually going on a date with *Jesse.* He is *so* cute!" a dragon girl she could never remember the name of said to one of her phoenix classmates.

Usually, the rumor mill made Juliet want to run away, but this time she quite enjoyed hearing their opinions. She couldn't hold back her smile as she listened to their compliments.

If only Nik could see her now.

She stopped dead in her tracks when she turned the corner. There in the grand hall was Myreen, walking right toward her. For a moment, Juliet hoped Myreen was looking to squash the bad blood between them, but by the way Myreen's lips were pursed, it didn't look like that was her intent.

"So, you're really going through with this?" Myreen got

right to it. Not even a *Hi*, or *You look good!*

"Um, yes. I'm not going to stand Jesse up just 'cause *you* think it's a bad idea. Who knows, it might go well." She was pushing Myreen's buttons, but she didn't care. All thoughts of apology were gone, thanks to Myreen's attitude.

"Juliet, come on. Don't do this to yourself. You're better than this." Myreen crossed her arms and lowered her eyes to Juliet.

"So let me get this straight. You want me to move on from Nik, but not with Jesse. All while you and I continue this stupid fight. So what you're expecting from me is to be okay with being alone at the same time accepting that we don't talk anymore while you date my ex's best friend? Sorry, but no thank you." Heat formed in Juliet's stomach, and she closed her eyes to concentrate on making it go away. She didn't need to lose control again and ruin her date.

"No, that's not what I want. I just don't want you to regret anything." Myreen's cheeks were red.

Juliet had to get out of there before Myreen blew up again. "Whatever. I have a date to get to. Don't you have a boyfriend to spend your Christmas Eve with?" Juliet brushed by Myreen without giving her a chance to respond.

***

Jesse looked effortlessly handsome when she met him at the Dome's exit. She wondered how much time he spent getting ready. Probably not much. Jesse's hair was ruffled and pointed in all different directions, like he'd tried to make bed-head look good. He'd succeeded. The fitted plaid button-down beneath his leather jacket completed the bad boy look, as did his dark jeans.

When he saw her, he whistled. It made her feel beautiful as he grabbed her hand and twirled her around.

"Damn, you look hot! Just as a phoenix should."

Juliet wasn't sure how to take his compliment, but his expression was earnest. He didn't seem to be making fun of her, so she just smiled and played with her hair.

"So, where are we headed?" she asked, assuming that as the guy he had something planned.

"Uh, well you asked me out. You tell me." Again, he was serious. Juliet thought he would laugh and turn it into a joke. He didn't.

"Oh... Um, we could get some pizza? There's a place right out of the station. Somewhere close would be best, I guess." Shocked, she walked slowly as she led the way.

The short train ride was just as awkward as she thought it was going to be, but not because of silence. Jesse had no problem rattling on about Christmas and how lame it was that they were stuck at the Dome. Like many of the students, his parents had forbidden him from leaving after the recent vampire attacks. He went on and on about missing out on the traditional ski trip his family usually took.

Under normal circumstances, too much talking alone would be annoying. But it was the way he kept *looking* at her, like she was something delicious to eat, that made her truly uncomfortable. He got all doe-eyed whenever their eyes met, and he kept linking their hands together and pulling her in close to his side. He even brushed his lips against her cheek when he whispered secret observations about the couple sitting across from them. She shivered whenever he did that, and had to swallow hard so she didn't gag on his thick cologne.

He was definitely more of a hands-on kind of guy. She was thankful when the train let them off, and the Chicago air made it too cold to stop and talk.

Jesse flashed a big, bright smile—his best feature, in Juliet's opinion—as they walked against the cold wind. Once they turned the corner, Juliet saw the pizza shop and ran for the entrance. She hated the cold, and cursed the sky whenever the chill started up. When Jesse followed her inside, he rubbed his hands together then took Juliet's small ones in his. The gesture was endearing.

"How's that?" he asked, and she got another whiff of his thick cologne. It smelled of spice, and though Juliet wasn't a fan of the scent, she found herself growing used to it.

"I'm okay. Thanks." Juliet had had enough of his nearness, and took the moment to escape and walked over to the hostess.

As the hostess led them to their table, Juliet was glad to see they weren't being placed in a booth. She could already imagine Jesse scooting in next to her. Instead they took seats across from each other, in their own chairs.

"So, that mer chick is your best friend, right?" Jesse asked. His confidence irritated Juliet. Or maybe it was the mention of her friend.

"Her name's Myreen, but yeah." Sure, they were still fighting, but Myreen was the only best friend she'd ever had.

"Why does she sleep in the avian wing, anyway? She couldn't handle Trish and her minions?" His laugh grated her nerves.

"Well, she's also part harpy," Juliet said. "Which is why she was allowed to move to the avian wing."

Jesse's confidence slipped into all-out confusion. He rubbed his chin, then scratched the back of his head rapidly. Juliet couldn't help but picture a mangy dog doing the same thing. *Well, he is a hound,* she thought and stifled a laugh.

"No, she's a mer," he said. "I *know* she's a mer. There was some heavy debate on whether the blue tail or the dragon prince would get their hands on those pearly pink scales of hers—"

"That's my friend you're talking about!" Juliet snapped.

Jesse held his hands up in mock-surrender. "Sorry," he mouthed as their waitress appeared. "A cheese pizza and a milkshake to share," he said before the waitress or Juliet could say a word.

"Two straws please," Juliet requested.

The waitress, a pretty blonde with a severe case of acne, nodded and wrote down the order before turning on her heel to leave them to their conversation.

"Well, whatever happened," Jesse continued, "the blue tail couldn't even stay at the school, while I hear things have been getting hot and heavy between her and the prince." He lifted his eyebrows as if suggesting that *they* get *hot and heavy.*

She looked down at the table.

"She's a mer." He just wouldn't drop it.

"She's both," Juliet corrected. "She's a chimera. She's a mer *and* a harpy." It was probably best if she didn't divulge any more. If this stereotypical dumb-jock had his head buried far enough in the sand that he didn't know about Myreen's harpy nature, she should probably leave it that way.

He whistled low. "I didn't know that was possible. Damn! No wonder Dracul finally decided to settle down. Can you imagine how that girl would be in be—?"

"Stop right there," Juliet said firmly, her teeth gritted.

"Again, that's my *friend* you're talking about."

Fortunately, he finally took the hint and dropped the subject. Which was smart if he wanted to keep his pretty face free of burn scars.

They ate the entirety of the pizza and ordered another milkshake—there was only one incident of him trying to spoon-feed it to her, which she slapped away on impulse. She realized that Jesse could be smart and funny—when he wasn't using his kraken tentacles.

As they waited for the check, she was surprised he picked it up. She'd assumed he would make her pay, since he'd made her pick the place. The date was proving to be a roller coaster.

But him paying brought her hopes back up. Maybe he wasn't all that bad.

Then again, the date wasn't over.

On the cold walk to the train station, he kept true to his lack of personal space. Juliet wasn't complaining because of the cold, only, she might have given him the wrong impression.

"When we get back to the Dome, why don't we continue this date somewhere a little more private? See if you could make me sweat with something other than that fire of yours."

Juliet wanted to smack the smirk on Jesse's face right off. "You are a *dog*!"

With a shove, Juliet spun around and stormed off. Surely now Jesse would understand that all she needed from him was distance. Her bed called out to her, beckoning her to finish that Hallmark movie marathon.

But mostly, she wanted to never speak of this date to anyone. Ever.

Why did Myreen have to be right?

Chapter 31

Myreen

After an exhilarating flight with Ms. Heather, Myreen felt like she could conquer the world as she walked back to her dorm.

She couldn't believe how much she loved flying. And the shifting itself was so easy. Not forceful and agonizing like mer shifting sometimes was. Letting her tail out was different from unfurling her wings. With her tail, bones had to break and fuse together. That wasn't the case with her wings. It was almost like they were always there, just hiding in shrunken form between her shoulder blades. If anything, letting them out was a relief, and gave her more balance.

If she could, she'd have them out all the time, but that might anger a few students—especially the mer.

When she entered the avian common room, Kol and Brett were hard at work killing zombies. That made her smile, seeing Kol having fun rather than spending all his spare time pushing himself to his limits in the sim room. Kol acted like such a man that he—and many others—often forgot he was still a teenager. It was nice to see that side of him come out.

She walked behind the couch where they sat without interrupting, wanting Kol to savor his video-gaming. She had a paper to write on extinct shifters, anyway, for which she'd chosen alicorns. She didn't know the first thing about them, just that they were a unicorn with wings and were pretty. That had to be better than krakens or wendigos.

As she approached Juliet's room, she resigned not to look inside or acknowledge Juliet at all. She hated that they were fighting, but Juliet was acting so stupid, and all over a guy she had only technically dated for like a week. Myreen didn't want to get into that right now.

But as she passed by the door, she heard the soft yet distinct sound of crying.

Oh no.

Unable to do otherwise, Myreen stopped and took a step back. Juliet's door was open a crack, and Myreen nudged it enough to see Juliet sitting on her bed with her face in her hands.

Instantly concerned, Myreen pushed through the door. "Juliet?"

At the sound of Myreen's voice, Juliet turned her whole body away and began wiping the tears from her face with her hands. Juliet really hated for anyone to see her vulnerable, even Myreen.

"I'm fine," Juliet barked with a sniffle.

Myreen ignored the wall Juliet had put up and sat on the bed beside her. "No, you're not. You're crying. Did that hound hurt you? 'Cause if he did, I swear I'll—"

"No, he didn't do anything like that." Juliet shook her head. "And if he had, you wouldn't have to come to my defense right now, because he'd be ashes."

Relief flooded through her. Juliet may be a firecracker, but she was still a girl with a gentle heart. If her rebound guy did anything to betray it, Myreen would have parted the seas to make certain he'd regret it.

"Just so we're clear, you didn't burn him, did you?" Myreen felt she had to ask.

Juliet gave a sardonic chuckle. "No. He's unscathed."

"Good. So then, why are you upset?"

Juliet turned and looked at Myreen. "Because you were right. I shouldn't have gone out with Jesse. The whole thing just felt wrong, like I was somehow betraying Nik. And I know you hate hearing about him, but he's just... a hard guy to get over."

Myreen put her hand on Juliet's back and slowly began to rub up and down. "I'm sorry for being such a... *mer* about the whole Nik thing. I was just so conflicted about Kol's unrighteous anger that I didn't want to hear about anyone else's relationship woes. But that's no excuse. I should have been a better friend to you. I should have listened."

"I'm sorry, too! I really do talk about Nik a lot. And I shouldn't have gotten so pissed when you told me about you and Kol. You guys deserve to be happy, even if Nik and I don't work out."

"Thanks I shouldn't have bragged about it like that."

"I don't know. Getting the Dragon Prince to finally commit to a girl is a pretty epic feat." Juliet's tear-streaked cheeks scrunched in a laugh. "How's that going?"

"Um, pretty good, I think." Myreen bit her lip, thinking

about all the make-out sessions they'd shared the past few days.

"Good. I'm glad you're happy."

Myreen smiled. "So, friends again?"

"No. Best friends."

They wrapped their arms around each other in a long hug.

"Let's never fight again, okay?" Myreen said, still squeezing Juliet. "Christmas would've really sucked without you."

Juliet looked over her shoulder, then back at Myreen with a smile. "You know, I actually have a present for you. I bought it before our fight."

Then she hopped off the bed, slid open the closet and knelt to pick something up. She returned to the bed with a plastic shopping bag holding a mystery item and handed it to Myreen.

"I didn't wrap it because... well, you know," Juliet said. "Go ahead, pull it out."

Myreen spread the thin white plastic and pulled a bundle of blue fabric out. She unfolded it, revealing a t-shirt with Ariel from The Little Mermaid on it and text reading *Part of your world.* At the same time, she and Juliet burst out laughing.

"I saw this and instantly thought of you," Juliet said.

"I love it! Thank you." Myreen frowned. "I got you something, too! Hold on." Holding up her index finger, she scampered to her room and found the gift she'd bought for Juliet when they went shopping on Black Friday. The box was wrapped in plain brown paper, which she'd had done at the store so Juliet wouldn't see it. She took it back to Juliet's room and handed it to her.

With typical Juliet vigor, she tore off the paper and her eyes widened, her mouth forming an O.

"Wireless soundproof headphones!" Juliet exclaimed.

"I know the wires always get in the way when you're working out," Myreen said. "And this way you can cancel outside noise without having to blast your music."

"Thank you!" Juliet said, cradling her new headphones like they were a cuddly teddy bear. "You shouldn't have, but thank you!"

Myreen laughed. Juliet was always insisting on paying for stuff, even though Delphine had set up a small discretionary fund for Myreen. And though the gifts Myreen had bought took a bit of a hit from her account, it wasn't like she needed much, thanks to her schooling at the Dome. Besides, seeing the look on Juliet's face now, it was worth it. She got a flutter in her stomach just thinking about Kol's gift. She hoped he'd have a similar reaction to Juliet's, even though he'd probably be more stoic about it.

"So the hound you went out with..." Myreen began.

"Jesse," Juliet clarified.

"Right. Do you think you're going to see him again?"

Juliet shook her head. "Not likely."

"Was the date that bad?"

Juliet shrugged. "I don't know. It just felt weird."

"Because you felt like you were cheating on Nik," Myreen supplied.

Juliet nodded. "I know. It's stupid."

"Well, maybe you should keep seeing Jesse, I mean, if you like him okay," Myreen suggested. "Or date anyone. It might help you get over Nik. You might find a guy you like even better, and one who won't end things after a week."

"Maybe you're right. Maybe I should give this another try. It can't possibly go any worse a second time." Juliet sighed.

"Okay, enough talk about boys and apologies. Let's go kick Kol and Brett off the TV and put on a chick flick."

"That sounds wonderful."

Juliet snappily booted the guys off their game while Myreen floated in relief at having her best friend back. Sure, she'd had other plans for this night, but right now, nothing was more important than spending some quality time with Juliet. Her paper could wait.

Kenzie

"How's it going in there?" Adam asked, rapping on the dressing room door.

Kenzie was fighting with another shirt, the knit fabric squeezing like one of those Chinese finger traps. "Almost done," she called back. She grunted as the shirt finally popped off, and she threw it on the bench built into the alcove.

"Let me know if you want any help," Adam said. He must have been smiling wide, because it was practically audible.

Kenzie rolled her eyes, though she was definitely grinning. "You wish." It seemed the only way to stay out of trouble was to flirt with it. And she was definitely flirting.

This was their third store, the first two not really having anything that appealed to her. And it wasn't like the stores were clumped together, either. But she was having fun with Adam, their banter filling her mind until it chased away all the rest of the worries in her life. Kenzie liked that about him... a lot.

She threw on a turquoise shirt from the approved pile, not wanting to put her ruined sweater back on, and opened the door. Adam's attention was buried in his phone, but as soon as he heard the door, his gaze slid up.

"You look hot."

Kenzie flipped her hair over her shoulder. "What gave it away? The flushed cheeks?"

Adam stalked toward her, shaking his head as he slipped his phone into his pocket. "You, little miss, are a tease."

Kenzie raised her chin to keep her gaze pinned on him. His nearly-a-foot difference in height was always more noticeable when he was standing close. And right now, he was very close, his cinnamon breath tickling her nose. "Only because you, dear sir, are a wolf."

Adam snapped his jaw playfully, and Kenzie squealed. "Find everything you want?" His eyes searched hers, his brow quirking.

Kenzie took a shallow breath, her tongue darting out to moisten her lips. His eyes tracked her movements, his grin growing wider. She gently pushed him away and began gathering her stuff, shoving the pile of rejected clothing at Adam. "Here, hang these up."

Adam looked at her over the mountain of clothing, chuckling. "What did you actually choose?"

Kenzie pulled her lips in and shook her head. "Not until you get those clothes up."

Adam regarded her for a long moment, then went to the rack standing outside the changing area and began putting everything on it. Kenzie grabbed the three other shirts and her bag, then stood behind Adam, tapping her foot.

When he was finished, Adam clapped his hands together and pivoted to face Kenzie. "So, what am I buying?"

Kenzie chuckled. "Besides what I'm currently wearing, I've got this one," she said, holding up the purple knit she'd chosen. "And there's this one." She shuffled through the hangers, pulling up a red sweater with gems and sequins woven into the design. "And finally, there's this." The last hanger held a gold sequin shirt, which changed to a hot pink color depending on which way the sequins lay. "It's not a sweater, but I like it."

"Me too," Adam said, his brows flaring. "You should wear it."

Kenzie shook her head, amusement tugging at her lips. "It's far too cold today for this shirt."

"I'd be happy to keep you warm."

Kenzie's mind raced, and her cheeks flushed. She really was playing with fire with this guy, but not even the fear of getting burned could convince her to stop. For now. "Come on. Let's check out with these. I need to get home."

"What's the hurry? You haven't even found a dress yet."

"It's time to wrap it up," the store clerk said from across the floor, an elderly woman whose girth made her look cuddly and soft. "I'm getting ready to close down."

"Well, there's that," Kenzie said to Adam, casting a worried glance at the storefront. She hadn't realized how much time they'd spent together. "Wait, what time is it?" She reached for her phone, but Adam got to his first.

"A little after four."

"What? Let me see that."

Adam turned his phone around, and she stared at the mocking numbers, marking it as 4:08 in the afternoon. The sun would be setting soon. She was in so much trouble.

"Aw, fudgesicles. Come on." She looped her arm around Adam's and dragged him to the counter. Plopping the shirts down, she threw her thumb at Adam. "He's paying."

The woman nodded and began ringing everything up, including the shirt she was still wearing. She rattled off the total as she carefully folded the shirts and bagged them, and Adam handed over a card.

Kenzie looked at the window again, her foot tapping, her fingers beating a rhythm against her thigh. The Christmas display across the street was glowing in the darkened shade of the buildings, but it did nothing to warm her beating heart. This was taking too long, and she was already late. She'd need to send her mom a text, and soon.

The clerk wished them a Merry Christmas, and Kenzie gave her a quick smile before darting for the door. Halfway there she realized she'd forgotten to grab the bag, and turned back, but Adam was sauntering her way, swinging her purchases from two fingers.

Kenzie ducked out of the store and waited for Adam to follow. The clerk was just behind him, and as soon as he was out, she pulled the door closed and locked it.

Kenzie angled toward the L, expecting Adam to follow. After a moment, she turned to find him lagging behind. She hurried back to him and made to snatch her bag, but Adam held it above his head, just out of her reach.

"Hey! You bought those for me, remember?" She put her hand on her hips, putting on her best angry face.

Adam laughed. "And I think it's only fair I get to see them all on you."

Kenzie screwed up her lips as she tried to swallow her amusement. "Set up a proper date or two and you might."

Adam sucked in a breath in mock pain. "Oooh, is that a challenge?"

"Only if you find it challenge-*ing*."

"I should kiss you." He stepped toward her, his towering height making her turn her chin up to meet his gaze. Her heart hammered, both in pleasure and panic. She almost wished he'd make good on his threat.

"No," Kenzie said at last, stepping back but not lowering her chin. "You should give me my bag so I can go." Part of her wanted to continue their banter, but a bigger part was screaming that it was time to go home. And she still needed to send that text. Kenzie cast a worried glance at the last hints of pink peeking through the skyscrapers.

"I think I'd rather kiss you." Adam took another step forward and leaned in, but Kenzie pressed two fingers to his mouth.

"Then set up a date," she whispered. She spun on her heel and marched off.

"What about your shirts?" Adam called after her.

Kenzie gave him the one-finger-salute and kept walking, her hips sashaying to the sound of his laughter. She had what she needed for now. And Adam would be back, she was certain of it.

When she turned a corner and out of Adam's sight, she broke into a sprint, looking for the nearest L platform. A train decked-out with twinkling lights, Christmas trees, and Santa's sleigh, barreled past on the L above, broadcasting merry holiday tunes. On any other Christmas Eve, she'd be delighted to see the Holiday Train, but worry and hurry had her looking beyond it.

She spotted the accompanying platform and slowed, pulling her phone from her pocket. Twilight was gathering in husky blues, and her heart hammered against her chest as she sent a text to her mom, saying she was going to be late. Hopefully that little bit of forewarning and the magic of Christmas would ensure she got off easy.

She slipped her phone back into her pocket and took off again, but a force slammed into her, sending her sprawling and knocking the wind out of her. Hand to her head, she tried to steady her vision, searching for the source of her collision.

What she saw sent ice through her already-chilled body.

The pale face smiling down on her bore a wicked grin—one that didn't bring the same happy flips that Adam usually caused. Two sharp teeth glinted in the yellow glow of the streetlamp, dark hair styled into boyband perfection. But it was the eyes, with their red sinister glow, that turned Kenzie's mouth to dust.

The vampire took a deep breath, reveling in Kenzie's helplessness. "Ah, a selkie," he said, his voice carrying a heavy accent. Australian, if she had to guess. "I haven't run across one of your kind in a while. I hear magic makes the blood exceptionally sweet."

"Wouldn't you rather have a shrimp on the barbie?" Kenzie asked, trying to buy herself some time. That was something Australians said, right?

"You look like a shrimp, and I'd be happy to call you Barbie." His sinister sneer grew wider.

Kenzie's breath came in hurried puffs, the light playing off the escaping steam. She had to get out, away from this red-eyed creep. She needed to use her magic, but the words escaped her.

I'm going to die.

Something caught the attention of the vampire, whose head snapped in the direction of whatever he'd sensed. Kenzie stumbled to her feet, tried to run, but the man cornering her was faster and stronger than she could ever hope to be. He wrapped her in a bear hug after barely a step, pinning her arms to her side and hampering her frantic breaths.

"Mmm. Fast food," he said, then clamped down on her neck.

Kenzie screamed, flailing against the pain spiking in her neck. She kicked and squirmed, but his icy limbs were like rocks, locking her in place. And her terror was just feeding him faster.

As he continued to draw her blood, a silky coolness filled her veins. A kind of lull dampened her mind, and she stopped struggling. She needed to escape, but why? This was nice, luxuriant, intoxicating. A shuddering sigh escaped her lips, and the strong arms hugging her loosened. Why had she thought his smile so different from Adam's? They were the same—dark, sexy, and with just the right promise of danger.

But the welcome lips at her neck produced a pulling sensation that sparked a memory, a frantic hammering just on the edge of her mind, screaming this was wrong. It all felt so distant. Still, they shouted a series of sounds at her that her lips ached to produce.

"Fiáscha na olch," she started in a whisper. Warmth slid through her, fighting off the ice sloshing through her veins. The draining feeling in her neck slowed, then stopped, but her eyelids were still so heavy. "Tóggo boggé na folía," she continued between shallow breaths. "Diúltódha darsha-a-ahhh." The final word slurred, and the strong arm holding her upright let go.

She fell to the ground, an unwelcome coldness chilling her legs, her hands, her face. Her body took to coughing, and she pulled her knees to her chest to try to fight against the pain blossoming there. A stinging in her neck brought a hand to clamp over it, something warm and sticky coating her fingers. Kenzie scrunched her face.

Where had that mysterious man gone and why had he let her go? A chime rang from near her leg. "Go away," she moaned, her frown deepening.

"What the blooming—?" came a voice that sent a shiver down Kenzie's spine, cut off by a loud bang.

I'm in danger.

Loud thumping approaching from one side, while a whispered breeze left a vacuum behind her. Kenzie tried to push herself up, but her jelly limbs were slow to respond, even in her renewed terror. She looked up, wide-eyed, as a dark form swam into view, clamping a hand over her mouth as she opened it to scream.

"No, Kenzie, it's me. Wes."

Wes. Wes was good. Not as good as the Adam-Man, but good enough. She could see Wes now, his granola face ringed by his granola hair, a granola light behind his head. Kenzie reached for his cheek, but frowned when her fingers came away red. Was he hurt?

"Kenzie. Are you okay? Kenzie!"

"Immafine," she mumbled, her head lolling back.

"Kenzie, hang in there. You're gonna be okay. Please, be okay." Wes swore as his strong, warm arms cradled her. She tried to speak, to tell him about her Adam-Man and Christmas and sweaters and mom, but the words slurred and muffled against his firm chest. His granola scent was the last thing she took in before darkness claimed her.

Leif

Leif sat in the chair he'd held onto from the Frost Boarding house, the old, familiar wood of its arms surfacing memories of a happier Christmas over one hundred years before—one spent amid the company of his non-blood sister, Camilla, her parents, and even the Fullers and their high-energy children.

"This *has* to be the worst Christmas I've ever had," Piper said, pulling him away from his memory-indulgence. She sat cross-legged on her mattress in front of the fireplace, her fingers outstretched to gather warmth from the licking flames, her back to him. "No tree, no presents, not even *music*!"

"I could play you a tune on the piano, if you'd like," Leif offered.

She turned and regarded him hopefully. "That would actually be wonderful."

Leif stood and walked to his baby grand piano. Its typical

black sheen was muted by a layer of dust; he'd fallen behind on the upkeep he usually had plenty of time for in the past. Ever since rejoining the vampires at Heritage Prep, his apartment had fallen into disarray. The accumulation of not one, but two cats hadn't helped with the cleanliness of the place, either. In the closet near the door, he heard their melodious meowing, and Leif wondered if they were *trying* to harmonize.

Shrugging it off and stretching his fingers as he sat, he said, "Name your favorite Christmas song."

"Okay, but don't laugh," Piper replied.

Leif chuckled as his fingers began to play *Christmastime is Here*, skating across the keys like ice skaters on a frozen pond.

"I like that one," Piper said, getting to her feet and moving next to him, leaning against the piano. "My favorites are the jazzy ones, though. You know, like *Jingle Bell Rock* and *Rockin' Around the Christmas Tree.*"

Leif nodded as he continued to play. "Those are great ones," he said. He finished playing the first verse of his song, then moved into *Rockin' Around the Christmas Tree.*

Piper began to sway her hips and bob her head back and forth and she closed her eyes. Leif couldn't help but smile.

"Yes," she said. "Now this is more like it. Now, if only we had a Christmas tree to rock around."

"Can't help you there," said Leif. He had no desire to put one up, especially *on* Christmas Day.

Piper paused for a moment and held up a finger as he continued playing. "Do you hear that?"

Leif played a little softer and listened for what Piper had heard. From the closet where his vampire cats were stowed away he could hear mewing—but not just any mewing. The two cats were harmonizing perfectly to the song he played.

Leif stopped playing and laughed.

"Leif, you can't tell me that's normal behavior for cats," Piper said.

"You're right," he said as he stood and walked toward the closet. "Rainbow and Goldie are far from normal, but they're one of a kind."

"*Two* of a kind, you mean," she corrected.

Leif ignored her as he reached for the door handle. "I used to hate cats, but these ones... well, I can't help but feel like I'm a part of them."

"They're crazy," Piper said. "I don't know why you've taken a liking to them. Did you know their eyes have turned completely red? I think it's from the amount of blood they've been drinking. But they don't glow like the eyes of hungry vampires do."

The cats *had* been consuming a fair portion of his blood bag stash, but that was normal for newer vampires.

"How does a cat even become a vampire in the first place?" she asked, narrowing her eyes at him.

Leif ignored Piper's question. He hadn't taken the time to explain to his Initiate that—using his own life force, and with the help of a selkie witch—Rainbow had been brought back from the dead. Opening that particular door would lead to a conversation about Gemma, and he wasn't ready to talk to Piper about his deceased soul-mate.

Opening the closet door, the gray-and-white shorthair and the tabby sprang out and rubbed the lengths of their bodies against Leif's leg. Rainbow purred at his typical middle-C pitch, and Goldie harmonized a fifth up.

Crouching low, Leif petted his furry friends, one with each hand. It sounded like they were ready to burst into song. Seriously, what wasn't there to love about these cats? They were far better than the typical feline.

Indeed, their eyes looked blood-red, but Leif didn't feel as if it made them appear demonic. They were different in an endearing way.

"They give me the creeps," Piper muttered as she folded her arms.

To this, the ears of both cats pointed backwards, and they hissed at the Initiate. Leif kept a hand on each of their backs, noticing their fur rising.

"How about we *don't* insult the kitties?" Leif suggested softly.

Before he could react, Goldie bolted like a lion sprinting to an antelope. Except an antelope would have at least tried to get away. Piper stood frozen in place by the piano, her eyes and mouth widening in perfect synchronicity.

Leif watched in horror as Goldie pounced at Piper. He never considered that the vampire cats might have inherited enhanced strength, but that was confirmed as the impact of the cat sent Piper crashing against the baby grand. One of Piper's elbows slammed into several keys as she fell.

Goldie had latched her paws into the thick sweatshirt Piper wore, and she went tumbling along with the shrieking young woman.

Piper sprawled on her back as she landed on the floor, then screamed in pain as Goldie lunged for her neck.

"It's biting me!" she cried, trying to tear Goldie away. "Get it off!"

Leif ran to Piper's side and slung an arm under the attacking cat, feeling Goldie's tight, coiled muscles. He pulled gently at first, but the cat had sunk its claws deeper into Piper—past her clothing. And the cat didn't budge. He threw Rainbow a look just to make sure he didn't jump into the fray, and found him sitting on his hind-end, watching them with humored interest.

Pulling harder, Goldie still didn't yield, and the attempt only increased Piper's screaming. It also increased the cat's wildness.

Piper squirmed and cried, begging the cat to stop. Blood soaked through her sweatshirt. The smell was fresh and warm, and it called to him—tempted him. He gritted his teeth, ignoring it just as he'd forced himself to do so many times in the past.

At last, he resigned himself. Goldie wasn't about to stop.

"Don't watch this, if you can help it," Leif yelled above the screams, not knowing if Piper had the capacity to even try to hear him at this point. Reaching a hand up, he grabbed Goldie by the neck, closed his own eyes and set his jaws, then twisted and pulled with all his vampire strength. Ignoring the sickening sounds that followed, he felt Goldie's body go limp, her claws retracting in the process.

Piper jumped to her feet, holding a hand to her neck. She teetered for a few moments, and Leif dropped the two parts of Goldie to help stabilize his Initiate. He noticed that her glasses had fallen off, and there were several cuts along her face and chin.

Through painful sobs, she said, "I *told* you those cats aren't normal. That monster was drinking my blood!"

The mere mention of blood caused Leif to lick his lips

subconsciously, but he caught himself. He hated this curse—was disgusted by his need for blood.

"Let's get you cleaned up," he said, helping her to the bathroom. Rainbow ran by them and began whining as he approached the lifeless body of Goldie.

"They're vampire cats," she said in a crazed tone. "Nobody has ever told me about vampire animals. None of my classes at Heritage Prep—"

"I... think they're a new thing," he interrupted quickly, not wanting to explain further.

Thankfully, a knock sounded at the door.

"I'd better go get that," he said. "I'll just close the bathroom door and let you take care of yourself. I'm afraid I don't have any bandages, but there are towels under the sink."

He heard Piper curse under her breath as he shut the door, just in time to hear his doorbell ring.

An anxiety he hadn't had time to think about crawled up his spine. Who had come knocking? *Nobody* ever came to his door, especially not on Christmas. In fact, this was the first Christmas in a long time he'd had *any* company. What if the hunter who'd attacked him four days prior had managed to track him back to his apartment?

He bent over to look through the peephole in the door and relief washed over him. It was the concierge... holding a present?

Hesitantly, Leif opened the door and poked his head out.

"Hello there," Leif said, eyeing the man. "Can I help you?"

The concierge bowed, then handed Leif the holiday bag that was decked out in silver and gold with white snowflakes all around. "Merry Christmas, sir. A young woman stopped in yesterday and asked that I bring you this gift. Unfortunately, with the holidays on my mind and family commitments, I forgot to bring it to you before I left for home last night."

Kenzie, Leif immediately thought. There was only one young woman who'd have the audacity to give him a gift—like a certain t-shirt with a kitten and a rainbow on it that had somehow managed to make its way into his closet.

Leif accepted the bag and tipped his head forward. "Thank you, and Merry Christmas."

The concierge smiled and nodded, then turned away. Leif quickly shut the door.

Sure enough, there was a tag attached to the handle, and on it was written a single letter—a *K* with curly ends where each stroke ended.

"Who was at the door?" Piper asked from the bathroom.

Leif rifled through the bag quickly and discovered a piano solo book entitled *Pop Your Socks Off*, complete with arrangements of the top Pop hits from the past ten years.

He shook his head and mumbled, "Kenzie."

"Who?" Piper asked. "I couldn't hear you."

Leif cleared his throat. "That was just the concierge dropping off some... sheet music I ordered."

"On Christmas Day?" Piper asked, opening the bathroom door. Leif quickly turned away in embarrassment. She'd removed her shirt to take care of the cuts underneath, and was wearing a white sports bra. "Hey, that's not a package. That's a present!"

Leif fumbled with the bag, spilling the rest of the contents onto the hardwood floor. He was mortified at the two items that had fallen. Their colorful packaging bolded the brand *Cat Capes* with a real selling one-liner on it: *Add sophistication to your feline friend!*

Rubbing at his forehead, he chanced a look at Piper.

"Cat Capes?" she read. "Leif... who else knows about your cats?"

Struggling to force down a swallow, he jumped as another knock sounded at the door.

"Back into the bathroom," he said, rushing to her side. The cuts along her skin had somehow shut, and then he noticed a small container of superglue on his counter. It seemed like a smart move, and suddenly, gluey-blood sounded absolutely repulsive.

"Are you expecting someone else?" Piper asked, entering the bathroom with a little push from Leif on the back.

He shook his head. "This might come as a surprise, but no, I don't really come to expect anyone. Anytime."

A deafening boom sounded at the entrance, and the metal hinges holding the wooden door in three places popped. The door teetered inward, then came crashing down.

Piper screamed from the bathroom, watching in terror.

In the doorway stood a vampire Leif hadn't seen since the destruction of the shifter school on Framboise Island fifteen years ago.

"Solomon?" Leif said softly. It was late morning, which meant the vampire had been within the large apartment complex at least since sunrise.

Solomon's eyes were red, revealing his thirst. His short, dark hair was messy, as if he'd just been through a scuffle of sorts.

"You're in trouble, mate," the Australian vampire said, stepping inside, on top of the door he'd just knocked down.

Leif straightened his back and side-glanced at Piper.

Solomon followed his gaze and saw the Initiate with her fresh wounds.

Solomon snickered. "Looks like you've been having a bit of fun on Christmas, Leif."

Piper grabbed the crimson towel she'd been using to staunch her bleeding from the wounds Goldie had inflicted, and quickly wrapped it around herself, covering up her skin. Leif knew the bloodied towel would only attract the thirsty vampire that much more.

"What are you doing here, Solomon?" Leif moved protectively toward Piper. He didn't trust the other vampire around her, not with his eyes glowing red.

Solomon's face formed into a wicked snarl. "Cleaning up a small mess for Draven."

Leif stood his ground, putting on the show he'd gotten quite used to displaying since Oberon had asked him to get involved with the vampires again.

"What mess?" he asked.

Solomon took a few more steps forward. "You think we're a bunch of drongos? You go crying to Draven on the telephone, saying hunters are trying to kill you at the subway station. That sounds mighty convenient, considering your mission, mate. How'd the hunters find you? And what about the selkie girl you've been visiting? Meeting up in a hotel with her, right? She must make for some fun play. But she didn't play so nicely with me."

Leif froze. Solomon had gotten to Kenzie? What had he done to her? Was she okay? His mind raced as he pictured her lying on the street somewhere, dead eyes staring into the sky, body drained of blood. How much did Solomon know? What had he reported to Draven? Was he here on Draven's orders?

"What's he talking about, Leif?" Piper asked, her voice quaking.

Leif didn't reply, but took a defensive stance as Solomon continued approaching.

"My rank and status at Heritage Prep is about to skyrocket," Solomon said, a smug expression forming on his face. "Oh, the rewards I'll receive for bringing Draven the pitiful head of the infamous Leif Villers, traitor to his own kind."

The threat bounced off Leif like Vancouver raindrops off an umbrella.

"I think I'll keep my head, *mate*," replied Leif.

Faster than a hunter's gunshot, Solomon reached with both arms for Leif's neck, attempting a death strike. But Leif had been taught by one of the greatest combat specialists: Beatrice Morton. With ease, he smacked the underparts of Solomon's wrists with his own arms, then counter-attacked with a fist to the other vampire's chest.

Such a punch would have crunched the ribcage of a human, but all it did was push Solomon back a few steps.

"Still as quick as ever, old man," Solomon mocked.

If the Aussie thought he'd be able to win the fight with insults, he had another thing coming. It took a lot more than that to get under Leif's skin.

Solomon jabbed a far-reaching kick that Leif blocked with his wrist.

"If you manage to land one blow before you run away, I'll consider this a loss," Leif said, shoving some trash-talk at Solomon. The other vampire was far more likely to lose control, based on the fact that he was thirsty.

Solomon growled and threw a flurry of punches his way, which Leif simply evaded.

"Nobody will be running away today," Solomon barked. "And after I'm done with you, I'll have my way with your Initiate, too. She's as guilty as you are."

Leif could handle threats when they were aimed at him, but he couldn't ignore such things when they targeted those he protected.

"Then let's get to that part where you're done with me, shall we?" Leif put his hand forward and urging Solomon to come at him.

"With pleasure," the other vampire said, grinning wickedly.

Solomon feigned a right-handed punch, and Leif took the bait. In the same motion, the other vampire spun and stretched his leg forward, striking Leif in the shins and throwing him off balance. But Leif knew this attack method from his own training, and as soon as he hit the floor, he rolled to his left. Solomon's knee landed right where his neck would have been, snapping the floorboards like they were twigs.

Lashing out with his own foot, Leif kicked Solomon in the face with such force that terrible popping sounds came from the vampire's neck as it whipped backward. A second later, the same sickly sounds popped again as his body repaired itself.

Solomon set his sights on Leif with such fiery fury, Leif knew he was on the verge of losing complete control. At that point, he'd be vulnerable. Keeping things together in a fight was crucial, especially when a vampire was fighting another vampire. Unbridled attacks were rarely timely or efficient.

"You must be pretty low in status these days," Leif said, keeping his fists in the air. "Banking on such a high-end target as me? Sounds like desperation."

And that did it.

Solomon yelled with rage as he charged Leif. Before the other vampire could smash his shoulder into him, Leif sidestepped, smacking Solomon in the back of the head as he went by. But what Leif hadn't expected was Solomon grabbing Leif by the legs as he sprawled, causing Leif to lose his balance, too. Solomon was on top of him in an instant, pummeling his face over and over again.

Leif brought his hands up to protect his face and to try to gain some sort of advantage on the other vampire, but the strikes were coming in too fast and too hard. He found it was getting harder and harder to think of ways to get away.

Solomon took advantage of Leif's confusion and wrapped his firm hands around his neck, sending stars through Leif's vision. All Leif could think about was the day of continuous drowning in Draven's madness chamber.

Suffocation.

But this time, he didn't have the coolness of water to soothe his aching lungs. The suffocation would bring on unconsciousness, and then Solomon would tear his head from his shoulders.

So this was how it was going to end. Not at the hands of Draven, but one of his lackeys.

Gemma, I tried.

Yes, this was how he was meant to die—thinking of Gemma, her porcelain face, her fiery hair, and her emerald eyes.

I'll be with you again soon.

And then the strangling stopped, and a sickening gurgle came from Solomon's mouth. Leif's blurred eyes slowly came into focus and he saw something sharp protruding from his attacker's chest. Behind Solomon was a trembling Piper, holding the attacker steady.

Solomon stared down at the tip of the copper knife that had stabbed him through his heart, then brought his harrowed gaze back to Leif. The gurgling stopped and Solomon's eyes went distant.

Coughing, Leif felt his body rejuvenate, healing from the damage Solomon had done. Quickly, he pushed the vampire to the side before the coppery point jutting from Solomon could stab him, too.

"Piper!" he said in surprise, finding her staring at the dead vampire on the floor of his apartment.

She looked at him with tearful eyes, then slowly melted to the floor and wept.

"You saved me," he said, running to her side and throwing an arm around her.

"I had to," she wailed. "You saved me a few days ago."

Leif looked at her in confusion. Why was she crying? Had killing a vampire who'd threatened to do terrible things to her been too much for Piper?

"Hey, it's going to be okay," he comforted.

She shook her head slowly, sobbing heavily. "They'll never let me become a vampire now."

And that was it. By killing Solomon, she'd thrown out her opportunity. But that was only if Draven found out what happened.

"But you didn't kill Solomon," Leif said, and she gave him a questioning look. "Hunters have increased their scouting in Chicago, remember? They were the ones who killed him."

"I'm a terrible liar," she said, sniffling.

"So am I," replied Leif, rubbing her towel-covered shoulder. "But we'll make it through. Where'd you get that knife from, anyway?"

Piper looked at her hands. "I'm a human living among vampires. After I saw the danger on the streets with the hunter, I realized I should take my mortality a little more seriously. So I stashed a knife... just in case."

Leif nodded. It made sense, although it was a little disturbing that she'd chosen a copper knife, of all things.

She snorted.

"What?"

She looked at him. "You know what the funniest part about this is?"

"What's that?"

She looked down. "After having gone through what I've been through the past two weeks, I don't know if I want to become a vampire anymore."

It was music to Leif's ears. But with Draven around, she'd never be free. If Myreen could fulfill the prophecy, then maybe she'd have a shot.

"You've been through a lot," he said. "And I know this Christmas has only gotten worse for you. But after saving me, you've made my Christmas pretty fantastic."

She chuckled, and so did he.

Kenzie

Kenzie groaned, lifting a hand to her pounding head. Everything was fuzzy. She wanted to roll over and go back to sleep, but there was no more bed to roll onto. And the shape was all wrong. Frowning, she sent a hand out to feel around. Couch. She was on a couch, but as she cracked her eyes open, the room that came into view wasn't her own living room.

She sucked in a breath as she bolted upright, but groaned again as the room set to spinning. Her stomach did flip-flops, and she leaned against the armrest, trying to gain her bearings.

"Kenzie?" Wes's golden honey scent preceded him, and he was kneeling next to her in a matter of moments, smoothing back her hair.

Kenzie blushed, wiping at a damp spot on her chin, wondering just how much of a nest her hair was in at the moment. "What happened?" she croaked. She cleared her throat, then swallowed.

"What do you remember?" Wes's eyes clouded as he watched her, his hand finding hers.

"I—" *I what?* She'd come to Chicago to deliver presents. And afterward she'd run into Adam... Had he roofied her? But no, she was with Wes, not Adam. The jackhammer digging at her brain made it hard to think, and she wanted to close her eyes again and slip into blissful sleep.

Wes opened his mouth, then closed it again and swallowed, rubbing the back of her hand with his thumb. "What am I thinking? You need to eat and drink something."

Kenzie licked her cracked lips, but she wasn't sure she could eat anything right now. Just thinking about food made her stomach clench.

Wes walked behind her, and she tracked his movements. The apartment was small and simple, not at all the luxurious space Leif had. Everything about Wes's place was as beige and granola as he was. But as curious as she was, the more important question lingering in her mind was how she'd gotten here. Although the small glimpse into one of the rooms down the hall had her a little worried. *Maybe he's just a gun enthusiast?*

An ache lanced her neck, and her hand clamped on the spot, meeting a soft bandage. *Why is there—? The vampire.* The memory of the attack rattled her nerves—the glowing red eyes, the lancing pain at her neck, the animal desire that spread into her from the bite. Cool fear washed over her, and her eyes darted around the apartment. "Where is—?"

"He's gone." Wes bounded over to her, carrying a granola bar and a bottled sports drink. He set them on the end table beside her head, then grabbed her hands again. "You're safe.

You're gonna be okay. I'll make sure of it."

"Did you kill him?"

"No." A small part of her was relieved at his answer—a part that very much scared Kenzie. Wes frowned and turned his head to the side, mumbling, "That's two now."

"Two what?" She reached for the sports drink, and Wes grabbed it and loosened the top before handing it over. She gingerly sipped at the liquid, marveling at the sweetness coating her mouth. She usually hated the sweaty-feet taste of those kinds of drinks.

Wes held out the granola bar, but Kenzie shook her head.

He put it back down, casting his eyes at the floor. "Just, don't worry about it."

"Shouldn't I be in a hospital right now?" She groaned as she clutched her neck again.

"I couldn't risk— You're okay. I checked. The light—" Wes sighed. "You're okay."

Kenzie slowly scooched up straighter, trying not to trigger another dizzy spell. Her body ached in places she'd never noticed before, and her head still buzzed angrily at her. "Wes, do you know what attacked me?"

Wes stood and turned away from her, locking his hands behind his neck. He paced around the room, and she watched him, wondering what secrets he held. He seemed too plain, way too granola to be anything *other*. There wasn't a sinister, non-normal, dangerous bone in the guy. She was certain of it. Right? So why couldn't she shake the growing dread?

"What do you *think* attacked you?" Wes asked, turning to face her.

Kenzie set her mouth in a line, looking him directly in the

eyes. "*I* know. I wanna know if *you* know."

Wes gave her an incredulous look. "Or trick me into telling you something you don't know."

Kenzie folded her arms. "Fine. Then we'll both say it. On the count of three." She lifted her brows.

Wes nodded.

"Okay. One. Two. Three."

"Vampire," the two said in unison.

Wes stopped to regard her. "How did you know?"

"You mean besides the glowing red eyes, the inhuman strength, and the fact that he was *drinking my blood*?"

Wes shrugged. "Chicago has all kinds."

"Not like that," she mumbled. "How do *you* know?"

Wes chewed on the inside of his cheek for a moment, then ran his fingers through his hair. It stuck up in odd places, completing the day-off vibe his t-shirt and sweats were giving her. He looked cute and kinda vulnerable like that. "I'm with a group that protects people like you from monsters like him."

"Hunters." The whispered word barely escaped her lips when Wes's gaze hardened on her.

"How do you know that?"

"Where am I?" Kenzie asked, ignoring his question. She put the drink down, tempted to try the granola bar, but not before she had some answers.

"My apartment. Now answer me! How do you know about vampires and hunters?"

Kenzie folded her arms, wincing at the fresh pain in her neck and back and arms. This was just great. Her mom would—

Mom! Kenzie swore as she reached for her pocket. "My mom is gonna kill me." But her pockets were empty, and she patted them, hoping maybe she'd missed something.

Wes grabbed an object from the end table at her feet and handed it to her. Kenzie took it, recognizing her phone, the screen smashed. She must have landed on it when the vampire knocked her sideways.

"Your mom sent you a text. Told you to stay with Myreen until the sun came back up."

Kenzie sagged back against the couch. What was she going to tell her mom? Citing a vampire attack was sure to get her freedom restricted, and she needed that now more than ever. And she was missing Christmas, no less. What a rotten day this was turning out to be. Her head throbbed in agreement.

A text chimed, and the broken display lit up.

Mom: Please let me know you got this.

But the broken screen prevented Kenzie from replying. It looked like there were a dozen or so more texts, too. "Give me your phone."

Wes grimaced. "Not until you tell me how you know about vampires and hunters."

"Why? So you can play judge and jury? Give me your phone so I can at least tell my mom first."

Wes shook his head, his eyes pleading with her. "I can't help you if I don't know."

Kenzie firmed her chin to keep it from wobbling. After everything she'd encountered in the shifter world, she didn't hold much hope that hunters would be any different. The gun rack visible through the sliver of opened door pulled her gaze again. An ending from him would probably be permanent. Hunters weren't exactly known for their mercy. Her magic wasn't much help at the moment, either. Her fuzzy head couldn't pull up anything useful—and there was little that she knew that was actually useful. She should've studied more, focused on learning more than just resurrection spells.

"You're not a vampire," Wes said, trying to prompt her into answering.

Kenzie shook her head.

"Are you a hunter? A shifter?"

Kenzie kept shaking her head, not looking at him. Wes must have spotted her glancing at the door, because he closed it. "Dang it, Kenzie. I'm not going to hurt you."

"And what if that vampire had turned me? Then what?"

Wes looked away, his head tilted toward the floor.

"So what does it matter what I am? You're a hunter. Anything not *you* is considered a danger."

Wes frowned. "I didn't take you to them, did I? Do you see any other hunters here?"

Kenzie fell silent, staring at her phone in her lap. The broken screen mocked her, and she couldn't help but feel it was now what she'd always been—useless. She closed her eyes, hoping she was making the right choice. Her pounding head wouldn't give her enough peace to try to weigh the pros and cons, but she needed to tell her mom she was okay.

"I'm a selkie," she whispered.

Wes took a step back. "A magic user? I thought... I didn't realize there were any more selkies left."

Kenzie glared at him, her chin attempting to wobble again. "We're not extinct, no thanks to *hunters*."

"Why haven't you used your magic on me?"

"Who says I haven't?"

"You wouldn't..." His brows pulled together, his fingers

knotting together. "There's no such thing as love spells, right?"

Kenzie snorted, but a second after she did so, it hit her. Was Wes saying he loved her? That wasn't even possible. They'd only been on one date. "Even if I had a spell like that, why would I use it?"

Hurt crushed Wes's boyish features. Kenzie looked away. That hadn't come out right, and judging from the look on Wes's face, he'd taken it the wrong way, too. But it wasn't her fault this was all so screwed up. Why did he have to be a hunter, anyway?

She held out her hand. "Your phone?"

Wes regarded her with skepticism.

"To tell my mom I'm okay. You said I could." She curled her fingers several times, then held her hand out again. Wes put the phone in her waiting palm, grimacing.

Kenzie sent out a quick message, saying her phone was broken but she was fine and she'd explain later. Maybe she could come up with something on the way home. She held out the phone for Wes, but he shook his head.

"You might as well keep it. I'll have to burn it anyway."

Kenzie raised her brows. "Why? Because I touched it?"

"No." Wes looked at her for a long moment, as if he expected her to understand, but she didn't have the brain power for puzzles right now. Wes sighed. "Because I don't want them tracing you through me. Here, give me the sim card."

"Oh." Kenzie turned the phone off and began prying off the back panel. She didn't know what kind of information they could glean off a cell phone number, but she didn't want to find out. Who knew if Mom and Gram had a spell to protect them from hunters? She assumed not, since hunters were human.

She got the sim card out and handed it to Wes, who broke

it in half. He might as well have been tearing up the last shreds of their relationship. Kenzie couldn't take any more.

"I should go." She pushed herself into a standing position, but the sudden movement sent her world spinning again. She caught herself on the arm of the couch and waited for the room to stabilize.

Wes was by her side again, his arm around her waist. "Whoa, you lost a lot of blood. You need to rest."

"No, I need to go home." She tried to push Wes away, but her arms shook with the effort, and Wes still held on tight. "My mom is going to kill me."

"Better than vampires."

"Vampires only come out at night."

"Not all of them."

Kenzie's startled gaze riveted to Wes's. Did he know about Leif? "Just the bad ones," she whispered, unable to wipe the shock from her face.

"Kenzie, they're all bad."

Kenzie shoved harder this time, earning a grunt from Wes. "That's the problem with you hunters. You think everything that's different than you is horrible. You kill them without even knowing if they're good or bad."

"You can't just—"

"I can't? If I'd been identified by your organization before you had a chance to get to know me, what would you have done?"

Wes looked away, his silence saying so much more than words could.

Kenzie sniffed. "Exactly."

"But you're different."

Kenzie clenched her teeth. "Not nearly as different as everyone seems to think."

Feeling sturdy enough, Kenzie pushed off Wes again, this time breaking free. She limped a few steps, but she still needed her bag, and she wasn't sure where the exit was. There was a door next to the kitchen that looked right.

"At least let me take you home."

"Why? So you can tell your buddies and shoot me and my family down?"

Wes grimaced. "No. I would never."

A spell she'd found in the grimoire came to mind, a simple one to verify his promise. She turned to Wes, holding a palm toward him. "Fírrineth." The magic tingled through her fingers, a green pinpoint of light hitting Wes in the chest, the color rippling out and then fading. He rubbed the spot, then looked back at her, concern etching his face. Kenzie gave him a half-smile. "There. Now you've been magicked. Tell me you won't rat on me and my family."

"I promise. I won't tell anyone about you, your family, or where you live."

Kenzie nodded. "Good. And tell me you're not in love with me."

Wes's brows scrunched. "Easy. Of course I'm in love with you. Wait. What?"

Well, dang. That backfired. The magic wouldn't let him lie, but at least she knew he wouldn't rat her out. The rest of it she'd deal with later. Maybe.

Her shoulders slumped, and she closed her eyes. "You can take me home."

Wes nodded, his face ashen. "What you did to me... it

won't last, will it?"

Kenzie shrugged. "I don't think so. We can test again when I get home." *And I can verify with my grimoire.* But that was a whole other matter she didn't feel like bringing up.

Wes nodded, then went around a corner. A door opened and shut, and he came back out with her winter gear and backpack. He helped her put it on, apologizing every time she winced. He held out an arm, and she leaned on it one more time.

"You know we can't see each other anymore after this," Kenzie said, her vision going blurry.

Wes nodded, but kept his gaze forward. Kenzie discreetly wiped at her eyes, hoping to erase the evidence before he noticed. She shouldn't be this broken up about a guy she'd only been out with once, one she'd practically ignored ever since she'd begun to imbibe in the dark draw of Adam. His granola must have infected a part of her heart, because she felt it going chewy and crumbly at the thought of never seeing him again.

If only he hadn't been a hunter.

She was getting tired of pulling the short stick.

Kol

Christmas at the Dome was normally quiet. Most students would spend the holiday with their families, the halls and common rooms emptying until the New Year's Eve ball.

This Christmas, it was decidedly *overcrowded.*

With the recent vampire activity, parents had either insisted on their children staying in the safety of school while they remained at home, or they'd covertly entered and intruded on the dorms themselves. Very few students were actually permitted to leave.

Kol hated it.

The avian common room was currently packed with Leya's loud family of harpies. They were a strange bunch, since harpies were normally more... peaceful, living up to their angelic nature. This group whooped and hollered with each present opened, like a bunch of hounds. Why they didn't confine themselves to

Leya's dorm like the other families was beyond him.

The noise—topped with the fact that Kol was avoiding certain dragon and phoenix families who kept trying to get information about how they could either get in or *back* in the good graces of his father—forced Kol to escape from the avian wing altogether. So he'd snuck into the gardens for a moment of peace after downing a stack of pancakes and a handful of brown sugar bacon at breakfast.

Since the Dome had a controlled climate—completely separate from the bitter chill of Chicago—Kol was perfectly comfortable lounging on the faux-snow in a t-shirt and shorts. He was smart enough to have his tablet on him, too, and played the ancient Atari classic, *Asteroids*, to pass the time. He'd pinged Myreen an hour ago to meet him. He wanted to give her the gift that was neatly wrapped and stashed in the bag at his feet.

The fake snow muffled any footsteps, and the fountain he leaned against burbled a happy tune, so he didn't realize that two small boots approach until they stood right next to him.

A small smile emerged. He didn't look up right away and savored the blossoming feeling in his chest. It amazed him that he didn't even need to look at her for the happiness to swell.

She tapped the side of his sneaker with her foot gently.

He looked up expecting to meet those blue eyes he so often found himself drowning in. Instead, she stared at the roof of the Dome. He stood and circled his arms around her. She didn't tear her eyes away, even with the gesture.

"It's so... magical," she said, finally wrapping her arms around him, hugging him back. She lowered her head to meet his eyes.

"Mr. Suzuki," Kol said as if it were explanation enough.

Myreen's eyebrows pinched together.

"Ren?" The professor preferred students to refer to him formally, unlike Oberon, but maybe not Myreen? She seemed to be the exception on many things *shifter,* so he wasn't entirely sure.

But she still looked confused and returned her gaze to the sky. Kol followed suit and watched the ribbons of green and blue dance across the star-filled, black-blue projection.

"It's beautiful." Myreen sighed.

It was. Seeing it through Myreen's eyes really opened his own to beauty in a way he doubted he could ever see alone. After all, he had been sitting underneath this majesty for more than an hour, and only now looked up.

"Northern lights?" she asked, those piercing blue eyes meeting his. Finally.

Kol nodded and pointed. "It's a real-time projection of the North Pole," he explained. "Mr. Suzuki probably rigged it up like that because so many are stuck here for Christmas."

"You think he did it *just* for Christmas?"

"Well... the tech was always there. Mostly it's used to make the Dome disappear if anyone above gets too close, or if word gets out that someone is looking."

"Like a camouflage?"

"Exactly like camouflage." Kol ducked his head to kiss Myreen briefly. "Besides that, it's only used on the first and last days of the school year."

She still smiled in surprise from the kiss. "And what is projected on those days?"

He wanted to kiss her again and make the smile wider, but he also liked having conversations with her—something he never cared for with other girls. Which is probably why Myreen was his first girlfriend. "Stick around long enough, and you'll find out," he teased, then kissed her again.

After a moment they pulled apart and her head snapped right back to the curvature of the Dome. Mesmerized. He couldn't help but feel a little jealous that the sky was getting so much of her attention.

"You said real-time, but it's dark?"

Kol nodded once. "The North Pole won't see the sun again until March. So, real-time."

Myreen smiled and nodded. "Of course. I knew that... it's just different in person." Then she laughed. That bell-ringing, heart-swelling laugh that had grown so dear to him. "You know what I mean."

Suddenly Kol noticed her attire. "You're not... leaving, are you?" Panic built at seeing her donned in her winter clothing, complete with gloves and a hat.

Her cheeks flushed as she swiftly unwrapped the scarf and shrugged off her coat. "There's snow!" she protested with another laugh and waved a still-gloved hand at the very real-looking, fake snow. "What is it, anyway?"

"I dunno," Kol said, a little embarrassed that he *didn't* know. "Another of Mr. Suzuki's creations, I'm sure."

"Well, he should sell it on eBay or something. He'd make a fortune!"

That comment, so mundane and yet so *Myreen*, caused Kol to throw his shoulders back in a booming laugh. "And he'd probably be offended that you even suggested it," he said when he'd finished.

She shrugged like she might suggest it anyway. But when

she looked over Kol's shoulder, glistening tears formed in her eyes. Tearing away from him, Myreen took a few steps toward the grand, ten-foot evergreen decorated elegantly with expensive, round, red and green balls—Kol knew the price tag since they were donated by his mother—LED lights, bells, tinsel and hundreds of tiny, intricately carved and hand-painted figurines of snowmen, Santa Claus, reindeer, candy canes and everything else Christmas or Hanukkah or Kwanzaa or Omisoka or other December holidays Kol could not name, including a small nativity and menorah near the top.

Myreen tentatively stepped toward the tree until she was within arms-length, then reached a hand out and gently touched a small silver bell with a red bow tying it to a low branch. "We had these," she said.

"Hmm?"

"We had these on our tree at home," Myreen clarified. "You know... with my mom."

"Ah." That was enough for Kol to walk up behind her and wrap both arms around her. He rested his chin on the top of her fruity-shampoo-scented, silky hair.

She leaned into him, her hand still cradling the bell, the other reaching up to grip his arm.

"I'm sure this one doesn't even make it in your top five, but this is definitely *my* favorite Christmas to date," he said softly into her hair.

She twisted in his arms until their noses met. "But you're stuck here," she said. "Don't you miss your family?"

To Myreen, it probably felt like an innocent and straightforward question. If Kol's family was anything like Myreen's mother surely was, it would have been. But he also didn't want to discount the fact that his family was alive, while hers was either dead or unknown.

Kol pushed back a few inches so he could see her face. "I miss my mom," he said truthfully. "And my sister, Tatiana, but she hasn't come home for Christmas since she graduated from the academy, anyway."

"But not your father?"

Kol dropped his arms, releasing her. "I respect my father in a lot of ways," he said. "But I dunno... Christmas was always an afterthought to him."

"He still, like, bought you gifts and stuff, right?"

Yeah, like tutoring sessions at age six to push him to shift early, which was his present from ages six through eleven. "Probably only when my mom nagged him about it. After a while she just took over all of the shopping."

"The things a man will do for the woman he loves," Myreen said. Kol noticed a hint of pink in her cheeks when she said it. "But what about your mom?" she said quickly. "Didn't he buy things for her?"

"Yeah?" He didn't mean for it to come out as a question, but after that comment about his father actually loving his mother, he was suddenly out of sorts. He wasn't ready for Myreen to learn about the curse. What he'd said wasn't a lie, his father *had* bought his mother things for holidays and important anniversaries and birthdays—Kol suspected Eduard tasked Tatiana with the job more often than not—but it was never out of love. Only respect. Kol suspected that was why his parents were still together. Because Eduard respected Victoria. That, and he was concerned with appearances. Still... there weren't many Draculs who were divorced. All were aware that the grass wouldn't be greener elsewhere.

"Speaking of," Kol said before Myreen could comment on his question-answer. "I have a gift for you."

"Oh?" Her eyes sparkled with anticipation.

Taking her hand, he led her back to his spot near the fountain where he'd left his bag and tablet. Sitting cross-legged, he patted the space beside him for her to join. He chuckled when she hesitated, probably remembering the *snow* wasn't actually cold.

When she'd settled, Kol's heart thudded at a faster pace. This was new territory for him. His interactions with girls in the past consisted of leading or being led by a girl somewhere secretive for a brief physical moment of kissing. It rarely happened twice with the same girl, if he could help it. And sure, he'd had several of those with Myreen, but this was nerve-wracking, pulling the small gold-wrapped box from his bag and placing it in her waiting palm.

Slowly, she untied the thick red ribbon that had been so adeptly tied by the store clerk and was careful not to create a single tear in the gold paper before revealing the square white box.

Kol's heart hammered harder, threatening to push through his ribcage. Time seemed to slow to a stop—*sheesh!* It was just a damn Christmas present, not an engagement ring! But he snapped his thoughts away from *that* line of thinking immediately. He was seriously in danger of losing Myreen forever if he wasn't careful.

When she gasped, seeing the silver bracelet contrasted against the black velvet, he had to bring his knees up to his chest and put physical force against his beating heart.

She lifted the charms delicately and slowly, as if any other way would make them turn to ash.

"Kol," she said, her voice breathy and barely a whisper. "This is..." she trailed off, inspecting the five charms he'd chosen—with the help of Nik—with purpose and care. "This one is obvious," she said, grinning as she held up the open seashell with a blue back and silver mermaid sitting inside. It was that mermaid from the animated film, but the store had no others. "And this one..." she teared up as she looked at the single silver wing with a tiny golden heart attached to a ring surrounded in clear gems.

"Because flying is better than swimming..." Kol prompted, teasing.

Her smile met her eyes and she shoved him lightly.

Myreen furrowed her eyebrows at the next one, the silver origami crane with its wings folded up.

Kol touched it with a fingertip and rolled his eyes. "Jewelers need to grow imaginations." He felt his neck grow hot with sudden self-consciousness. "They didn't have any dragons."

"Ah." Her eyes widened and he wondered if she saw any resemblance between the tiny paper crane and Kol's own alter-form. He felt a little chagrined, thinking maybe she was merely humoring him. It seemed more obvious when he picked it out in the store, but Nik had expressed his doubts.

The next was a silver locket. Simple, with embellished swirls on the outside. Myreen opened it carefully. "What, no picture?" She asked, winking. "Am I supposed to ask for a tiny picture of my boyfriend so I can take him with me wherever I go?"

"Actually, I thought you could put your mom in that one," Kol said, hearing his voice go flat. Probably because of his previous embarrassment.

She nodded and swallowed.

"And this one is just pretty," Myreen said, her voice a bit shaky. She held the rose-gold sphere, diamond in the middle and spokes of gold pointing outward to more diamonds, then more spokes and diamonds. It had reminded him of one of his fireballs, but again, like with the crane, he felt foolish for thinking so. "No... actually..." She paused and turned it to the side. "It looks like... a fireball."

Relief washed through him. A silly feeling, but this girl was doing all sorts of crazy things to his emotions, so he wasn't surprised. He nodded. "And I thought..." he took it from her fingers and held it carefully between his thumb and finger. "You could put some of your light inside."

"I love it!" Myreen threw herself into Kol's arms before he was ready, pinning one of his hands again his chest.

He breathed another sigh of relief. "I'm glad."

"I have something for you, too!" she said after clasping the charms around her thin, porcelain wrist. It somehow looked even more beautiful against her skin. "But I don't have it with me. Come back to my dorm?" Now it was Myreen's turn to blush fiercely.

Kol couldn't help but smile at that and nodded—after secretly praying he could slip in without being noticed by the ones he avoided.

A few minutes later they sat knee-to-knee on the edge of Myreen's bed. They had successfully snuck back in without issue, since most of the families had migrated to the dining hall for lunch. Myreen pursed her lips when she handed him a brightly wrapped gift with cartoonish green Christmas trees on a red background. It was the shape and size of a Blu-ray or DVD.

He wasn't so careful about the unwrapping and blurted out the title before the paper hit the floor. "*Flesh Eaters 4* the *Collector's Edition!*" Kol held in his hand the newly released zombie killing video game Brett had been going on and on about for the better part of the last six months. Though Kol hadn't been as vocal about it, he too had been anticipating its release. "How'd you get it?" he asked, gripping Myreen so tightly he realized too late that he might crack some bones.

"The mall?" Myreen said when he'd released her.

"But how? It's been sold out for months!" Kol couldn't help the giddy-kid grin he had on his face, but he didn't care. He couldn't remember the last time someone gave him a gift that was absolutely nonessential to his advancement in the shifter or dragon community.

"They had a bunch at that gaming store on Black Friday," she said, looking a little fearful for her life suddenly.

Kol willed himself to calm in order to wipe the look from her face. "They had them in?"

She nodded. "And not that it matters, but I got it on sale, too."

"Do you have any idea just how much I lo—?" he choked on his words, but pulled her close and kissed her anyway. A hard lump formed in his stomach as their kiss deepened and almost as quickly as he'd reached for her, he broke the kiss and jumped apart. "Thank you," he said, touching his mouth and trying to hide the fact that he'd pushed her away so suddenly.

"You're welcome."

Something caught his eye just over Myreen's shoulder. A rose sitting on the nightstand. It hadn't been there the last time he and Myreen...

"Where'd you get that?" he asked, not realizing that it could be from another guy until the words left his mouth. Great. Now he sounded like the jealous boyfriend.

"Kenzie."

He nodded and made a noise of approval.

"So... I hear the New Year's Eve Ball is pretty fantastic," Myreen said, suddenly sounding nervous. It was a yearly tradition at the Dome, and while a lot of the students made a big deal out of it, he usually didn't care.

But this year was different.

"Yes." Kol had been meaning to ask her, but between embarrassment over silver cranes and the excitement and anticipation of fighting brand new zombies, it had fled his mind. "And you're coming as my date." He injected confidence into his tone, hoping it put her sudden *un*ease at ease.

She smiled, then laced her fingers through his and squeezed before turning her chin upward to meet his lips in a gentle kiss.

Kol's tablet buzzed in his bag next to the bed, breaking the moment. He glanced at the clock and realized it would be his parents calling. "I should take this," he said, standing. "I need to make sure Mom got the plate I sent her."

"Plate?" Myreen scoffed. "You got your mom a *plate* for Christmas?"

Kol made a face, then leaned in for one last kiss. She was quickly becoming more and more irresistible to him. Like a drug he couldn't shake. "It's gold-plated and hand-painted ceramic. She's wanted it for a while. It's a collector's item."

"Ah, like the zombie game, *collector's edition*," she whispered the last part in a mocking-tone.

"Exactly!" He pointed at her. "We Draculs are collectors." He winked before exiting.

Kol managed to play secret agent, ducking through the hallways and making it to the boy's dorms and his room without being stopped. The call ended before he could get there, but he called back as soon as he was in the safety of his room.

Victoria answered, her thick auburn curls filling almost the entirety of the screen. Kol almost couldn't tell what room she was in.

"Merry Christmas, Malkolm," she sang. Her smile brightened the screen and his father's office behind it.

"Merry Christmas, Mom," Kol said.

Her eyebrows twitched downward a fraction of an inch.

"Is everything okay?" he asked. "Did you get the plate I sent?"

Her eyebrows returned to their rightful positions. "Yes, sweetheart!" she said. "Thank you so much!" She clutched a hand to her chest.

Kol smiled and ducked his head in a semi-nod.

"Malkolm." Eduard's face filled the screen.

"Hello, Father," he said, donning the mask he'd always worn around his father, ever since he could remember. "Merry Christmas."

Eduard nodded. "And to you as well, son," he said. "Your mother and I are coming to the Dome for the New Year's Eve Ball. We have some business to discuss with Oberon and some others who will be there, and your mother would like to spend some time with you, since she didn't get to see you today."

Kol nodded, his brows furrowing as he contemplated just how he would juggle what he'd planned to be a night to remember for Myreen at her first New Year's Eve Ball and whatever his parents expected of him.

"Did the connection cut out?" Eduard asked.

"Hmm?" Kol asked, inwardly kicking himself for using a non-committal noise in front of Eduard. He was sure to get scolded like a three-year-old any minute.

"Malkolm?" Eduard asked, the video shook as if he was tapping his screen. "Did you hear me?"

"What did you ask?" He felt partial relief that his father blamed Kol's momentary daze on the quality of the video connection and rolled with it.

Eduard's face smoothed. "How are things with the siren? Have you seen her? Any word if she's been able to tap into her voice yet?"

"I hear she's still struggling," Kol lied. He knew the second word got out that Myreen actually *could* use her siren voice, shifters such as his father would snatch her from the school. "I overheard Delphine talking to someone about it."

"Has she said anything to you about it?"

"Nope," he said. "And anyway, I broke things off with her, like you asked. I thought you were done with me staying close to her?"

Eduard's frustrated face flashed across the screen, and he rubbed the skin between his eyebrows, mouth tight, jaw set.

"Did you want me to *befriend* her again?" It could solve the reason he stayed near her at the ball.

"No. No, that's not necessary," Eduard said dismissively. "I want you to stay away from her. You were right to follow my instructions to break things off with her. You've done enough in that area. I'm proud of you, Malkolm."

Kol gulped. "Thanks, Dad." He hated lying to his father and hated even more to think what would happen if he were caught in that lie.

"And while we're on that topic, Charlotte Stern says hello."

Char? Kol hadn't thought of her even once since Myreen arrived at the school. Charlotte Stern was one of Kol's oldest friends and a dragon who had graduated recently and joined the shifter military.

"Tell her 'hi' for me," he said.

Eduard nodded and Kol wondered if there was still an understanding between his family and hers about their eventual union. As much as he cared about Char, he hoped not.

"Could I speak with him again?" Victoria asked in the background, for which Kol was grateful. He wasn't ready to go down that naga hole of arranged dragon marriages.

"And how is your Christmas?" Victoria asked when she was back on the screen. "You got our package?"

"I did," Kol said, relaxing onto his bed and eyeing the opened packages across the room. Shoes and suits and books—with extensive detail about rare shifters in Eastern Europe and tactical maneuvers for the military—littered the area in organized chaos. "Thank you."

"Well, we've missed you," she said. "I hope you haven't been too lonely stuck at the Dome this Christmas." It was almost like she'd forgotten Kol would have stayed regardless of recent events. He'd done so last year, and there was nothing preventing him from going home, other than the fact that his childhood home was also empty, since his parents spent the holiday in the Alps. For whatever reason, his mother missed him more this Christmas; Eduard had all but said it when he mentioned she wanted quality time when they came on New Year's Eve.

Kol suspected it had something to do with him almost dying recently.

"I haven't been lonely," he said, thinking about his time with Myreen.

Victoria's eyebrows dropped like they did before.

Kol glanced at the small video of himself in the top corner, wondering what made her face do that—if she thought he'd lied about not being lonely. But when he looked at the tiny video of himself, his heart dropped. He recognized that look. He'd never seen it on his own face, but it was near identical to the one his mother had worn his entire life.

For her sake and his, the damned Dracul curse *had* to be broken.

Juliet

Myreen's blessing was just what Juliet needed, and she didn't even know she needed it.

Although the date with Jesse didn't go great, the thought of Kol and Myreen brought her hope. If they could be happy after such a horrendous first date, then maybe Juliet could find some happiness with Jesse.

Even with that option open, Juliet still wasn't completely sure she should try to move on. Especially now that she and Myreen had made up. She was happy with just that. And with Myreen dating Kol, she knew that she could still sneak away for some alone time in the Defense Room. She was happy for them, but she didn't want to be around them *all* the time. Kol was still connected to Nik, after all.

But it had finally clicked; she deserved someone who actually wanted her. Someone like Jesse. He definitely let her know he was attracted to her—and his straightforwardness made it obvious. That thought alone made her stomach turn into a million knots. She didn't want to be sappy by calling them butterflies, but that's almost exactly what they felt like.

Or maybe it was the excitement of the ball. Even if she didn't have a date, she vowed to herself that she would have fun. Now that things were back to normal with Myreen, Juliet felt unstoppable.

She should've devoted the day to getting ready for the ball, but she wanted to get in some workout time. Nothing that would exhaust her too much, but enough to help keep her calm and collected.

There were only a few students in the Defense Room, and Jesse was one of them. He had a thin, black headband in his hair to keep it out of his face, and Juliet felt her attraction to him escalate. He kept his distance, but he also wouldn't stop giving her the side-eye and wiggling his eyebrows. Which made it hard for her to focus on her workout reps. But Jesse made her smile the entire time she was there, and the time flew by.

As she grabbed her water bottle and towel to leave, Jesse jogged up to meet her.

"Hey, you looked great out there doing your little workout reps."

Juliet didn't know if he knew how offensive he sounded. "Little? I would murder you in there. Gotta get ready for the ball, though." She didn't intend to bring up the ball, but there it was.

"Ooh sounds fun. Who's the lucky guy?" For the first time, Jesse didn't hold eye contact. She'd never seen this softer side, and she had to admit, she liked it.

"I don't have one."

Jesse's confident smile returned. It kind of annoyed her, but at the same time, the way his eyes scrunched together made her go weak in the knees. By the way he took a step closer, she figured it was written all over her face.

"Well, we can give our first date a second chance. What do you think? Wanna go with me?" Jesse smoothly took Juliet's hand and linked his fingers with hers. Her cheeks heated up, and she knew she must have been as red as a tomato. Jesse's smile grew twice as big and he pulled her even closer.

"Is that a yes?" he said, reminding her that he'd asked a question.

Juliet completely forgot where they were or that anyone was around. Everything faded away as he locked his deep, dark brown eyes with hers.

Juliet had to blink several times to remember how to speak. But her mouth was dry and her breathing heavy. She didn't want him to think she was saying no, so she nodded.

Jesse—embarrassingly—howled a loud *WOO* and twirled her around. "I'll meet you in front of your common room. Can't wait to see how hot you're gonna look." With a kiss to the top of her hand, Jesse jogged back to his friend, leaving Juliet with her stomach butterflies moving around in a frenzy.

She didn't even realize when her hands began to heat up. It was only when she saw the smoke escape her fingertips that she knew she had to get out of there. With one more look at Jesse, Juliet fled the Defense Room to cool down with a shower.

She couldn't wait to tell Myreen.

***

"Okay, I only have a few minutes before I have to go meet Kol. Any last-minute adjustments I need to make?"

Myreen spun like a princess in her white, empire gown. White heels hid beneath the skirt, which had tiny gold sequins spread sporadically to her waistline, making her look taller. A thin white-and-gold tiara crowned wispy, beachy waves. Her makeup was subtle and natural, the light colors and gold highlights making her look like a fairy princess. Myreen was a beauty of light, and Juliet knew Kol would be floored.

"Not a thing, girl. You sure are a sight to see. What about me?" Juliet mimicked the same spin while Myreen giggled.

Juliet was the dark to Myreen's light. Her quarter-sleeve, all lace, burgundy, tea-length dress flowed around her, a thin black studded belt cinching the waist. Her bright orange hair was pin-straight—thanks to the help of a flat iron she'd never used before—and a thin braid crown woven with a black ribbon, circled her head like a headband. She paired her dress with all-black jewelry: a choker, long earrings that almost reached her shoulders, and wrap-around bracelets that covered both of her wrists. Smoky eyeliner lined her eyes so thickly that it made their yellow-green color even more piercing. Juliet completed her look with black Mary-Jane wedges that made her almost as tall as Myreen.

"You look like you could set the room on fire. But really, don't do that."

The girls laughed as they added an extra layer of lipstick to their already-painted lips.

"I still can't believe Jesse asked you last-minute like that. I would've paid anything to see your face." Myreen gently nudged Juliet's arm, which made her blush all over again. Every time she thought of Jesse now, her stomach flipped and twisted—a feeling she thought she could only get from Nik.

"Shut up! But yes, I was so freaked that I couldn't even verbally answer him. My cheeks were so hot I swear I turned all shades of red. He's so sure of himself and playful. It's different from..." Juliet stopped herself.

But Myreen already knew what she meant. "From Nik. You can talk to me about how you're feeling, J. Anytime, anywhere. And just so you know, different isn't always bad. Maybe someone like Jesse is just what you need. I'm proud of you for putting yourself out there." Myreen pulled Juliet in for a quick hug before she let go and grabbed her clutch.

"Parting is such sweet sorrow that I shall say goodnight till it be morrow." Myreen faked an old English accent as she walked to the door.

Juliet's hand flew to her forehead as she laughed at Myreen's *Romeo and Juliet* quote. "Oh jeez. Please don't." Juliet shook her head and smiled.

"It is the east, and Juliet is the sun," Myreen said, again using her fancy accent. She switched back to normal and said, "Ooh! That's a good one, 'cause you're a phoenix. See you at the ball!"

Juliet's cheeks hurt from laughing so much—Myreen's excitement only excelled her own.

Jesse would be there any minute, so she grabbed her velvet pouch and nervously walked to the door. Her hands were sweaty as she gripped the knob, so she gave herself one more second to regulate her breathing.

She walked through to the common room, taking in how beautiful everyone looked. There weren't many people, but everyone she saw was dressed to the nines.

Juliet turned the corner and almost crashed into Jesse. He leaned against the wall, his hands in his pockets. His hair was slicked back, which really opened up his face. He had on an all-black tux with a black button down shirt, which wasn't buttoned all the way up. He'd never looked so clean-cut. Juliet knew she was staring, but his eyes moved down her body, doing the same thing. He looked devilishly handsome, and she thought she wouldn't mind his lack of personal space so much.

"Wow. You look... ravishing." He closed the space between them and took her hand in his to kiss the top. His light cologne smelled of citrus, a scent she'd probably remember forever. "I am the luckiest guy here."

Jesse's spoke so smoothly that Juliet felt weak and faint—but she wouldn't give him the pleasure of a full on swoon. "You don't look so bad yourself. Did you have to go to a groomer for that hairdo?" She was trying to sound cute, but her nerves poured out with her words.

Jesse gave a cute snicker. He kept his hand intertwined with hers as he led the way to the ball. They were quiet on the walk, which was weird for Jesse. Maybe he was just as nervous as she was.

The second they walked into the ball, Juliet's breath hitched. It was an all-white winter wonderland, complete with fake falling snow and an elegance that only Mr. Suzuki could put together. It looked like something only seen in dreams: true magic.

"Whoa," Juliet whispered.

"Yeah, it's nice. But not as nice as how you look. Now that is *whoa.*"

Juliet blushed again. "You're killing me here."

"Oh, I know. I like seeing your cheeks get red. It's kind of my favorite thing about you." Jesse playfully winked at her, then pulled her closer as they walked through the ballroom.

"So, what do you want to do first? Get some refreshments? Hit the dance floor? Or maybe the photo booth? I'm down for it all." He was so much more outgoing than Juliet, but like Myreen said, maybe that was what she needed.

"Let's get a drink. Then we'll see where the night takes us." Juliet didn't want to do anything just yet. She just wanted to take in the decorations a little longer.

After two drinks of punch and a round of appetizers, Juliet felt a little more comfortable. Not comfortable enough to dance, though, even if the music called to her.

"Ready to visit the photo booth?" she asked Jesse, and he stood right up. If he had a tail, it would've been wagging. Juliet giggled as they ran over to the prop table. She grabbed a stick with nerdy glasses on it and Jesse put on an elaborate velvet crown.

They went behind the curtain and waited for the countdown. Jesse moved behind Juliet and pulled her into his chest. She went along with it, and they did three different poses that way. When there was one more picture to be taken, Jesse bent down and kissed her cheek. Her blush came just as the camera flashed, and Jesse laughed.

"I am the happiest were in the world." He raced out of the booth to wait for their strip of pictures to be printed. As soon as it finished, he pulled them out and stared at them in awe. "These are perfect. I'm gonna keep them forever. That blush of yours—damn, you are so hot!"

Jesse was so vocal with his feelings. Juliet was going to have to get used to that. She was terrible with compliments, mostly because she never got them growing up, and she didn't know how to react to his. Juliet shook her head, a wide smile on her face as she gazed at their cute photos.

"They did come out pretty perfect," she admitted. Jesse flung his arms around her and spun her around in a tight hug. She laughed and squealed until he stopped.

When she tried to regain her balance, she thought she was hallucinating. There, across the room, was Nik. He stood by General Dracul's side, but this time he didn't hide that he'd noticed Juliet. His eyes looked sad as he watched Jesse smile at her.

Nik looked just as handsome as she remembered. He wore his military uniform with white ceremonial pants and jacket over it, and he cut quite the figure. But she missed his dimples, and it saddened her that she might never see them again.

He leaned over to say something in the general's ear. She might have imagined it, but she thought he nodded his head to her. She didn't want to miss the chance if he did.

"I'm going to run to the ladies' room for a second. Don't go anywhere." She didn't want to mess up what was growing between her and Jesse, even if Nik *did* want to talk to her.

"Trust me, I'll wait for you all night." Jesse looked back at their pictures as Juliet walked to the exit, knots in her stomach.

Nik waited in the dark part of the hall. Juliet stepped slowly to where he stood, afraid he would run away if she walked too quickly.

"Juliet, you look incredible. And happy." Nik's voice was low, his fingers twitching as if they wanted to take her hand in his. It broke Juliet's heart all over again.

"You look really nice, too. And busy." Juliet's eyes were glued to the floor, afraid if she looked at him, tears would appear.

"Always busy. But really, you look happy. You deserve the world, Juliet. Even if it's not me who's able to give it to you. And it kills me to know that it's not me bringing that smile to your face."

This time Nik did touch her. He brought his hand to her chin, softly lifting her face so she would look at him. "Don't ever stop shining that beautiful smile of yours. You never know whose day you might brighten." He ran his fingers through her straight hair, then turned and walk away.

Just like that.

Juliet felt like she'd just taken ten steps backwards. Jesse had made like her heart could be repaired, but Nik had just torn it in half again. His words were sweet, but he left her wanting more. Had he done that intentionally?

Like a zombie, Juliet walked back into the ballroom. Thankfully, Myreen was walking toward her, and Juliet was glad for the break from the guys. Myreen's lips pouted, her arms crossed in front of her chest. She didn't look happy.

Juliet went straight into defense mode. "Are you okay? What's wrong?"

"I could ask you the same thing. You look like you saw a ghost." Myreen hooked her arm in Juliet's and led her to a quiet corner.

"Yeah, I'll tell you later. I'm going to need to vent, but I don't want to do it here." Myreen bobbed her head, and Juliet was grateful her friend was willing to wait.

"Okay. Well, you'll never guess. Kol's been flaking on me! He abandoned me as soon as we got here, and has been at his dad's side ever since. He knows I wouldn't dare go near his father. I just don't understand. Why would he do that? We've been so good, then he pulls this." Myreen spoke rapidly, her pitch rising.

"That does sound weird. I thought you two were done with the whole hot and cold crap. Doesn't sound like Kol. Maybe he's afraid of his dad or something? Everyone else is. Do you want me to go and beat him up for you?" Juliet was only half serious, but she comically began to remove her earrings as if getting ready to fight.

Myreen smiled and nudged Juliet. She took a deep breath, then shook out her shoulders. "You know what? You're right. It doesn't sound like him. Something must be up. I'm gonna go back in there and enjoy that gorgeous ball. With or without him. But I'm definitely going to kill him when this is over. Hope you don't mind a third wheel?"

Juliet laughed as Myreen led the way back into the ballroom, her head up and back straight.

When Juliet caught sight of where Jesse was, her heart skipped a beat. She wanted to go back to him, but Nik's words echoed in the back of her mind like a broken record. She was confused and bummed, but she wouldn't let it show. Jesse was sweet and fun and deserved to have a good night with his date.

She was going to do her best to give it to him, even if she fell apart on the inside.

Chapter 37

Oberon

"Ren, you've done it again," Oberon whispered to himself as he marveled at the simulated snow falling to the gymnasium floor. It was obviously a trick: the "snow" didn't stick, nor did it melt. The flakes merely disappeared, like stars in the sky as twilight approached.

The doom he'd felt ever since the vampire attack on Myreen and her friends seemed a distant thing now. The New Year's Eve Ball took him out of that reality and placed him in one where shifters had no fears. Students were smiling, mingling, and singing along to the music. Some were dancing. Even a few of the teachers had decided to join in the fun—Ren was currently performing a breakdance move he'd labeled "The *Real* Electric Slide," complete with energy manipulation and rapid phasing from side-to-side.

Oberon shook his head.

"Poor fool sometimes forgets he's not a teenager anymore," Delphine said, startling Oberon. He hadn't heard the mermaid approach. She was wearing a form-fitting forest-green dress that matched her jade eyes, accentuating her red hair beautifully.

It was a good thing Ren was too busy showing off his dance moves, otherwise he'd be ogling at Delphine.

Oberon couldn't help but chuckle. "I don't think Ren will ever truly grow up."

Delphine laughed softly, shaking her head as she watched the kitsune dancing away. "Still, the school wouldn't be where it's at today without Ren Suzuki."

"Very true," Oberon agreed. He shifted his eyes from Ren and back to Delphine. Her smile slowly faded into a hard expression, and her eyes looked on distantly. The joyful feeling that had filled his heart dashed away like a candle blown out by a sudden breeze. "Delphine, is something the matter?"

She bit her lip before she returned his gaze. In a whisper, she said, "I've had another vision."

Oberon's brow raised. "About Myreen?"

She shook her head ever so slightly. "It was about—"

"Oberon!"

A firm hand clapped him between his shoulder blades, nearly causing Oberon to lose his balance. He whirled to find Eduard Dracul standing next to him, grinning broadly in his military uniform. Behind the general was his lovely wife, Victoria, who wore a dark purple dress, holding a glass with both of her hands and looking quite out of place.

"Another successful year at the Dome," Eduard said, reaching a hand out. Oberon took it, feeling the strength of the military leader's hand. "The school has always thrived under your direction, my friend."

Seeing the general so jolly was somewhat disconcerting. The way he wore his emotions looked contrived and unnatural.

Oberon forced himself to smile. "Thank you, Eduard. Although we've met some difficult moments this year, no doubt the school will continue to thrive as we bring more and more shifters here to guide them in mastering their abilities." Looking past the general, he said, "It's good to see you again, Victoria."

A warm smile formed at her lips and she nodded. "Thank you, Oberon." Victoria glanced at the mermaid next to him. "And Delphine, I swear you never age. How are you doing?"

Delphine laughed, swatting the air in front of her. "Oh, Victoria, you're always so pleasant with your words, even when they're untrue. I'm doing well. Thanks for asking."

Eduard cleared his throat loudly, a flash of annoyance flitting across his face. "Victoria, dear, why don't you locate Malkolm. He seems to have slipped away. Perhaps he needs the gentle touch of his mother?"

Oberon looked at his dark shoes out of pure awkwardness. The belittlement that seemed to come so easily to Eduard mocked the relationship he had with his wife and child. It irked Oberon to witness: he'd have done anything to have his sweet Serilda at his side tonight, as well as his child.

"And Miss Delphine," Eduard continued, "if you don't mind, I have a few matters I need to discuss with the director. Alone."

Oberon didn't even have to look at Delphine to know how she was feeling.

"Actually," Oberon said, "why don't we go for a walk through the greenhouses? It's a bit loud in here, and I could use the fresh air the plants provide."

"A wonderful idea," Eduard replied. "Very well."

Oberon nodded at both women. "Delphine, Victoria. We'll return shortly. Shall we, Eduard?"

Side-by-side, they made their way toward the eastern elevator that would drop them into the Were Training Room.

Upon entering the chrome interior, Oberon looked out among the sea of students dancing in the falling simulated snow. Right before the doors closed, he saw Myreen with her friend, Juliet Quinn, chattering off to the side.

He released a long breath, not even knowing he'd been holding it. The last place he wanted to be was confined to a small elevator with Eduard Dracul.

"Eduard, this better be important," Oberon said as he tapped the button labeled *Were Training Room*, causing it to glow blue. "My place is with the students and faculty of the school."

Lord Dracul waved his hand rapidly in front of himself. "I will be quick and straight to the point, Oberon. After all, I value the importance of time much more than most."

And there it was. Oberon didn't even need to hear what Eduard had to say. The general had come to speak with him about Myreen. *Again.*

The elevator dinged open, and the pair exited. Oberon took long strides, and the general effortlessly kept up with him. Before long, they were in the hallway heading toward the greenhouses in the southern portion of the Dome.

"It's about the girl," Eduard specified.

Oberon stopped dead in his tracks, and Eduard took one more step before coming to a halt, too.

"Every time you come to the Dome, it's always about Myreen," he said, raising a finger in the air.

A few voices could be heard in the adjacent hallway, along with the sound of sprinting feet moving away from them. He didn't even want to think what a couple of students were doing out here while everyone else was in the gymnasium, but he wasn't about to go after them, either.

Eduard narrowed his eyes toward where the noises dissipated. Through clenched teeth, the general said, "Perhaps we should wait until we reach the greenhouse before we continue this conversation."

Oberon agreed, but didn't say it. Instead, he speed-walked down the hallway again.

Although the greenhouses were close to the gymnasium, to Oberon it seemed as if an age had passed before the long, white structures came into view.

Stopping at the first one, he pressed his hand to the panel by the wide door. Upon scanning his hand, the mechanism controlling the door started, and on small, thin wheels, it opened from the side, as if hands were pulling it right to left.

Eduard raised an eyebrow. "A little secure for a place full of plants, don't you think?"

Stepping inside, Oberon said, "The structure is anti-flammable, but all it takes is one stray fireball *within* a greenhouse to burn everything to ashes. We lock them up as an after-hours policy."

The air was powerfully wonderful, and seemed to clear Oberon's head almost immediately. The scent of the youthful greenery was clean and therapeutic.

Lord Dracul entered behind him. "I suppose this was a

lesson learned the hard way?"

"Years ago," Oberon said with a nod. "But I'd hate to bore you with such details. Let's move on to more pressing matters, since time seems to be of the essence."

Dim ultraviolet lamps hung low from the ceiling, an elaborately timed system designed to encourage the best growth from the plants they nurtured.

Eduard snorted. "You are quite snippety this evening, Oberon. More-so than usual. But yes, I've come back to the Dome to discuss the siren."

"Was your last visit not telling enough, Eduard?" Oberon asked as civilly as he could. "You saw with your own eyes; Myreen is not ready for military training."

The dragon shifter walked to the nearest plant, raised a hand to it and felt at one of its leaves. After a few moments, he lifted his thumb and finger to his nose and sniffed. "Basil?"

Oberon sighed and looked away in exasperation. The air that had helped him before was doing little to subdue his building agitation.

Eduard cleared his throat. "Hear me out, my friend. This basil plant sits in a climate-controlled environment, receiving the appropriate amounts of water and UV light to grow and thrive. At this very moment, the young plant could handle losing multiple leaves without any real harm done to it."

"That's very intuitive and educational," Oberon said, rubbing his forehead. "How does this apply to Myreen?"

A smirk crawled upon the general's face. "I'm glad you asked. You see, Myreen is like this basil plant—full of promise and potential. But unlike this particular plant, she is in an environment that is stunting her growth."

A fiery fury kindled within Oberon, and he felt his face turning red. "Her environment is stunting her growth?"

Eduard stood tall and lifted his chin, but did not reply.

"How dare you!" shouted Oberon, also straightening his back. He would not be daunted by Eduard Dracul. "For years, this school has prepared hundreds of students. Many of them are your own soldiers. Your own children have thrived here. Malkolm is an exemplary student."

The general shook his head slightly. "Come on, Oberon. I'm not attacking your school. But you saw Myreen's pitiful performance in the simulation room. Your *siren* couldn't conjure a voice to save her life."

"Her siren abilities are much harder to master," Oberon countered. "Delphine is doing her best to instruct her, but she's no siren herself. And besides, her water and light manipulation abilities are admirable. Even you can't deny that."

Eduard held a hand up. "The prophecy states that it will be her siren abilities that bring down Draven, not her other abilities."

"So what would you have us do? Focus her studies purely on increasing her abilities as a siren?"

"Oberon, my friend, it is not within Myreen's best interests to remain here at the school."

Oberon snorted. "And who's going to train her in her siren abilities? You?"

"She needs military supervision. She needs *my* supervision."

"She's sixteen years old, Eduard," Oberon countered. "She belongs here in the school with other students her age."

"Myreen is an orphan," the general refuted. "As such, there are no legal issues with her joining the military at her age."

Oberon wanted to explode with the revelation that Myreen was not entirely an orphan—that her father still existed, and that he was the very being she was prophesied to destroy. But he held his tongue, not wanting to give General Dracul another reason to pull Myreen away from the Dome.

Pointing his finger under Eduard's nose, he said, "High winds, stop looking at Myreen as a tool for the military. Your complete disregard and disrespect for the girl as a person is distasteful. The prophecy says *nothing* about her and military involvement."

Eduard smirked. "On the other hand, the prophecy says nothing about Myreen attending school."

Oberon slammed his hand on one of the wooden tables, causing dozens of flats of plants to shake.

"Myreen is a ward of the school, and she will never—I repeat, *never*—be in military custody as long as I am director of this school. Is that understood, General?" Chest rising and falling, every muscle in Oberon's body went taut.

Eduard's features clouded in the dim light of the UV lamps. "You'll regret those words, my friend," he hissed.

Lord Dracul studied Oberon for a few moments, then moved past him, brushing him out of the way in the process with one of his sturdy arms. The door of the greenhouse opened as he approached, the sensors within triggered to let him out.

As the general disappeared into the hallway, Oberon turned and looked at the nearby basil plant. Lord Dracul had been wrong: Myreen wasn't like the plant. She was the lamp shining above, the light protecting the life beneath it from being swallowed in darkness.

Myreen

After such a wonderful Christmas break, it was hard getting back into schoolwork. Myreen woke up late and walked around until noon, unaware that she'd put her pants on inside-out. Then in shifter history, she'd arrived only to realize that she never finished her paper on the alicorn, which was due today. Thankfully, she wasn't the only one who had forgotten, but those other students weren't exactly known for their stellar academic records.

To make matters worse, Kol's behavior at the ball weighed on her, and thanks to his dad being back around, she hadn't had a chance to speak to him about it. The whole thing felt off, though she couldn't quite put her finger on why. It seemed she was destined to be the last one to know pretty much everything that affected her life.

So when she arrived at defense training and saw Oberon motioning her over, she couldn't help but groan.

"Hello, Myreen. I'm sorry to do this to you on your first day back, but I'm going to need you to stay for an additional hour today. We need to step up your training."

"Of course, we do," she sighed, unintentionally letting the sarcasm seep into her voice.

Oberon didn't seem to notice. "We're going to try you in another sim," he went on.

She kept her disdain to herself this time, though the sim room was not her favorite way to train. When she sparred against Oberon, she always knew he wouldn't really hurt her. With the sim room, there was no guarantee of her safety. It was all so real. She understood that was the point, to prepare her for real life battle. But she wasn't any more eager for it than she would be to get a root canal.

During defense class, she held back, saving her energy for what was to come. After all the other students trickled out, she went directly to the sim room to await Oberon's instructions. When he arrived, he wore the same wearied expression as the day he'd told her about displaying her skills to the general.

"If you don't mind me asking, what did the general think of my test?" she ventured as he tapped instructions into the sim's control tablet. "Did anything come of it?"

Oberon looked up, caught off guard by the question. Then he closed his eyes and sighed. "I'll be frank with you, Myreen. The general is concerned your training isn't progressing quickly enough. If he had his way, he'd pull you out of the school and oversee your training himself."

She scrunched her brows. "Can he do that?" she asked, her voice wobbling.

Oberon kept eye contact as he promised, "Not as long as

I'm the director of the Dome. But either way, it's wise to kick your training up a notch or two."

She nodded, understanding the need for it, but doubtful she could keep up with anymore notches.

Oberon tapped the tablet with finality. "Alright, you're ready to go."

She shook out her hands, flexing and stretching her fingers as she walked into the bright white room and closed the door behind her. She vaguely noted that the lights had been repaired since her tryst with Kol—just before they faded away.

The walls pixelated away at the same time as water pooled at her feet, the level quickly rising up her legs. The familiar prickle told her it was saltwater, and as fast as she could, she pulled off her shoes, socks and sweatpants before her tail could come out, tugging her shirt down past her hips as she did so.

By the time her legs had merged together, the water had risen meters over her head, leaving her completely submerged. She appeared to be floating in the lake outside the school, the Dome's glass twinkling below her in the filtered light of a midday sun. It struck her as unfair for a moment, as the lake water wasn't saltwater, but maybe he'd forced the transformation to ensure she didn't drown.

Myreen stayed still for a moment, recovering from the forced transformation and the embarrassment of having to disrobe in front of Oberon because of it. She didn't wear her swim top anywhere outside of the mer training room because she never expected to need it, but the sim room never failed to shatter her expectations. She vowed in that moment to never go anywhere without it again.

Something rammed into her from behind, sending her

hurtling through the water. She twirled around in the stony arms that trapped her. A male vampire bared his fangs in a wicked smile mere inches from her face.

Her reflexes took over and she repelled him with a pulse of water that radiated in all directions. The vampire was flung a few feet away, and she sucked water through her gills with the shock of using such an attack. She didn't realize she could do that with water.

The vampire found his bearing and jettisoned toward her once more, swiping his clawed fingers through at her. She shimmied backward, dodging his attacks the best she could. His speed was too much for her, and he landed a gash across her upper right arm, red liquid seeping upward from the wound.

Clutching her arm with anger and wounded pride, she turned tail and torpedoed into the open water with speed she didn't know she was capable of—but then again, she'd never been chased in water before. She looked over her shoulder and saw that the vampire was gaining on her. She willed the water to part and push her through faster, but with each inch she gained, he gained two.

Before she knew it, he had chased her toward the surface. She had no choice but to leap out of the water.

The naked air chilled her body instantly, and before she could dive back into the lake, another pair of hard arms closed around her waist and yanked her upward. She flailed like a fish on a deck trying to get free, but her tail was surprisingly heavy out of water, and she had no idea how to maneuver herself. She stretched and tugged until she could see enough behind her to know what had happened.

Her captor hung by a rope from a helicopter that ascended

with increasing speed. The space between her and the lake's surface was getting bigger and bigger with each rapid beat of her heart, and she soon realized that a fall from such a height would wound even a mermaid.

She couldn't fend off the vampire without her legs—her balance was too thrown off. But her deeply rooted sense of privacy reminded her that she couldn't shift back because she had nothing to cover her bottom now, and she wasn't willing to put herself on display in such a way for the sake of a simulated fight.

No, she would have to win this fight in the air as a mermaid.

She gritted her teeth and swung her tail backward at her attacker with all her strength. Her strike loosened his grip enough for her to turn around in his hold. Now face to face, she scratched at his cheeks and neck. His skin was so thick and hard that her nails hardly grazed him. *Stupid vampires!*

Suddenly, she had a thought. It made no sense, but she went with it anyway. Just as Ms. Heather had shown her, Myreen flicked out her fingers, and to her amazement, her nails extended into long, sharp talons.

She stared at them for an instant, stunned by her ability to use harpy moves while in mer form. Then she curled her fingers into claws and dug them into the side of the vampire's neck.

The vampire shrieked and released her, and gravity grabbed hold of her. She flung out her hands, grasping for his clothes, but she grabbed nothing but air.

True panic filled her as she hurtled downward, the mirror-like surface of the lake coming up to meet her dangerously fast. Even in a sim, if she landed on that water, she would need an urgent trip to the infirmary. She couldn't land. What was she supposed to do, fly?

She gasped as she realized that's exactly what she would do. If she could use her harpy nails in mer form, then she should also be able to use her wings in mer form! It was her only option, so she had to try.

Her panic over her situation was so great that she didn't need to try very hard. As soon as she willed her wings to come out, they did, and with such urgency that they ripped through the back of her shirt.

As soon as they were fully extended, she cupped them like parachutes, catching the air and putting an immediate stop to her fall. Catching her breath, she flapped them hard until she was ascending again. She flew upward, a hysterical laugh bubbling out of her chest at the fact that she was both a mermaid and a harpy in this moment. It was almost too incredible to be true!

Something small and dark whizzed past her from behind, stealing this moment of fascination. She looked to see the helicopter coming after her, one vampire shooting at her as another pulled the wounded vampire up by the rope from which he dangled.

Dang it, I just can't win!

She narrowed her wings over her back and darted through the sky like an eagle chasing prey—even though she was the prey in this situation. More shots fired and bullets sailed by her, barely missing. As fast as her wings could carry her, she still never gained distance.

It became clear that running wasn't going to win this fight. She had to put an end to them.

She soared upward and arched back down in their direction.

Aiming right for them, she could see the bullets coming and dodged them just in time. She had no idea what she was going to do when she reached the copter, but she knew it was the only way to end the sim, one way or another.

As she got within yards of them, she wondered if she could create a large enough gust of wind with her wings to throw them off course. Not knowing what else to do, she flapped her wings toward them with all her strength. The wind that emanated was strong enough to knock a pedestrian off their feet, but not enough to alter the helicopter's flight in the slightest.

It kept coming, and the gunman kept shooting. One bullet grazed the upper right side of her tail, and she growled at the pain. Now she was mad.

Like she had done with her fingers to extend her talons, she flicked her right wing out toward them. Amazingly, feathers, like blades, flew from her wing and shot at the copter. One pierced the shooter in the chest, causing him to fall out of the helicopter. Several stabbed into the black metal of the copter's outer shell and through the glass of the windshield. But the winning shot was the one feather that stuck in between the spinning blades on the top, seizing their rotation. The copter plummeted like a rock toward the lake below.

Before the scene around her finished pixelating back to the white walls and floor of the sim room, Oberon opened the door and applauded her.

"Myreen, that was... Wow! I've never seen anything like that before," Oberon praised as he picked up her sweatpants and brought them to her.

She took them and he immediately turned around to let her unshift and slip them on.

"I still can't believe I did any of it," she exclaimed, standing back up with her pants on. "And my wings—I didn't know harpy feathers could do that!"

Oberon turned back around to face her. "It's a higher level skill, one that takes many harpies years to master, mostly because harpies are mild by nature and tend more toward healing than offense. Not only were you able to shoot your feathers well before expected, but you were able to do it while in two different shifter forms."

The excitement in Oberon's animated face made him look young for a moment, and she could almost imagine him at her age. The fact that she was responsible for this change in his usually dower demeanor made her swell with pride.

Well, she was swelling with pride for several reasons.

"I have no doubt that you'll be the salvation of us all," he said, leading her out of the room.

That comment should have made her smile, should have fattened her head to the point of exploding.

But it didn't.

She'd done something unheard of today—existing in two shifter forms at once—and she'd beaten a more advanced level simulation than she'd ever done before. But that didn't mean she could save the world.

Hugging her tennis shoes against her as they walked across the defense room, Myreen prayed she wouldn't let everyone down, Oberon most of all.

Kenzie

It took a lot of convincing to get her mom to buy her story of Christmas Eve's events. Thankfully, the granola bar and sports drink had helped ease her headache by the time she arrived home, so she had enough brain power to work up those explanations.

Mom bought that she'd lost track of time and spent the night with Myreen at her school. She'd begrudgingly accepted that Kenzie had slipped on some ice and smashed her phone, and no one could lend one to her until the next morning. She'd eyed Wes hard when Kenzie explained that the new shirt she wore—which was now also ruined, thanks to her "fall"—was a result of the old one having coffee all over it. Though for that part of the story, she actually had evidence by way of her old, coffee-stained shirt, still in her bag.

But Mom frowned through Kenzie's explanation of the

new phone—even with Wes to back her up—and she wasn't entirely convinced that Kenzie wasn't hiding something. Which she was. A little makeup and some smaller bandages helped conceal the scabbed fang-holes in her neck—both items Wes had readily bought for her—but she was especially careful to keep her hair over said neck until she was alone in her room.

Explaining everything took far longer than she'd wanted.

Which was in part due to Wes's presence.

Wes had ceded to her every request—like stopping to find some place that served soup to go. And when he'd arrived at her home, he'd escorted her inside and corroborated her story. All the while he looked her mom in the eye, speaking with respect and an air of wholesome honesty that helped soothe Mom's flaring anger.

All the while, Kenzie's heart crumbled just a little more.

It was one thing to know she would never see him again, but another to have him care for her so sweetly for the next hour and a half. And he lied so well. She was rather impressed—and relieved that the spell she'd used on him wasn't a long-term thing.

Even Wes couldn't get Kenzie completely out of trouble. She was grounded for two weeks.

It felt like she'd never recover.

Which was why, not even a week into her detainment, she'd decided to sneak back out. There'd be no reasoning with her mom, and the text from Adam had set fire to a burning desire she wasn't willing to ignore. She needed something to break up the monotony of Christmas break, to make her forget Wes and the attack and the fact that Leif still hadn't contacted her. Mr. Dark and Dangerous was all that. Plus, he still had her shirts.

And he was a normal human—not a hunter or a shifter or a vampire. She needed some of that normalcy in her life right now.

Thanks to the healing spell she found, she could wear her hair in the high ponytail she had it in, no turtleneck to squash her already short-ish neck. Porcelain skin had replaced the scabs, making her look—even if she didn't quite feel—like she'd never been bitten at all. Kenzie wasn't going to let anything slow her down.

She turned on the radio in her room to her favorite channel, adjusting the volume so it was loud enough to dampen sound, but not so loud as to draw the attention—or annoyance—of her mom. And then she slid the window open and swung a leg out. She lowered herself down, then dropped to the ground. It took a few minutes to get the chair from the back patio so she could close her window, as she had to check that her mom wasn't in the kitchen, which had a direct view into the backyard. But she managed to do it all without getting caught.

Quietly, she slipped out of the back gate, then raced down the street.

Guilt tried to eat at her for sneaking out on her mom after everything else, but she set her mind to Adam and ignored the bothersome gnaw.

This was one date she didn't want to be late to.

***

She met Adam just outside the city and he ushered her to a warm car. She gave him a questioning look, but he met her with a mischievous grin and waggled his eyebrows before getting in. Kenzie shrugged and hopped into the passenger seat.

"Where we going?" Kenzie asked, sinking into the warm

leather. They were heated seats, and that—combined with the pristine interior—screamed that this was a rental. Not that she minded.

"Someplace a little more private."

Based on their interactions so far, Kenzie wasn't too surprised. To be honest, it was what she was looking for, anyway. She was ready to shake off the funk Wes had put her in, and a little bit of Adam sounded like the perfect cure. Chances were, Adam didn't have much privacy at his cousin's place, anyway. Or wherever he was staying.

They drove until they found a secluded parking lot. Adam climbed in the back seat first, then beckoned her to follow.

"You know we can just go around. The car is a four-door."

Adam smirked. "Not as much fun. Plus, you'll let all the warm air out."

Kenzie had a feeling that wouldn't be much of a problem, but she climbed through the center, landing not so gracefully on Adam's lap. They laughed.

"Absolutely perfect," Adam said, toying with one of Kenzie's curls.

He leaned in for a kiss, but she put a hand to his chest, stopping him. "Do you have my shirts?"

Adam laughed. "Feisty today, aren't we? Maybe I should've stopped and gotten you that dress I promised you first."

Kenzie snorted. "You wish. So?"

Adam leaned forward again, riveting her with his wolfish grin. "What do you need a shirt for?"

Kenzie shook her head and chuckled. Adam pulled on another curl, then let it go, watching it bounce back.

"You should take it down. I like your curls."

Kenzie lifted a brow, but raised her hands to her hair and unwound the band holding it all in place. Adam ran his arms down her sides as she worked, openly ogling. She threw the elastic on the floor, and Adam lanced his fingers through her hair.

Her breath caught in her throat as he pulled her close, and she closed her eyes as his lips found hers.

The passion ignited, as it always did, red-hot and delicious. But this time Wes's boyish face swam through her mind. She pushed back at the memory by moving so she was straddling Adam's lap. He purred against her lips, his hands sliding down her back, brushing the waist of her jeans. Kenzie opened her mouth, letting their tongues and lips do a sensual dance. Her heart hammered against her chest, pleading with her to slow down, but she didn't dare. Regret was trying to worm its way in and ruin her fun, but she needed this. Just normal, teenage stuff with a normal, teenage boy. No shifters, no magic, no hunters, and no vampires.

Adam's fingers slipped beneath the hem of her shirt, his warmth seeping into her skin. The cold had clung to her more deeply ever since the attack, and she savored the way his touch chased that chill away.

Their lips broke apart, and he traced a trail of kisses down her jaw and to her neck. She closed her eyes and moaned, though something stirred at the edge of her mind, something that feared such close proximity to the site of the last set of lips and fangs.

And then his teeth were clamped on her flesh, and Kenzie yelped, pushing away from Adam as fast as she could. Her breathing came in ragged, and she cast a wary eye on Adam. "What the heck was that?"

"Aw, just a little nibble. What's wrong?" Adam leaned forward again, but Kenzie kept her hand out, blocking his approach.

"Why would you do that?" She was just being paranoid, right? But she still needed him to explain himself, just to calm her nerves.

"Because it's sexy. Twilight and crap. See?" He leaned forward to do it again, but Kenzie pushed back.

"No." Panic was threatening to choke her, ruining all her fun. Why did he have to be such a creep so soon after her attack?

"I thought you of all people would appreciate a little love bite," he grumbled.

Kenzie's eyes widened. She blurted out, "Fírrineth," before she had time to think, the green light pulsing out from where her hand touched Adam's chest.

"What are you?" she asked now that he'd been spelled to speak the truth. After her experience with Wes, that was the first thing she wanted to know.

"An Initiate," Adam replied, then paled.

Initiate. She'd heard that word before... Leif's roommate. He said she was an Initiate. "As in a vampire Initiate?"

"Yes. Aw, damn. What did you do to me?"

"I'm the one asking questions. What are you doing here?"

"Besides kissing you?" Adam smirked, but she thought she saw a tremble behind that confident façade.

"Duh." She crossed her arms over her chest, feeling almost naked after their little make-out session, despite still having all her clothes intact. She wasn't sure if she wanted to hide behind her hair or pull it back into a ponytail again.

"I've been sent by Draven to spy on Leif. Seriously, what

the hell did you do to me?"

He was spying on Leif? This was not good. "So why date me?"

"You're working with him. I wanted to find out what you two were working on."

Hurt clouded her face, and Kenzie clenched her teeth at the wobble threatening to take over. "So you were just mining for information."

Adam shrugged. "And you're hot. Two birds, and all that."

Kenzie glared. "Of all the selfish—"

Adam's face scrunched in concentration. "You're a selkie, aren't you? Your eyes, they glowed white when you said that foreign word thingy."

Crap. Crap, crap, crap. Of course she couldn't just pick a normal guy. Vampire, hunter, Initiate. If the shifters didn't hate her so much, she probably would've picked up one of them by now, too. She'd befriended Myreen, after all, and she was a shifter.

"How do I get you to leave me and Leif alone?" Kenzie asked.

Adam shrugged again. "I don't think you can. I've got orders direct from Draven. If I went back empty-handed, he'd be very upset."

"It would serve you right! You little— Ugh!" She couldn't even find the right words, she was so angry.

"Aw, Kenzie, you don't mean that, do you? I thought we had something good going. And it will only get better once I become a vampire. Then you can dust that Leif character."

"You think he *feeds* off me?" Kenzie scowled.

"I saw you two at the hotel the other day. What else does a

vampire and human do behind closed doors?"

"Ugh! I should burn you alive."

Adam's cool façade melted, his eyes widening. "You wouldn't burn me alive. You— you—"

"I wouldn't?" Kenzie looked at her fingers as if they held something, then slit her eyes at Adam, who watched her with a look of uncertainty. She wanted to burn him, wanted to send him to whatever hellhole he'd crawled out of, but she couldn't risk hurting Leif in the process. No, she had a better idea.

"Leich ín dhearmandah," she said, channeling all her anger into the magic those words released.

Adam snapped to attention, his face going blank.

"You will forget this conversation, and every piece of damning information you have against me or Leif." She narrowed her eyes as she considered her next words. "And you will forget where you're living." Her lips curled into a smug smile as she imagined him riding all around Chicago, looking for his place but unable to find it. Adam shook his head, his eyes beginning to refocus, so she rushed to seal the spell. "Dhearmandah," she blurted.

Adam blinked a few times, then looked up at her. "What happened?"

Kenzie slapped him across the face. "Take me back where you got me. I want to go home." She crossed her arms and looked away.

Adam stared at her for a long minute, his brows scrunched, then sighed and returned to the driver's seat. He wrapped his arm around the passenger seat as he backed out of the spot he'd been parked in, throwing a worried glance at Kenzie.

Kenzie stared out the window, chewing on the inside of her

cheek. She had her hair pushed forward, trying to give herself some sort of privacy. First Wes, now Adam. Not to mention her first choice was actually a vampire. Probably one old enough to be her great great grandfather.

Her chin trembled and her eyes brimmed, but she refused to shed any tears for this creep. The fact that he'd used her like he had made her feel so ugly. Sure, she'd been using him, but she thought the attraction had been mutual, at least. He was just taking advantage of her attraction to get information on Leif.

More puzzle pieces fell into place as the suburban Chicago landscape fled by. Of course Adam would only show up when she was near Leif. All his questions were only as personal as the information he was trying to pry out of her. And if he really thought she spent her time with Leif doing— Kenzie shook that thought out of her head. Whatever he thought, he'd pegged her as an easy target. She wondered how much he'd already reported back to Draven.

She needed to tell Leif.

Kenzie hardly waited for Adam to park at the transit station, getting out and slamming the door.

Adam turned the car off and stood in his open door. "What about the sweaters?"

Kenzie flipped him the bird, not bothering to look back. "Burn them. Along with my number." And then she sauntered to the bus that would take her back home.

***

Kenzie used her magic to let Leif know about Adam. Their talk was brief—he was with his *Initiate*, of course—but she'd been able to convince Leif that her magic had done the trick. At least for now. But there was no way to know how much damage had already been done. She should've asked, but it didn't occur to her until after she'd made him forget everything important about her and Leif.

Kenzie watched out the window the rest of the ride home, a lead stone settling in her stomach. She should've seen this coming. She must have mentally kicked herself about a million times for being so dense.

The text from her mom came about twenty minutes before she arrived home. She'd been caught. In a way, she was kinda glad. She was too tired to keep holding it all together. If she couldn't talk to Myreen about stuff, then her mom would have to do. She just had to be careful about how much she revealed. There were still some secrets worth keeping.

As her front door loomed ahead, she resigned herself to whatever hell storm her mom had planned. Still, she crept through the front door as quietly as she could. Maybe if she came in meekly, things wouldn't go so badly.

What she didn't expect was the look of disappointment on her mother's face, or for Gram to be there as well.

Kenzie hung her head as she took off her winter gear.

"What were you thinking?" her mom said, arms crossed, eyes glistening.

Kenzie looked at the ceiling and blinked, the full emotion of everything that had happened threatening to spill. "I wasn't thinking."

"I don't know what's gotten into you! Your grades have been slipping, you've become forgetful and secretive, and now this. I don't even know who you are anymore."

Kenzie bit her bottom lip. She hardly recognized herself

some days. "I was stupid, okay? Stupid and selfish and just... stupid. But you don't have to worry about me anymore." Not like she had anywhere to go now. Leif was tied up, there were no more boys to keep her busy, and Myreen was locked away in a school she could never attend, let alone visit.

" *What* was stupid?" Gram asked, leveling a gaze at Kenzie. If she didn't clarify, that gaze promised a magical punishment. Kenzie didn't fancy another go with one of those.

But she couldn't tell them the whole truth, so she stuck with the truth in its simplest form. "A boy."

Concern etched the weary lines in her mom's face. "Was it that Wes kid that brought you home the other day? If he hurt you and you're covering for him—"

Kenzie shook her head. "No, not Wes. He was... decent. It was another guy." She looked at her feet, her toe tracing invisible letters of magic spells on the hardwood flooring. Too bad that wouldn't help her.

"And this other guy wasn't decent," her mom said, filling in the blank.

Kenzie nodded. Heat burned her cheeks as she thought of Adam and the carnal passions he'd roused.

"Aw, honey. Are you okay?" Mom wrapped her arms around Kenzie, and the dam she'd been so carefully constructing burst, her tears coming out in wracking sobs.

"If that boy did anything to hurt you, just let me know," Gram said, adding her warmth to the embrace. "I'll set a curse on him he'll never forget."

Kenzie hiccupped a laugh, mirth struggling against anguish. "No. Nothing I didn't allow or was uncomfortable with." She grimaced. "He was just using me, though. I thought..." she shook her head. "But he wasn't really interested in me. I was just a means to an end."

"What end would that be?" Gram asked, pulling her back so she could look Kenzie in the eye.

As Kenzie's head was mashed against her mom's shoulder, it wasn't like she could look away, either. Kenzie released her mom with a sigh, then wiped at her eyes. "Oh, you know boys."

Mom pushed Kenzie back quickly, her eyes wide. "We don't need to take you anywhere to get you checked or get you a pill or—"

"Ew! Relax. I can take care of myself." Kenzie crossed her arms, feeling doubly embarrassed.

Mom rubbed her arm. "What I still don't understand is why you would do this. I thought you were doing okay."

"Yeah, I was." *Until my best friend turned out to be a mermaid and her mom was killed by vampires.*

"So what changed?"

Kenzie looked to the side. How much should she tell them? Maybe just a little wouldn't hurt. She didn't have to tell them about Myreen or the grimoire or Leif... "What if I told you there's a school for shifters and I want to go?" She didn't dare look her mom in the eye, afraid of what she might see there.

Gram crossed her arms. "You want to go to a school for shifters? I'd say you're crazy."

"Why would you want to do that, honey? You know shifters aren't very fond of selkies."

"No! I don't really know, now do I? You and Gram have kept me in the dark about everything—magic and shifters and vampires." She pointed to her chest, feeling years' worth of anger bubbling out like a river of hot magma. "I have to figure out everything on my own because you two are too worried I can't handle it. But guess what? I'm sixteen! I'm not a little girl anymore."

Mom's chin had hardened, the stubborn look in her eye telling Kenzie this conversation wasn't going anywhere. Big surprise. "Maybe if you'd stop acting like a kid, lying and sneaking around, I'd stop treating you like one."

"I wouldn't have to be sneaking around and lying if you two would just stop hiding things from me."

"Things that are dangerous! You're reckless, Kenzie. You can't be trusted to boil a pot of water. What makes you think you should be using magic? Dangerous, volatile magic?"

"I'm capable of more than you think!" Kenzie stood tall and stared at her mom, despite the sting from the verbal stab her mom had just given her. Gram's gaze kept darting between the two, a measure of uncertainty hanging on those furrowed brows.

"Lita," Gram said, reaching out a hesitant hand.

"Mom, not now," Mom ground out, not taking her eyes off Kenzie. "And you, young lady. Go to your room and stay there. Mom, can you do something about that window so she can't escape again?"

Gram nodded. "Come on, Kenzie. Just walk away."

Kenzie had half a mind to walk right back out that front door, but she had nowhere else to go. So despite a huff of protest, she followed her Gram down the hallway to her room.

Kenzie plopped on her Rainbow Bright comforter and grabbed her black decorative pillow, hugging it to her chest. Mom must have turned off the radio after she'd discover Kenzie's escape, and the silence made her want to scream. It was so unfair. Mom's rules about magic were a typical catch-22, and

Kenzie had a feeling Mom would never really see her as anything but a little kid.

Gram finished muttering whatever spell she'd put on the window, then sat on the bed next to Kenzie, putting a hand on her knee. "For the record, I think you're mighty capable when you put your mind to it."

She appreciated the confidence, but she was still too upset to be grateful for the compliment. "Not like there's anything to put my mind *to*."

"What if I could change that for you?"

Kenzie sat up straighter, leaning forward. "Really? Like, you'd teach me about shifters and magic and vampires and… everything?"

Gram laughed. "Not everything, but as much as I know."

"Behind Mom's back?"

Gram pressed her mouth into a thin line. "Perhaps."

Kenzie's brows rose.

"I've stood back and let your mom handle things the way she'd like for a long time, now, but when your father passed, I think she lost her way."

Kenzie looked at her lap. She knew that feeling, though maybe not to the same extent her mom did. Losing her dad when she was just nine to that car accident had sent her through a very black phase, one that took her years to come out of. Heck, there were times she wasn't sure she ever came out at all, just floating along on a little magic until the blackness dragged her down again.

Gram looked at Kenzie, pity in her eyes. "There's something you don't know about that accident. Something your mom has kept you from. But if you really want to pursue magic, you have to know."

Kenzie's brows furrowed. "Know what?"

"Your dad's death wasn't just an accident. Your mom was testing out a spell, one that would protect you and your father and—"

"And she suffocated him." Gram had told Kenzie that story a few times, though the details were different.

Gram nodded. "It was an accident, of course, but you can see why she wouldn't want you involved in the stuff."

"And the rest? The shifters and vampires?" *And hunters*, her head screamed, though she refused to give it voice.

"It all led back to magic. Getting involved with them would have meant getting more involved in the magic needed to protect you."

Kenzie sank back, trying to process it all. So much of her life suddenly made sense. The secrets, the fights, the constant worry. Mom's guilt must have been eating at her. "Why wouldn't she just tell me?"

Gram sighed. "She can barely admit it to herself."

Kenzie nodded. "But you're still willing to teach me stuff, right?"

Gram nodded. "You'll have more of a chance of botching stuff up if you try to do this alone. I'd rather be there to help guide you."

Kenzie wore a sad smile. "Thank you." Her eyes darted to the headboard, considering showing Gram the grimoire, but decided against it. Trying to explain where that thing had come from would cause more trouble than it was worth at the moment. At least now she could ask Gram more about grimoires and why they didn't try to make a new one. Maybe she'd be able to unlock those sticky pages and the magic they held.

Gram patted Kenzie's leg as she stood up. "Don't thank me yet. Come to my place tomorrow and we'll get started." She left the room, closing the door softly behind her.

After the day she'd had, Kenzie didn't know how to feel about this new development. On the one hand, she was thrilled Gram was opening up to her. It would make life so much easier to have an ally at home. But learning about her father's true death made everything so heavy.

Not like she had anything else weighing on her, right?

She picked up the turquoise sweater Adam had gotten her. She'd balled it up and thrown it in a corner, hoping maybe she could fix it with some magic. But now?

"Dóicheáhn," she said, and a spot of fire sparked in the blue-green fabric. She let it go for as long as she dared, then threw it in the tin wastebasket she kept by her desk and poured the remnants of a glass of water over the flame. It wasn't Adam, but it would have to do.

She crossed her arms, the tears welling back up. She wished she could tell her best friend, but Myreen might as well be a world away in that school.

"For now," she whispered through her glum. Leif needed to hurry up and knock that vampire problem out.

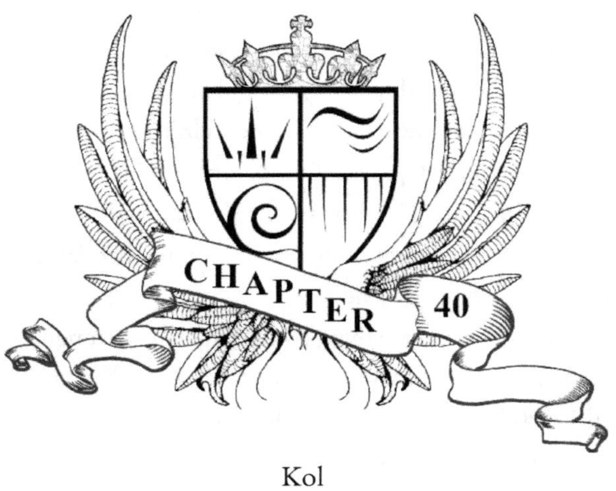

Kol

Kol felt like a piece of—

Which was why he flew today. Pumping his powerful wings through the frigid Illinois atmosphere—nope, Lake Michigan was behind him, he was well into Michigan state now—his thoughts wouldn't stop running loops around his recent actions.

Physically, he was in top form. Feeling the icy air rush through his dragon-sized lungs was euphoric. Feeling the fire run through his veins was invigorating. Feeling his invisible scales shift with the movement of his body and knowing that not a soul on the ground below—shifter or human—would be able to see him despite it being a clear, cloudless afternoon, made him feel powerful and invincible. He felt he could continue flying for hours, until Chicago and the Dome and the danger—and Myreen and his father and his responsibilities—were thousands of miles behind him before he would need a respite.

A tiny part of him still felt like a hypocrite for leaving the Dome in the first place. He still cringed at the memory of shouting at Myreen for leaving all those weeks ago to shop. He still thought it was stupid and reckless, but he shouldn't have caused such a scene. He wasn't even her boyfriend at the time. Not that being her boyfriend was any excuse, but still...

No, Kol felt like crap because he was a horrible person. More specifically, now that he had the title, he was a horrible *boyfriend.* Myreen should have been able to trust that his on-again off-again behavior was behind them, and then he went and avoided her at the New Year's Eve Ball—and ever since. All because of Eduard Dracul. He was a coward and couldn't bring himself to tell his father that not only did he lie about cutting all ties with Myreen—i.e. discontinuing their friendship—but that they were more than friends, and were in an actual, real relationship.

He'd made a commitment. He asked her to be his girlfriend and she'd said yes. He had no excuse to be avoiding her—even Eduard Dracul.

Coward. Hypocrite. Liar. Worst boyfriend ever.

So, true to his predictable behavior, he fled and flew. It was too bad that ever since he'd laid eyes on Myreen, flying was no longer the mindless activity it used to be.

White fields stretched below him. Snowbanks quiet and sparkling in the sunlight almost looked like a blanket of diamonds from his dragon's-eye view. It was beautiful. He suddenly wished his eyes weren't the only ones enjoying them, and it wasn't Nik's or Brett's company he wanted.

Kol shook his head, blowing out a breath of hot air that probably looked like a small cloud that suddenly appeared, if anyone was watching. But he knew no one was.

Adjusting downward, he pointed his nose into a dive. He tucked his wings back to reduce the air friction and allowed his speed to increase, with the help of gravity, and aimed at the perfect and untouched snow below. Building the heat inside him, he sped the pace of his heart to increase the circulation of fire running through his arteries and veins until enough built at the base of his fire chamber. Taking a deep breath, he veered at the last second and let out a jet stream of blue-white fire, evaporating and eviscerating a perfect line in the snow and uncovering the brown grass beneath. He smiled when he noticed the edges had turned to smooth ice.

Kol went on that way, building fire and creating lines and curves in the snow until he rose and could see the shape he'd created—a heart with letters inside reading: KD + MF.

It was simple. It was unoriginal. It wasn't math equations or history facts or anything intellectually amazing, although it was larger than two football fields. He felt better for doing it and briefly wondered if he could convince Myreen to come back with him to see it.

Pushing against the air again, Kol lifted higher and higher into the sky until his creation was a tiny dot below him. Only then did he shake the color of his scales to a deep rich blue color, the color he wished he'd chosen over his typical dark gray, because they were the same color as Myreen's eyes.

He thought about the way she looked that night. All white and gold and *angelic*. Her face had never looked so beautiful, her skin never looked so smooth, and yet he didn't allow himself more than a few looks in her direction when she should have remained in his arms all night.

With his feelings increasing, Kol became more and more panicked that he'd wake up one day having finally fallen deeply in love, and then rush to find the face that could not and would not ever look at him with any hint of affection again. It happened to his mother—of course she was already married to Lord Dracul and knew the risks and inevitability—but it could and *would* happen to him, too.

The air grew thinner the higher Kol climbed, and the oxygen decreased, making Kol's head fall into a fuzzy haze. He'd need to plateau or dive back down soon or else he'd pass out, but through the fuzzy haze he finally had a moment of clarity.

The vision of the Frost Boarding House history book forced itself to the forefront of his vision. He'd been studying it earlier in the day, desperately looking for more information about the Dracul curse. Questions ran through his head in rapid succession as he skimmed through the text and studied the few pictures peppered throughout.

What horrendous thing did Aline Dracul do to deserve the curse?

Was she an innocent victim?

Who put the curse on her?

And why?

On the outside, Aline was the model shifter. She was proper and kind. She assisted other shifters in learning to use and control their powers, including an entire pack of ursa weres. She and Evandrus Quinn—her bodyguard—protected the humans at the house and surrounding Vancouver from a rogue vampire. During the Arctic Winter of 1899, they not only kept the boarders of the house alive, but helped an entire orchard of apple trees survive—a major income source for the Frosts. Not a single apple tree was lost. Which was hailed a miracle.

Aline also stood and fought until she nearly lost her own life when the old vampire line—the Fausts—attacked and ultimately destroyed the boarding house. Leaving it in ashes.

The description didn't specify, but Kol was pretty sure the violet scales, scorched and littered around what was left of the house, in addition to several red-orange feathers in the same condition, belonged to the dragon-shifter Aline and phoenix-shifter Evandrus.

A story that didn't seem important at the time suddenly connected in Kol's analytical mind. It teetered on the tip of his tongue. Just out of reach. So he adjusted his position, no longer climbing, but not diving as if the exact quantity of breathable air would lend him the answer. He hardly dared to move a single scale that would cause him to fly in any direction but straight ahead. He could see the glow of sunlight along the curvature of the earth at this altitude, but could hardly appreciate it until he received his answer.

A boarder, Gemma MacLugh, who stayed at the house less than half a year, unexpectedly died at the claws of a dragon. It was reported as a random act of violence. The newspaper clipping had been printed right on the page and said in the unbiased, unfeeling language, that it was suspected that a migrating dragon mistook Miss MacLugh for a vampire due to recent vampire sightings in the area.

A Tragedy.

The story alone, a human girl being killed by a dragon shifter, was certainly a tragedy, but nothing noteworthy.

Except a few months later, a family of *selkies,* five sisters in particular, visited the house. Their name was *MacLugh.*

Kol bent into a nosedive immediately and felt the rush of oxygen fill his nostrils and muddle his mind with rapid-fire thoughts again. But he finally had an answer!

What reason would a family of selkies with the same name as the girl who died—he suspected this *Gemma* was also a magic user—have to travel to the place of their close relative's death?

Unless it was for revenge.

Whether Aline was to blame, whether she was the dragon who killed Gemma or merely the scapegoat, it was possible—no it was *probable*—that the group of magic users *cursed* Aline for Gemma MacLugh's violent and tragic death.

Kol shouted a stream of profanities. All the ones he knew at least. Which were a lot.

What creature could bring themselves to inflict such a miserable existence on an entire family line? Murder was horrible, yes, but what they'd done was despicable and disgusting and soulless. Kol wished he could get just one of those damnable seals into an interrogation chamber and flip pictures of his mother's face over the years at them. The ones that were forever burned into his mind.

But that was ridiculous. Aline lived at the turn of the twentieth century. The villainous selkies were long dead and six feet under.

Kol increased his speed. He could fix this. Maybe. He could ensure his mother and his sister, every living Dracul and every future Dracul, that they would never have to live another day wearing that heart-wrenching expression again. He needed to get to Chicago and back to the Dome, *now.*

***

"Here you are!" Kol said when he finally tracked his girlfriend down.

It was past dinner when he returned to the Dome. It was nearly lights-out when he finally found Myreen hiding in Juliet's room.

"Can I help you?" Juliet asked, holding her door halfway closed, braced to slam it at Myreen's word.

"Yes, I need to speak with Myreen."

Juliet looked over her shoulder, silently asking a question.

Myreen raised an eyebrow at her in response.

"Whatever you have to say to her, you can say in front of me."

"It uh... I..." Kol fumbled, running a now-human hand through his hair. He didn't have the actual words planned out. He knew he needed to apologize for avoiding her, but mostly he wanted to get to her tablet. "I'm an asshole, I know that," he said. "I'm a horrible, horrible boyfriend."

Myreen's expression thawed.

Juliet's smile suggested she'd stifled a laugh. "Go on," she prompted.

Kol's eyebrows frowned briefly at Juliet. He really wanted to get Myreen back to *Myreen's* room and he was getting nowhere.

"Please, Myreen?" he asked, surprised that it sounded like he had actual emotion inflected in his tone. "Could we speak in your room a minute? Alone?"

Myreen shot up immediately and shrugged at Juliet.

Now Kol held back a smile.

Juliet pointed a finger at her friend in mock annoyance and rolled her eyes when Myreen met Kol in the hall.

He grabbed for her hand the instant Juliet's door was closed and squeezed it gently. She looked up at him with a small smile, but neither said a word until they were safely behind Myreen's door.

Kol eyed the tablet in the middle of Myreen's bed when they sat knee-to-knee on the edge and wondered how he could get to it without telling her the actual reason he wanted it.

"I'm stupid," he said, going with the apology that was needed anyway. "It's my dad and it's stupid that I keep letting what my father thinks..." He wasn't sure where he was going with the sentence, so he ran his hand through his hair again to buy a few seconds.

Myreen pulled his hand away from his hair and used the other one to touch his face. "It is stupid," she agreed with a snarky smile. "And you're being stupid."

Kol ducked his head and laughed. "Then we're in agreement."

"We're in agreement."

C'mon, Kol, he thought. *Tell her you need the internet? To check your email?* Nothing seemed important enough to trump the current conversation. Except the truth, but he was *not* divulging that.

"I uh..." he scrambled again.

She put a finger against his lips. "Hold that thought. Want popcorn?"

Kol nodded with more enthusiasm than necessary. He had skipped dinner looking for her. His stomach rumbled audibly to sell the enthusiasm.

"Or a sandwich?" She twisted her mouth in a teasing way.

"Both. Please." He shrugged. "I missed dinner."

"Great. I'll be right back," she said, jumping up. "Don't go anywhere."

"Actually, could I use your tablet a minute?" he asked, praising whatever gods dropped this window of opportunity right into his lap.

"Of course!" she said, but then waved a finger at him. "But you're not out of the doghouse yet—or dragonhouse." She giggled.

Kol raised his hands. "Nope. But I plan to get out of that *dragonhouse...* tonight." He winked at her and watched with pleasure as her cheeks reddened.

Without another word, she spun on her heel and left him alone in her room.

Kol snatched up her tablet and located her email icon.

He remembered a specific shifter party, the one he invited Myreen to. She'd dragged along Juliet and that *selkie* friend of hers. The one who was outed and ridiculed for being a magic user and not a phoenix like she'd claimed.

Kenzie.

He quickly located her email and clicked the button to draft a message. Normally Kol would avoid a selkie like the plagues of the earth they were, but if a selkie laid the miserable curse on his family... then maybe a selkie could remove it.

Kenzie,

I miss you! Meet me at Mack's diner in Chicago tomorrow at noon.

I can't wait to see you.

Myreen

Kenzie

Kenzie bounced in her seat as she waited for Myreen to meet her. Technically, she wasn't quite off her punishment, but her mom had made an exception when she saw who the request had come from. Mom had insisted on coming into town as well, just to make sure Kenzie didn't do anything stupid or end up stranded, but at least she'd left Kenzie alone for her girl time.

This time she was definitely going to tell Myreen about Leif. It wasn't like that relationship was going anywhere, so there wasn't much to tell, but at least she could stop lying to her friend. She owed it to Myreen. Maybe she could explain the plant while she was at it. She only hoped her friend hadn't thought she'd gotten a lame Christmas gift in the meantime.

But today she could fix all that. She bounced in her seat again, a big grin on her face.

A waitress came up, brandishing a pad and pen. "What can

I get you?" she asked, smiling brightly.

"Um, I don't know. My friend should be here soon."

"We'll start with a plate of your chili cheese fries," came a male voice.

Kenzie spun around to see who it was. Tall, Dark and Brooding was standing there, looking pained as he attempted to smile. Kenzie sat back, rolling her eyes.

"Sure thing, sweetheart!" the waitress said, then turned to wink at Kenzie. "I'll give you two a few more minutes."

Kenzie was miffed. Myreen had sounded so excited to catch up, and here she'd brought along her boyfriend—one who had clearly expressed his distaste for selkies. If she wanted to bring a friend, why not Juliet? At least that girl didn't care if she was a shifter reject.

Kol slid into the seat across from her, his forever-long legs crowding her space, his hands forming a little tent on the table. And he was studying those hands of his like he'd never seen them before.

Well, this was awkward.

Kenzie casually looked around again. "Where's Myreen?"

Kol let out a long breath. "She's not coming."

"Is she okay?"

Kol shook his head. "She's fine."

"Was it something I did? Because I swear—"

"No. Let me explain—"

"Okay, so why'd she flake?" She didn't want to be rude, but she felt panic clawing at her throat. She searched her memories for anything that might've miffed Myreen enough to call off their friendship, but she was coming up empty.

Kol cleared his throat. "She didn't '*flake*.'"

Kenzie raised a brow. "I don't follow."

Kol looked to the side. He had yet to meet her gaze. Maybe he thought he'd turn to stone if he did. Kenzie snorted at the thought, and Kol looked at her like she was crazy—still not in the eyes, but at least he'd looked at her.

"I asked you to come here be—"

"Whoa, whoa, wait a minute. *You* asked me to come here? Because the email was specifically from Myreen." And now the wheels of her mind were turning in a different direction.

Kol at least had the decency to redden. "I sent that email, and will you just shut up for a minute so I can get this out?"

Kenzie shook her head and stood. "Look, I don't know what stick you have up your butt, but I'm not going to just sit here because you're my best friend's boyfriend. I get it. You hate—" She looked around the diner, but no one was paying them any mind. "You hate my kind. But whatever hazing you have in mind, I'm not in the mood."

But the chili cheese fries arrived, and Kenzie backed into the booth again to make room for the waitress. The woman set the steaming fries on the table. Kenzie's mouth watered and her tummy rumbled, reminding her she was ready for lunch. She glared at the plate and then the guy who'd ordered it.

"And what else can I get you two?" the waitress asked.

Kol threw a quick glance at Kenzie. "Two cheeseburgers and chocolate shakes."

The waitress smiled and left again.

Kenzie grabbed a fry and sank back in her seat, glaring at Kol. Did he know she was a foodie? Dang, if he didn't play her like a harp with that carb load. The cheesy, gooey, meaty, chewy bliss of a chili cheese fry filled her mouth, and she let out a soft sigh. "What if I was allergic to cheese?"

"You're not. You're eating cheese right now."

She smirked. "Oh yeah." She grabbed a few more fries and pointed them at Kol, though the rebellious things refused to remain straight. "Fine. I'll hear you out. You have until the burgers get here to convince me not to take all this to go. Oh, and you're paying." She popped the fries in her mouth, not taking her eyes off Kol, daring him to challenge her.

"Not a problem." He grabbed his own handful of fries and threw them in his mouth, grabbing a napkin to clean up his fingers and face.

Kenzie smirked. "You should've left the cheese on your face. You almost looked human."

Kol didn't even crack a smile.

Kenzie grabbed another fry. "Tick, tock."

Kol rolled his eyes. "Look, I've got this problem."

"Don't we all," Kenzie sighed. She knew she should slow down on the fries—she probably looked like a freaking pig scarfing them down like she was—but they were sooo good.

"I can't—" Kol stopped and pursed his lips, his face reddening as he glanced around the room. When he started again, his voice was softer, his gaze firmly planted on the table. "I can't... fall in love."

Kenzie stopped with a fry halfway to her mouth. She lowered it as she looked at Kol. "Can't? Or won't?"

Kol shook his head. "My family was cursed." He looked around again, then leaned forward—which for all his lank was at least halfway across the table—and hissed, "By selkies."

"And they turned you into a robot?"

Kol growled. "Will you take this seriously?"

Kenzie shrugged, bringing the fry to her mouth at last. "Nah if I won' haf foo," she said around her food.

Kol scowled. "If I fall in love with Myreen, she'll hate me."

Kenzie swallowed. "Geez, how'd you manage to tick them off that bad?"

"*I* didn't. My ancestor did."

Whoops. He'd said that already, hadn't he? *Blame the impending food coma.* "Wait, so you're saying the curse has been passed down—?"

"Generation after generation. Yes."

Kenzie took a sip of water as the waitress dropped it off, then let out a low whistle. "That's harsh."

Kol ran his hands through his hair. "Tell me about it."

The waitress came by again, doling out the two burgers. She only set one shake on the table, dropping two straws next to it.

Kenzie eyed the shake, then turned a questioning brow to Kol.

"You two enjoy," the woman said, giving them another wink.

"I ordered..." Kol began, holding up two fingers, but the waitress was gone again.

Kenzie shrugged and dragged the shake towards her. At a look from Kol she said, "What?"

Kol scowled.

"Okay, so you have this curse, but you're still dating my best friend."

"Yeah, and I don't want to hurt her."

"So you set up this little meeting with me—"

"To see if you could break the curse."

Kenzie took a big gulp of shake, appraising Kol. Kol returned her stare as he grabbed the last of the fries, but broke it as he dug into his burger. Kenzie liked him. She didn't know what it was about him, but she wanted to see him turn into a real boy. Maybe it was that stubborn chin of his? Or maybe it was the chili cheese fries talking—or the chocolate shake. At the very least, the transformation should prove amusing. And her best friend obviously liked him, if she was dating the guy. Right?

But he was asking her to lift a curse, one she knew nothing about. What if there was no way to break the curse? What if she did something stupid and the curse rebounded on her? Of course, it wasn't like she had any love prospects at the moment, so that was the least of her worries. Still, messing with unknown—and ancient—selkie magic could be dangerous.

But this was for Myreen. If her friend had any hope of finding happiness...

Kenzie sighed. "I can't really promise anything—"

"I figured. This was a dumb idea."

Kenzie held up a finger, giving Kol a pointed look. "You're the one who came to me, so let me just say this before you go climbing on that high and mighty shifter horse of yours. Selkies don't just go casting curses for the fun of it. That stuff is serious crud, and if you want me to try to remove it, you'd better treat me with a little respect."

Kol opened his mouth, but Kenzie held up her finger again. "Not done. I'm doing this for her more than I am for you, but that doesn't give you the right to treat me like crap. And don't go thinking I can just wave a magic wand and lift this curse. It's going to take some time and research, and even then, I don't know if I'll be able to lift it. But for Myreen's sake, I'm going to do my best."

Kenzie grabbed the milkshake and sucked on the straw until she got past the melted part and back to the thick and creamy bit. Kol's jaw twitched as he regarded her. He sighed and grabbed a bite of his burger, throwing it back on his plate as if it suddenly repulsed him.

"I don't know how much time I have left."

Kenzie lifted a brow. "Are you like, dying, or something?"

"No. The curse. I'm... She makes me..." Kol shook his head. "It could activate any day now."

"Oh."

"I've spent my whole life trying to compartmentalize my emotions because I didn't want *this*. I've watched what the curse has done to my parents. I thought I'd have more time, but Myreen... She's special. I tried to stay away, but I couldn't. And now?" He held out his empty hands.

Kenzie couldn't help herself. Her heart broke at the anguish on his face. He was clearly smitten, and it was making him miserable. She couldn't imagine anyone was deserving of such a curse. To never even be able to hope for love; what would that do to a person?

Maybe the tin man in front of her really did have a heart. And from the looks of it, it was in serious danger of breaking.

Kenzie slid the shake to Kol. "I think you need that more than I do."

Kol chuckled and shook his head.

"How is everything?" the waitress asked, seeming to materialize out of nowhere.

Kol nodded. "Fine, but I'd like another shake." He moved the one Kenzie had been drinking back her way.

"Something wrong with that one?" she asked, eyeing the second straw, which was still unopened.

"We just wanted two," Kol said, his tone curt.

The waitress pasted on a saccharine smile. "Of course. I'll be right back." She started to leave, muttering something about a lover's quarrel.

"We're not lovers!" Kol and Kenzie said at the same time.

If she heard them, she didn't acknowledge it.

Kenzie leaned forward. "What is her *problem*?"

Kol shrugged.

"Okay, so tell me more about this curse." She bit off some of her burger, marveling at the amount of grease dripping out the other side.

"I will, once you promise me you won't go telling anyone about it."

Kenzie raised a brow. "Who am I gonna tell?"

"Myreen."

Kenzie barked out a laugh. "Yeah, Myreen's got a lot on her plate at the moment." But as he continued to stare at her she lifted her hands. "Okay. I promise. I won't tell your girlfriend you can't fall in love with her."

Kol glowered at Kenzie, who gave him her sweetest smile in return. "It was placed on an ancestor of mine—Aline Dracul. I don't know what she did to piss off the selkies who cursed her, or who exactly those selkies were, but I have some ideas."

"Like?"

"Like, there was a boarder at the school she was staying at that mysteriously died. Then a bunch of selkie sisters traveled to the area, with the same last na—"

"Kenzie!"

Kenzie whirled in her seat to see her mom storming toward their table. She sank down, wishing she could make herself invisible. She wasn't expecting her mom back so soon.

Kol raised a brow.

"I thought we had an understanding," her mom said, her fists on her hips. "And now I find you sneaking around with another boy."

Kenzie groaned. "Mom, it's not—"

"I don't want to hear any more of your lies."

Kol cleared his throat. "Actually, it's not her fault. I sent an email from Myreen's account asking to meet with her."

"Because?" Kenzie's mom asked, fixing Kol with a hard stare.

"He's planning a surprise party for her," Kenzie rushed to fill in. She didn't need her mom knowing that Kol was a shifter. She had a feeling that would only make things worse. "And since he and I haven't really seen eye-to-eye on things in the past, he wanted to meet in person so I didn't mess anything up. But I think we've come to an understanding, right Kol?"

Kol nodded, still looking confused. Whatever. Let him think what he wanted about her relationship with her mom. If he knew what was good for him, he'd take her lead.

Mom sighed. "Well, I'm sorry to say Kenzie won't be able to attend your party. She's been grounded for the foreseeable future."

"But Mom!" Kenzie groaned.

"Don't 'But Mom!' me! You should've notified me as soon as you knew this meeting wasn't with Myreen. *And* that you were with a guy."

"*Moooom!*" Kenzie was beyond mortified.

Kol stood, towering well above Kenzie's mom. "Sorry. I didn't mean for you to—"

"There's no need for you to apologize, uh..." Kenzie's mom

began, and Kenzie stifled a snicker as she measured the two against each other.

"His name is Kol," Kenzie said, crossing her arms.

Mom smiled. "Kol. I'm sorry you got caught up in the middle of this. Kenzie, let's go."

Kenzie stood with a sigh. But the look on Kol's face made her gut clench. "Don't worry, I'll still work on that *gift* we discussed. I'll let you know when it's ready so you can come pick it up?" Kenzie said, then mouthed the word "sorry" to Kol.

Kol nodded.

Kenzie drained the rest of her shake and grabbed her burger and a handful of paper napkins as she followed her mom out the door. No sense wasting good food. Kol was paying for it, after all.

She just hoped she could fix his problem before he ran out of time.

Sorry, Leif, but you'll have to wait a little longer for Gemma. Not like she was getting anywhere with that, anyway.

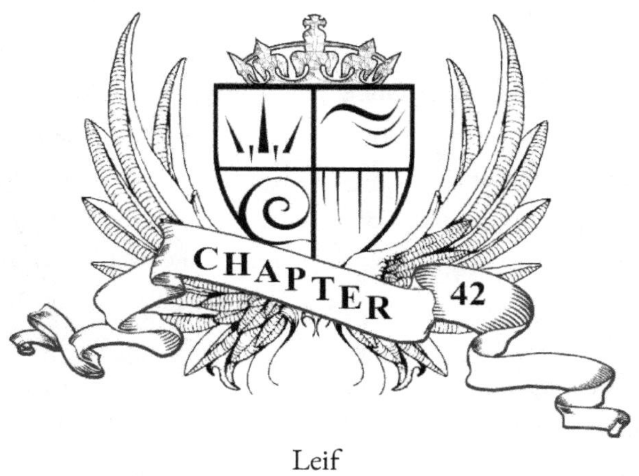

Chapter 42

Leif

To his dismay, Leif was summoned back to Heritage Prep. Draven had even sent his own private jet to pick him and Piper up, but was too busy with other matters to come along himself.

Now Leif found himself back in the trophy room, noticing a few new prizes mounted to the wall. The vampire leader was stroking one of them—a long black tail that Leif could only assume had belonged to a mao. The tail reminded Leif of Rainbow, who he'd left behind in Chicago. He highly doubted Draven would be happy to discover such a creature, and he really didn't want to explain how he'd been involved with a selkie.

"I warned you what would happen if you failed me in snatching Myreen," Draven said casually, as if he were talking about the weather.

"As I told you on the phone, the subway station is far too dangerous to be around," Leif replied, keeping his eyes on Draven.

He wouldn't put it past the other vampire to suddenly attack him. He'd been a witness to the vampire leader's ruthless brutality before. And he also knew Draven always made good on his threats. "Human hunters are swarming like hornets at that staircase."

Draven turned his attention to Leif, a cruel smile forming on his face. "You know, most vampires would have died trying to complete their assigned mission. But not you." He gently tapped a finger against Leif's chest. "Some would say that's cowardice. But you're no coward. You're a survivor. You always have been."

Leif wished he'd just get on with it. If Draven wanted to sentence him to three years of drowning, then so be it. Perhaps by then, Kenzie might be able to find a resurrection spell for Gemma.

If Kenzie survived the next three years, that is. Draven had yet to confront him about his selkie friend, which made him think that Solomon and the Initiate, Adam, had not reported everything back to Heritage Prep. At least, that's what Leif hoped.

Draven chuckled, and Leif shuffled his feet as he returned his attention back to the vampire leader.

"To be honest, I'm surprised you didn't turn into a fugitive after I requested you return." Draven placed a hand on Leif's shoulder. "And now that you're here, I know I shouldn't be shocked to find you unapologetic for your failures." His smile disappeared and his eyes narrowed, all humor erased from his features. "I'm used to begging and pleading for mercy when my followers are unsuccessful in their missions."

Leif felt no fear at Draven's words. Had the vampire leader intended to kill him, he'd already be dead.

Draven removed his hand and turned his back on Leif as he analyzed his trophies again.

"I have spent enough time around you to know you don't deal out second chances," said Leif. "But you allowed me to return once before, and for some reason, you're letting me return again."

Faster than a blur, Draven moved. The leader wasn't the typical vampire—he was an inheritor of one of the ancient sire lines, which meant his abilities were even more enhanced.

Leif didn't have time to react, and felt his ribs crack as Draven's palm slammed into his chest. The momentum lifted him into the air and flung him across the room. He went crashing hard into one of the stone walls, knocking a few shifter body parts off in the process.

He hurt all over, but the internal pain that burned within him was excruciating. He tried to inhale, but his body refused to let him. Leif guessed he'd punctured a lung. Moments later, he felt relief flood in as his body mended itself. Bones snapped back into place, and flesh restitched like water rapidly freezing into ice.

Slowly, Leif rolled over and got to his feet.

"Consider *that* your punishment for failure," Draven said, wiping his hands together as if he'd just taken out the trash. He shook his head. "You're one-of-a-kind, Leif. But you could be *so* much more."

Leif felt at his pocket, ensuring Gemma's brooch was still there. As much relief as his body had just been through regenerating, it was nothing compared to the comfort he received feeling the outline of the metal through his slacks.

Looking at the trophies he'd knocked off the wall, Leif said, "Sorry about your harpy talon collection. I'm afraid I crushed a set."

Draven snorted, lifting a hand in disbelief. "You apologize for breaking replaceable talons, but not your inability to bring me my daughter?"

"That was an impossible task," Leif said, doing his best to prepare for another punch. Nobody talked back to Draven. But he was sick of dancing around the vampire leader. And again, had Draven intended on killing him, he'd already be dead.

"Impossible for the incapable, perhaps," Draven said, approaching Leif again with narrowed eyes. "Quite possible for the capable. Have you ever heard the cliché 'If I want something done right, I'll do it myself'? It applies to the mission regarding my daughter. I'll see to her capture personally, which means the task is no longer yours."

Leif didn't know how to respond. Draven rarely let his followers just *hang around* the school. If he had his way, he'd race back to Chicago and work with Kenzie to find a way to bring Gemma back. But somehow, he didn't think Draven would just let him go. Leif still wasn't entirely sure how much the vampire leader knew.

"What does that mean for me?" Leif finally asked as he straightened the black jacket he had on. He wondered if the crushed talons had punctured the back of it. Such a thing would only fit his luck.

Draven studied him for a few moments—about three feet away this time. The space between them brought Leif some comfort.

"I have another assignment for you," Draven said at last. Turning to the side, Leif followed his eyes to the two sets of wide wings mounted above the doorway of the trophy room. Gryphon wings. The smaller set was white-feathered, while the larger was a deep, dark brown.

Does he know about my contact with Oberon?

"Back in Chicago?" Leif asked, hiding his hopefulness. Although he didn't consider Chicago *home*, his greatest hopes were there.

Draven chuckled, returning his attention back to Leif. "Old friend, you are done with Chicago for a while. Your new mission is something of a more personal nature."

Leif kept his gaze steady, but he didn't like the sound of that.

"We've received intelligence about a flock of gryphons that has been spotted."

"A flock of gryphons?" Leif asked, raising his eyebrows. "The last sighting of gryphons was on La Framboise Island twenty years ago. And you killed all but one of them."

"Indeed I did," Draven said, looking back up at his precious trophies. "So you can imagine how badly I'd love to add the wings of an entire flock to my collection."

Oberon would kill for this information. The wings on the wall belonged to his parents. Apparently, his wife had died in the attack on the old school, too, but she hadn't been in gryphon form. Throughout their meetings over the years, Oberon had explained everything, and that he was still going out on expeditions during his summers looking for more of his kind. The poor gryphon had never found any, and had admitted to Leif that he was beginning to think he was the last gryphon on earth.

Instead of exuding wonder, Leif sighed heavily. "How accurate are these reports? Will I be chasing ghosts?"

"They're accurate enough for me to send you to investigate," Draven replied without hesitation.

"And what do I do if these reports prove to be true?" asked Leif. "Do I move to engage?"

Again, Draven laughed wickedly. "If you seek your own death, then by all means."

Leif had only ever fought against one gryphon before, and

that was Oberon. During the attack on the school at La Framboise Island, the young gryphon had entered a store Leif and Beatrice had camped out at. It had been a trap, but Oberon and his friend managed to escape. And even then, he hadn't seen the full force of the gryphon's attacks. But Draven had.

"So whether I find gryphons or not, I should return and report?" Leif asked.

Draven nodded.

"And where have these sightings been? Where will I be going?"

"Not far, actually," replied Draven as he started pacing the room again. "The sightings have been in Yukon, Canada. In the mountains."

"Sounds cold," said Leif.

"And snowy, especially this time of year," Draven added. "Yukon is home to the highest-elevated mountain in Canada, called Mount Logan. Our reports indicate that the gryphons have been seen circling it."

"Do they live on the mountain?" Leif asked. He had a hard time believing any creature would force themselves to dwell in such an unlivable place.

Draven shrugged. "Who knows? They could be living in one of the small townships. There's only one actual city in Yukon, and they could be there, too."

"So I'm to search the city and towns, as well as the mountains?"

Draven smirked. "That's what I would do, yes."

It seemed easy enough. Leif had been assigned a similar task back when he'd first joined Draven. The former shifter school had eluded Draven and his followers for years, and Leif had been assigned the task of finding it. He'd been successful in that mission, and he'd regretted it ever since, as Draven had destroyed it. If Leif found gryphons in Yukon, he'd never admit it to Draven.

"Is Piper assigned to come along with me?" He'd grown fond of his Initiate over the past few weeks. He felt a responsibility to her—a fraction of what he'd felt for Camilla from his boarding house days, but still a responsibility.

Shaking his head, Draven said, "No. I need her expertise here at the school. We're on the verge, Leif. The day of the vampire-shifter hybrid is near."

The vampire leader's eyes lit as he spoke, as if he could see his dream just inches away.

Leif set his jaw. Draven was mad. Such an abominable goal had to be stopped. The question was, would Myreen fulfill the shifter prophecy before Draven's hybrids came to be?

"Where will that put people like us?" Leif asked.

The light in Draven's eyes snuffed out, and he gave Leif a hard look. "People like us?"

Leif shrugged. "Average vampires with standard abilities. When your hybrids come waltzing in, they will crush us."

Draven laughed loudly as he made his way back to Leif. "If you elect not to become a hybrid, that's your own choice. But I would advise you to start considering which shifter powers you'd like added to your compendium of current abilities."

"I will think on that," Leif said, lying through his teeth. He longed for an escape—to be able to hide where nobody would come looking for him. Somewhere with Gemma, where they could live uninterrupted and make up for all the lost time—

A knock sounded at the door of the trophy room, pulling him out of his thoughts.

"Enter!" Draven boomed, turning around.

The door opened inward, and Leif saw a young, dark-haired

boy—the same nine or ten year-old he'd seen embracing Draven the last time he was here—sheepishly step inside.

Leif cast a look at Draven, finding the vampire leader's features warm.

"I've lost track of the time!" Draven said excitedly, then looked back at Leif. "You may begin your mission now, Leif. I have other responsibilities I must see to."

Leif bowed ever so slightly. "Of course. I'll return as soon as I've learned more about these gryphon sightings."

Having to walk past the boy at the doorway, Leif gave him a half smile. The child returned the gesture with a chilling glare. What terrible plans was Draven involving such a young child in?

Pushing himself out of the trophy room, Leif decided he needed some fresh air rather.

Exiting the school, he went down the stairs at an easy pace, then began to hike the northern mountains. It was evening, and although there were clouds, Leif could see patches of the night sky glittering with stars.

He had a call to make, and he couldn't afford being heard. Once he felt confident with the distance up the easy climb, he pulled out his phone and dialed Oberon's emergency number, hoping the gryphon was in a position to talk.

After several buzzes, he heard the gruff voice of Oberon on the other end.

"Leif?"

He could hear the concern in the shifter's tone.

"Oberon, I have some urgent news for you."

"About Draven and his plans?"

"No," Leif said quickly. "There's been sightings of a flock of gryphons."

Myreen

Myreen slammed the bleeping alarm, groaning as she tried to curl up under her covers. She felt like a truck had run over her while she slept. Her head pounded, her stomach rolled, and her teeth chattered as she kicked off the blankets. She groaned as the air cooled her again, but her sore body protested even the thought of moving to get the blanket again.

After a few minutes, the chill became unbearable. She needed to see Ms. Heather. There had to be *something* a harpy could do to fix this, and she didn't feel up to trying to figure it out herself.

Wrapped in her blanket, she slid into her slippers and shuffled from the room, keeping her half-closed eyes on the floor in the hopes she wouldn't face-plant on it.

"Myreen, what's wrong?"

Myreen winced as she looked up, the room starting to tilt.

Juliet's hand was on her elbow a second later, keeping her vertical.

"Are you okay?" Juliet asked, looping an arm around Myreen.

"I— I th– think I'm s– sick," she stuttered through her chattering teeth.

"Oh no! I'm so sorry."

Myreen shrugged. "M– Miss Heather?"

Juliet nodded. "Yeah, we should get you there right away. I'll help you."

Myreen was grateful for the assistance as they made their way down the stairs and through the Grand Hall and then left toward the Nurse's Station. What should've only been a couple of minutes seemed to drag out for an eternity. The halls were thankfully empty, as most students were either getting ready for the school day or were in the Dining Hall having breakfast.

Ms. Heather's forehead crinkled as she saw Juliet escorting Myreen in, and she took off her glasses. "What seems to be the problem?" she asked, coming straight to Myreen's side and helping her to a bed.

Myreen sat down and draped the blanket over the bed, letting her head fall into her hands as she leaned forward and groaned.

"I can tell you she's burning up, and I'm a phoenix," Juliet said, folding her arms as she cast a worried look at Myreen.

"Hmmm," Ms. Heather said, placing a hand on Myreen's forehead. "Have you ingested any mercury or lead?"

Myreen feebly shook her head. "N– not that I n– know of."

"And what other symptoms are you experiencing?"

"Aches, ch– chill, n– nausea."

"What's wrong with her?" Juliet asked, chewing on her bottom lip.

"I'm not sure. It sounds like a bad flu, but that shouldn't be possible." She turned back to Myreen, placing a warm hand on her knee. "Myreen, I'm going to draw some blood and do some tests."

Myreen nodded, pulling the blanket around her as the room seemed to shift temperatures again. "N– not possible? To get a c– cold? What, are shifters im– immune or s– something?"

"No, but harpies are." Ms. Heather's answer surprised her.

Juliet looked surprised, too. "How long will the test take?" she asked, shifting her weight to her other hip.

"Not very long," Ms. Heather said, grabbing Myreen's ankles and gently swinging her legs onto the bed. She pulled the blanket up to Myreen's chin and smoothed the hair from her face. The soft motion reminded Myreen of her mom, and she would've cried if she wasn't already feeling so miserable.

"Why don't you rest while I get everything taken care of?" Ms. Heather said.

Myreen nodded and closed her eyes.

"Is she going to be okay?" Juliet whispered.

Myreen idly wondered why her friend wouldn't at least voice her concerns a little further away, but when she cracked one eye open, Juliet and Ms. Heather were on the other side of the room. She was too tired and achy to care. She let her eye drop closed again.

"I'll take good care of her. Don't you worry. Now, off to class."

Soft footsteps retreated from the room.

Myreen scrunched her eyes tighter and pulled the blanket over her nose as a wave of chemical scents assaulted her senses. Her stomach gurgled in protest, but thankfully didn't go any further. It wasn't like she had anything to throw up, anyway.

She barely felt the needle as Ms. Heather took her blood and sealed the spot with her healing light. The last thing Myreen remembered before finally drifting back to sleep was Ms. Heather laying her hands on Myreen's forehead and speaking soft, soothing words that seemed to ease the ache.

***

Myreen groaned as a gentle hand rocked her awake. Ms. Heather smiled as she helped Myreen sit up.

"I apologize, but I have something that will help. Here." Ms. Heather handed Myreen a plastic cup filled with a clear liquid. There was no smell to it, but Myreen hesitated. She hadn't been sick much growing up, but she'd seen her mom shudder in revulsion after taking some medicines. Myreen wondered if this was one of the sweet ones or one of the horrible ones.

"It's best if you drink it all in one go," Ms. Heather said, as if reading Myreen's mind. She sat in the chair next to Myreen's bed. "And you'll need to drink the whole dose."

Myreen sighed. So it was one of the horrible ones. She held her breath and tried to still her chattering teeth as she lifted the drink to her lips. She only made it halfway through before she started coughing and spluttering. The bitter taste coated her throat and tongue, and she shuddered just like she remembered her mom doing. But as she threw back the last awful dregs of the drink, she noticed that the shaking and chills were gone, her sore muscles beginning to unwind.

"What the heck *was* that?" Myreen asked, handing the cup back to Ms. Heather. She tried to scrape the taste off her tongue with her teeth, but it just wasn't letting go.

"Here. Try this." Ms. Heather handed Myreen a mint. The flavor didn't quite cut through whatever was in the remedy, but at least it gave her taste buds something else to focus on.

"Better?" Ms. Heather asked, and Myreen nodded. "The drink is an old were remedy to help ease the change."

Myreen's brows furrowed. "A were remedy? Why would that help?"

Ms. Heather pushed her glasses up her nose. "Well, based on your symptoms and you being a chimera, it seemed prudent to run some diagnostics on your blood. The flu isn't really something a harpy would get—we don't get sick at all—and even with your mer side, your harpy should be strong enough to keep you free of illness. Something had to be blocking that ability." She looked down at her nails, and Myreen wondered what would make the woman so nervous. "It turns out that you have ursa DNA in your chimera makeup."

"As in a werebear? How's that possible?" Myreen clearly remembered from her shifter biology class that weres were bitten shifters, but she'd never been bitten. Not by anything any bigger than a bug, anyway.

Ms. Heather curled her hands in her lap, looking Myreen in the eyes. "It appears the ursa DNA has been lying dormant in your blood. I think your shift into your dual chimera form activated the latent ursa DNA, and you're now experiencing the effects of a first shift."

Myreen groaned as she leaned back. That's all she needed,

another shifter type lurking inside. "How long will the change take?"

Ms. Heather shifted in her seat. "I'm not entirely certain. Normally, it takes a were about a week, give or take, from bite to first shift. You, however, seem to be developing at a slower rate. I'm estimating two weeks, but it could be more, or things could change and your rate could accelerate. No one's ever seen a born were before, so I'm afraid we're out of our element here."

Myreen let that sink in, but a startling thought made her sit back up. "There's no other shifter types in me, right?"

Ms. Heather shook her head, giving Myreen a half-smile. "Ursa is the only other *shifter* DNA you carry."

Myreen nodded. She felt like such a freak. What kinds of procedures were done on her mom to produce a chimera with were DNA? For the first time since her mom's passing, anger bubbled up. What kind of person let people experiment on their unborn child? It was beyond sick. She wanted to yell or scream or do... something.

If her mom were alive...

But her mom was dead. And she'd done everything she could to keep Myreen away from her vampire father. Guilt cooled the white-hot anger burning through her. She was the worst, most ungrateful daughter ever.

Still, the anger gnawed at the edges of her guilt. Myreen felt almost dizzy from the mood swing.

"Knock, knock," came a deep voice from the doorway. Myreen recognized the man as Mr. Coltar, the world history teacher. It was one of her normal classes, the ones that helped her feel a little less like a fish out of water. What was he doing here?

"Ah, Henry. Thanks for coming." Ms. Heather stood as

Mr. Coltar came in. "Myreen, Mr. Coltar here is an ursa shifter. I asked him to come talk to you about what you'll be going through in the coming days."

Myreen straightened the sheet draped over her legs. If Mr. Coltar knew, how many others did, too? "Um, where'd Juliet go?"

Ms. Heather smiled. "I sent her to her classes."

"You didn't tell her anything, did you?"

Realization lit Ms. Heather's angelic features. "Oh, no dear. Oberon and Mr. Coltar are the only people I've told."

"Do you mind if we... keep it that way? Just for now?" Myreen asked, twisting a corner of the blanket around her finger.

Ms. Heather nodded slowly. "You want to tell the others in your own time."

Myreen gave her a hopeful smile.

"Mum's the word." Ms. Heather winked. She closed the door leading to the rest of the school, then returned to her desk, giving Mr. Coltar space.

Mr. Coltar took the chair Ms. Heather had been sitting in and turned it around before taking a seat and resting his arms on the backrest. He appraised Myreen for a long moment. "Feeling a little lost, are we?"

Myreen nodded.

"I've always maintained that being a were shifter is the most difficult of shifter types. Not only does getting bitten suck, but the change from being a regular human to a magical shifter is a bit like going through puberty. You may have skipped the bite, but I'm afraid you'll still have to go through that ugly, awkward phase." Mr. Coltar chuckled.

Myreen's face reddened. This was not the conversation she

wanted to have with anyone, let alone a male of any age. The thought of telling her friends—or Kol—was enough to make her cringe. They'd understand, she was sure of it, but this part of herself felt so much more personal—not to mention embarrassing. It probably didn't help that the weres carried an obvious stigma as the only non-born shifters. She'd never thought of herself as prejudiced, but now?

And things were just starting to get comfortable at the school.

"So, you'll be experiencing some mood swings, some cravings, and surges of strength and sensory input as your body adjusts to the shift," Mr. Coltar continued. "It's one heck of a ride."

Myreen sighed. "And the were juice?"

Mr. Coltar laughed. "Never took the stuff myself, having been unlucky enough to stumble into being a shifter by accident, but the illness bit only lasts a day or so."

"Which is all the remedy really addresses, I'm afraid," Ms. Heather cut in from her perch at her desk. "And with your rate of progression, it might be a few days before you're past those symptoms."

"Of course," Myreen grumbled.

"But hey, better a few seconds of that gunk than a day of the shakes." Mr. Coltar laughed, but Myreen didn't see the humor.

"And if you ever want to talk, me and the other were instructors are happy to help."

Myreen tried to conjure a smile, but it felt flat. "Thanks."

"Man, a mermaid, a harpy and an ursa. What do you call something like that, a murpy? A mersagryph? Dang, kid. I think you've got the whole shifter kingdom covered in that one body of yours."

Myreen could tell that Mr. Coltar was trying to lighten the mood, but tears still sprung to her eyes. She held her knuckles to her lips as she tried to keep the flood of emotion at bay.

"Oh, man, I'm sorry. Bad time to make a joke," Mr. Coltar said, grimacing.

Myreen shook her head. "It's okay. I'm sorry, I just—"

"Feel like a pile of emotional goo? Yeah, I get it. It's been a while since my first shift, but the power of that transformation..." Mr. Coltar shook his head, a faraway look in his eyes. "I know you want to keep this to yourself for now, but you should probably tell your friends, at least. It'll be hard trying to keep the shift under wraps now that it's started. And this really isn't something you should *bear* alone. Catch my drift?" Mr. Coltar smiled.

Myreen tried—and once more failed—to smile at Mr. Coltar's corny joke.

"Well, is there anything you want to ask? Anything else I can do for you?" Mr. Coltar asked.

Myreen shook her head. She wanted to disappear. "No. Not that I can think of."

He looked to Ms. Heather, who shook her head.

"Then I suppose I'd better grab some grub before break's over."

Just like that the guilt was back. He'd used his lunch break to try to ease her mind about her new shifter form and she was too miserable to be grateful. "I'm sorry I—" she began, but the door clicked. Myreen looked up, a smile tugging at her lips as she recognized the familiar red hair of her friend.

"Myreen! You're up!" Juliet bounded over to the bed and gave Myreen a big hug.

Mr. Coltar gave Myreen an encouraging nod as he slipped out of the room.

"Are you all better?" Juliet asked. "I was so worried. I mean, it's so weird you getting sick, being a harpy and all."

Myreen laughed. "I'm doing some better, but I guess it's not over yet."

"It's not contagious is it? Because you looked like crap, and I don't think I want whatever you got."

Myreen gave her a half-hearted smile. "I don't think you have to worry about that."

"Why?"

Myreen glanced at Ms. Heather, who was studiously focused on her paperwork, though Myreen had a feeling the nurse was still listening. But Myreen wasn't ready to share her news yet. She hated the thought of lying to her friends, but they'd all find out soon enough. And she had a feeling she should tell Kol first, anyway. It was hard to sort out the details when her mind was spinning so furiously.

"It's kind of a chimera thing. You wouldn't be able to get sick from it."

"Oh, cool. I mean, not for you, obviously, but I'm glad I can't catch it."

"Me too."

Ms. Heather's lips were pressed in a tight line, but she didn't correct Myreen's lie.

"Was that Mr. Coltar?" Juliet asked, glancing at the open door.

"Yeah," Myreen said, her face heating.

"What was he doing here?"

"Um—" Myreen began.

"I asked him to help me with something," Ms. Heather filled in, and Myreen shot her a grateful look.

Juliet hopped up as her tablet chimed. "Oh, dang it. I need to go back to class. I ate before I came over here. I hope you don't mind. Are you going to still be here after school's over?"

Myreen looked to Ms. Heather.

"If she's feeling okay, she's welcome to rest in her room," Ms. Heather told Juliet with a smile. Juliet looked to Myreen for her verdict.

"Yeah. That would be nice. I think I will go back to my room." Maybe she could sort through this mess of thoughts before school let out for the day.

Ms. Heather nodded, and Juliet clapped her hands. "Okay, I'll be in to check on you as soon as I'm off. Ping me if you want me to bring you anything. Even if school isn't out yet."

"Okay, thanks."

Juliet jetted from the room and Myreen chuckled. She sure was grateful she had Juliet in her life right now.

Ms. Heather grabbed what looked like four water bottles, but Myreen was sure their unlabeled contents held the antidote she'd taken earlier. The memory of the drink made her cringe, but she supposed if she was desperate enough, she'd get over it.

"You'll want to keep these in case the chills and aches come back. One a day should suffice, but only take it if you're still experiencing flu-like symptoms. Here are some mints to help with the aftertaste." She grabbed a tote and put the bottles and a large bag of mints she'd pulled from her desk inside, then brought it to Myreen.

Myreen nodded as she swung her legs off the bed and grabbed her blanket. The ursa thing was a bit of a shock, but at least she didn't feel like death warmed over anymore.

"Bring any unused bottles back when you're done with them."

"I will. Thanks, Ms. Heather."

Myreen reached for the bag, but Ms. Heather held on a moment longer. "And please check in once a day. We'll need to monitor your progress closely, along with the phases of the moon. Most weres experience their first full shift during a full moon, and we have one coming up soon."

"Of course," Myreen groused. Just her luck.

"And Myreen?"

"Yes?"

"Please consider Mr. Coltar's advice carefully. I know this particular shift is kind of a sensitive thing, but it might be easier on everyone if you don't try to deal with it on your own."

"I'll keep that in mind. Thanks."

Myreen would tell them. She just needed a little time to process first. Hopefully a few hours would be all she needed.

Oberon

The late-morning Canadian winter air was bitter cold, but Oberon's gryphon form was well equipped to withstand the biting currents. After all, he was master of the weather. And the possibility that he'd finally run into other gryphons ignited a fire within his soul that no chill could bite through.

Without any hesitation, Delphine had approved the funding to get Oberon to Yukon by plane. He'd worded things in such a way that protected Leif's identity, and he was set to meet the vampire at the only city in the province: Whitehorse. It was just under two hundred miles east of Mount Logan.

But Leif wasn't due to arrive until the evening, so Oberon checked into a hotel, went to his room, and stripped down to his smart clothing. After opening his window, he'd jumped out six floors above the ground, and shifted in mid-air. His wings had formed first, and they'd caught the harsh wind that was now carrying him.

A surge of liberation unfurled as his wings whipped through the air. The confinement of the Dome wasn't obvious, probably due to its technological majesty, but being above *everything* and away from it really showed how stifling the underwater school really was. Still, Oberon wouldn't trade his experience as Director for anything.

But that didn't mean he couldn't enjoy himself while he was away. Oberon swooped, climbed, spun, and drifted. The sky was his playground, and he felt like a teenager again, allowing the air to blow away all his concerns and worries.

He was flying toward hope—a hope he hadn't felt in a long time. The kind of hope that invigorated his body and outmaneuvered exhaustion. Flying two hundred miles without stopping? It would be a *breeze*.

Seeing other gryphons with his own eyes wouldn't be Oberon's greatest indicator that there were more of his species alive. He'd be able to *smell* them first. Although he couldn't smile with his razor-sharp beak, his heart burst with joy as he recalled the scent of his wife, Seri. That was how she'd been found in the first place—Oberon's father had discovered her while she'd been living with her foster family.

On the wind, Oberon could almost smell the crushed-rose scent of his sweet Seri, her memory was so vivid.

He could even recall how his mother and father smelled, and he missed them sorely. Perhaps finding the flock of gryphons Leif had heard about would better stitch the wounds their emptiness left behind.

Such were his thoughts as he soared through the air, all thoughts of vampires, the Dome, and the siren of prophecy shoved to the corners of his mind.

It seemed no time had passed at all when the tall, snow-covered mountain came into view.

This is it, Oberon thought. *Mount Logan.*

It stood as a single pointy peak like a volcano. While one part sat higher than the others, the entirety was a big piece of landmass, like an island cropping out of the snow. From such a high elevation, the late-morning sky was a gorgeous blue background to the blanket of white snow. Sure, the water above the Dome was a sight to behold, but the shifter-made structure seemed to pale in comparison to the natural wonder before him.

The place looked untouched and remote—a perfect place for gryphons to hide from the rest of the world.

But there was only one problem. Oberon detected no scent of another gryphon. Had there been a flock that gathered here, it hadn't been for a very long time.

He swooped lower, circling his way down until his large talons grabbed the snow-covered rocks below.

Grateful for the chance to rest, he tucked his wings in and felt his muscles burn from the long trip. He couldn't remember the last time he'd flown so far in one go. Oberon made a mental note to exercise his wings better when he returned to the Dome.

With his eagle eyes, he looked around for any potential signs that gryphons had been on the mountain recently, but the snow looked untouched. If gryphons had been spotted here, it had been a while ago.

He pressed on, keeping to his talons to give his wings a break, hoping to smell even a stale scent on the verge of disappearing. The powerful hope that had filled his heart during the flight began to wane, and a sudden panic struck his heart.

Was this a setup? Had Leif convinced him to leave the

Dome because Draven was ready to make his attack?

Oberon's phone was in his hotel room, and he wished he'd had the foresight to bring it. With how cold it was, though, chances were the phone wouldn't have worked. Even less likely was the possibility of a cellular signal on top of the mountain.

His heart filled with a chilling terror, as if confirming Oberon had made a grave mistake in traveling away from the school so rashly.

Leaping and unfurling his wings, he ignored the aches of his sore muscles and let fear-filled adrenaline send him shooting through the air. He had to get back to Whitehorse. He had to get in contact with Leif!

***

Whitehorse was a smaller city, its population just under one percent of Chicago's. Oberon wasn't too concerned with being spotted as he rocketed through. Although it was late afternoon, the sun had already set—an outcome of the geographical location.

His eagle eyes saw his open window on the sixth floor of the hotel, and he decided to attempt the acrobatic maneuver of shifting back to human form mid-air just in time to clear the opening and shoulder roll into his room.

It had been decades since he'd tried, but he figured it was better than walking into the hotel lobby in his smart clothing.

Slowing his momentum, he climbed the air just a tad higher than the open window, then tucked his wings in and began the rapid transformation. His claws shortened into feet, and his large, feathery body shrunk just in time as he entered his room, the drapes blowing side to side from his velocity.

As he impacted on the carpet, he tucked his shoulder down

and rolled easily, coming to a stop before slamming into the wall that separated the bedroom and the bathroom.

He slowly got to his feet. "Looks like I still have it in me, after all."

Oberon shivered. The smart clothing was doing its best to compensate for the freezing temperature, but the window had been wide open for hours. He made his way to it and shut it with icy fingers.

He wanted to take a shower to help himself heat up, but his anxiety superseded that desire. He needed to call Leif. Oberon settled for slipping on the warm clothing he'd brought along with him, then reached for his phone.

The screen illuminated, showing he'd missed two calls from the vampire. Of course, Leif hadn't left a voicemail. He wouldn't want his voice recorded, directing a message to a shifter. That would put him in too much danger, and Oberon would hate to be caught with a message from a vampire.

Tapping on Leif's missed call, Oberon held the phone to his ear. He didn't even hear the first ring before the vampire's voice was on the other end.

"Oberon, I've been trying to call you."

Oberon's nervousness spun at the urgency in Leif's voice.

"Have you arrived in Whitehorse?" Oberon asked. "Are you here?"

"Yes, I'm at the *Snow Eagle Inn*, just as we'd planned," said Leif.

"So am I. Leif, we need to talk."

"I'm in my room, but we can meet at the hotel café by the lobby," suggested Leif.

Oberon made for the door. "I'm already heading that way."

Verifying he had his hotel key in one of his pockets, he slid his phone into the other and pulled the door closed behind him. Walking down the narrow hallway, he skittered past a member of the hotel's housekeeping staff.

"Good afternoon, sir," she said, flashing him a smile.

Putting on a smile of his own, he nodded and returned her greeting, then scuttled to the elevator. Oberon mashed the button pointing down, and it lit up with golden light.

Moments flicked away, and Oberon spun his thumbs around one another. He trusted the vampire. At least, he thought he did. Leif had his own agenda, and Oberon didn't exactly have the time to help him on his quest to find a way to bring his deceased fiancé back to life. Perhaps Draven had found a way, and had reached a deal with Leif?

The elevator chimed and the doors opened. Leif was on the other side.

"Oberon," he said, cocking an eyebrow.

Oberon hesitated a moment, finding himself unable to enter the elevator. In such confined quarters, Leif could snap his neck faster than he could react.

"Is everything okay?"

Setting his jaw, Oberon said, "I need to know, Leif. Did you bring me all this way just to kill me?"

The elevator doors began to close, but faster than a blink, Leif threw an arm out to catch it. He matched Oberon's gaze.

"I have no qualms with you, and have never wanted to kill you."

"Even if Draven has bought your loyalty?" growled Oberon.

At this, Leif's features darkened. "Not with one thousand promises could Draven buy my loyalty."

"Why is it that there are no other vampires like you?"

Oberon asked. "Why are you not driven by the same motivations as Draven and his followers?"

"You know precisely what my motivations are," Leif said as his dark features softened into sadness and his posture relaxed. No longer did he seem to be a threat.

Still, Oberon kept his guard up.

"Does Draven know them, too?"

"Draven," Leif spat, shaking his head as he looked down. He stepped out of the elevator and the doors closed angrily behind him, as if they knew they'd been held up. "If Draven knows my motivations, he has no desire to aid me. But I can promise you that bringing Gemma back is not my only purpose in life. Do you want to know the greatest difference between me and Draven? I respect life. I think the diversity of shifters, vampires, and humans strikes a great balance, and that instead of trying to kill each other, we should be finding ways to *live* among each other. But Draven? He's on the verge of making his own version of peace between our species. But that's by making his vampire-shifter hybrids."

Oberon shuddered. He'd spent so much time working with Myreen and trying to forge her into the siren the prophecy spoke of, he'd forgotten about Draven's ultimate goal.

Discovering that his hands were balled into fists and his muscles were flexed, Oberon slowly released them, breathing deeply.

"What happened, Oberon?" Leif asked, stepping forward and placing a firm hand on his shoulder. "You seem so unlike yourself—so scattered and apprehensive."

The elevator dinged again, then opened. A man and a woman, bundled up in winter gear, stepped off and walked past them.

Oberon's eyes followed them until they turned the corner, then he looked back at Leif.

"I already made the trip to Mount Logan," he said. "There was no sign of gryphons there."

Leif's brow furrowed. "What? That's impossible. Draven said the reports came from good sources."

Oberon shook his head. "We've been duped. And I fear something terrible will happen because of it."

Leif stared at him seriously. "You're sure there weren't any signs of gryphons?"

"The mountain was untouched. Gryphons put off a scent that is easily detectable by other gryphons, and there wasn't even a slight chance they were there."

Leif raised his hand up to his forehead, his eyes flashing with worry. "It could've been a setup. But it's possible Draven was given bad intel."

"Either way, I'm returning to the school immediately," Oberon said.

Leif nodded and let his arm fall to his side. "And I'll return to Draven and report that his intel was wrong."

The vampire swirled around and hit the button to call the elevator.

"It's likely we'll need to stay in better touch," Oberon said. "Going forward, I need to learn all I can from you on what Draven is planning."

The door dinged open once more, and Leif stepped inside. "I'll do my best, but I'm afraid Draven is catching on to me. But do be careful, Oberon. I believe Draven is going to make his move soon, though I don't know what he's planning. The sooner you can get your siren ready, the better."

The door closed, leaving Oberon alone in the hotel hallway.

He sighed. "High winds, don't I know it."

Juliet

With how things went at the ball, Juliet decided to give Jesse a chance. He made it clear that he was into her, and he wanted to be exclusive. That was a little too fast too soon for Juliet, though. She asked that they take things slow, and not put a title on it. A title wouldn't make much difference, anyway. So they kept it to themselves.

Even with Nik's confusing conversation haunting her, she didn't want to pass up the possibility of a happy future—with Jesse or any other guy. Still, it didn't feel quite right. She liked Jesse, but she wasn't sure if he was right for her. Myreen could've helped Juliet sort through it, but she'd been so sick when she woke up. And Juliet could hide it a little while longer.

After Juliet left Myreen with Ms. Heather, it was hard to focus on her classes. She wanted to get back to her friend, but she'd already missed so much this semester. Her eyes kept drifting back to the clock, which made the time feel like it went even slower.

So when the class finally finished, she threw her things into her bag and ran out, pushing through her classmates. She didn't care about the grunts and the dirty looks she received. She only wanted to get to Myreen.

A knot formed in her stomach as she made her way through the halls. There was something off about Myreen's sudden sickness. Juliet didn't know what that was, though. But with Myreen out of the clinic, it would be easier for them to talk.

When she finally approached Myreen's door, she didn't bother to knock, and she burst in like someone was chasing her. If she wasn't so concerned about Myreen's health, she would've laughed at the way Myreen jumped, her hand over her heart and her eyes bulging out of their sockets. Juliet threw herself onto Myreen's bed and hugged her knees to her chest, and Myreen finally relaxed.

"Did you really have to come in like that?" Myreen's voice was low as she scolded Juliet.

"How are you feeling? Do you need anything? Are you okay? Do you hurt anywhere?" Juliet spoke rapidly, afraid of the answers.

"Slow down, J. Yes, I'm fine. I just..." Myreen avoided eye contact and played with a string on her sheet.

"You just what? Come on, don't do this to me! Are you dying? How long do you have?" Juliet's heartbeat raced faster as her worry grew.

"What? No! I'm not dying. You're so dramatic sometimes." Myreen buried her face in her hands and mumbled something.

"I can't understand you. What are you saying?" Juliet

leaned forward on her knees and tried to pry Myreen's hands away from her face. Juliet was happy when she heard Myreen's giggles through her hands.

"Okay, okay. I'm sick because..."

"Because what, Myreen? You've got to stop taking these long pauses."

"Because I have ursa DNA in me. Happy now?" As soon as the words left Myreen's mouth, she hid her face in her hands again.

"You have what?" Juliet heard what she said, she just couldn't believe her ears.

"I'm an ursa. On top of being a mermaid and a harpy."

"Holy..." Before she could spit out profanities, she stopped herself. Myreen didn't need someone freaking out; she needed someone to be there for her. Juliet scooted over and wrapped her arm around Myreen's back. "Whatever it is, Myreen, you're going to get through it and you're going to come out stronger." She tightened her hold for a second, then let go as she turned back toward Myreen. "Honestly, though, that's pretty extraordinary. Even *I* know what a rare situation this is, and I'm almost as new to this stuff as you are. So cool. *My* best friend is a badass mermaid, and harpy, *and* ursa. Ah-may-zing! I mean, how do you feel? I could only imagine you feel like a rock star. Well except for the getting sick part. I'm sure that sucked. But still, I wouldn't want to mess with you now that you're a freaking bear!"

"Juliet..." Myreen's voice was almost too low for Juliet to hear.

"Oh my gosh, just wait until Kol finds out. Who else knows? Are you going to tell everyone? Or keep it...?"

"*Juliet!*" Now Myreen's voice was loud enough to stop Juliet's rambling.

"Okay! Fine, I'll take it down a notch. But you haven't even answered any of my questions." Juliet raised her eyebrows and opened her eyes wide, which caused a smile to crack on Myreen's face. Juliet was glad she could still make her friend smile under such circumstances.

"Well if you took a breath, it would've given me the chance to answer you." Myreen laughed as she shook her head in her hands. "Yes, I know how bizarre this is. I feel fine, thanks to this were stuff I'm drinking. No, I haven't told Kol yet. And only a handful of people know. Which now includes you. I would love for this not to blow up, by the way."

Myreen took a deep breath and Juliet finally realized how stressed she looked. Her skin was flushed and she had dark circles under her eyes. Juliet's heart sank as she looked her friend over.

"Sorry. I'm not good with controlling my emotions. We can definitely keep this between us. I'm honored to be part of your secret circle. Do you need anything? Anything at all?"

"Thanks, J. I'm okay for now. Worried about having to go through yet *another* transformation. And this one's not pretty. I'm just tired. I think I'm going to take a nap, if you want to come back later." Myreen gave a big loud yawn, and Juliet couldn't help but giggle.

"Now I can see the ursa in you. Sleep tight. I'll be back in a little bit." Juliet shut the light off for Myreen before she exited. She knew how worried Myreen must've been if she needed a nap. Poor girl had been through enough. Juliet felt sorry for her friend, who kept finding new things about her life with little-to-no answer why. No one had ever heard of a born ursa, but

Myreen had never been bitten. Chances were, Myreen hadn't gotten a valid explanation—nor would she.

Glumly, Juliet walked back to her room. She knew Myreen was okay, especially now that she knew what was wrong. But seeing Myreen look so weak and frail... it worried her. As bad as Juliet wanted to lean on Myreen's shoulder about the boy drama, she knew it wasn't the time—even more-so now that Myreen was headed to dreamland.

Juliet got to her door and as soon as she put her hand on the knob, she knew she couldn't go inside. Not without doing something first. If she did, she would slump into a never-ending cycle of negativity. She withdrew her hand and spun around. If Myreen wasn't in commission, there was only one other person that Juliet felt comfortable enough with.

In a rush, Juliet pulled out her phone and made her way towards the Dome exit. It was a long shot, but she hoped and prayed it would be enough.

"Fire Girl, what's up?" Kenzie said after a few rings. She always sounded so lively, and it was one of Juliet's favorite things about her.

"Hey Kenzie. I know this is random and last-minute, but are you busy tomorrow? Could you possibly meet up with me somewhere?" Juliet didn't want to sound like it was a dire situation, but she also didn't want Kenzie to decline her invitation.

"Um, yes! Wait, hold on a sec." There was a noise and the sound muffled, but Juliet could still hear Kenzie yelling. "Mom! I wanna meet a friend in the morning... Yes, she's a girl! ... I've got her on the phone now. You want to talk to her?" The same crinkling noise came as the sound cleared back up. "So sure, where do you wanna meet?"

Juliet's smiled again. "If you're sure it's okay, we can meet at the frozen yogurt place in town."

"Yum! Healthy ice cream. I'm in. Text me the deets and I'll meet you there."

The second they hung up, Juliet sent her the pin to the location.

***

Out of habit, Juliet looked around to see if her father was there to stop her from going out. It varied from day to day, but today Juliet saw him leaving the security room. He hadn't turned in her direction yet, and she didn't want him to see her—if he did, he'd keep her there for hours. So before he could turn, Juliet opened the platform door a crack and squeezed through. Without a look back, she ran to the train and hopped inside.

With her mind running in circles, the ride seemed to move a lot faster, which she was grateful for. The minute the cool air hit her face, she felt like she could breathe again. She savored the fresh air, then ran to the yogurt shop with a little more pep in her step.

When she arrived, Kenzie still wasn't there. Juliet made sure to grab a table in a place where they could have privacy—though, the customers were mostly young kids with their parents, or young adults on dates, and probably wouldn't be interested in a couple of girls chatting.

She only had to wait another four or five minutes before Kenzie loudly made her entrance. "The yogurt queen is here!"

Forget about privacy now. Juliet jumped out of her seat and ran to her friend. They embraced each other with a quick hug, then went right to the buffet line, Kenzie waving to a woman who looked like an older version herself. The woman gave a curt nod and disappeared. Juliet thought about asking Kenzie about it, but figured if Kenzie wanted to talk about it, she would.

No one else was in front of them, so Juliet was sure their table would be fine. She decided to go with a safe flavor and chose coffee froyo and s'more toppings. Kenzie, on the other hand, had gummy bears, cotton candy, and fruity pebbles toppling over on her strawberry froyo—it matched her personality perfectly.

After they were seated, they took a moment to cherish their delicious masterpieces.

"So, is Myreen okay?" Kenzie asked between bites. "I'm not saying I don't appreciate your invite, but either something's wrong with Myreen, or you two are fighting."

"Well, she's sick and going through... a lot. My problems aren't exactly important at the moment. I just felt selfish bringing my issues up, you know? But then your beautiful face flashed through my mind." Juliet shrugged, then gave Kenzie a straight-lined smile.

"Aw, poor Myreen. She's tough as nails, though. Let me know if you guys need anything." Kenzie leaned forward, lowering her voice conspiratorially. "Meanwhile, I'm soooo glad you called 'cause my mom is driving me nuts. That was her, by the way. She's gone all helicopter parent lately. What exactly is going on in the secret world of the Dome?"

"Too much, Kenzie. It's insane! And even with the tornado of events going on down there, I still manage to have boy problems." Juliet felt embarrassed now that she'd said it out loud.

"Girl, you and me both. Boys absolutely suck!"

It was exactly what Juliet needed to hear. "Amen!" Juliet shoved another spoonful of her concoction in her mouth, then let out the flood of emotions built up inside. "I mean, they tell you one thing, then do another, then expect you to be completely okay with their crappy choices. The games they play are maddening. I'm over them all." Juliet couldn't believe how sour she sounded, but she didn't care.

"Dang straight. They don't deserve our tears." Kenzie raised her spoon, and Juliet, taking it as a high-five, raised her spoon and tapped it with Kenzie's. They both broke out in giggles.

"So, what jerk tore you apart?" Kenzie asked. She went straight for things.

"He was my first boyfriend, my first kiss, my first lo..." Juliet stopped herself. She couldn't say the word love out loud. She didn't think he deserved hers, since he tore their relationship apart.

"Nik, right? I remember hearing you guys talk about him. He broke it off the last time I saw you, didn't he?"

Juliet could only nod.

"Listen, the first *anything* is always the hardest to get over. But think of it this way, after all the firsts are out of the way, you can make room for the other numbers." Kenzie winked at Juliet, almost causing her to choke on her yogurt.

"Well, I'm dating someone else right now..."

"Ooh, go girl!"

"He's nice. But I just don't feel like we belong together. Something feels off to me. And I can't figure out what it is." Juliet put her spoon down and leaned back in her chair.

"Then dump him. Why waste your time? Unless he's giving

you something you need—but even that can be messy. Trust me. What feels off is the pedestal you placed Rebound Guy on. No one's going to compare to Nik until you're over him. But who's to say there isn't someone better? Maybe not Rebound Guy, though. Am I right?"

"Jesse, his name is Jesse. I never really thought of it that way. I think you're absolutely right, Kenzie."

"You don't need any guy to make you feel good. You're hot and you're a *phoenix*." She whispered the last part, but Juliet wasn't afraid—there wasn't anyone around them. "You make even *me* jealous."

"Thanks. You really don't know how bad I needed to hear that."

Kenzie reached her arm across the table to pat Juliet's hand. "No problem. It's the truth. Girls are so quick to rely on a boy to fix them when the fixing really only comes from yourself. It's part of the reason I gave you that necklace."

"Aww, thanks! I liked it before, but now I know the meaning behind it, I love it." Juliet gave Kenzie a big smile, then took another bite of her froyo. "Okay, *Chicago's Best Therapist*, your turn. What guy has you so wound up?"

Kenzie snorted. "More like *guys*, with an S. There's an older man, and he's just... too good to be true. Seriously. But he's hung up on some long lost love, so I pretty much have no shot with him. And the last two guys I went out with were dirty, rotten, no-good liars. It's like a curse. I'm like a magnet for weird crap." Kenzie paused and leaned forward, lowering her voice. "One of them wants to be a vampire. Like a real, honest-to-goodness vampire. Sick, right?" She straightened up, loading her spoon and waving it in the air. "But I'm done with guys. Too much drama."

Kenzie's told her story so freely. That was something Juliet wanted to learn from her—the ability to not give a crap.

"Sounds like no fun. I wish I had some powerful advice to give you, but as you heard, I'm a newbie to this boy world. And already I want out."

"Ha! Then get out. I am. We don't need them. We have each other. And a sick Myreen. But hopefully she'll be better soon. And then we can rule the world."

Juliet fed off Kenzie's positive energy. "Yes. I agree. A hundred percent."

"And just so you know, I'm not exactly an expert in the dating field, but at least my flops have hopefully helped you."

"I really needed this. Thanks again for meeting me here." Juliet didn't want to get sappy after such an empowering talk, so she stopped there.

"I'm sooo glad you called. I needed this too and I didn't even know it. Maybe we can make it a little tradition—eating healthy ice cream while bashing boys." Kenzie winked.

"Now that sounds like a plan." Juliet promised herself that she would make this call more often. She felt like a weight had been lifted off her shoulders. Kenzie's advice was spot-on and made total sense. Kenzie's confidence ran through her and it was intoxicating.

Juliet knew what she had to do. And she wasn't the slightest bit nervous.

Myreen

Myreen woke the next day with a groan. The aches and chills were back with a vengeance.

Eying the bottles sitting at her bedside, she scowled. She didn't want to take more of that stuff, but it was Saturday and she didn't want to spend the day in bed and miserable.

She sat up and grabbed a bottle of were remedy. Opening it, she stared at its contents, willing the vile liquid to sweeten. She took a deep breath and held it as she chugged everything down as fast as she could. Thankfully, she didn't choke on it this time. When she had it all down, she shuddered and stuck out her tongue. Throwing the bottle to the side, she grabbed one of the mints and popped it in her mouth.

The flu-like symptoms cleared up almost immediately, just like the last time. At least the bad taste was worth it.

Myreen threw on a t-shirt and jeans and pulled her hair into a low ponytail. Juliet had said she was going out today, but Myreen had to admit she felt a little lost without her friend around.

She was just about to go to the Dining Hall for breakfast when a soft knock sounded on the door. Opening it, she found Kol on the other side. His eyes seemed to smolder as they took her in, and he winked, setting her heart aflutter.

"Got any plans today?" Kol asked, an almost boyish uncertainty behind those honeyed eyes.

Myreen had the sudden urge to pull Kol into her room and close the door. She cleared her throat, hoping the heat blooming from her neck didn't make her look guilty. "No. Nothing today."

"Good. Let's grab some breakfast and then I want to show you something."

Myreen slipped her hand into his and closed the door as she followed him to the Dining Hall. It was so strange still—and yet so comfortable—being Kol's girlfriend. She cast a sidelong glance at him, wondering what had held him back before. Whatever it was, it seemed to be gone, though the brief setback when his father came to the ball had unsettled her. Still, he'd apologized, and fully made up for it. Her cheeks reddened again as she remembered their late-night make out session, the taste of buttered popcorn still fresh on their lips.

Those thoughts melted away as she spotted Trish and her posse sitting near the entrance chatting away. They stopped to glare at Myreen and Kol. Trish opened her mouth as if to say something, but then closed it again, getting a faraway look. As her eyes began to uncross, she slouched in her seat, folding her arms. Myreen smiled and waved, wondering what kind of nightmare Trish had just lived through at the hand of her own cruelty.

"What was *that* about," Kol asked.

Myreen shrugged, holding Kol's hand a little tighter. Delphine was the only person who knew about her little siren experiment on Trish—not even Trish remembered what happened—and she wanted to keep it that way. Being able to manipulate people like that was frightening, and she was tired of being the main topic of the rumor mill.

Myreen and Kol got food from the buffet line and sat down at their usual spot.

"So, what did you want to show me?" Myreen asked. She took a bite of sausage and sighed. She was craving meat like nothing else, and had loaded her plate with anything even closely resembling protein. Again, she thanked whoever had made that drink. The flavor was nearly gone, but she didn't have to worry about nausea getting in the way of her voracious appetite.

"It's a surprise." Kol looked at her plate with a quizzical expression on his handsome face. "Are you on a special diet or something?"

After her heart-to-heart with Juliet last night, she'd nearly forgotten that Kol still didn't know about her latest news. "Actually—"

"Dude! Who's up for smashing some serious zombies?" Brett said, dropping into the seat next to Kol. "Most of our clan should be online today. You in?"

"Maybe later. Myreen and I already have something planned." Kol winked at Myreen, then grabbed his own bite of sausage.

"Gee, thanks Myreen. You finally get this guy to loosen up and then you monopolize all his time." Brett smirked, but Myreen felt her blood beginning to boil.

"Maybe if you did something besides play games all day he wouldn't be so opposed to hanging out with you." She glowered, aware that she was overreacting, but the anger seething inside her needed an outlet, and Brett had become it.

Brett leaned back, holding up his palms. "Whoa. Okay, then. Not like *I* got him the game for Christmas." He leaned toward Kol and muttered, "PMS much?"

Myreen narrowed her eyes as she leaned forward, placing both her hands on the table. "I'm sorry, but does me being a *girl* offend you? You want to see what this *girl* can do? Because you wouldn't stand a chance."

Kol placed a hand on Myreen's shoulder, and the tension coiling in her stomach unwound. "Are you okay?"

Myreen blushed, shrinking in her seat. "Yeah. Sorry. Not much of a morning person."

Kol gave her a quizzical look. She wanted to tell Kol about being an ursa—an ursa heading for a first shift, no less—but she didn't want to talk about it here. She didn't really want to discuss it in front of Brett, either, considering the way she'd just snapped at him. Maybe she could tell Kol during whatever he had planned.

"Whatever," Brett said and went back to eating as casually as if they'd just had a minor disagreement.

Myreen was grateful he wasn't making a big deal of it.

"I'll just have to beat Flesh Eaters 4 without you," Brett said, ducking out of Kol's reach with his tray. "Later suckers!"

"You be careful with that game," Kol called after him. Brett waved and laughed. "It's a collector's edition!" he yelled over the din of the Dining Hall.

Myreen shook her head and popped a piece of bacon in her

mouth.

Kol turned back to her. “Seriously, though, are you okay?”

Myreen half-smiled, covering her mouth as she spoke. “Yeah, I’m fine. We’ll talk later.”

“Do you feel up for a flight?”

Myreen’s eyes lit up. “Yes! Ohmygosh, that would be a-may-zing!” She bounced in her seat, laughing giddily. “Where’re we going?”

Kol smirked. “You’ll see.”

Myreen squealed. “Oh, I can’t wait. Are we going—” Myreen shifted her eyes back and forth, then leaned in and whispered conspiratorially, “in the Sim Room?”

Kol laughed. “No. I have someplace better.”

“Outside?” Myreen clapped her hands. Yeah, she was overdoing it, but it felt impossible to control just how much emotion she had coursing through her system. “Wait.” She folded her arms, fixing Kol with a stern stare. “Last time I went out you went berserk on me.”

Kol smiled. “Yes. And I believe I’ve apologized for that. Besides, now that I’m your boyfriend, I can go with you and personally see to it that you’re safe.”

“Ooh, *boyfriend.* I like that word.”

“It’s a good word. Almost as good as *girlfriend.*” Kol nudged her with his shoulder, and Myreen leaned her head on it.

She wondered what kind of surprise Kol had in store for her, though she had a feeling whatever it was, she was going to love it.

***

Myreen blushed as Kol stripped down to his smart clothes,

grateful that her harpy form allowed for a lot more privacy. The smart shirt she wore today was long-sleeved, and warm enough to wear without a coat, despite the deep chill in the air. Her toes felt like they might freeze when she took her shoes off, but as soon as those black talons emerged, she was good to go. She reveled in the transformation, circling her shoulders as her wings came out, enjoying the lightness in them, the soft feathers tickling her hands.

Kol smirked at Myreen as he rounded his shoulders, letting the shift happen in a flash. Myreen stood mesmerized at the sheer size of her now-dragon boyfriend. She'd seen him in action several times, but it still seemed startling. He flicked his scales and his image melted into the evergreen foliage surrounding them.

"Try to get above me once we're in the air. You shouldn't be too conspicuous at the height we're going, but it doesn't hurt to be safe."

"How will I know where you are? I can't even be sure where you are right now, and I just saw you disappear."

"Here." There was a sound like playing cards being shuffled, and a strip of gray scales appeared, marking Kol's back. "That will let you know where I am."

"Neat trick."

"Yeah, about that," Kol said, the gray strip bending back and forth like a snake. "It's not really widespread knowledge that I can change the color of my scales."

"Oh. That's not some advanced dragon thing?"

"No. So I'd prefer that we keep that knowledge just between us."

Myreen shrugged, the gesture feeling a little odd with her wings out. "Yeah. No problem." The trust he'd placed in her would've made her heart swell if it weren't for the fact she hadn't told him about her upcoming ursa transformation yet. She almost spilled everything at that moment, but she hesitated and the moment was lost.

"Good. Ready?"

Myreen nudged her discarded coat and shoes a little further under the bush with her talon. "Whenever you are."

"Then come on!"

There was a whoosh of air as Kol launched himself, and Myreen followed behind him. It took a minute to climb to a decent height, but once they leveled out, she was able to find a current to soar on.

The air flowing over her felt delicious, the bite of cold dampened both by her shifted form and the heat regulation of the smart clothing. She knew it would be different than flying inside, but she didn't expect it to be so exhilarating. It was like they were in their own world up there, only the sound of the wind and their flapping wings to keep them company.

Myreen decided to test out some of those trick maneuvers Ms. Heather had shown her, and managed a shaky loop the loop once they'd traveled far enough past the city. "This is amazing!" she yelled over the wind rushing past her ears.

"I always love a good flight topside. The Sim Room is great, but there are subtle things missing. But today is the best."

"Why's that?"

"Because you're with me."

They were well away from Chicago by now, the wind at their backs speeding their flight.

"I want to try something," Kol said, letting all his scales turn red.

Myreen gasped at the stunning display, but it was him shifting back into a human that stole her breath.

"Catch me!" he called to her as he flipped over and spread his arms and legs wide.

Myreen dove, her heart hammering in her chest. Had something gone wrong? Was there some sort of attack happening? But she could only see her and him. She tucked her wings in to reach top speed. It didn't take long to catch up to him, and she grabbed him around his firm chest.

"What are you doing?" Myreen gasped.

"This."

And then Kol's lips were on hers, delicious and warm with that tantalizing hint of cinnamon. For a second, she almost forgot they were falling.

Kol broke the spell as he pulled away from their kiss. "Spread your wings."

"What if I can't hold on?"

Kol smirked. "Then I'll fly."

Myreen spread her wings, slowing their fall and altering their course so it better paralleled the ground. She still had Kol tightly wrapped in her arms. She broke into a grin. "I did it!"

"Yeah, and you're crushing my ribs. Let go."

"Oh!"

Myreen's eyes widened seconds after she released Kol, realizing just how close to the ground they'd gotten. He twisted in the air, bursting back into his dragon form and pulling into a glide barely a tree's-height from the frozen earth. She hoped she hadn't hurt him too bad with her new ursa strength.

Kol banked to the side and pulled up into the air again, hovering over a certain spot.

"What is it?" Myreen asked as she came beside him.

"Aw, it's gone already."

"What?" As Myreen hovered there staring at the snow, she could see the faint traces of a giant heart, KD + MF in the center. "You did this?" she asked, grinning.

Kol nodded, giving her a pointed look.

"You're not thinking of taking another dive are you?" The thrill of that trick was a dead match for the terror he'd put her through, and she wasn't sure if she wanted to try it again or punch him in the arm for it.

"No. We're too close to the ground. Hey, that was some strength back there."

This was it, the opening she needed to tell Kol about her ursa DNA. But something held her back. They were having so much fun, she didn't want to ruin it with her news.

Myreen shrugged. "It was probably the adrenaline. You scared me half to death."

"Yeah, sorry about that." Kol lifted a brow, a mischievous glint in his large dragon-eye. "Wanna go again?"

Myreen laughed. "Actually, I think one death-defying stunt in a day is enough. Hey, what do you say we head back to the Dome and you can go kick Brett's butt at that zombie game? If we hurry, you might be able to catch up with your team."

"It's a clan. But thank you!"

A kernel of guilt crept in, but she flicked it away. She'd tell him soon. She just needed a little more time to process. Today she just wanted to enjoy her time with her boyfriend and at least attempt to feel somewhat normal.

Kol

Kol tapped his pencil against his desk in English. Mrs. Coltar was reading a lengthy passage of *The Great Gatsby* to prove a point, but his thoughts were trailing. He doubted Gatsby would have any importance in his life past this moment and his grade.

Instead, his thoughts trailed to the weekend when he'd taken Myreen for that flight. He cringed a little at the lovesick way he'd acted, but reminded himself that she had been acting the same way:

> *"Ooh, boyfriend,"* she'd said. *"I like that word."*
> *"It's a good word. Almost as good as girlfriend."*

He tapped his pencil quicker, as if the steady drumming would erase the memory of his tone when he'd said the word *girlfriend*, like he was some lovesick hound. His shifting mid-air had been cool, if corny. And maybe he wanted to show off a little, but he really was curious about the amount of weight Myreen's harpy wings could hold—he'd never been good enough friends with any of the others to find out—but that was just an excuse. Mostly, he'd just wanted to kiss her right then in that moment.

Like he couldn't wait until they were back on the ground and being a dragon wasn't exactly an ideal form to be kissing girls in.

And *that,* right there, was why he needed to snap out of the sappiness.

For the first time since his initial shift, there was something he wanted to be doing that trumped being a dragon. Sure, he had responsibilities and didn't hate being in human form, but that was the first time he had no reason to be human and he desperately wanted to be.

He'd seen Myreen briefly that morning and fortunately, she still seemed to like him, so that told him one thing—that he wasn't in love with her yet, and therefore the curse hadn't been triggered. By the way he was feeling things he'd never allowed himself to feel before, Kol feared he was dangerously close.

"Kol." Mrs. Coltar pulled him from his thoughts. "Will you read the next few lines?"

A naga sitting next to him pointed at the place in the book and Kol quickly flipped to it without missing a beat.

He cleared his throat: "'I wouldn't ask too much of her,' I ventured." Kol read the lines, Gatsby insisting to Nick Carroway that he could change the past. "'I'm going to fix everything just the way it was before,' he said, nodding determinedly. 'She'll see.'"

"Thank you Kol," Mrs. Coltar said. "This passage is probably Gatsby's most famous quote. Why do you think that's so?"

Joanna, one of Trish's minions, raised her hand and was called on.

"Well it shows the contrast between Nick's worldview and Gatsby's," Joanna said.

Mrs. Coltar smiled, the way she always did whenever a student seemed to *get it*. Kol was the usual recipient, but his daydreaming wasn't conducive to literature dissection.

"Exactly, and what is Gatsby's worldview?" Mrs. Coltar asked.

"He's naïve," Joanna continued, this time without raising her hand. "He thinks that he can recreate everything as it was back in Louisville, like it will somehow be the key to winning Daisy back. Gatsby is delusional, if optimistic, in thinking it's possible if he wants it enough."

"Precisely," Mrs. Coltar said, then flicked her tablet to project an image on the screen behind her.

Kol was no longer paying attention. Something Joanna said caused him to lean forward in his seat. Panic ignited and grew.

Kol raised his hand, but was instantly impatient and asked his question without waiting for Mrs. Coltar to look in his direction. "Does Gatsby ever win her back?" He ignored the stares around him that quickly snapped away. "By re-creating the past, or whatever. Does it work?"

Mrs. Coltar didn't look irritated for being interrupted mid-sentence. "Has anyone read to the end yet?" she asked the class.

A hand must have shot up in the back, but Kol didn't turn and waited for whoever it was to speak.

"I've finished." It sounded like Myreen's friend, Juliet. Kol suddenly felt self-conscious. "Is everyone okay with a tiny spoiler to answer Kol's question?"

Everyone nodded, or voiced their agreement. It wasn't like she was spoiling the ending to the latest superhero movie or anything.

"All right, Juliet," Mrs. Coltar said. "Go ahead. After all of Gatsby's antics in buying a mansion across the bay from Daisy and attempting to re-create the past, believing that he could somehow win her back... does it work? Does he win her back?"

"No... he doesn't," Juliet said. "She never intended to leave Tom."

"Thank yo—"

"So what's the point?" Kol blurted. "What's the point of him doing all of that? What's the point if he doesn't get her back?"

Mrs. Coltar looked at him, unsure of the answer.

"Sorry..." Kol muttered, feeling the eyes of everyone in class on him again. "Go on. Symbolism, whatever. Go on."

She paused for another brief moment before moving on, but Kol didn't move on. He couldn't move on. He was acting so stupid. He was being so careless with his feelings, first with Christmas and then taking Myreen on that flight...

He didn't even know if breaking the curse would work—*if* Kenzie could pull it off.

Kol tuned out the rest of class and was the first one out the door as soon as it was over. He wasn't sure why Gatsby had gotten to him so badly. Their situations were worlds different, yet felt tragically parallel. Besides the fact that the characters in Fitzgerald's novel were human and that Kol didn't promote infidelity—he wasn't trying to win an ex-girlfriend back who happened to be married—but Gatsby's situation, though futile and tragic, actually seemed... possible. Gatsby's situation happened in the real world. It wasn't a happy ending for the Tom's of the world, but it was possible.

But curses? Generation-long curses, no less. He wasn't sure if those had happy endings.

Kol checked his tablet again. He'd been waiting to hear from Kenzie far longer than he would have liked. Nothing from the selkie, but there was a message from his father.

It was a vague question about how he was doing, or something about school, but before thinking, Kol responded with a quick: *Gatsby is stupid, but I'm fine.*

He realized too late that it was not the response he should've given Eduard, because immediately his tablet rang with a video call.

Kol groaned, but quickly found an empty classroom and called him back. There was no sending his father's calls to video mail without repercussion and school wasn't an excuse. So to avoid the consequences, Kol always called him back within minutes. His teachers—annoyingly—didn't seem to mind, even if he had to slip out in the middle of an exam.

But when the familiar pose of his father—the beginning of the general's video mail—popped up, he ended the call and sat for a moment. His dad was sure to call him back in a few minutes, so there was no point in Kol heading to his next class.

Ping. Kol's instant messenger alerted.

He pulled up the app.

Myreen: Hey, are you alright?

Kol racked his brain for a reason why he wouldn't be. But

another message pinged before he could respond.

Myreen: In English, Juliet said you were acting like you were...

Ah, he should've suspected the phoenix would go blabbing about his strange behavior over Gatsby. He could see it now. Juliet's orange hair flying as she warned her friend about her crazy boyfriend who freaked out over literature. He typed a response.

Kol: What? Weird? Crazy?

Myreen: No... upset?

Upset? Wow. The girl was observant. He absently wondered if Juliet was a mind-reader.

Kol: It's nothing. Gatsby is drama.

*Myreen: Like Gatsby the character? Or is an assignment giving you drama? Because I can help with that (study buddy) *winky face* *kissy face**

Kol laughed aloud. He wasn't one to use emojis, but it sure had a way of saying words without the words. His mind drifted to what that might look like... Myreen *helping* with his imaginary Gatsby assignment. Mrs. Coltar hadn't actually assigned anything for Gatsby. Not that he could remember anyway.

Kol: How about another flight instead?

The memory of falling through the frigid Michigan air in human form flashed through his memory. It was exhilarating. His adrenaline had pumped through his veins, even though he knew full well if Myreen couldn't hold him, he was skilled enough to shift back into dragon form before splattering onto the ground.

But she had held him.

And he'd kissed her in his human form in the altitude of the clouds.

Kol's tablet rang with Eduard calling again right as Myreen's last ping came through.

*Myreen: Deal *blushing smile**

He answered the call before his face was ready and he knew he had an uncharacteristically, almost goofy, smile on it. So he said the first thing that came to mind as if it would cover his dreamy look. "Did my insult of a great American literary character prompt an immediate call to set me straight? Or are you also of the opinion that Gatsby is maddening?"

Eduard's face flashed brief confusion, then shifted into something Kol wasn't used to seeing. It almost looked like concern.

"Is everything alright, Malkolm?" he asked.

"Everything's fine," Kol said quickly. Plastering on his mask immediately. "I'm fine."

Eduard's eyes narrowed. "Meet me in three hours. At the *tree.*" No obscure restaurant in Chicago. No teachers or director's office. Kol knew the exact coordinates his father meant. It meant they were meeting alone.

"Three hours," Kol nodded, his stomach knotting. If they were meeting alone, something must be wrong, but he didn't think he was in trouble.

Maybe Eduard *knew* something. Perhaps a certain something he'd made a point to keep secret from his father about a certain siren girl.

Kol ended the call and shoved the tablet into his bag before rushing out the door. Three hours meant he had to leave right then.

The flight took at least three hours.

***

Shifting and flying was different this time than it had been with Myreen. There would be no shifting mid-flight. There would be no daredevil antics to impress. There would be no exhilarating kisses or gigantic hearts melted into the ice and snow.

Instead, he pumped his wings hard over Lake Michigan, the Dome far behind him as the fire churned within. At least flying this time cleared his head. He was able to sink into the dragon part of his brain, avoiding all the complications behind and in front of him.

It felt good, flying for so long. He might've enjoyed it if the human side of him didn't insist on reminding him who he was meeting.

Kol circled, then landed in the familiar spot in the middle of Hiawatha National Forest—right by the *tree* his father had mentioned. It was a dead northern hardwood. A massive one that, despite the paleness and lack of green, remained standing like a skeleton amid the living.

Kol only waited a few moments, still in dragon form, wearing his usual dark gray scales, when the silhouette of his father appeared. Wearing scales jet-black in color, his father was even more intimidating in his shifted form, but he began his transformation the instant his claws touched ground.

Kol did the same and hoped their meeting was quick, since deep snow covered every inch of the ground, even the spaces beneath the trees, and his smart clothing didn't do much to protect him from the elements, other than a bit of temperature regulation. He was a dragon, though. He wouldn't freeze to death.

He waited for his father to speak first.

"How are things?" Eduard asked, standing stiff with his arms behind his back. Not looking cold in the slightest

"Things are fine," Kol said, resisting the urge to lift an eyebrow and comment that this wasn't the sort of conversation that needed the secrecy of a three-hour flight to the middle of a forest.

"How are things with the girl...?" Eduard squeezed his eyes tight for a moment, as if searching for her name. "Myreen?"

Kol's stomach lurched. Did his father know he'd disobeyed orders and was dating the girl he was supposed to cut all ties from? "Myreen?" Kol asked, injecting an aloof tone into his voice. He wasn't sure if it worked, but his father looked distracted enough by his own thoughts that he hoped it was.

"Yes." Eduard waved a hand, like he wanted the conversation to move quicker. "How are her... abilities coming? Do you know if she's been able to use her siren voice yet?" He seemed impatient and Kol wondered why he was being asked these questions and why Eduard wanted to know. It worried him more than he could let on. No, it terrified him. What did his father want with Myreen?

"I'm not seeing her anymore," Kol said, suddenly speculating if it was just a trap to find out if Kol had followed orders. "Remember?"

Eduard took several steps forward until they were only a foot apart. "Don't be ridiculous, Malkolm," he said. "You must know *something*. And I don't believe that you haven't seen the girl or had any interaction with her for one second."

"Wha– why?" Kol stammered, wanting to step back, but

not wanting to show weakness.

"You don't just cut ties like that, especially as a teenager in a *shifter high school*." The words sounded like a scolding, but Eduard's voice didn't match it. "I know you didn't follow orders *exactly*. You must have some relationship with her."

Kol felt the heat rise in his face. He hoped his father didn't notice, and looked down at the untouched snow near his feet. "I don't—"

"You don't want to tell me, that's fine. But I know more than you think, Malkolm."

Kol swallowed and nodded, meeting his father's eyes again.

Then Eduard's face softened and Kol wondered what he saw.

But he didn't really wonder. He *knew* what Eduard saw there. The same expression he'd seen on Kol's mother's face for decades. The expression that meant Kol was very nearly—if not already—in love with Myreen.

Kol didn't affirm or deny any of it.

After a few more inconsequential questions, and Kol inquiring after his mother and sister, they parted ways.

Kol hadn't even reached the tree line in flight before the overwhelming feeling filled the immense volume of his dragon form. From the tips of his wings to the end of his tail, he needed the curse to be broken.

ASAP.

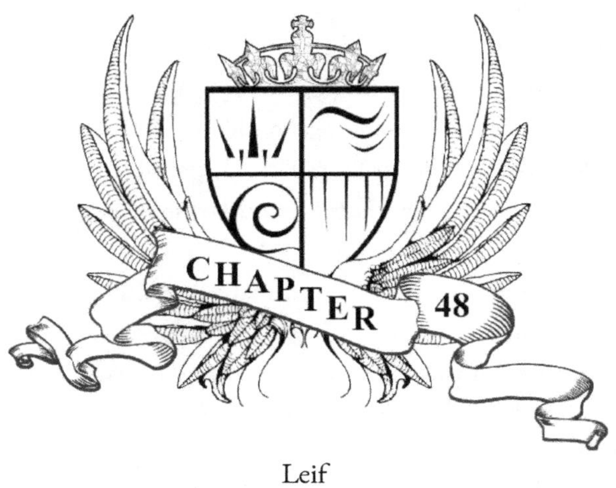

Leif

It had been four days since Leif met with Oberon in Whitehorse. He'd been back at Heritage Prep for three days, spending the entire time in his quarters, away from the worries of the world. Draven was out on one of his missions—perhaps finalizing his great scheme for capturing his daughter, or maybe the destruction of the shifter school.

Probably both, he thought.

But Leif spent the time well. He'd brought along his new piano book—his Christmas gift from Kenzie. And while he didn't care much for contemporary pop music, it was at least somewhat enjoyable to play something outside of his usual repertoire on the piano.

His eyes bounced along the notes while his fingers followed suit in practiced perfection. Sight-reading was a skill he'd worked hard on over the years, but now it came so easily.

All the while, his mind was on Kenzie. Although her personality was different than Gemma's, he couldn't help but sense a bit of his lost love in her. When he'd first seen Kenzie, he'd actually mistaken her for Gemma. Ever since then, he'd compartmentalized that aspect. He couldn't afford to project his fiancé on Kenzie. The girl had shown a playful interest in him, and had he not the hope of bringing back Gemma, perhaps there might have been something there to explore. But he couldn't act on that. It wouldn't be fair to Kenzie. And it wouldn't be fair to Gemma.

Leif's fingers danced along the keys, and from time to time, he'd tear his gaze from the sheet music to Gemma's brooch that he'd placed next to the piano book. He was playing for her. Someday, he'd play for her in person, and surprise her with how far he'd increased his talent.

A soft knock came at the door, and Leif's fingers stopped. Swiping the brooch away from the piano, he brought it to his lips and gently kissed it, then placed it safely in his pocket.

Leif closed the lid on the keys, then hid Kenzie's piano book inside the bench—he couldn't afford unwanted eyes to see that modern collection on the antique piano.

He opened the door to find Beatrice standing on the other side, resting a shoulder against the stone doorway. She was in her typical black getup, her black hood up to the crown of her head, and her blonde hair trailing like locks of light. Her arms were folded, and her face held a mischievous smirk.

"*Bad Blood*?" she asked. "Really, Leif? I'd never have marked you as a Taylor Swift fan."

Had he been capable of blushing, Leif knew his cheeks would have been as crimson as a cardinal.

Leif scratched at the back of his head. "I thought I'd try something new."

I thought I was playing softly. He must have been too distracted with thoughts of Kenzie and Gemma to notice just how loudly he'd been playing.

Beatrice snorted, then straightened her pose. "The boss is back and wants an update from you. But I can tell him you're too busy busting out pop music up here, if you'd like."

Kenzie! That girl was trouble, even from a distance.

"That won't be necessary," Leif said quickly, stepping past Beatrice and pulling the door shut behind him.

Beatrice smacked him on the arm. "Oh, you're no fun. But your nervousness is extremely cute."

Leif stopped dead in his tracks and cocked an eyebrow at her. "Cute?"

Beatrice snickered. "Sorry, was that not formal enough for you? How about endearing? Charming? Adorable?"

Sighing, Leif tore his gaze away and kept walking down the stone corridor toward the staircase.

"Leif, wait up," Beatrice called, a moment later grabbing his arm. "What I'm saying is that it *normalizes* you. That's not a bad thing." Her grip gently dropped from his arm down to his hand, and he felt her familiar fingers against his own. Long ago, before they'd become vampires, he'd found great pleasure in holding her hand. He'd looked forward to any chance at physical contact with her after working in the Frost orchards all day. But that was before she left. And that was before Gemma had come into his life.

At the thought of Gemma, Leif pulled his hand away from Beatrice and shoved it in his pocket. Beatrice's shoulders slumped.

"Why?" she said, her sad eyes piercing into his own. "Why won't you give *us* another chance?"

Leif shook his head. He was tired of this question. It was this question that had ended with him turning into a vampire. It was this question that had led to the death of Gemma. It was this question that she'd thrown at him after saving him from hunters before he'd first joined Draven.

And still, she persisted.

"I've spent my whole life forcing myself to become more than what I was," she continued. "I've done it all in the name of increasing my status here at Heritage Prep. Our fellow vampires respect me. Draven respects me." Tears beaded at the corners of her eyes, and she gritted her teeth. "And you know what? It wasn't for them. It wasn't even for me. I've spent the past one hundred years trying to become worthy of your love, Leif. That is *all* I've ever wanted. For a few years, long ago, I had it. And I want it back."

Leif returned her gaze, although it pained him. He had cared for Beatrice, before she'd left the boarding house. Back then, he had seen a potential future with her. But after experiencing relationship with Gemma, he knew that what he'd felt for Beatrice was a grain of sand in comparison. And that's all it would ever be.

"My heart is not mine to give, Beatrice," he replied softly. "I gave it to someone else a long time ago."

She shook her head, as if his words simply bounced off her. "I've learned from our past, and I'm ready to do whatever it takes."

"Beatrice..."

"No, hear me out." She lowered her voice to a whisper. "Right now, I will leave with you, abandon Draven, forsake the life I've created. We can run away together—anywhere you want to. I know you desire solitude. I will join you in that solitude if it means we can be together." She tapped his chest, then hers. "You and me, like the keys of a piano—the white and the black, making an eternity of harmonious music together."

Her words were enchanting, and he wondered for a moment if she'd learned real magic. Her talk of music and her willingness to let everything go just to be with him. Her loyalty was not solely with Draven. He could go and live in the peacefulness of—anywhere other than Heritage Prep and the watchful eyes of the vampires. Somewhere remote, like Scotland or New Zealand. Even Whitehorse, for that matter.

But Beatrice's mistake was her analogy of their relationship and a piano. She wasn't the black keys; Leif was. And the white keys were Gemma. There was no room on the keyboard for Beatrice.

Leif sighed. In that moment, Beatrice seemed as delicate as a butterfly. He placed a hand on her shoulder. "I'm truly flattered by your words. But your dream of exile with me would never be enough for you. Not while I'm unable to reciprocate your affection."

She inched closer to him until their bodies touched. Leif's instinct was to step backwards, but he held his ground as he stared into her rich brown eyes. They stood like that for several moments, studying each other, until Beatrice made a slight movement and pressed her lips against his.

Again, Leif's instinct was to step away and reprimand her for her actions. Instead, he let their lips remain together, but he didn't kiss her back. He ensured that no spark flared between them, no passion ignited.

Her eyes were closed, and he felt her lips tremble against his until she pulled away.

At last her eyes opened, tear-filled and pained, as if he'd stabbed her through the heart with a copper dagger.

But she didn't weep or groan. With a sniff, she said, "Draven's waiting."

As she stepped forward, Beatrice's shoulder coldly bumped into his. Leif stared after her for a few seconds before following.

Was she really that surprised? She couldn't have thought that, after all this time, he'd simply throw away his only purpose for living just to be with her.

Beatrice's shoes clicked on the stairs, echoing through the passageway leading down to the main floor of the school. Upon reaching the Great Hall, he was surprised to find the large room completely empty. Besides their footsteps, not a sound filled the air.

Something didn't feel right. A dread filled Leif's being, causing cool tingles to run up his spine and his mouth to suddenly thirst. Beatrice's quick pace didn't slow, and she kept her eyes forward.

Leif had walked to Draven's trophy room countless times, but this time there was a heaviness settling on him, and for a moment, he wanted to turn around. But he'd been summoned, and Draven wouldn't just let him walk away this time.

Beatrice pulled the door open without knocking, which surprised Leif. It was an unwritten rule that Draven demanded the option of allowing visitors to enter or be sent away.

Leif followed as Beatrice slipped into the trophy room.

Across the room, Draven sat at his desk, pouring over three tablets angled up, illuminating his face.

Leif stood at the entrance, waiting for the vampire leader to acknowledge him and invite him in. He looked at Beatrice, who stood just a few feet away from him, leaning against the wall next to the doorway with her eyes downcast.

A minute of uncomfortableness went by before Draven finally looked up.

"Ah, Leif, forgive me," Draven said, scooting his chair back and straightening his spine. "DNA is such a fickle thing to study—more detailed than an image with a trillion pixels, more intricate than a hand-woven rug, and more delicate than love." He gestured to Leif. "Come in, come in."

Leif stepped forward, and a loud clang sounded behind him. He whirled to find Beatrice standing in front of the now-closed door, crossing her arms as if she were guarding it. The pained look was still in her eyes.

"We need to talk, Leif," Draven said, his tone resounding with disappointment as he got to his feet.

Panic jabbed at Leif, and he knew that what he'd felt in the Great Hall had been a warning he'd ignored.

Forcing himself to swallow, Leif said, "About what?"

"A lot of things, I think," replied Draven. The vampire leader approached Leif with authority in his stride. "Let's start with your mission. How did your hunt for the gryphons go?"

Leif faced Draven, planted his feet, and stood his ground. "Something tells me you already know the answer to your question," he answered, matching Draven's fiery gaze.

"Of course I know," Draven snapped. "I asked you a question. Now answer it!"

Leif licked his lips, noticing their dryness. When was the last time he drank? He couldn't remember. The days had blurred over the past few weeks.

"There were no signs of gryphons at Mount Logan," Leif replied. "Nor in Whitehorse. You were given bad intel."

A wicked grin formed on Draven's pale face. "Oh, there was a sighting of gryphon activity."

The vampire leader strode back to his desk and removed one of the tablets from its docking station. With several quick taps, he approached Leif, then handed him the device. "For your viewing pleasure. This footage was taken four days ago by drones equipped to handle extreme temperatures. Go ahead, push play."

Setting his jaw, Leif looked at the screen. The date-stamp embedded on the video read *January 13, 1:11pm.* He tapped the play icon, and the top of Mount Logan showed against the light-blue sky. Seconds ticked by, and a large brown gryphon suddenly flew into frame. Leif gasped.

Oberon!

"So there *was* a gryphon in the Yukon Mountains on the day you went to check for yourself," Draven said in a mysterious tone. "But you just told me there were no signs of them. Tell me, old friend, why did you lie to me?"

He'd been caught. How was he going to talk his way out of this?

"It seems you're a bit tongue-tied at the moment," Draven said. "Perhaps I can elaborate for you. Of course, I don't have *all* the pieces of the puzzle, so please, do correct me if I'm off. First of all, you know exactly who that gryphon is. His name is Oberon Rex, the director of the shifter school."

Leif didn't acknowledge his recognition of the gryphon.

The less he verbalized, the better off everyone would be.

Draven waited a few moments before continuing. "Perhaps a little more dissemination is in order? Let's go back to the evening you voluntarily came back to Heritage Prep. You smelled of gryphon the moment you entered my trophy room, which means you had dealings with one. And it stands to reason that those dealings had to have involved Oberon Rex, the last living gryphon in the world. Am I right so far?"

Leif blinked, but didn't say anything. Still, Draven continued to study him, his eyes piercing through, as if reading his mind.

Draven chuckled and extended his hands forward. "Your silence speaks volumes, Leif. So Oberon sent you here, but for what purpose I have yet to discover. You came back and suffered a full day of drowning, followed by three awful days of hallucinations. You sacrificed much to join me again; I can only assume the great gryphon promised you something in return."

Oberon *had* promised to help. He was going to do his best to find a way to bring Gemma back. But he hadn't come through—not yet. Oberon was too busy dealing with school matters, as well as Draven's daughter.

"Whatever he promised is of little consequence now," Draven said, his wicked smile growing wider. "You played your part well. You caused the accident that blocked access to the subway station in Chicago, but you stood by as we fought my daughter and her friends. You knew I was watching then. And then your assignment to catch Myreen and bring her to me... it was all a ploy. I sent you back to Chicago so I could keep eyes on you. And those eyes saw much. On Christmas day, one of those vampires suddenly disappeared."

Leif glanced down as he recalled the fight in his apartment with Solomon. The Australian vampire had nearly killed him, but Piper had come through and saved him at the last moment.

"Ah, yes, it seems you remember that particular detail," Draven said. "It didn't take much for your Initiate to spill what had happened."

He couldn't contain the panic. Everything was spiraling down. Draven knew everything.

"What did you do to Piper?" Leif hissed.

Draven's brow raised. "Do I detect concern for your Initiate? Good heavens, Leif, you're growing soft. You'll be happy to hear that her punishment was minimal, and she's back at work helping me. As of a few days ago, she's unassigned."

If Draven was telling the truth, Piper likely was still alive. Leif just hoped Draven hadn't done something terrible to her. The greatest relief was that Draven hadn't said anything about Kenzie, which was a good sign. He hoped it would stay that way.

"You're a traitor, Leif. You're a traitor to your species. You're a traitor to those who once called you friend. Your disloyalty eliminates any status you once held. You are below the humans and shifters you sympathize with. And your silence magnifies your guilt."

Draven kept his gaze poised on Leif, and the silence screamed at him to retort, to argue, to give the vampire leader an earful.

He breathed deeply, then found words tumbling out of his mouth. "Whatever you decide to do to me today, I need you to understand why I left you and your vampire legion fifteen years ago."

Nodding his head, Draven said, "Go on."

"You seek for peace in this world, but you go about attaining it the wrong way. Your motives are barbaric and genocidal. You'd destroy the majestic shifters because you feel you're somehow greater than they are. But at the same time, you're envious of them—you want to take what they have and throw their corpses away once you have what you want. I left because I knew there was another way to live peacefully with the shifters. I *talked* with them. I *learned* about them. And I *cared* about them. I care about all life.

"So tear my status away—it means *nothing.* Kill me and you'll finally set me free to be with my beloved Gemma. But know this: I was done with you fifteen years ago, and that fact hasn't changed since I've been back."

Draven shook his head like a pendulum. "Leif, Leif, Leif, I'm not going to kill you. I'm not going to give you the freedom you've been wanting since that selkie witch was buried."

Anger surged within Leif like a thunderstorm.

"How dare you talk about Gemma that way!" Leif shouted, and he couldn't withhold his bursting abhorrence any longer. Fueled by the desire to protect Gemma's name, he moved faster ever before, slamming a fist into Draven's jaw and sending him flying backward. The vampire leader slammed into his desk, and the hardwood cracked from the impact. Leif leapt through the air and planted a knee into the crook of Draven's neck, then clapped his hands on either side of his head.

"Your rule ends today, Denholm Heir," Leif hissed. Flexing his muscles Leif clenched his teeth as he prepared to tear the vampire's head from his shoulders.

His hold slipped as something impacted his back, and his head smashed against the desk, leaving him dazed. Something pulled on his shirt, tearing it in places while being thrown to the ground. Leif's head cracked against the floor, and stars blasted into his vision. They cleared fairly quickly, and he found he was looking up at Beatrice, who was now sitting on top of him. He'd forgotten she was in the room.

She punched him once in the side of the head, causing another burst of stars to pop in his vision like fireworks. It happened again, then again, and then it stopped.

Before his vision cleared, he heard Beatrice crying nearby. She'd gotten off him, but had proven where her loyalties remained.

"You broke my desk," Draven said. His voice sounded distant, but Leif could see the vampire leader towering over him, holding... something. Leif couldn't focus enough to see what it was.

"Like I said, I'm not going to kill you, although you more than deserve it. And the three years of drowning I promised you before? That's not nearly enough of a reward."

Draven bent closer and grabbed Leif's wrists. He was too weak to resist. Metal clanged shut, and Leif saw he'd been handcuffed.

"Your eternal punishment?" Draven continued. "I'm turning you over to Beatrice for whatever purposes she intends."

Leif wiggled his arms uselessly against the cuffs.

"You get to test a new invention we've created." Draven grabbed the chain holding the cuffs together. "These are called probe manacles. Let me just push this little button."

Leif's eyes were slowly coming back into focus enough to see what Draven was doing. There was a small button on the middle chain, and when the vampire leader pushed it, Leif felt a prick as something within the manacles inserted into both of his wrists.

"The probes are detecting what kind of creature you are, and after a few moments..."

The dull pain in his wrists flared as if he were being branded by hot iron, causing him to cry out.

"Ah, see? The probe has discovered that you're a vampire. Every six hours it will insert a minuscule speck of copper into your wrists to help keep you in a weakened state. In this manner, Beatrice will be able to have her way with you." Draven looked up at Beatrice and smiled. "Will this suffice, my most loyal friend?"

Leif's head slumped to the side as he looked up at his ex-girlfriend and new captor.

"I've waited a long time for this," she said, her eyes growing distant, perhaps remembering something from their past.

Leif couldn't think clearly. The sharp pain was one thing, but whatever copper had been placed in his body was messing with his thoughts. What would Beatrice do to him? How would he escape?

"On your feet," Beatrice said, grabbing at the chain and pulling Leif up. He swayed back and forth. Dizziness threatened to throw him back to the floor, but Beatrice steadied him. "Let's get you to my chambers and make you a little more comfortable."

Leif discovered his will to resist was gone. His legs moved maladroitly, following Beatrice's guidance like an injured animal.

Crossing through the doors and into the Great Hall, Beatrice whispered, "You should have taken my offer."

Juliet

Kenzie was such an inspiration that Juliet decided to use her as a muse. Juliet woke with a confidence that she hadn't felt in a long time. Something about getting reassurance from Kenzie flipped a switch inside of Juliet. Her stomach didn't sink when she thought of Nik anymore, and now she felt at peace with ending her relationship with Jesse. It was as if she was walking on air as she got ready for her day.

Juliet threw her high heeled boots on and kept her hair loose, the wild curls bouncing with extra life. To add the final touch of closure, she slapped on her dark lipstick. She knew she looked like she was ready for a night out, but it made her feel bold and courageous. And then she snapped on her necklace, the perfect reminder that her heart was her own. She wouldn't let anyone else play with it.

She was ready for her day of freedom.

She walked around her room and collected the small objects that she'd kept to reminder herself of Nik—a keychain from Mack's, a small stack of books, and two hoodies that she'd taken from him. She left her room with her hands full and her heart open.

Before Juliet's class started, she went back to the library. She hadn't been to *their* spot for so long, but she didn't even hitch when she stepped through the front doors. He could gather his things the next time he came here—and she was positive he'd return.

Hopefully, he wasn't there now.

Then again, she didn't think it mattered anymore.

Even so, she was still grateful that the small space was empty when she arrived. Everything was the same, even after all the time that had passed. Nothing had moved or changed.

Which was weird because Juliet had changed—for the better. She didn't need to rely on a guy for happiness. She could find that on her own.

She placed his belongings on the empty, dusty chair, and when she let it go, a weight lifted off her shoulders. She was officially ready to let go of her first relationship.

Juliet clapped her hands clean and spun around with a bounce to her twirl—only to find Nik standing behind her wearing a heartwarming smirk, dimples on full display.

"So, that's where my two favorite hoodies went." His eyes looked forlorn, but his smile was as genuine as ever.

"Thought you might want them back." Juliet shrugged and gave him a playful smile that bared all her teeth. She was no longer nervous around him, just appreciative of their history. Their relationship wasn't something to mourn, it was something to celebrate and learn from. "Well, gotta get to class. See ya 'round."

His smile faded into a frown, and for a second, Juliet wanted to console him. But she'd already had her fair share of grief.

She slowly walked past him, but he gently took hold of her wrist. "You look beautiful, Juliet. I keep wanting to apologize but I know it doesn't help. Under different circumstances..." Nik paused, still holding her hand.

Games. That's all boys want to do is play games. Juliet had had enough. She didn't get angry, she got cocky.

"No, don't. No need for sorry's or explanations. I'm good. But like I said, gotta go." She flipped her hair a little too dramatically, but it was just enough for her to get a good look at Nik. His lips were in an O shape and his eyebrows almost reached his hairline.

Only a small part of her wanted to run back and tell him it was okay—an incredibly small part. Kenzie's advice played over and over in her head, and she touched the heart and key pendants hanging against her throat. She didn't need a guy to make her happy.

And Nik clearly didn't know what to feel. He just kept leading her on.

Without a look back, Juliet sashayed her way out of their secret spot for the last time. She was proud of herself for not giving in and for not falling apart, and she couldn't wait to tell both Myreen and Kenzie. Her strength seemed to double, and it felt like she'd drunk a potion of adrenaline. She couldn't let it overtake her, though, because class was about to start. The last thing she needed was the rumor mill bringing her into their stories.

Juliet quickly got to class and took her seat. She noticed the looks that the guys gave her and wondered if it had always been that way. Was she just too blinded by Nik to see it? But although it boosted her confidence even more, she was still on the no-boy train that she and Kenzie had jumped on.

As class began, she found herself looking at the clock and counting down the minutes before she could see Jesse and make it official. She was about to be single and *not* ready to mingle.

Though she feared that her spark of courage would fade away by the end of class, Juliet was relieved when the bell rang and she still felt the fire of determination. Jesse would be in the Defense Room. She had another class to get to, but if she didn't stop to have the talk with him, she thought she might explode. She walked at so brisk a pace—almost running into other students in the hall—that she had to stop and catch her breath before she entered the Defense Room.

Juliet looked around until she spotted Jesse by the target area. He had on a tight black t-shirt that accented his biceps, and his hair was pulled back in a thin black headband. It was her favorite way to see him, which made the situation ten times harder to face. He was attractive—insanely attractive—but he wasn't right for her. She didn't feel intensely enough to want to stay with him. He was the perfect rebound guy, but to her that's all he would ever be.

"Jesse, hey."

He spun at the sound of her voice, then whistled and circled her like a wolf in heat. "Well, damn! You are a snack, a meal, *and* dessert." Jesse grabbed her from where he stood behind her and pulled her into his chest. His playful behavior made her laugh, but she had to remember what she was there for.

"Can we go somewhere private for a sec?" She didn't mean

for it to sound like she wanted to get steamy, but Jesse sure thought she did. With a deep moan in her ear he grabbed her hand and led her to the sim room.

"How's this for private?" He leaned in and placed his lips on Juliet's.

She was so stunned that she didn't move or tell him to stop. She went with it—for a second. It was her goodbye kiss.

She pulled away and looked at the floor. "I've never done this before and I'm a little nervous."

"That's okay. Nervous is good. We can take it slow. Just know that when you look so hot, I can't promise I'll be able to control myself." He tried to go in for another knee-weakening kiss, but this time Juliet couldn't let herself.

She turned away and steadied her breath, making herself aware of the warm metal of the necklace against her skin. Thinking about Kenzie's words of wisdom, she straightened her back and looked into his eyes. "Look, Jesse. I came 'cause I wanted to talk."

"About?" He still wasn't catching on. Jesse took her in his arms and leaned down so his lips touched her shoulder.

Juliet cleared her throat and took a step away. His closeness made it extremely hard to focus.

"About us. I just don't think..."

"Oh, I see what kind of talk this is." His grin was gone, but he still stood close. Grabbing her hand, he gave her his best puppy dog eyes. "Are you sure that's what you want?" Jesse batted his thick eyelashes, managing to make Juliet smile.

"Yes. I think it is. I just need some me time. I mean, the time we spent together was... wonderful. But I can't be with someone until I'm ready, until my heart is healed." This seemed harder than breaking up with Nik, but maybe it was because she was doing the dumping this time.

"I get it. I'll miss you—and your kisses. But you'll be back." His smirk grew so wide that he looked like the Cheshire cat.

Juliet rolled her eyes. "Very funny. But I won't. Not before you come begging for me to take *you* back." She knew flirting was not how breakups worked, but for Jesse, it seemed to be the only language he understood.

He laughed and pulled her in for a tight embrace. "Really, I'll miss this. My arms will be wide open for whenever you want to come running back to me." With a kiss on the cheek, Jesse walked to the door and held it open for her. As she walked past him, he whistled like he did before and gave her a wink. Juliet shook her head and walked out—again without a look back.

She felt free, and it pleased her that the day had gone so well so far. Jesse could be her friend—if he learned to accept her personal space—and Nik was left with his mouth hanging open because Juliet had finally stood up for herself.

Juliet felt electric with pride.

She pulled out her phone and opened her music app. She'd created a new playlist and added songs by artists like Christina, Demi, and Miley. The list had a massive amount of girl anthems, and it had become her new favorite song list. Juliet named the playlist and texted it to Kenzie.

As she pulled out her headphones and clicked *Random*, she felt like she was on top of the world. With one last look at her phone before she put it in her pocket, she could only smirk at the title. It ran across her screen, giving her goosebumps of self-confidence.

#GirlBoss

Kenzie

After school, Kenzie listened to the playlist Juliet had sent her, loving the #GirlBoss vibes. She'd just barely managed to convince her mom that she should be allowed her freedom again—specifically another trip to Chicago. But seeing Juliet had been so good for her soul. It was nice talking to someone her age about her boy drama, even if she had to leave some of the best bits out. And now she had a song list to commemorate their time. It was awesome.

But hearing that Myreen was sick reminded her of Kol's request. Based on the twenty or so messages she'd received from Lover Boy within about an hour's span the other day, he was dangerously close to tripping that hazard. She needed answers, like now. But how to get them? The dang book sure wasn't yielding. Still, it seemed it was her only resource. It's not like she could ask Gram about it, even if she *was* spilling the magical beans.

Kenzie angled herself toward Gram's place next door. She had taken to doing her homework there, getting extra magical training from her grandma while she was at it. Her mom must have known what was going on, but if she did, she made no mention of it. And Kenzie wasn't about to bring *that* back up and break the uneasy truce that had settled in the house.

"How's my favorite granddaughter?" Gram asked as Kenzie came in.

"I'm your *only* granddaughter," Kenzie said, shaking her head.

Gram laughed. "And I wouldn't have it any other way. You ready for a little fun today?"

Kenzie shrugged. "What you got?" She wasn't in much of a mood for lessons, but it didn't hurt to find out what was on the agenda.

"I wanted to show you a spell for erasing your scent."

Kenzie frowned. "Didn't I already learn that one?"

"Yes, but that was specific to vampires. There's a variation on the spell that helps with weres—hounds, specifically. You know, I dated a hound once. He was a real dog." Gram winked, and Kenzie burst out laughing.

"Are you pulling my leg, Gram?"

"Maybe. Maybe not. So, you want to learn that spell or what?"

Kenzie tugged on a lock of hair, digging the toe of her shoe into the wood floor. "Actually, I think I'm going to skip the lesson today, if you don't mind. Homework." She shrugged.

Gram gave her an appraising look. "I suppose that's fine. We can continue again on Monday. Or tomorrow, if you're so inclined."

"Thanks!" Kenzie gave Gram a quick peck on the cheek before heading to her own house. She said a quick hello to her mom, snagged a bag of chips and tub of dip and took everything to her room. She turned on her iPod again and set the volume to low, still playing her #GirlBoss list—talk about mood music—then performed the reveal spell and retrieved her grimoire.

The *grimoire, not mine,* she reminded herself. Kenzie sighed. It didn't seem fair, being in possession of the key to unlocking her magic and still not being able to use most of it. Stupid magic rules. *But the rules are there for a reason,* her grandmother's admonition rang in her head. Kenzie couldn't help but be reminded that her dad had died at the hands of unguided magic. At least she had something, even if the grimoire refused to yield all its secrets.

And she didn't need all its secrets. Just two. If she was lucky.

She flipped through the pages to the love spell she'd marked, hoping to find inspiration to Kol's dilemma.

"Ow!" she hissed, jerking her stinging hand from the offending edge. "Papercut. Ack." She examined her finger, squeezing it and then shaking it to relieve the pain and banish the endless instant replay her mind wanted to perform.

A speck on the book began to glow, and Kenzie's eyes widened. That was her blood on the page. And the book was reacting to it.

"Oh no!" She licked her thumb and tried to rub at the spot, but her attempts only managed to spread the blood further. And the light was growing.

"Crap, crap, crap!" Gram had said something about blood

and magic, so whatever this was couldn't be good. Not that she'd realized the book would actually *react* to her blood, or she might've been more cautious. Maybe. Her heart hammered, and she tried to slam the book closed, but it felt as if a weight was on top of the pages.

In a flash of brilliance, the light disappeared. Kenzie did a quick inventory of the book and herself, but nothing seemed wrong. Hopefully that was a good sign.

Except the pages felt different. When she turned it, the thick one she'd been on turned into four, revealing relationship spells of all sorts... Had her blood unlocked it?

One spell in particular caught her eye, sending that question to the back of her mind. It was the one marked LOVE UNREQUITED.

Kenzie held her breath as she read through the description and then how to place the curse and how to break it.

There was no mistaking it. This was Kol's curse, the one that had followed his family through generations. The one that stood in the way of her best friend's happiness. She should be smiling right now.

But there was no way she could do the counter-curse alone.

"Awww, crap." She was already in hot water as it was, and revealing the grimoire could mean she'd lose it. Forever. But she'd need at least two more selkies, according to the instructions for the spell. Or counter-spell, rather.

Basically, if she wanted to lift this curse, she'd need to reveal the book. The book that had just magically responded to her blood. She had so many questions.

She wrestled over the decision only a moment. Myreen needed this break and Kenzie needed answers. She'd figure out a way through the rest of the mess later.

Kenzie stuffed her face with a few dip-covered chips, then gathered her book in her bag and ran back over to Gram's.

"Okay, I have a confession," Kenzie said as she burst through the door.

"Hold up!" Gram said from another room. There was a flush and some running water, and then Gram came out from down the hall drying her hands with a towel. "What's up?"

"I have a grimoire and I accidentally got blood on it and it glowed and crap."

"What?" Gram hurried toward Kenzie, the towel in her hand forgotten. Kenzie held up the ancient tome, and Gram took it, gingerly turning the pages.

Kenzie couldn't quite look at her grandmother. Even at seventy-five, she was an intimidating figure, not by stature but by presence and knowledge of magic. Kenzie hoped the whole grimoire revelation thing wouldn't incite a riot, as so many conversations about magic had done in the past. Though, to be fair, most of the rioting had been between Kenzie and her mom.

"Where did you get this?" Gram asked, marveling at the various pages.

"Um, that's not important. What *is* important is that I just magically unlocked this thing with my blood."

At least she didn't seem mad. Yet. Hopefully Gram would drop the origin thing. Kenzie wasn't ready to spill the beans on Leif, especially since she had no idea the part he played in this whole thing. Just one more mystery she needed to pull out of the guy. If he'd ever talk to her.

Gram looked hard at Kenzie for a long moment, but eventually she turned her gaze back on the book. "MacLugh," she said, and the pages glowed again.

"Oh, sure. Throw that in my face." *Had it really been that easy this whole time?* "Does this mean that it's ours?"

Gram sighed. "I think this is a conversation best had sitting." Gram sat on the dingy floral couch and patted the seat next to her.

"Yes, this is our grimoire," Gram continued once Kenzie was seated. "If it wasn't, chances are all your hair would've fallen out, or your joints would've become as gnarled as an old tree. Selkies aren't exactly known for their sharing nature. Your blood probably would've activated a curse if the book didn't belong to us." She looked at Kenzie, and Kenzie reluctantly met her grandmother's gaze. "Where did you say you got this?"

Kenzie pulled her lips in and clamped down on them. "I didn't. And actually, I need your and Mom's help releasing Myreen's boyfriend from a curse that I found in this book."

"How would Myreen's boyfriend be cursed by a spell from our book?"

"I was hoping you might know something? Here." Kenzie opened the book in Gram's hands, flipping to the page with Kol's curse. "It's this one."

Gram stared at the page for a long moment. "Is he by chance a dragon or a vampire?"

"A dragon! Kol's a dragon shifter."

Gram leaned back, looking up. "There is one story, though it's hard to say how much of it is truth and how much is fiction at this point. But what I heard is that a vampire stole our grimoire, after killing a member of the family. Apparently he was in league with a dragon and they ran off together afterward. The selkie sisters were upset, as you can imagine, and placed a curse on them both. If I were to guess, I'd say it's the spell you found."

Kenzie ran through a gamut of emotions, from concern to anger to disbelief. Could she have really been so wrong about Leif? He didn't seem the type to steal a grimoire or kill his beloved, though he still hadn't told her the full story. Maybe if the vampire didn't keep vanishing on her, she'd have been able to mine a little more information from him by now. She'd have to contact him soon, if only for her own peace of mind.

"So you'll help me convince mom to undo this curse?"

"I don't like it. Our ancestors placed that curse on his family for a reason."

"A reason that's centuries old and has hurt countless people in the process. They cursed that dragon's family—*not* just the dragon. And if that dragon's descendant, Kol, falls in love with Myreen, she'll hate him if we don't lift that curse. Love *unrequited*." She tapped the page for emphasis.

Gram shook her head. "I don't know. I think our family has suffered enough at the hands of magic."

"But we've got the book to guide us now. Please, we can't just let Kol and his whole family suffer like that. And Myreen. You and Mom like her, don't you?"

Gram frowned. "How exactly did Myreen get caught up in all this?"

Kenzie looked at her hands, resting in her lap. "She's a mermaid. Or actually, she's a chimera, and her mom was killed by a vampire—but she doesn't deserve this and neither does Kol!" Kenzie rushed through the information, hoping to rip off the remainder of her lies like a bandage. Well, almost all of them. Now wasn't the time to bring up the vampire who had given her the grimoire.

She dared to glance at her grandmother, who wore a look of disappointment that nearly broke her heart. "That's a lot of lies, Kitten. I thought there might be more, after we caught you in the one, but this..."

"I'm sorry."

"You've had our grimoire for some time, and you lied about your friend and her mom."

"Technically, yes, but I didn't know it was our grimoire until you told me, and I've just been trying to be a good friend." She gave Gram a hesitant smile.

Gram's grim expression wasn't budging. "Is there anything else you'd like to tell me while we're at it?"

Kenzie grimaced. "Um, there's a school in Chicago for shifters and I want to go?" She pasted on a pained smile, hoping her grandmother would go easy on her.

Gram pursed her lips. "I've heard of this school, but shifters aren't exactly known for their acceptance of selkies."

"But I can change that! I know I can. I just need a chance. The director said he's working on getting me in... They just have a little vampire problem they're trying to resolve first." Kenzie gave her grandma a sheepish grin.

Gram shook her head. "Kenzie Renee MacLugh, your mother should've named you trouble. How did you plan on getting in that school without us noticing?"

Kenzie shrugged. "One step at a time. I'm still not *in* yet."

"Hmph." Gram looked back at the book in her hands, her expression finally softening. "You've been gone for far too long, friend," she murmured, softly stroking the cover.

"So you'll help me convince Mom to break the curse?"

Gram sighed, looking toward the ceiling as if it held her

salvation. "Okay. I'll talk to your mother, but you have to promise—no more lying to us. I'll find a spell if I have to, to make sure you comply."

Kenzie reddened. "Heh. Yeah, already found that one."

Gram raised a brow.

"I'll be a good girl, I swear. Well, as good as I can manage." As Gram continued to stare, Kenzie added, "What? *You're* the one who said Mom should've named me trouble."

Gram pulled Kenzie into a side hug. "You're trouble, all right. But I wouldn't have you any other way."

"Aw, thanks Gram."

"Okay. Let's go break the news to your mom."

Kenzie gave Gram a hopeful smile as they stood. Mom wouldn't be happy, but with the book to guide them and Gram in her corner, Kenzie felt confident Kol's curse would be lifted in no time.

One magical problem down, one to go. Hopefully Leif could hold on just a little longer.

If she decided he was still worth helping.

Kol

When Kol finally got the ping from Kenzie Saturday morning, he dressed in record time and flew out the door. He only remembered at the last second that it was the middle of January and a coat might be a good idea outside of the controlled climate of the Dome.

It shouldn't have surprised him that it took Kenzie over a week to find something, but the fact he could almost taste the freedom from the curse made him antsy and anxious.

He might've texted and emailed her at least a dozen times... a day.

Fortunately it was early, and he slipped out easily, but as soon as he settled in the Uber, he became jittery again. Kol pulled out his phone to make sure he hadn't imagined her message.

Kenzie: Found it. Meet me?

An address outside of Chicago was listed in the next message—the location he was headed to. Kenzie was smart to be vague. Kol just hoped that what she'd *found* was the counter-curse, and that the text hadn't actually been meant for Myreen about a missing sweater or something.

Probably should've called to verify. He was half-tempted to do so now, but wondered what sorts of looks he'd get from his driver and decided against it. It was too late, anyway. His hopes were up and if he'd been mistaken, he'd want to be far from the Dome. He wouldn't make contingency plans for the day just yet.

When they pulled up to the small townhome more than an hour later, Kol blinked a few times.

"Is this it?" he asked.

"It's the address you gave me, man," the guy, a few years older than Kol—and definitely human—said.

Kol double-checked Kenzie's message and agreed that the address was correct. He stepped out and onto the curb, took a deep breath and then strode up to the door.

Looking at the mailbox, he did a double-take. *MacLugh.* It sounded familiar. Had Myreen ever mentioned Kenzie's last name to him? He couldn't think of a reason it would be important and brushed it off.

When Kol lifted a hand to knock, his heart began to pound, and his arm froze in mid-air.

This could be it.

This could be the last moment Kol would ever worry about allowing himself to fall in love. His sister Tatiana could have a happy marriage with a husband who loved her. Dozens of aunts and uncles, cousins twice and three times removed could love their spouses, their boyfriends and girlfriends, and be loved in return. This could be the last moment of pain his mother ever went through being married to a man who didn't love her—well… realistically he couldn't expect his father to return the feelings overnight. But after this moment there might be hope that he could, someday.

After this moment, Kol could allow himself to fall completely for Myreen, and she might love him back.

He knocked.

Wavy brown hair swung the door open and met him with a smile.

"You look like you're gonna throw up," Kenzie said, leaning against the door. "You okay?"

Kol frowned, attempting to mask his face, but knowing he failed. "Fine. I'm fine."

"'Cause we can do this another day…"

"No, Kenzie," he growled low. "Now. Please, now."

"The good news is, I'll probably feel about as green as you look in about five minutes." She stepped aside for Kol to walk in. He handed her his coat, which she dropped on a bench by the wall.

Kenzie waved him into a room just off the entrance that felt almost like a closet. Kol filled the whole of it, yet somehow two other women, plus Kenzie, also fit. He was too nervous and distracted by his racing pulse to notice details, but the entire room had a buzzing, chaotic feeling.

Kol met one pair of hazel eyes, then another. The women were clearly relatives of Kenzie—wavy brown hair with varying levels of gray—probably her mother and grandmother.

"Kol, this is my mom, Lita," Kenzie said. "You probably remember her from our little *meeting*."

Instinctively, Kol held a hand out to Lita who took it firmly, giving Kenzie the "mom" look. "Kol Dracul," he said.

"And my grandmother, Marjorie."

He did the same with Marjorie, nodding at them both.

"Mom, Gram, this is Kol, Myreen's boyfriend." Kenzie gave an awkward smile and held out her hands like Kol was some sort of display.

Kol stepped back, clasping his hands behind him, unsure what to do next. He didn't know if it was common for Kenzie's family to vet guys who wanted to hang out with her, or if they were aware of Kol's situation and his reason for being there. Either way, the way everyone stood looking at one another felt awkward.

Kenzie reached behind her on the desk for an ancient-looking, large bound book. It made Kol's stomach leap into his throat and beads of perspiration gather around his hairline. Kenzie stared at the book for several seconds as if gathering her thoughts.

"So... I found the spells," she said, still not glancing up. "The curse and the *counter-curse*. Sorry it took so long, but the grimoire only started cooperating yesterday."

Both of Kol's eyebrows rose in surprise. "It was in your family grimoire?" he said, not exactly sure what he was asking. It seemed pretty incredible and almost too easy that the exact spell they needed just happened to be in the spell book of the first selkie he'd sought out. Kol felt his skepticism rise, but shoved it down.

He needed this. His family needed this. His *mom* needed this.

Kenzie nodded, still not looking at him. "The spell requires the magic of several selkies." She finally lifted her eyes to meet his. "So Mom and Gram have agreed to help."

That's why they're here.

Lita shifted her feet uncomfortably. Marjorie merely smiled as if they were about to do something mundane, like making a sandwich.

They weren't just there to make sure Kol acted like a gentleman and treated their daughter and granddaughter with respect. They were there to add their own powers and strengthen the spell.

Kol swallowed. "Is three enough?" he asked, feeling the gravity of the situation. It was only natural and logical that it would take several to break the curse. He remembered reading that several of the selkie sisters placed it. He wasn't sure of the exact number, but he thought it had to be more than three.

The women looked amongst themselves. Kenzie shrugged.

"It should work," Kenzie said, then opened the book to a marked page and handed it to Marjorie who propped it on a yellow music stand she'd retrieved from the corner. The old book looked ridiculous on its perch.

Lita pulled a small black pocket-knife from her back pocket and handed it to Kenzie who thanked her with a grimace.

Blood. It must need blood. Without thinking or being asked, Kol pushed up his sleeve and offered his hand.

Marjorie cupped his palm with her own beneath and looked expectantly at Kenzie.

Kenzie's face contorted again—she'd been right, she did look a little green now—and she flipped open the knife, then took a breath.

Kol attempted to pull his hand back again, realizing it

wasn't his blood that was needed, but Marjorie held it firm and motioned for Lita to also place her hand beneath.

Kenzie squeezed her eyes tightly for a moment as if bracing herself. It didn't seem like a good way to draw blood. Kol would hate for her to accidentally hit an artery and bleed out on the rug—curse or no curse, his chances with Myreen would plummet indefinitely.

When she opened her eyes again, her face was stoic and determined. She placed the edge of the blade firmly on the tip of her finger until a deep red bead appeared. She then handed the knife to Lita.

Kenzie smeared the blood on Kol's palm, gagging. "Fuathah chailliút," she said, drawing a circle.

Lita then cut her finger and did the same over Kenzie's blood. "Fuathah chailliút."

Marjorie took the knife for her turn.

"Grá'arais," Kenzie, Lita, and Marjorie said simultaneously, re-tracing the circle. "Flaisch shoun flaisch," the three said almost together, then drew a line through the circle, Kenzie shuddering. "Follah shoun námash."

Falling into a chant, the MacLugh selkies repeated the spell. "Fuathah chailliút, grá'arais, flaisch shoun flaisch, follah shoun námash." And they retraced their mixed gore on Kol's palm over and over.

A warm sensation began on the skin of his palm, which could have been the blood, but when the heat sunk down into the bones of his hand, he knew it couldn't be. Taking stock of his own fire, he realized it was low on reserve, dormant inside and nowhere near his hands.

The warmth spread down his arm and through his

bloodstream, taking the same route his fire traveled, but it was a different sort of heat. Not exactly the same physical heat he was accustomed to, but more of an ethereal or spiritual *light* coursing through him.

Once it reached his heart, it spread everywhere like an explosion. Down his legs, across his shoulders, up the back of his neck, making his scalp tingle. He even saw red and purple flashes dance in front of his eyes, which continued even when he shut them. The feeling raced around, seemingly erratic and almost frantic. It was a little overwhelming, so he kept his eyes closed.

Then suddenly, the sensation vanished.

When Kol opened his eyes, Kenzie and her family continued to whisper the words of the spell, their eyes shut in meditation. He involuntarily twitched his hand, and Kenzie opened her eyes and ended the chant.

Kol lifted his hand from theirs. The blood was gone from it, vanished as surely as the strange warm light.

Kenzie raced from the room, a hand over her mouth.

Kol looked to Lita. "Is she alright?"

"Just give her a minute," Marjorie answered.

His eyes glued to his hand while they waited. He looked for any trace of the blood, or any difference. Would he be able to see if the curse had really been lifted?

"So?" Kenzie asked when she returned. "Do you feel like a real boy yet?"

He lifted his eyes from his unmarked palm to her. "I don't—"

"Kenzie!" Lita said. "And I doubt his ancestor felt much after the curse was placed on him or her. It wasn't until they fell in love that they truly knew. Unless they weren't aware a curse was placed on them."

"Aline," Kol said. "Her name was Aline Dracul. And she knew. Maybe not right away, but every Dracul knows."

"So go find out if it worked!" Marjorie said.

Just the thought made Kol a little sick.

"Let yourself fall in love with our sweet Myreen," she continued. "Then you'll know."

Kol looked to Kenzie as if she'd know how to respond, but she merely shrugged and gave him a half-smile.

And then Kenzie was walking Kol to the door. "Well, that was crazy. But nothing strange is falling off, so it must've worked." She picked up his coat from where it had slid to the floor and handed it to him.

"I hope so," he said, then lowered his head in a half-nod. "Thank you."

Kenzie waved a hand. "Whatever." She opened the front door, letting in the cold air. "But just so you know, if you break her, I'll break you."

Kol went a little cross-eyed looking at the newly bandaged finger pointed straight at his nose.

"And you know I can," she said with a smirk.

He knew she was serious and so saluted in response. "Got it."

"Are you all set? Need me to call anyone?"

Kol shook his head. He held back the smile until she shut the door behind him, leaving him on the porch.

The smile got wider. *It worked,* he thought. He somehow felt different.

Hopeful.

Like he could have a happy ending.

Like his mother could have a happy ending.

For the first time in his life, Kol let himself dream of a future that wasn't stocked-full of military life to avoid the cold glances at the dinner table. Or seeing a face identical to his mothers, but unable to do anything about it because the person he loved was not the person he shared a life with.

Kol glanced back at the selkie house as he waited on the curb for his Uber. Reading the name that was so familiar—*MacLugh*—he racked his brain, trying to remember where he'd seen it. It was almost like a cold blast of high altitude air when his brain provided the answer and the connection.

MacLugh was the name of the woman who mysteriously died at the boarding house. Gemma MacLugh. It was Gemma's sisters, the MacLugh sisters, the *selkie* sisters who traveled all the way to Washington in order to curse his ancestor, Aline Dracul.

The realization filled Kol with even more confidence and relief that the spell had worked. If MacLugh's placed the curse on his family, it was only fitting and logical that the counter-curse *would* be in the MacLugh grimoire. And who better to break it than the very family who placed it?

He was half-tempted to fly home because he couldn't wait to get back to Myreen, but the Uber had finally arrived. Kol practically sprinted into car, every nerve sizzling with anticipation.

Chapter 52

Oberon

Oberon's eyes glowed purple as he called upon the crackling thunder high above. Leaping at the nearest vampire, his beak tore through its neck, while another was struck by a targeted bolt of lightning. The unfortunate vampire was thrown fifty feet through the air and into the Missouri River, skipping several times like a stone before submerging.

Torrents of rain pattered down, and Oberon caused a mist to form, hoping it would decrease the visibility of his seemingly countless enemies.

A heavy weight slammed onto his back, and Oberon angled his head swiftly, his razor-sharp beak grabbing the head of the vampire who'd jumped onto him. With the strength of his muscles surging in his neck, he pulled, separating his attacker's head from his body in a matter of milliseconds.

The body slid off his back like the pouring rain, and

Oberon cast the head aside, launching himself into the air with his powerful wings. He had to get a better vantage point. It was this part of the simulation where Draven made his entrance—when he went for Oberon's parents and his pregnant wife, Serilda.

Years ago, Oberon had asked Ren to create a simulation of the attack on Framboise Island. It pained him to relive the experience in such a real way, but it also gave him the opportunity to change the outcome. On top of it all, there was a certain satisfaction that came from killing Draven.

Diving and with a fierce shriek, Oberon stretched his talons out at the distracted vampire leader. Rage filled his soul as his claws went for Draven's shoulders. He opened his beak to kill the murderous vampire before he could get to his family again.

But before he could taste the victory of the win—something he'd done time and time again since the simulation's creation—Draven disappeared, and the simulation room went white.

Oberon tucked in his wings as he crashed hard to the floor, spinning over and over, the air taken out of his lungs. He came to a stop, dazed and in pain. Who had pulled the plug?

The sound of several marching footsteps approached, and Oberon began shifting back to his human form. As his body popped and cracked, shrinking in the process, he was relieved to feel no breaks in his bones.

Flat on his back and in nothing but his smart clothing, he propped himself up to see who had entered.

"Eduard!" he growled, pushing himself up. "You stopped my simulation."

Lord Dracul was accompanied by Nikolai Candida, both in their standard military uniforms. Malachai Quinn was also among them, as well as four other shifters from the military. Behind them all, he saw Delphine. Her face was pale and filled with dread.

Pluck my feathers, what is going on?

Oberon brought his attention back to the general.

"Oberon," Eduard said with an acknowledging nod. "I'll have you know that I did not terminate your program. Your access to the simulation room was removed."

Oberon's brows scrunched as he got to his feet, and he shook his arms. "Excuse me?"

Eduard gave him a hard look. Unnamed emotion boiled behind his eyes, just barely suppressed.

Setting his jaw, the general said, "As of this morning, you are dismissed from your position as director of the Dome."

Dismissed? Nobody had the authority to dismiss a Director. For a moment, his mind flashed back to the director of The Island—the only school director Oberon had ever known—Zabrina Slegr. She was a brilliant leader and was a quick thinker. The mao had helped hundreds of students during her time as director. But she'd never been removed from that leadership—not until a vampire murdered her. He'd witnessed the cruel death as it happened. Had he arrived at her quarters just moments before, he could have saved her.

But this was different. A *shifter* had come to toss him out. He wished he was facing a vampire.

Oberon laughed humorlessly. He took in the surrounding soldiers giving him distasteful looks. "Is this some kind of joke?"

The military leader's eyes widened. "A joke? Oh, I'm quite serious, Mr. Rex. It has become very apparent that you are unfit to lead this school."

Oberon's eyes flitted to Delphine and he gave her a questioning glance. She cast her gaze to the white floor of the sim room. Did she have a part in this? He didn't want to believe she did, but why else had she come?

What was this madness? A bombardment of questions assailed his mind. Oberon hadn't anticipated anything like this.

Straightening his back, he said, "Is this about Myreen?"

At this, Eduard let loose a hearty laugh. "Every time I come here, that's your assumption, isn't it?" His humored expression dropped. "I have come this time because of your betrayal to the school and to our shifter world."

The general's words were icy-cold, chilling Oberon to the heart. Betrayal? How could he be accused of such a thing?

Gritting his teeth, Oberon said, "Since the loss of the last school, as well as my wife and unborn child, I have dedicated my entire life to the Dome. Everything I have done and everything I do is for the shifters who live here."

Eduard snorted. "Does that include vampire dealings?"

Oberon froze. Had Lord Dracul been spying on his every move? Did the general follow him to Yukon to see what Oberon was up to? How could he explain the Leif situation?

"Your silence is a witness to your guilt," Eduard said. "Do you choose to deny this accusation?"

Sighing heavily, Oberon said, "I have had dealings with *one* vampire who is a defector of Draven's group."

"Do you think labeling any vampire as a defector makes your crime any less tarnished?" Eduard aimed a finger at Oberon, his eyes heating with rage.

"Believe me when I say that I understand that mentality all too well," Oberon said. "But this particular vampire saved my life years ago. He's on our side."

"Then why have you not brought this individual up before?" the general hissed.

"Because you would have thrown me out!" Oberon shouted, feeling the warm heat returning to his heart. "Just like you're doing now. That vampire has been instrumental in the protection of this school and—"

"No more lies, Oberon," interrupted Eduard. "We have video footage of several meetings you've set up with this vampire, as well as logged phone calls. Even Lady Delphine spotted you meeting with him recently in a restaurant in Chicago."

Oberon felt a violation of privacy, and it very nearly caused him to shift into his gryphon form to take on the general. But the spike of his anger was at the mention of Delphine. He gave her a sorrowful look, feeling the jabbing claws of betrayal. She must have seen them together the time they'd met up, right before Christmas. Why hadn't she come to him first about Leif?

"If you've been listening in on my conversations with Leif," Oberon growled, "then you'll know he's on our side and that he's been our eyes and ears in the heart of Draven's fortress."

The general snorted. "You've been played, Oberon! Never in this world has there been a *good* vampire, and there never will be. It's been proven by over a millennium of war between our peoples. This Leif... he's got you right where he wants you—right where Draven wants you." Eduard shook his head. "Since I've known you, I've taken you for a reasonably intelligent man. How wrong I was."

Lord Dracul's words pushed him over the edge, and the rage that erupted within Oberon caused him to shift. Brown feathers sprouted along his skin like flames on wood, and he grew in size. His hands and feet molded into dark talons, and the muscles in his body flexed with familiarity. Through his newly-formed beak, Oberon released a shrill call, a voice of challenge to Eduard.

At the same time, the five soldiers—including Malachai Quinn—shifted as well. Their uniforms were smart clothing, expensively made, but imperative for military use.

However, Eduard and his assistant, Nikolai, did not shift. Terror was spread across the Candida boy's face. It was apparent he didn't want to be in this situation. Delphine stood back, the depth of sadness on her face dropping even more.

While Oberon's intelligence had been insulted, he wasn't stupid enough to take on a phoenix, a naga, and three weres—all military-trained. He knew the fight was over before it had even begun. Slumping his wings in surrender, he shifted back into his human form.

"Smart move," Eduard said, holding a fist in the air. Oberon assumed it was meant as a command for the other shifters—they didn't shift back to their human forms, but kept wary eyes on Oberon. "Thank you for complying, Mr. Rex."

Oberon hung his head. "So what happens next?"

"Well, now that you've been relieved of your duties, you will move on to wherever your heart desires," replied Eduard as he narrowed his eyes. "*Away* from the Dome. You are no longer welcome on school grounds. And if you are caught attempting to return, you'll find yourself under military imprisonment. Is that clear?"

Oberon's heart dropped. He no longer felt anger or rage, but a deep sadness he hadn't known since the destruction of The

Island and losing Seri. Still, he nodded slowly. "May I ask who my replacement is?" He sent Delphine a hopeful look, as she was easily the best candidate for the job.

A slight smirk—barely detectable—inched its way on the general's face. "Me, of course. The Dome is now officially a militarized school. All teaching will be supervised by higher-ranking officers, and *proper* combat training will be taught to each student."

"You're turning this place into a military school?" Oberon asked.

"The future of the shifter world relies on the strength of the military. Why would we teach our students any other way?"

Oberon's mind raced. When he was younger, he knew the school needed to have classes based around combat—he'd ensured it was an integral part of every student's education. They *had* to know how to protect themselves from the vampire threat. But an advanced focus on military training? That had never been the plan.

"I will go peacefully," Oberon said softly, if regrettably. "But heed my advice, Eduard: be careful not to turn our people into what makes vampires our enemies. A lust for battle and death—all they bring is darkness and emptiness. There's a whole lot more to life than these."

"Oh, the wisdom of the gryphon," Lord Dracul said with disinterest. He raised his hand again and unfolded his fingers, spreading them wide. His soldiers shifted back to their human forms, but they still watched Oberon fiercely.

"May I speak, General?" Delphine said, her soprano voice pinging off the white walls.

Eduard turned toward the leader mermaid—the person

Oberon had come to love and trust as a sister as they made her vision of the Dome a reality—and nodded.

Delphine took several graceful steps forward. "Though it pains me to see you leave, Oberon, it is alarming you've had *any* vampire dealings at all. I know your past. Nevertheless, I can't let you leave the school without help. No matter what has happened, you have done a lot for the lives of hundreds of shifters. They will be forever indebted to you. Therefore, I have opened an account for you, and have supplied you with funds to help you get started on whatever life you decide to lead now."

Oberon wanted to spill everything to her right then and there. Of all the people he knew, she would be the only one who could understand what he was doing with Leif. But it was too late. Eduard had seen to that. Still, it hurt to know that she had shifted her loyalty. Had their years working as a team meant so little that she was willing to betray him?

"A parting gift I didn't agree with," the general added. "But Lady Delphine does make an excellent point. You have done well over the years." He narrowed his eyes. "But even the best fruit can go rotten."

Oberon forced himself to bridle the bubbling anger that started rising within him again. Eduard's abrasiveness was relentless.

"You may return to your office," the general sighed. "You have the rest of the day to pack your belongings and say your goodbyes. When you're ready to depart from the Dome, you will notify me, and I will *personally* escort you out. Is that understood?"

Oberon ran a hand through his tousled brown hair. This was it. The end of his life at the Dome. Biting his lip, he nodded.

Eduard moved closer until he stood nose-to-nose with Oberon. Whispering, the general gloated, "You should have let me have control of Myreen when I first asked."

Oberon blinked a few times, processing what Eduard just said.

"So that's it," Oberon said, loud enough for everyone in the simulation room to hear. "All of this because of the siren?"

Lord Dracul kept his maddening smirk as he moved away from Oberon. "Lieutenant General Quinn?"

Oberon watched with disappointment as Malachai stepped forward. He considered the teacher-military man a friend—had been the one to give the man his teaching job at the Dome when Malachai first found out his daughter was a shifter.

"You and the others will escort Mr. Rex back to his quarters and remain with him until he is prepared to depart," Eduard continued. "Keep your sharp eye on him, will you?"

Malachai saluted, and no pained expression formed on his freckled face. "It will be done, General."

Eduard swept his hand forward, as if he were dusting a dirty spot on a table. "Then escort away. The sooner he's gone, the sooner we can improve the school."

Again, Malachai saluted, as well as the other shifter soldiers. "Come along, Oberon," he said. "Let's get this over with."

Oberon had no choice. For all the talk of betrayal, the irony was not lost on him that he was the one who felt it the most, and the sting was worse than any gold-covered weapon could ever inflict.

Myreen

"I need to tell him," Myreen whispered to herself as she left Saturday morning training and crossed the grounds in search of Kol.

The week had been one of her most difficult yet. She couldn't remember a time in her life that her hormones were so off-balance, that her emotions were so erratic, or that every sensation, even the dullest ones, felt so intense. Every time she had tried to tell Kol during the week, something had come up or the timing just felt off. She needed to just come out with it now. The full moon was in a few days, and even through a mile of water, she could feel the prickle of an impending shift. The last thing she wanted was to lose control and turn in front of Kol without warning.

She should have told him a week ago. The truth was, she was scared he wouldn't want her after he found out. Ursas weren't like the other weres. Hounds were cool to look at, and every mao she'd ever seen was just downright gorgeous. Ursas, though—they were terrifying!

She'd always wondered why they never let out their shifter in defense class, or to show off like the other weres sometimes did. Then she seen one shift, when she'd happened to look into the Sim Room when one of them was training. That day, she learned why. Ursas in their shifter form were mammoth, grisly creatures that could scare the pants off a skilled poacher. There was nothing pretty about them. And when they got angry, there was no limit to the destruction they could cause.

A little voice in the back of her head whispered all week long that Kol would be disgusted with her if he found out. But she had to trust that what they had was stronger than that. Despite his random flakiness, they shared something... real. She felt it every time they were apart, and saw it in his eyes whenever they were together.

Now to put it to the test.

At this time on a Saturday morning, Kol should be playing the game she got him in the avian common room. So that's where she headed, treading with purpose.

"Miss Fairchild, there you are," boomed a commanding voice from across the hall.

She knew that voice.

She stopped and turned to see Kol's father marching toward her, an eerily satisfied smile on his face. As he came closer, she couldn't quite pinpoint what about the smug smirk made him look so deadly. Except for maybe the wicked glint in his amber eyes, as if he had just won a very bloody battle.

"Good morning, sir," Myreen said, her tone flat with hesitation.

"You're just the person I wanted to see," the general said as he stopped in front of her and clasped his hands.

"I– I am?" *This can't be good.*

"Yes." His smile widened as he put his arm around her shoulder in a gesture that assumed too much familiarity. "I have taken the position of Director of the Dome, and as such, I will now be overseeing your training."

"Wh—? Uh– What about Oberon?" Myreen stammered, shaking her head, her brows drawn down.

"Yes, poor Oberon. He's taking a personal leave of absence, and I've been chosen to take his place." His chest was so puffed with pride that it almost looked swollen.

Oberon's leaving? This doesn't sound right. He would have mentioned something to me.

"Well... Is everything okay? With Oberon, I mean."

"Everything is exactly the way it should be," General Dracul said with a nod. "Now, about your training, Oberon and Delphine have been handling you with kid gloves for far too long. They don't see the strong, independent woman I see when I look at you. They don't realize that you can handle so much more. Your skills have not been nurtured as they deserve. We're going to change that. I'll train you myself every single day from now on. Starting tonight."

"Tonight?" Every word that came out of his mouth filled her with unease. Oberon had said the general wanted to train her himself, and now suddenly Oberon was out of the picture and General Dracul was the school Director? Something smelled fishy, and it wasn't her tail.

"Will that be a problem?" The way he asked it made it clear he didn't care if it was—that it would happen anyway.

She paused before shaking her head. "No, no problem. I just..." She was pretty sure that Kol hadn't yet told his father about the two of them being together. If he was going to be the director, he would find out very soon. Despite her better judgment to let Kol be the one to tell him, she spit it out anyway, relinquishing control of her decisions to her inner ursa. "I had plans to spend the evening with Kol."

He dropped his hand from her shoulder and raised a thick black brow at her. "Kol? *My* Malkolm?" The scrutiny in his eyes was heavy.

"Yeah, we're kind of dating," she said with a shrug.

General Dracul threw back his head with a hearty laugh that made her jump. "Oh, my dear girl, that's not possible."

"Excuse me, but why not?" she asked, the sting of insult simmering inside her chest. Like she wasn't good enough to be with his son. *Honestly, why does every shifter species feel superior to the next?* Maybe she really shouldn't have mentioned it—not when she was so temperamental. She knew that Kol had a reason for keeping this from his father, but she didn't expect the general to be so blunt about it.

He put his hand on her shoulder again, and this time it was all she could do not to shove it off. "I know you think that Malkolm was genuinely interested in you before, but that was only because he was following my orders."

Myreen's heart squeezed, as if someone had just punched her hard in the chest. "What?" *Following his orders?*

"You see, when you arrived at this school, rumor had it that you were the siren from Delphine's prophecy. Oberon and Delphine weren't making any progress, and I needed to know with absolute certainty. So I tasked Malkolm with getting close to you to find out if you were indeed who they suspected."

Her head was shaking as he spoke, her ears refusing to

believe a single word that went through them.

That couldn't be true. Kol couldn't have been using her like that. Not Kol.

"When your siren abilities were discovered, I ordered Kol to cut his ties with you," General Dracul continued. "Surely you understand why. You're dangerous, my dear. Which is exactly why it's imperative that I help you learn to control your powers. All of them."

Her blood boiled inside her veins, making steam build beneath her clothes. A growing hatred for the general teased her already-unhinging grasp on her emotions, and the truth of Kol's betrayal threatened to let it loose completely.

"Perhaps Malkolm wasn't clear when he ended things," the general suggested, as if discussing the weather. "He's never been very good at dealing with emotional situations. I'll have a talk with him about it."

"That won't be necessary," she said, her voice deep with the weight of her anger and hurt. "Message received."

"Excellent." The general clapped his hands. "I want you at the Defense Room at seven o'clock sharp. Be prepared to train late into the night." He marched away with a spring in his step, and Myreen was left to stand alone in the middle of the empty Grand Hall.

She clenched her fists so hard that her nails cut into her palms. Every muscle in her body was tense with anger, creating a constant state of oddly-satisfying pain. All she could feel was the overwhelming need to break something. Everything. Smash it all to itty-bitty pieces.

So that was why Kol had been so hot and cold with her all this time. He never really liked her. He had only been following *Daddy's* orders. All those times he had brushed her off were his true colors coming through the mask of his princely duties. He really was the unfeeling robot she always teased him of being.

She hated him. More than she had ever hated anyone in her entire life.

Her body was no longer her own as her feet stomped out of the Grand Hall. Her vision was fogged and tinted with red, and she existed only as the singular desire to vent the rage that consumed her. Suddenly, she found herself in front of the greenhouse—*the* greenhouse, the one where she and Kol had made out for the first time.

Without a moment's hesitation, she clutched the handle of the door and pulled, wrenching it completely off its hinges. Frayed wires snapped and hissed in confusion as the connection that kept the doors locked outside of school hours severed. Myreen paid them no mind. Or rather, she had no mind with which to pay them. She took one look at the spot where she had sat on Kol's lap, and everything went blank.

When next the fog cleared, she was standing in the wreckage of the once-vibrant vegetable and herb garden. Water spurted from broken irrigation lines. Shards of glass and smashed pottery littered the ground, covered in the green shreds of what used to be healthy plants.

Over the sound of her own snarling, she heard someone say her name behind her. She snapped her head in that direction.

Mr. Coltar stood in the vandalized doorway, Mr. Suzuki standing skittishly behind him.

At the startled looks in their wide eyes, Myreen's temper started to cool, her grizzled breath easing. Slowly, she realized what she'd done. She'd destroyed the greenhouse.

Her panting quickly turned into hiccupping as guilt

crushed her. "Ohmygosh, what did I do?"

"It's okay, Myreen," Mr. Coltar soothed, stepping over the debris to come to her side. Putting his hands gently on her arms, he said, "These things happen during first shifts. Not usually to school property, but they do happen. Luckily there was no one here. Let's get you to Ms. Heather."

"B– but w– what ab– bout all this?" She shook so hard she could barely speak. It was all she could do not to break down, she was so filled with self-loathing.

"Once you've calmed down, we can deal with cleaning up the mess," Mr. Coltar said, leading her out of what remained of the greenhouse. "Isn't that right, Ren?"

"Yes, of course." Mr. Suzuki said the words with a dazed look, staring at the rubble before him.

"Come, let's get you taken care of," Mr. Coltar urged.

Myreen allowed his enormous hands to push her forward. She was feeling so much that she didn't really feel anything at all.

She had thrown a tantrum and destroyed one of the Dome's resources. Everyone at the school depended on those plants, and she'd ripped them to pieces. Over a boy. She was the worst.

Still. She despised Kol. She had been so certain they were somehow cosmically linked. Fated. She even thought she... *loved* him.

It was all a lie.

Kol had manipulated her. Lied to her. Used her just as he had used other girls before her. He was just as horrible of a human being as his father. They may be dragons by birth, but they were snakes in practice.

Part of her wished he had been the receiver of her rage instead of the greenhouse. *He* deserved it.

She never wanted to see him again.

Kol

Kol should've flown home.

It was the middle of the day and not exactly discrete to be shifting into an enormous dragon in the middle of suburbia—although, it would've been fun to see Kenzie and her mom's and grandma's expressions from the window if he had.

Still, he should have. He could've turned invisible before taking off.

But he didn't, and the new Uber driver drove at least five miles under the speed limit the entire way back to Chicago.

Kol wanted to rip his hair out.

In fact, he diverted the destination to the end of the L line and opted to ride the subway the rest of the way to the Dome.

He couldn't wait to see her.

For the first time, *ever*, he didn't need to be as cautious with his feelings. He didn't need to hold back and prevent his heart from giving itself away. For the first time, *ever,* he had hope that he'd get hers in return.

Kol continued to stare at his palm as the subway rushed back in the direction of the Dome. His hand looked the same—not that he expected it to look different—but he somehow *felt* different. Like he could plummet himself off the cliff he'd stood firmly on for seventeen years—fingers gripped around the guard rail—and actually allow himself to fall.

Part of him felt that he already had, but that was near impossible. Myreen still had feelings for him the last time he saw her, so it couldn't have happened yet. Plus, as close as he was, falling for Myreen might still take a bit of time. People didn't change overnight.

Either way, Kol was anxious to see her.

He was ready to tell her everything. He would tell her about his father's assignment when she first arrived at the Dome. That he'd been tasked in befriending her to find out if she was the siren from the prophecy, but that she actually had become his friend. He'd tell her that his father wanted him to seduce her to get the information, but he'd grown real feelings for her. That his father then ordered him to cut ties with her, but he'd asked her to be his girlfriend instead.

He hoped the latter would save him from all his former indiscretions and lies at the beginning of their relationship.

He would tell her about the curse. That it prevented him from allowing himself to fall too deeply for her—because he was terrified. And that it had driven his behavior more than he'd like to admit. He hadn't always treated her the way he should. And he wasn't proud of it.

And then... he would tell her that he'd gone to Kenzie, to

her trusted friend, who had finally lifted the curse.

For his entire family.

Kol made a mental note to call his mom later, even if he needed to be realistic about the timing in his parent's situation. Lifting the curse wouldn't change Eduard's personality, but Kol knew his father had a heart. He loved Kol and Tatiana in his own way, and he had respect for Victoria. It just might take a little bit of time for the *love* part to happen.

Dropping his coat in his room, Kol left immediately to seek Myreen out. She wasn't in the avian common room and it was a Saturday, so she could be almost anywhere. He would be methodical in his search for her. He'd start at one end and work his way to the other until he finally found her.

He headed to the greenhouses first. As soon as Kol rounded the corner and saw them, he immediately hoped she wasn't anywhere near the vicinity.

One of them was a pile of rubble.

What happened? he wondered, seeing the glass and structure scattered and smashed. Limp greens and dirt peppered the obvious destruction. It looked like an ursa had a tantrum. Whatever happened, Kol was finally distracted from his linear thinking and walked up to Mr. Coltar, who embraced a clearly upset Mrs. Coltar.

"It was an ursa," said Shawn—the dragon who often sparred with Kol in defense. He stood gawking at the scene.

"Figured," Kol said. "Who was it?"

Shawn shrugged. "A new one, clearly."

Kol scoffed in agreement. Ursas could be volatile. It wasn't exactly noteworthy, just an issue for the teachers to prevent future property damage. "Hey, have you seen Myreen lately?" he asked, already losing interest.

Shawn shook his head. "She's that mer-harpy right? The hot one?"

Kol nodded, but his eyebrows twitched downward at that last part. "And my girlfriend," he added, injecting fire into his tone.

"Right," Shawn said, though he seemed unfazed by Kol's hint of protectiveness. "No, I haven't seen her. She hangs out with that equally attractive phoenix, Juliet, though, and I thought I saw her heading to the training room earlier."

"Thanks," Kol patted him on the shoulder, then raced toward the Defense Room.

He caught sight of the silky dark hair just ahead of him before he reached the Defense Room. She was walking toward the main building.

Her name stuck in his throat and his palms felt clammy before he took two steps to catch up. He was nervous to see her. Everything that had happened, everything he planned to say in the next few minutes made him nervous. So much had changed, and she had no idea about any of it.

Swallowing loudly, he clenched his fists, then took a deep breath. Kol had no idea how she would take everything, but he also planned to tell her that he was falling in love with her. He hoped that would soften the blow of everything else.

"Myreen!" he finally called, the smile on his face genuine and big—and borderline giddy.

She stopped and stiffened. Kol felt a jolt of trepidation and met her in a few quick strides. *Something's wrong.*

When she turned, he could see the *wrongness* in her expression. Pursing her lips, her hand smacked against his jaw before he knew what happened. Orange and purple flashes zinged his vision for a split-second. Kol recovered quickly, but instinctively rubbed his cheek as tears rolled down Myreen's beautiful face.

And the *wrongness* wedged itself between Kol's ribs.

"I h– hate you, Kol!" she said, her mouth twitching into a frown. Then the sobs came, though he could see the fire in her eyes blurred behind the tears.

What? He glanced around, looking for witnesses—or hoping for the lack of them, he wasn't sure—but they were alone between the buildings.

Kol was surprised that the enormity of what happened registered so late.

No.

That cliff he thought he'd been so firmly planted on? The one he thought would be difficult to jump from because he'd held onto the guard-rail for too long? He was pretty sure the damned hope from Kenzie's pseudo-spell severed that handhold before blasting him right off the rock.

Kol was in love with Myreen.

He'd finally fallen in love. He'd finally done the one thing he swore he'd never do. He finally felt everything his mother surely felt for his father.

Myreen hated him.

The curse wasn't broken. His foolishness triggered it instead.

The spell hadn't worked.

"Don't look so surprised, because I *know,*" Myreen said through her tears. Kol had a hard time understanding her words through the emotion, but got the gist of it. *I. Hate. You. Kol,* bled through every word.

"Ca– can we talk?" he asked. He was clearly a glutton for

punishment, rubbing salt and lemon-juice on the wound and all.

She jerked away when Kol reached for her arm. He hadn't even realized that he'd reached out to touch her. The feelings had taken such a hold that he no longer had complete control of his actions.

"What's the point? Your father explained it all."

"My father?"

"Eduard?" She folded her arms across her chest, tears still on her cheeks, although she'd regained some composure. "Lord Dracul? The *General?* He told me everything."

Kol staggered back a step, then side-stepped to lean against the side of the building. The concrete was cool through the back of his tee shirt, giving him a grounding effect.

This was happening.

"Yeah," Myreen continued. "He said that he *told* you— er... *ordered* you to become my friend when I came to the academy."

Kol nodded once. He'd planned to tell her all of this; there was no point denying it. "That's true."

Her eyes widened a split-second, but her surprise was immediately replaced by the former fury.

"It's true," she whispered. "That you were only *pretending* to be my friend in order to find out if I was '*the siren.*'" She used air quotes and a sarcastic tone for the last phrase.

Kol lowered his head.

"And he also said something about you not being clear enough when you ended our relationship..."

"I didn't—"

"So, *will you be my girlfriend* is really dragon-code for: *I never want to see your face again?*" She spoke over his words, waving a hand to illustrate.

"It's not—"

"Sorry if I don't speak dragon-ese, or whatever." She pursed her lips, maybe because they began to tremble. "I'm sorry that I *misunderstood* the breakup."

"Myreen." He reached for her hand. Again, she jerked it away. He almost explained everything. He almost told her that yes, he was ordered to break things off, but that he couldn't. That he *didn't want to* because he was falling in love with her.

But it felt like a moot point.

It didn't matter.

Whatever he said at this point, even if he could somehow help her understand... as long as he was in love with her, she would forever despise and hate him.

It didn't matter.

Myreen gritted her teeth and wiped her face once more. The gesture had a finality to it that wedged itself further into Kol's ribs until he could physically feel his heart begin to fissure.

"I hate you," she said. "I never want to see you or speak to you ever again."

Kol nodded once more.

Myreen turned on a heel, then walked away.

After she'd disappeared around the corner, Kol slid his back against the wall behind him until he sat on the ground.

Then buried his face in his hands.

***

Kol disappeared to the one place he'd been avoiding since the invisible dragon incident. The sim room. He would've preferred flying in the real world, specifically deep in the Alps where he could disappear for hours—or days—but he couldn't build enough energy or motivation to sneak out. An unusual commotion was happening around the school, and he suspected his father had something to do with it, since several of his military minions were milling around.

But whatever it was didn't seem to concern him. And he didn't care to answer questions. Two of the corporals were guarding the sim room, but merely nodded when he walked in. If someone was banned from the room, it wasn't Kol.

He flew through blackness, his powerful wings pushing against invisible air when the scene should have had none. A large orange-and-yellow swirling planet lay before him, but he positioned it behind him. It was beautiful and didn't match his mood and so he didn't even allow it to make an appearance in his peripheral. The only illumination came from the tiny lights of faraway stars—mere pinpricks—not enough to really do anything.

Kol's scales were also black—the perfect camouflage, though he needed none in the darkness.

It wasn't somewhere even a dragon could go, and most likely one of the masterpieces Mr. Suzuki created for entertainment purposes only, which meant Kol didn't expect any form of simulation enemies to appear.

It was one of the many reasons he chose this one.

He groaned when he felt the presence of another creature to his right. Maybe some modifications had been added?

Relying on his extensive training and muscle memory, Kol pretended he didn't notice the intruder and waited until the being was closer, then veered right and extended his talons to immediately grip the sim enemy.

He blew a breath of fire to shed light on his attacker and strategize the quickest way to dispatch whatever it was. He nearly lost his grip at the familiarity of the deep red scales on a dragon that looked a lot like Nik.

"Hey!" It *was* Nik.

Kol released his grip and dropped into the abyss until he hit the sim floor, then scrambled to end the program and shift back.

Nik dropped seconds after he did and did the same as the scene melted back to reveal the stark white walls.

"Don't sneak up on me like that!" Kol said, stalking toward his friend, who still flipped red scales into skin and smart clothing.

"I thought you knew I was here," Nik said with a smirk.

"How could I know?" he shouted.

Nik kept his tone cool despite Kol's fury. "Because you nodded when I asked if I could join you? Remember?"

Kol ran a hand through his hair, gripping it tightly and scrunching his eyes closed. He didn't remember, but he also didn't exactly remember starting the simulation. He'd flipped a switch to auto-Kol-mode the instant he walked in the room.

But now that he thought about it, he vaguely remembered his best friend's tense smile when he'd entered. Nik was stressed about something, and Kol probably figured he could use a flight too.

"I guess?" Kol said. "I don't know." He walked to retrieve his clothes, which were in a pile next to Nik's, and pulled them back on.

"Everything alright?" Nik asked, then pulled a gray sweatshirt over his head.

Kol slipped back on his jeans. "Myreen hates me."

Nik froze. "Wait. Did you...?" His face twisted into a sort of sympathy Kol despised.

"Did I activate the curse?" Kol nodded, feeling his face twist in an emotion he wasn't accustomed to. "I'm ninety-nine point ninety-five percent sure."

"So you love her?"

Kol rolled his eyes to distract from the despair. "That is the key to activating the curse. So, yes. I believe the answer is yes, I'm in love with her."

"*Wow*," Nik slumped to the floor against the wall. One knee hitched up with an elbow resting on it.

Kol remained standing, but leaned against the wall and stared at nothing.

"Is that why she destroyed the greenhouse?" Nik asked. "Didn't you two, like, make out in there or something?"

Kol felt his eyes and the crack in his heart widen. "That was her?" Did she do it because she hated him that much? "How?"

"Apparently she's also an ursa." Nik shrugged like it wasn't huge news to find out that the siren/mermaid/harpy was also a werebear. "It was her first shift, from what I've been told."

"*Huh*." Kol didn't have any other words, let alone thoughts about it. In the past, Kol would have been fascinated to hear of such a shifter. He would've asked a thousand questions and done a ton of research on the subject. But this was *Myreen*. She'd long ago gone from a shifter who made him curious, to a shifter who made him crazy and protective and clearly willing to break a curse he vowed never to break.

Apparently, she hated him so much that she would destroy school property because it reminded her of him.

"And not to add more to your plate," Nik said. "But your father has taken over the school."

Kol's head snapped toward Nik, who shrugged.

"What about Oberon?"

"He's leaving." Nik paused. "But that means I'm staying?" He looked happy and guilty at the same time.

Kol slipped to the floor next to his friend and nudged his shoulder. "Glad to have you back, man," he said.

"Wish it were under different circumstances, but yeah."

"My father, huh?" Kol said to the floor ahead of them.

"Did you know?"

Kol shook his head. "But I'm not exactly surprised, either."

They sat in silence for longer than Kol could measure. But he was glad for it. There was a reason Nik was his best friend.

Kol considered telling him about asking the selkie to break the curse, but decided against it, since it didn't work anyway. He supposed it wasn't Kenzie and her family's fault it didn't work. Maybe it was too strong a spell for the three of them to break. Kol would be stupid to think that another Dracul hadn't sought out another magic user in the past.

"It was bound to happen," Kol finally said. "It's not like I'm the first Dracul to trigger the curse."

"It still sucks," Nik said, then snapped his head to Kol with a strange expression on his face.

"What?" Kol asked.

Nik stood, prompting Kol to do the same.

"Look, the thing with Myreen..." Nik trailed off, then shook his head. "I just wouldn't wish the Dracul curse on my worst enemy."

"You and I both. Are you okay?"

Nik was anxious and jittery all of a sudden. "Yeah, I've gotta..." he tapped Kol on the arm as a smile spread across his face. "I've gotta win back Juliet."

Kol gripped Nik's shoulder. Maybe one of them would get the girl.

"Good luck!" he called as Nik sprinted from the room.

Oberon

The world was a blur.

Conversations fluttered around Oberon, muddled and muted. His mind couldn't concentrate as he packed a bag—one of Ren's inventions that compacted clothing by sucking out the air and compressing the fabric. He'd used the same bag just over a week ago when he traveled to Canada in the hopes of discovering a rumored flock of gryphons.

The trip had been a failure, as well as his attempt at being the Director of the Dome.

My life is one of continuous failure, he thought as he mindlessly placed more of his clothing into the bag. Failure to save my family. *Failure to save the school in South Dakota. Failure to aid Myreen appropriately.*

Myreen. The chimera's innocent face formed in his mind. She'd been a pawn in Eduard's game since Oberon discovered her, and she would only continue to play that part as long as the general was Director of the Dome.

A rush of panic flitted through his body, and he dropped a jacket on top of the bag. The rush of the vacuum-based device kicked on as it tried to suck the fabric in.

Oberon looked up at Malachai Quinn, the Shifter Politics and Phoenix Mastery teacher. "I need to speak with someone immediately," he said quickly.

Malachai's eyes stared at the jacket, and Oberon followed his gaze. The center of the thick fabric was being pulled in. The arms were caught on the exterior of the bag, as if it were struggling to keep itself from being packed. Oberon wondered if it was all a sign that he, too, should be struggling against being kicked out of the Dome.

"Lord Dracul is allowing you to say goodbyes," Malachai said. The other four shifters from the military were present, staring at him with expressions of contempt. "We will escort you to whoever you desire to speak with. But know that the more people you speak to, the more likely it is that word will get out about your traitorous actions."

Oberon had been around the school long enough to know that word of his *vampire dealings* would get out in no time at all. There would be grand speculations about his involvement with the blood suckers. Rumors would likely spread that he'd had a hand in Draven's attack on Myreen and her friends. And he wouldn't be here to protect his innocence.

"Malachai, will you send for Myreen Fairchild?" he asked, ignoring the venom he'd heard in the lieutenant general's voice.

The phoenix shifter tilted his head and studied Oberon. "Of all the people in the school, you desire to speak to a student?"

Oberon nodded. "If she's the only one I get to speak to before I leave, I'll consider that enough."

Malachai didn't immediately respond, but continued staring at Oberon, as if debating whether or not he should send for Myreen.

"Please," Oberon said. "There are things I've been meaning to tell her."

Malachai sighed heavily. "I don't think General Dracul would approve of such a visit." He held up a finger. "But... like Delphine said, you've done a lot for the shifter world. If this is the last time you get to talk to her, then I'll see it done."

Relief flooded Oberon, and he wiped at the beads of sweat that had built up on his forehead. The stress of leaving the school was taking its toll.

Tapping rapidly on his smartwatch, Malachai looked back at Oberon. "I sent her an emergency summons." His watch blinked with a green light, indicating she was on her way.

"Thank you, Malachai," Oberon said. He knew the man would probably never trust him, but at least they had the decency to aid him one last time.

Bending over, Oberon adjusted his jacket, and the bag finally drew the piece of clothing in and compressed it, the soft vacuum sound finally stopping.

Moments later, the door of his quarters flung open, sending the doorknob right through the wall. The five military shifters leaped protectively in front of Oberon, taking defensive stances.

Looking past their shoulders, Oberon saw a seething Ren Suzuki, his chest rising and falling rapidly, and his face flushed a wild crimson.

"By my ninth tail, what is going on here?"

"Mr. Suzuki—" Malachai started.

"Don't *Mr. Suzuki* me, you fire-spitting duckling. Has the shifter world gone mad? First, one of our greenhouses gets destroyed, and now Oberon gets ousted for supposed vampire dealings?"

"Watch your tongue, Ren," Malachai cautioned. "That kind of disrespect will not be tolerated here at the Dome."

"Respect?" Ren replied incredulously. "Do you honestly think I care about respect right about now? The greatest shifter of our time is being thrown out of the one place that needs him the most. Well, if you throw *him* out, *I'm* going with him."

Oberon's heart swelled at hearing his life-long friend speaking so boldly. He and Ren had been through thick and thin together. Their experiences had made them brothers, but he didn't want to risk Ren getting incriminated.

"Ren, don't do this," he said softly, although he threw his friend an appreciative look. "The school needs you."

Ren whirled on Oberon. "Don't even start. That *Lard Dracul* is the last person I'd ever work for. Can you imagine me having to report to his sorry face? No. I've already submitted my resignation, and I've packed my bags. I'm coming with you."

Oberon knew there was no changing Ren's mind, and he was glad. With his friend by his side, it would be like old times. The question was, where would they go? What would they do?

Malachai had pulled out his phone and was flicking his finger as he read. "The poor fool's right! The Master Tinkerer's no longer listed as an active teacher."

"Which means your military tech will be going down in quality," Ren said. "Sure, you'll be able to find plenty of other kitsunes to replicate my work—it's that well-documented. Just don't expect much when it comes to new research and inventing."

Oberon rubbed at his temples. He knew Ren was proud of his work, but bragging about it as he was departing from the school was a terrible idea. There were plenty of other brilliant minds among the shifters, and while Ren was extremely talented in his abilities, his hubris only made him look desperate.

A small cough came from just behind the seething kitsune, and Oberon's eyes fell on the next visitor.

"Myreen!" Oberon said, painting a smile on his face. It was harder than he expected. "Come in, come in."

The girl's eyes were red, as if she'd been crying recently, and her hair had been thrown into a messy ponytail, with strands jutting out this way and that. She looked tired and bent over, as if she were carrying a bag of bricks on her back. And metaphorically, she was.

Ren stepped to the side, and Myreen timidly entered Oberon's quarters. Her anxiety was justified: she'd been summoned to a room containing five military soldiers.

"Malachai," Oberon said, turning to the lieutenant general. "One more favor is all I ask of you. May I have a moment alone with Myreen?"

"You heard General Dracul's orders, Oberon," said Malachai as he shook his head. "We're supposed to keep tabs on you until you've left the Dome."

Oberon sighed. "That's why I'm asking you as a friend, not a prison guard. It will only take a moment, and then I'll be out of your hair for good."

Malachai mulled it over for a moment, biting his lip. "Five

minutes. You'll get five minutes with the girl, and then you're done."

"Sir," one of the other soldiers—the naga—said, "I must question such an allowance. General Dracul explicitly—"

"It's not an allowance, Captain Bender," Malachai growled. "It's an order."

The four shifter soldiers saluted, then spilled out of the room. Malachai followed behind them, but turned around once he reached the door's threshold. "Five minutes."

Oberon nodded, then looked at Ren. "The same goes for you, my friend. I'll be done in a bit. Why don't you go and get your things, then come back?"

Ren still looked as if he were ready to shoot sparks at anybody who got too close, but he nodded and swept out of Oberon's quarters, closing the door behind him.

"Myreen, you look out of sorts. Is everything okay?"

The girl's emotions were so raw, his words seemed to be the final blow to the cracking dam. She wept openly in front of him. Oberon went to her and drew her into an embrace. Myreen stood stiffly, but rested her head on his shoulder as fresh tears spilled from her eyes. He felt their wet warmth through his shirt.

"Hey, it's going to be okay," he said. The words were not just meant for her, but for himself, also.

"Nothing is okay," Myreen sobbed.

Did she already know he was leaving? Surely she wasn't this sad because of that.

"What's wrong?" he asked softly.

Sniffling, she said, "It feels like the world is falling apart."

He nodded in agreement, but didn't vocalize it.

"I'm an ursa," she said as a fresh sob released. "And I

destroyed one of the greenhouses. And you're leaving the Dome!" Her body trembled. "And Kol lied to me."

Her body shook against him, and Oberon held her closer, providing as much comfort as he could. The bit about Myreen being an ursa was something he'd been meaning to discuss with her, but hadn't had the time. Ms. Heather had explicitly told Oberon that she needed space and rest as she dealt with her new shift. And Ren had gone off about a greenhouse being ruined. Now he knew who the culprit was. And as for the general's son...

"Why are you leaving?" she wept. "Is it because of me? You can't handle teaching me anymore?"

"No, no, no," Oberon whispered. "Quite the opposite, really."

"Then why?"

He was running out of time.

"I've been forced to leave the Dome for reasons beyond my control," Oberon said. "I do not depart with a willing heart, for my purpose has always been here at the school. But General Dracul has decided that changes need to be made, and that is why I asked for you to come here, to speak with me before I leave."

She stepped back from him and looked up, her eyes shimmering with tears.

"Do not trust Eduard Dracul," he counseled. "He seeks to weaponize you. He doesn't see you as a person. He wants to use you against the vampires, even if it means it ends in your death."

"He's already spoken to me," she said. "He wants to personally train me every night from now on."

"You will learn much," Oberon said. "But heed my counsel. As I said before, do not trust him. Follow your heart. Stand up against him if you need to. His intentions are noble but misguided."

She looked at him with tired, worried eyes. "What should I do?"

He placed his hand on Myreen's shoulder. "You'll know when the time comes. But if ever you need additional help or guidance, my contact information is in your tablet. I might not be able to directly aid you, but I will do my best from a distance."

"I don't understand why you have to leave," she said.

"It's a political move," Oberon said. "I have a feeling you'll hear rumors crop up soon enough."

Her eyes were puffy. She looked small and weak. It pained him to know the rigorous future Eduard had in store for her.

"You're the closest thing to a daughter I've ever had," he said softly. "Know that I believe in you. I have *always* believed in you."

She came back to him then, wrapping her arms around him.

"I'll miss you, Myreen."

A knock came at the door, and Malachai reentered, along with the other shifter soldiers. "Time's up, Oberon," he said.

So it is, he thought. *So it is.*

Chapter 56

Juliet

With the millions of rumors floating around the Dome, Juliet had trouble controlling her emotions.

"I heard Myreen demanded to be the director of the school."

"Someone told me they're shutting down the Dome and everyone has to go home."

"Oberon went full Gryphon on Lord Dracul and went to military prison."

None of the stories made sense, and she knew none of it was true. But still, she needed answers. She had a bad feeling in the pit of her stomach, and everyone's idiotic craze just made it worse.

She went to her father, but he wouldn't tell her a thing. She looked for Myreen, but she couldn't find her anywhere. She even asked Jesse if he knew why everyone was acting off, but he wouldn't stop flirting with her.

It was no use. The only information she had was the misinformation from the other students.

All day, everything made her jump, and she'd tripped over her own two feet more than once. She wanted to close herself in her room, where it was silent and drama-free. Music couldn't even ground her enough to stop her jitters.

Juliet tossed and turned in her bed as she tried to go to sleep for the hundredth time. She looked at the clock almost every hour until she punched the sheets by her side and gave up.

Food was the only thing that could help clear her mind—a brownie ice cream explosion, to be exact. She put on her slippers, and knowing everyone else would be asleep, she didn't care that she was in her fleece pajamas with her hair up in a messy bun.

Even if someone did see her, she wouldn't care enough to change.

The shuffling of her fuzzy slippers reverberated as she trudged through the silent hallways. Finally making it into the kitchen, Juliet practically bolted for the freezer. She pulled out an entire tub of Neapolitan ice cream and deposited it on the counter.

Next, she made her way to the pantry, filling her arms with toppings and sides—sprinkles, chocolate chips, caramel syrup, and mini marshmallows. Lastly, Juliet skipped to the fridge to get the strawberries and the day's leftover brownies.

If she wasn't doing it in the middle of the night, she would be blasting music and dancing along to it. Instead, she hummed a tune to break the silence.

She pulled out a large bowl, a large spoon, and a knife for the strawberries. No one was there to watch her create her masterpiece, so she wasn't shy with her portions. She licked her fingers and sashayed her hips to the song she was singing to herself as she assembled her creation.

Juliet took handfuls of toppings and poured them over her overflowing bowl. She clapped her hands, then rubbed them together, her mouth watering.

As fast as she could, Juliet shoved the unused ingredients back where she'd found them. Excited to try her dessert, she twirled around to race back to her bowl, and almost fell on her butt.

"Ah!" Juliet screeched, and it was so loud she was sure she'd wake someone up. There was another person at the door of the kitchen, but when she saw who it was, she was more confused than afraid of getting caught.

"Juliet. Hi. I've been looking for you." His deep voice sent chills through her, leaving a trail of goosebumps on her arms.

She was caught off-guard—and without a chance to give herself a Kenzie pep talk.

"Oh? What for?" She wanted to sound like she wasn't fazed by his presence, but her tone came out borderline snotty, and she didn't like it. Still, it was better than giving him the satisfaction of knowing he affected her so much. Juliet hugged her bowl into her chest and dunked her spoon in it, filling it with each and every ingredient and shoved it into her mouth. She wanted to run before she ruined her new #GirlBoss persona. But she seemed rooted to the spot.

Eyebrows raised, she silently urged him to answer her question.

Nik cleared his throat and stepped into the light. He was in dark blue sweatpants and a gray pullover sweater. Even though he looked cozy and attractive, she didn't want him to know that. She started to walk by him so she could enjoy her snack in her room.

He placed his large, warm hand on her shoulder and stopped her. “Have you heard about the General?” Nik asked, again speaking low.

Juliet rolled her eyes and tried to walk away. “Gee, you really didn't have anything better to do than to go looking for me in the middle of the night to talk gossip? I'll pass.” She shoveled another spoonful in her mouth as she walked backwards toward the door. “'Night.” Juliet saluted him with her spoon and spun around to face the exit.

But again, Nik stopped her, running to the door before she could reach it and blocking her way out.

Juliet was so shocked that all she could do was stare at him with her eyebrows raised.

Nik grabbed the big, cold bowl out of her hands and placed it on the counter. She gasped. *No one should ever take away a lady's last-minute ice cream explosion dessert.*

Nik smirked, which only set her more on edge.

He softly took her cheeks in his hands and pulled her in for a kiss that swept her off her feet. She was so surprised that she couldn't move, but then she closed her eyes and melted into his embrace.

It felt like home.

She'd missed him so badly. She'd worked so hard to overcome everything they'd been.

Juliet pulled away and gently nudged him in the chest.

“ *What* are you doing?” Juliet's stomach turned into millions of knots, her mind spinning. She just wanted her ice cream and then to get some sleep. Now she'd be awake all night thinking of Nik—and how selfish he could be. He was the one that broke up with her *and* he was leaving any day now with *Lord Dracul.*

"Juliet, please. Just sit with me for a second." Nik's eyes were wide and full of sorrow. It was the only reason she actually took a seat.

Juliet grabbed her ice cream and shoveled large spoonfuls into her mouth.

Again, he smirked as he looked at her.

She waved her spoon in the air to encourage some explanation. "Let's hear it. Why did you just do that?"

"I'm sorry, it's just... this is my favorite way to see you—your hair's up, your cheeks are flushed, you're so comfortable."

Sweet, but she didn't want anything to do with his butt-kissing. Juliet rolled her eyes and scooped another spoonful into her mouth.

Nik snickered, then took the seat next to her. "Have you really not heard about the changes in the Dome yet?"

She shook her head as he reached over her and grabbed a clean spoon. Without asking, Nik filled it with the contents in her bowl. Again, Juliet gasped. After he moaned his approval, he put his spoon down and took the bowl out of her hands. He placed it on the counter again and took her hands in his.

So she'd be getting her information from her ex. Who knew? A stop to the rumors started with a conversation with someone she used to be with. *Go figure.*

"The general has been made the new Director of the Dome."

Juliet couldn't believe what she was hearing. So many questions flew through her mind that she didn't know where to start. “What? Could he even do that? Why? What about Oberon? What about the students?” She rambled off some of those questions as her anxiety rose.

Nik still had a hint of a smile on his lips, and that confused her even more.

“You're asking all the wrong questions. How about something more along the lines of ‘Does that mean you’ll be living here again?’ Because the answer to *that* question is *yes*.” Nik looked at Juliet with hope in his eyes.

He waited for her to catch on and when she finally did, she almost fell out of her chair. But Nik stood and with the softest touch, he kept her afloat, wrapping his hands around her head and leaning down to place his soft lips on hers.

This time she let the hopefulness of their reunion envelop all her senses. She suddenly didn't care about the ice cream, or the questions she had, or even the fact that he’d broken her heart. Juliet let herself get lost in their kiss. It tasted like chocolate and caramel and it was the most delicious thing she’d ever had. She didn't want it to stop, and when it did, she leaned in for more.

“How do I know you won’t hurt me again?” Juliet whispered after the ice cream had melted and their kisses had slowed.

Nik leaned his forehead on hers. “Jules, I love you. I didn't know it before, but after I lost you, it hit me. You were the best thing to ever happen to me. I was wrong to break your heart and that will always be on my conscience. But I promise you, that will never happen again. Whether it’s long distance or not, you and I are meant to be together. I know it. And I will spend every single day proving how much I love you—if you'll only give me the chance."

Juliet's breath caught in her throat. She swooned the second he said the L-word. He'd professed his love to her. After all this time, she thought he didn't love her because he left. But he wasn't given much of a choice. Maybe his feelings were as genuine as his words.

She looked down at their intertwined hands and nodded. Unsure why she felt shy all over again, Juliet's cheeks warmed with a blush she didn't even know she'd missed.

"Thank you, thank you, thank you!" Nik lifted her out of her seat and spun her around. She giggled until he pulled her in for another kiss—another heart-melting, mind-clouding kiss.

Nik gently put her down, and Juliet looked into his eyes, folding her hand in his.

"I love you, too, Nik." Her heart raced as she said the words she'd only thought in her head, but as she said them out loud, she knew just how true they were.

Juliet was on cloud nine.

And yet, something was still not right. Juliet remembered what news came with Nik living at the Dome again. Lord Dracul was the director of the Dome?

Oh no. This can't be good.

Juliet smiled through the bittersweet feelings fluttering through her. She would get to the bottom of all this—and without ruining what she and Nik had.

She was stronger, now, and ready for anything that came their way.

Myreen

"Again," Lord Dracul said for the millionth time.

Myreen growled. Her ursa nature still seemed to have the reins, despite having shifted for her first time. She hated him even more than she hated Kol at the moment, if that was possible. Two days. That's all it had been since General Dracul sent Oberon away—the only real father figure she'd ever had—and turned the school into a military boot camp. With her as their secret weapon.

Except she wasn't. Even after all the training she'd done at the school, she still wasn't the siren everyone wanted. So it had been two days of pure torture at the oversight of the new Director. Two days of his constant again's. The only thing she wanted to do *again* was tear something apart in ursa form.

Instead, she was working with her water manipulation abilities.

Myreen concentrated on the ocean in front of her, willing even a portion of its lapping waves to become like an extra limb. It bubbled and gurgled, but otherwise was useless.

Like every other time for the past. Two. Days.

Today, the simulation had taken her to the beach. She could almost feel the warmth of the sun on her skin and the sand getting into her shoes. A soft breeze carried a briny scent, lifting her hair. She was standing far enough away from the water not to trigger her tail—yet another failure that the general was determined to address.

The setting today might actually have been relaxing if it weren't for the men accompanying her. General Dracul was the only vocal one, but he always had at least two others with him. Which was probably smart, considering what she'd done to the greenhouse—which she still felt bad about. Given the opportunity, she didn't think she'd hesitate to show him a little of the courtesy he'd shown her.

The general scowled at her failed efforts, *again*—a look that nearly broke her heart every time as it reminded her so much of Kol. Kol the traitor. Kol the good little soldier. Kol the ex-boyfriend she wished she could just forget.

"It would appear that you need something a little more *motivating*." General Dracul tapped on his watch, issuing some sort of command, and the beach scene faded away, leaving the white walls of the simulation room behind.

Moments later, the door opened, and a large cylinder full of water was brought into the room, carried on some sort of levitation device. Another one of Mr. Suzuki's inventions, she was sure. His absence was yet another blow to the school.

Myreen's head spun as she considered what exactly the

general considered *more motivating*. The cylinder of water was odd, but nothing she couldn't handle.

Moments later, a harpy was dragged in by two more soldiers, begging to know what was happening. *Her name is Leya*, Myreen recalled. It was hard to forget the girl after her boisterous family had pretty much taken over the avian common room for Christmas.

Christmas. It had only been a couple of weeks since then, but it seemed a lifetime ago. She never thought, when flying with Kol, that he'd betray her, or that Oberon would ever be forced to leave the school as Director.

Or that she'd be so dehumanized by the new Director in order to force her to hone her powers.

The general snapped his fingers, and the guards guided Leya up the small set of steps that had been pulled to the cylinder of water while she'd been distracted.

"What are they doing?" Myreen asked, dread pooling in her stomach.

"Providing adequate motivation for you to use your abilities. This young woman has volunteered to be submerged in the water."

By the way Leya was kicking and looking around wildly as the guards tried to put her in, she wasn't exactly a willing volunteer.

"Once inside, we'll seal this harpy in. Your job is to command the water to drain through the tiny holes in the lid."

"And what happens if I fail?" Myreen asked, unable to take her eyes off Leya as the guards managed to get her in.

"Let's hope you don't."

Leya sent Myreen a pleading look. She obviously wasn't much of a fighter—none of the harpies were, preferring to stick more to their healing abilities. Myreen couldn't believe the general was willing to go to such an extreme. And yet, yes, she did. She felt her anger building, and she closed her hands into fists.

"Good. Use that. Time is ticking."

Myreen stared at the water, practically screaming at it mentally. The water paid little heed to her, bubbling out in spurts and glugs. Leya's eyes were bulging, bubbles escaping faster than Myreen could make the water move. Leya grabbed for her throat, then clawed at the top of the tank, but it was no use. The girl wasn't getting out, and Myreen wasn't emptying it fast enough.

Myreen couldn't take the stress any longer. She let the ursa in her take over, felt its power coursing through her veins, creating muscles where there were none, turning every appendage into a deadly weapon—tooth, nail and claw. She barely registered the shouts around her, hardly recognized the panic in Leya's eyes as Myreen charged toward the cylinder. With a mighty push, the cylinder toppled over, the tempered glass shattering, water pouring everywhere.

Leya was free. Probably cut up from the glass, but alive. She was coughing, at least.

Myreen turned her attention to the source of her ire. General Dracul's smug face now wore a look of wide-eyed terror. Her lips curled into a beastly smile as she charged toward him.

A sting in her side immediately threw off her coordination, and she tripped over her feet, sliding right past the dragon shifter. General Dracul was no longer human, either, wearing black scales that made him seem more shadow than dragon. His toothy dragon grin was every bit as smug as his human one—maybe more so. "You'll regret that, little bear. I *will* turn you into the siren of prophecy."

Myreen snarled once more, and then the tingle spreading from the tranquilizer in her back stole the rest of her will, putting her on the edge of blackness but not taking her fully under. The sim room shifted again, and Leya and the tank of water were all gone.

Myreen looked around in horror. The general had programmed that whole scenario? She thought she was back in reality before, but it had been another simulation. Another head game by the new headmaster.

"That's right," he said as he returned to human form. "I'm not the monster you think I am."

"You're worse," Myreen slurred. "No wonder your son hates you."

He smirked. "Hate is an emotion you know nothing about. And my son is none of your concern."

No. He's not. She vaguely felt her body shift back to human form. Hands grabbed her arms and legs and carried her a ways, then propped her up like some toy.

Or a weapon. Oberon was right. That's all I am to these people.

***

When the world around her began to clear again, she heard an unearthly scream. She struggled against the grog still clinging to the edges of her mind, trying to figure out what was going on. The scream issued again, sending chills down her spine. For a moment, she almost thought the scream was hers, the pain it carried felt so much like her own.

When she was able to pry her lids open, what she saw turned her blood cold. The vampire tied to a chair in front of

Myreen twisted and wriggled against the orange-tinted wires binding her.

Myreen made to move, but her limbs were securely anchored to her own chair. She growled as she did her own thrashing. The chair rocked, but the chains binding her bit into her skin, sending a searing pain through her wrists. She gasped and tried to pull away, but there was nowhere to go.

"Ah, you're up," General Dracul said, his hands clasped behind his back. "I'm sorry for the extreme measures, but we can't have you hurting your own people, now can we?"

"I'm not the one hurting them," she spat.

"And yet, you refuse to embrace your destiny. If you'd done as you were told, that wouldn't be necessary."

"I can't! I can't be what you want me to be." A sob choked her throat, but she swallowed it. She wouldn't cry in front of *him*. He didn't deserve her tears.

"Now, if we can get on with this." The general stepped behind the vampire sitting opposite Myreen. She snarled and snapped at him, then cried out again in pain.

"As you can see, this vampire is restrained with copper-infused wire. Whenever she moves, she gets a dose of her own personal brand of poison. Much like you, though your wires have silver in them to keep your *ursa* under control."

"What is it you expect me to do?" Myreen asked, jutting out her chin.

"Use your siren voice to convince this creature to kill herself."

Myreen's jaw dropped as she stared at him in horror. "Is this another one of your twisted simulations?"

General Dracul's expression didn't change, and he didn't offer any answer.

"I– I won't do it." Simulation or not, she wasn't a killer. She didn't think she could do it. Not even to a vampire, despite all her simulation training. Somehow she could compartmentalize things when she knew it wasn't real. But this? She had no idea how Delphine could have ever seen her killing Draven. It had to be some sort of mistake. "You can't make me!"

"Can't I? You, Miss Fairchild, belong to the military. You will fulfill your destiny. The fate of all shifters depends on it."

Myreen glared at him. If she was going to use her siren abilities, there was nothing she'd rather do than destroy the man who had made it his goal to force her to become a weapon.

As if anticipating this reaction, the general raised a brow. "And don't even think about using your abilities on me. My men and I all have earplugs capable of withstanding your siren voice."

Of course he did. He obviously realized she was dangerous, just not dangerous in a way he thought would be useful. "No," Myreen said again, shaking her head.

The vampire sitting across from her sent her a pleading look. "I'm scared to die," she said. "But maybe it's better this way. Please, just, get it over with. I'm in so much pain." She sent a wild glance General Dracul's way, and Myreen got the impression that she'd been in the military's custody for some time. If she was even real. Would a real vampire beg to die? Myreen's head felt dizzy trying to determine what was real and what was not.

Her shoulders slumped as General Dracul grinned, placing something in his ears—the plugs he'd been talking about, she assumed. She looked back to the vampire, who nodded at her, a resolute look in the young woman's eyes. Or whatever age she was.

This was wrong. Myreen felt that on so many levels, but she

couldn't see any other way out. She had no idea what lengths General Dracul would go through to get her to obey him, and she didn't want to find out. At least the vampire was willing to die. Not that it made this feel any better.

Myreen closed her eyes as tears welled in them. She didn't know this woman or what she'd done, assuming she actually was real. Maybe she was a horrible person deserving of death, maybe not, but she wanted to die. Or Eduard wanted Myreen to think she wanted to die.

Vampires killed my mom and attacked me and my friends in the alley, she reminded herself. She had every right to hate vampires as a whole.

Holding onto those tiny kernels, Myreen called on her siren voice. "It is your time to die," she said, her voice not her own, the musical timbre vibrating through her bones. She didn't know if it was enough, but it was the best she could manage considering the situation.

The vampire screamed as she thrashed against her bonds, but Myreen refused to open her eyes. She couldn't watch, couldn't bring herself to face what she'd just ordered. There was a shuffling sound behind the vampire, and then movement, something wild and *unrestrained* caught Myreen's ears.

Fear drove her eyes open. The vampire stood free of her bonds, her hands on either side of her head. And she was pulling.

At the last second, Myreen squeezed her eyes shut again. There was a sickening pop, and then two thuds and a soft rolling sound.

Myreen thought she was going to be sick.

General Dracul laughed. "Very good, Myreen. Very good. Guards, take her back to her room and keep watch on her at all times. I want everyone caring for her wearing their earplugs. No exceptions. Understood?"

"Yes sir," came two male voices.

The swish of fabric and clack of heels met Myreen's ears, and then she was being untied from the chair—though her hands were still bound—and led away. She tried to keep her eyes closed, but she had to know if it was real or not.

She glanced over her shoulder as she was led from the simulation room. The body and head were still there, the vacant eyes staring at Myreen as if accusing her.

It had been real.

You've got to be kidding me.

Bile rose in her throat once more, and she swallowed against it.

Someone had died by her doing. A stranger who, good or bad, probably had people who cared about her, people who would mourn her. A stranger who'd had a future, and now was nothing but a memory. The death hadn't even been quick and merciful, but gruesome and undoubtedly painful beyond measure. She'd done that, just as sure as if she'd been the one to pull off that vampire's head.

She was officially a murderer. No better than the vampires who'd killed her mom. No better than the general himself. Some hero she was turning out to be.

She seethed as she caught sight of General Dracul, standing over the body as if inspecting a new car. His cruelty was beyond measure. Oberon's warning rang in her head—*Do not trust Eduard Dracul.*

Well, she wouldn't trust General Dracul, and as soon as she had the chance, she'd leave this wretched school and never come back.

Leif

Leif was exhausted—which he was particularly unused to. His modified handcuffs dug into his wrists, keeping him weak and tired. He sat on a wooden chair with royal purple upholstery. Like everything else in the room, it belonged to Beatrice.

Fortunately, it was daytime, and since Beatrice was the most skilled at combat among the vampires, she was off training newly turned vampires how to best use their new abilities. Or, at least that's what Leif thought she'd said before leaving.

The taste of fresh blood still sat in his mouth. A few hours ago, Beatrice brought a couple of Initiates to drink from. Leif hated it, but he'd greedily drank from a willing male. His weakened state seemed to magnify his thirst. Blood at least brought some sort of pleasure to his tortured existence.

He'd been locked up for—he double checked the set of scratch marks in the desk next to him—five days. But it felt like an eternity.

Beatrice had been a far more merciful torturer than Draven. In fact, a lot of her old charm had resurfaced. There were times she even spoke in the older, proper English of the late 1800s. It almost felt like they'd been transported back in time one hundred years.

Almost.

But Camilla wasn't there, coming in for their beloved late night conversations. Mr. Frost wasn't around to talk about the orchards.

But the worst part was the lack of Gemma. Beatrice had taken her brooch from him, too.

Leif had weakly tried to stop her, but he was no match for her dominance. And now he didn't even have the comfort of that piece of his fiancé.

He used to hear her voice in his head, back when the world was simpler. At least, he liked to think it was her voice. But with all the noises that had come ever since Draven had recruited him, she'd been mostly silent.

"Gemma, how I miss you," he said. A stray tear formed at his eye, and he didn't have the strength to reach up and flick it away. Instead, it trailed down his pale cheek, clinging to his lower jaw, and then splashed down onto the shackles holding his hands in place.

He looked at the cruel needles jabbed into his wrists. They'd been made to subdue Draven's enemies. Well, the secret was out: Leif *was* an enemy. To himself, most of all.

All hope was gone.

A soft scratching noise came from the closed window and pulled him from his dark thoughts. Leif lifted his head, and the effort to do so almost broke him.

Though the room was dark, his vampire eyes easily cut through it. Beatrice's long, purple couch sat right against the large, covered window. Although it was sealed off, Beatrice had strung long, flowing silver curtains around it, framing it in elegance.

More scratching sounded from behind the metal covering the window, and Leif gritted his teeth as he attempted to get to his feet. His legs shook at the effort, then gave out. Leif found himself sprawled upon a fine purple-and-silver woven rug. Having fallen face-first, his nose had cracked upon impact—the rug had done very little to protect it from the hard stone floor beneath.

With difficulty, he pushed himself onto his knees. He waited for his nose to heal itself, and it took a painfully long time. He felt the sluggish cracking and popping as his nose set back into its proper place.

The scratching came again, this time more rapid, as if whatever was on the other side was growing eager to enter. Leif didn't care what was on the other side, be it friend or foe, or some random little critter. At least he wouldn't be alone.

Will trumped exhaustion, and he forced himself forward like a wiggling worm on dry soil.

He kept his head down as he dragged his legs behind him, and before long, Leif bumped his head on the couch.

Inhaling heavily, he placed his elbows on the soft, deep purple cushions and levered himself up. He lifted his knees up one at a time, and the effort nearly made him fall backward. He balanced himself with his hands on the top of the back part of the couch.

The scratching was loudest just in front of him. He reached up for an ancient locking mechanism that kept the metal slate in place.

His shackles clanked as his arms shook while grabbing the horizontal lock.

Leif cursed under his breath. “Accosted things.”

Taking a few more breaths, he used what little strength he could muster to try to pry the lock up. It didn’t budge, not even a little.

He let himself fall back onto the couch in disappointment. For so long, he’d taken his superhuman strength for granted.

Laying back, he looked up at the stuck window again, and noticed the scratching had stopped. He’d failed whatever was on the other side. Not that it mattered. Nobody knew about his imprisonment. Nobody was coming for him.

And then a deep, crashing reverberation sounded like bells chiming in his ears.

The ringing continued, slowly tapering off like a glass being clanked by a knife.

“What was that?” he muttered.

And then the clanging noise boomed again, followed by the screeching of metal on metal. Sunlight streamed in, brightening the room with regal brilliance. Leif had to admit that Beatrice had a knack for interior design. The place looked fit for a queen.

His mind was slow on the uptake. He was seeing everything so well because the window had opened. And it hadn’t just been opened; the metal cover had been entirely ripped off. If that wasn’t surprise enough, Leif stared in wonder as a certain gray cat appeared at the window ledge and looked down at him with red eyes.

"Rainbow?" Leif muttered, wondering if his mind was playing tricks on him. His cat had torn away the metal window cover?

But Rainbow leapt from the window sill and landed on the top of the couch, then stepped down onto Leif's chest. His mind hadn't been playing tricks on him.

Leif lifted his bound hands and petted his vampire cat behind the ears.

"You followed me?" he said with wonder. The cat's senses must have been enhanced by its vampiric abilities. Leif marveled that Rainbow had made such a journey and had actually been able to find him.

In reply, Rainbow rubbed his head against Leif's arms and purred, his voice hitting that perfect Middle C timbre.

Leif wasn't alone anymore.

But if Beatrice came back and saw the cat, she'd kill it in a hurry.

"It's not safe for you here," he said.

If Rainbow understood him, the cat made no sign of it. For the time being, Leif didn't care. He was grateful to have the cat with him, however odd it was.

Time passed, and Leif remained on the couch, closing his eyes and stroking at Rainbow's fur. He felt empowered not being alone anymore.

While he could tolerate the sunlight just fine, he typically didn't care for it. Right now, though, it was a breath of fresh air. It brought Leif serenity in his weakened state. Mixed with the coming of Rainbow, it was a sign of hope. He closed his eyes and took in the moment of peace.

Leif.

His eyes flew open.

"Gemma?" he muttered. Her voice sounded vivid, as if she were there in the room.

You win two out of five points for at least being in the right family.

Leif's mind reeled. The same family? And what good was said point system? The blasted copper flowing into his body made it impossible to think.

"Who is this?" he asked, still speaking out loud. Vocalizing the words made it a little easier to focus.

It's Kenzie. You know, the girl with your grimoire? Remember me?

Leif furrowed his brow. "Kenzie? You're here?"

Um, I'm here in your head.

Ah yes, she was using her magic to reach out to him. He couldn't remember the last time she'd used her selkie abilities to communicate—much of their latest conversations had been over the phone or in person. Maybe she'd tried texting or calling him? He hoped not. Beatrice was in possession of his phone.

Hey, are you there? she asked.

"Yeah," he groaned. "Just spacey, is all."

Yeah. I hadn't noticed.

Normally, Leif would have replied with something just as sarcastic, but his mind couldn't formulate a counter.

Anyway, I haven't heard from you since before Christmas and thought I'd check up on you. I also have some good news.

Kenzie's words were crystal clear, and his heart pushed against the poisonous copper afflicting his body and mind.

"Did you find the spell?" he asked, a jolt of excitement spreading through his limbs, reinvigorating them and causing him to sit upright. Rainbow circled in his lap, then perched, staring at him curiously with red eyes.

Slow down there, eager beaver. First off, I need you to tell me Gemma's last name.

The question was an odd one.

"MacLugh," he replied. "Why do you ask?"

This time, Kenzie didn't immediately respond.

"Kenzie?"

Okay, so you know Gemma's grimoire?

"Of course," he said.

Apparently, she's a relative of mine, Kenzie said. *This is our family grimoire, the same one that was lost long ago. The story is that you killed its owner and took it.*

Her tone felt almost accusatory, and a fiery defensiveness welled within Leif.

"Aline Dracul killed your ancestor," he said. "I helplessly witnessed Gemma's murder with my own eyes and was nearly killed in the process. Whoever claimed that I was responsible for her death has mocked my pain. I loved Gemma more than anything in this world."

A few moments passed before Kenzie replied.

That actually makes a lot of sense. And it didn't sound like you. But I had to ask. Just in case... But I believe you.

He felt another shot of minuscule copper inject into his wrists, and it instantly clouded his mind, like an oily hand pressing on clean glass.

"I... I can't think," he mumbled, easing himself back into a laying position on the couch.

You can't think? Leif, is something wrong?

Leif moaned. "Trapped."

...Trapped? You're trapped?

Leif closed his eyes, wishing that darkness would come, rather than just toy with him.

"I got caught."

Leif! Where are you? In Chicago?

She seemed so distant, as if her voice was coming from a dream.

Stay with me. Are you in Chicago?

"No," he moaned. "In Beatrice's quarters. I'm... her prisoner."

Beatrice? Who's Beatrice?

The response bounced around his head faster than he could focus on it. The words eluded him.

Okay, let's try the yes-or-no game. Are you at the vampire school? In Washington?

Leif nodded slowly, disregarding the fact that Kenzie wasn't actually present to see the motion. "Yes."

Are they hurting you?

"Yes."

Well, crap. I'm assuming you can't escape on your own.

Leif shook his head. "No. I'm... they found me... traitor... Draven... Beatrice..." The words made sense in his head, but he could tell they came out wrong.

Okay, okay, I get the gist. Thanks to you, we've got the grimoire back now, and I finally unlocked it. Congratulations, you've earned yourself one selkie fairy godmother. I'm breaking you out.

"No!" Leif shouted. "Dangers... everywhere. Death."

Yeah, yeah, big, bad vampires and all. Yada, yada, yada. I'm not leaving you to rot. You can't... She hesitated for a second

Just... stay alive, okay?

"Yes," Leif replied lazily.

Good. See you soon.

The voice departed, and Leif was left to swim alone with his thoughts.

Kenzie was coming. She'd found a way to unlock the grimoire's sealed pages. She was related to Gemma. That explained a lot. And the way she'd spoken to him, being adamant about coming to rescue him... she reminded him so much of Gemma.

Renewed hope pushed against the venomous cloud swirling around his mind. Perhaps a portion of Gemma lived within Kenzie. Maybe they weren't so different after all. Was there something between them? Something for him to explore?

Confusion overshadowed the hope he was feeling, and his thoughts slowly came to a stop, leaving him feeling gray and empty. It all took too much effort. All he really wanted was to fall into nothingness, at least for a while.

Kenzie

Kenzie sat at the dinner table, smiling at a conversation she didn't hear, chewing on a beef stew she didn't taste. Her conversation with Leif kept replaying in her mind. He was in trouble, and she was determined to rescue him.

Maybe she was a fool for it.

But she really did believe his version of events regarding the grimoire. And he didn't sound like he was in any condition to lie about anything. Which was perhaps the most worrisome part.

More than anything, though, the moment she heard his voice, the same attraction she'd been trying to avoid rushed back. She didn't know what there was between her and Leif, but she was darned if she'd let him die before she had a chance to find out. Besides, he was a vampire. He wasn't supposed to die at all.

But facing the vampire leader and his cronies at that school had her stomach in knots. How was she going to get in? Or get

Leif out? She'd need her magic. Something in that book had to be helpful, but Mom and Gram had it locked up tighter than Fort Knox ever since breaking Kol's curse. Figured.

But she had a plan. Sort of. She just had to get Gram or Mom to take the grimoire out, and she could perform the hiding spell on it when they weren't looking. Once they were asleep, she'd grab the book and escape to rescue Leif.

After that, though, things got a little sketchy. And she worried about just how long it would take to get that book out. Leif was suffering, and though he hadn't been in any condition to elaborate, it still killed her to think what he was going through. Her mind was quick to supply the details he'd been unable to.

She had to get him out. Then, maybe she'd give him a good magical slap upside the head. Maybe.

"Kenzie, did you hear me?" Gram asked.

"Huh?" Kenzie replied, sitting up straighter as she focused. "Sorry. My mind must have wandered off."

"I asked if you've heard from that Kol fella? How are he and Myreen doing?"

Kenzie shrugged. "Dunno. Hopefully no news is good news. Like maybe they're so busy kissing their faces off they can't be bothered to send a message." She tried to play it off, but the radio silence was killing her. She'd even messaged Myreen to probe for info, and still nothing.

Now she knew why Kol's family was cursed. She supposed she should be mad with him, but she couldn't fault the guy. It wasn't like *he'd* killed her ancestor, and that kind of magical punishment sure didn't fit the crime. One day, she'd like to hear the whole story—yet another reason to break Leif out of his prison.

Gram snorted. "Yeah, like they're just kissing."

Kenzie blushed. "Gram!"

"What? Like I haven't been young and in love before. Ha! Speaking of kissing," Gram said, turning her attention to Mom, "what's this I hear about you and the clerk from the Health and Wellness store?"

It was Mom's turn to redden. "Oh, Mom, it's nothing. We talk. He's nice."

Kenzie leaned forward, smirking. "Really? When did you start talking to guys?"

"That's none of your concern," Mom said. "And I talk to guys."

Kenzie leaned back in her chair, raising a brow. "Yeah, for work."

Mom lowered her full spoon. "And I speak to Roger for work, too."

"Oooh, on a first name basis, are we?" Kenzie teased.

"Lita and Roger, sitting in a tree," Gram sang.

Mom rolled her eyes. "Honestly. I'm surrounded by children."

"Join the dark side," Kenzie said, deepening her voice for effect.

Mom laughed, shaking her head. "*Some*one has to be an adult around here."

There was a knock at the door, and all three ladies stopped to look at each other.

"I wonder who that could be?" Mom asked, her brows crinkling.

Kenzie shook her head. "I can't imagine." She hopped up

and went for the door, hoping for a little news. Or maybe a package. That could be fun.

What she saw was the last thing she expected.

Wes slumped against the frame, propping the storm door open.

Kenzie frowned. Was this his version of a drunk dial? She hadn't had much time to spare him any thought since their breakup, but she couldn't quite forget his confession that he was a hunter—or the rack of guns she'd seen in his apartment.

"What are you doing here, Wes?" Kenzie asked, folding her arms.

All chatter had ceased from inside the house, and Kenzie could practically feel Mom and Gram straining to hear the conversation.

"I didn't know where else to go. I'm sorry." Wes finally looked at her, his pained expression turning her anger into alarm. There were long, scabbed-over slashes on his cheek where something had ripped into him, and she suddenly realized that his pants and shirt were dirty and tattered. But the most alarming sight was what looked like a deep bite on his calf—visible through the punctures in the material left by whatever had attacked him. Her mind immediately turned to Rainbow, though these marks were clearly larger than that of a house cat, even one as big as him.

"Wes, what attacked you?" Kenzie asked slowly, breaking out in goosebumps.

"A mao," he replied, his voice soft and strained. And that's when she noticed the sheen of sweat on his forehead—odd for this chilly time of year—and the pallor of his skin.

He collapsed at the same time as utensils clattered onto

plates, and Mom and Gram rushed to the front door. Kenzie did her best to catch Wes, practically diving under him to keep him from face-planting. The storm door banged against Wes's body before Gram had a chance to push it back open. Mom helped Kenzie drag Wes into their office, and Gram cast a wary eye around the neighborhood before locking up.

"Is Wes from that shifter school too?" Mom asked as they laid him out on the love seat tucked into a corner of the office. His legs hung off the end, and his head lolled to the side until Gram could find a pillow to prop it with.

Kenzie avoided eye contact and kept her voice low. "He's not from the school. He's a hunter. Or was, I guess."

"A hunter!" Mom practically shouted, then brought her voice back down. "Kenzie Renee MacLugh, are you out of your mind?"

"I didn't know he was a hunter at first. I broke it off with him as soon as I found out."

"Was this before or after you brought him to this house and accepted his phone?"

"I found out that day, just before— But he promised not to hurt me or my family."

"We can't keep him here," Gram said.

"He was bitten by a mao, Gram. Where can he go?"

Mom shook her head. "We'll patch him up and help him with his first shift, but then he's got to go."

Kenzie nodded. "Yeah, of course. It's not like I'd expect you to move him in or anything."

"Speaking of, we need to lay down a few ground rules about your interactions with him."

"Mom, he's lying unconscious on a couch. I don't think I

can get into that much trouble."

"He's a were going through a first shift. He's going to heal quicker than you might think, and then he's going to be more emotional than you can imagine. I don't want him marking you as his territory."

Kenzie rolled her eyes. "Mom! First off, ew, and second, I don't think you have anything to worry about."

Mom crossed her arms and eyed Kenzie. "We'll have a little chat again once Wes wakes up."

Kenzie let her head drop, but nodded. There was no way this situation would *not* be embarrassing. And Wes's confession that day she found out he was a hunter made her doubt her own words of reassurance. If he really did love her, how would that affect things as he moved toward his first shift? She couldn't deny the possibility was both frightening and strangely thrilling. Of course, there was no way to know if he still loved her. There was a good chance he hated her by now. Maybe.

She was so caught up with Wes that she almost didn't realize Gram had pulled out the grimoire. "Let's aid his healing with a little magic, shall we?"

Kenzie gave Gram a grateful smile. "I can take it from here."

Mom shook her head. "No. We'll all heal him together. Ready, Ma?"

Gram nodded her head.

The ladies all laid a hand on Wes, Kenzie by his foot, Mom and Gram taking his chest and head. Gram had set the book on the old music stand in the corner. "Leasheth'asa," Gram said, nodding at Kenzie and Mom, who repeated the spell one at a time.

Kenzie could feel the warmth of her magic passing through

her hand and into Wes, the scabs falling off, leaving crinkly, too-pink skin behind. The warm fuzzy feeling that using her magic created nearly always brought a smile, but this time she still felt so sad.

Wes's ragged breathing evened out as the healing took root. Kenzie wanted to trace the scars on his face, wanted to hold him until he looked at her with those granola brown eyes of his again and assured her he was okay. Her fingers certainly lingered over the bite on his leg, and she idly wondered how he'd gotten it. She was surprised—and a little annoyed—to realize just how much she'd missed him.

After her talk with Juliet, she'd thought she left her guy troubles behind. Well, most of them, anyway. But Wes coming back into her life—as a werecat, no less—just made things a lot more complicated. *Figures.*

Gram groaned as she stood back up, then brushed off her hands. "Nature's calling. I'll be right back."

Mom nodded, but didn't look Gram's way as she tried again to make Wes comfortable. Or at least look comfortable. That couch was way too small for his nearly six-foot frame, and his head kept rolling away from the pillow.

Kenzie eyed the room, suddenly aware the grimoire was unattended. "Coinnash i fholacha," she whispered under her breath, keeping her gaze on the book. In a blink it was gone. She quietly slipped to the cabinet and closed the door, praying Wes's distraction would be enough.

"Kenzie? Do you mind helping me with Wes?" Mom asked. "I'm going to move him to the couch in the living room."

Kenzie spun around, trying to calm her startled expression. "Yeah. Sure. You sure you want to take him in there?"

"We're cautious, not animals. And this love seat is just not working."

"Of course."

Kenzie helped her mom as they half-carried, half-dragged him to the living room couch. Both women were a bit out of breath by the time they arrived. Gram, who was just returning, lent a hand as well, and between the three of them, they managed to get him up on the old tan couch—which had probably been nearly white at some point in its long life. At least Wes looked a little more comfortable.

Mom went back to the office, and Kenzie followed her in.

"Hey, did you see Gram put the grimoire away?" Mom asked, scratching her head.

"Yeah, I think so," Kenzie said, then began chewing on her lower lip.

"Come on. Let's finish eating. Wes will be fine for now."

"Right."

Mom left, but Kenzie stayed a moment longer, staring at the love seat. What a mess this all was. Her appetite didn't look likely to come back for a while.

Gram poked her head in. "You should eat."

Kenzie shrugged.

Gram came in and put an arm around Kenzie's shoulders, drawing her into a warm side-hug. "It's going to be all right, Kitten."

Kenzie nodded, though she couldn't see how. She had so much on her plate with Leif, and now Wes, and she hated that she had to revert to secrecy because of it.

Yeah, this was a royal mess.

"Oh, did your mom put the grimoire away?" Gram asked.

Kenzie put on her most convincing smile. "I think so."

"Very good. Now come. Your food's getting cold."

Kenzie nodded. At least she'd managed to hide the grimoire. For now. But she'd need to leave with it before they figured out what she was up to. And she still had Wes to deal with.

Kenzie rejoined the table, looking at Gram and Mom. If anyone could handle the werecat's first shift, it was probably them, but she still worried about their safety.

She took a bite of her food—which had definitely gone cold, though it didn't much change the flavor in her current state of disinterest—and snuck a glance at Wes. He looked almost peaceful now, the color coming back to his face, which was still handsome despite the scars forming. Or maybe more handsome because of them. *I'm hopeless,* she chided herself.

Yeah, she was a magnet for supernaturals. For better or worse, she kind of liked it.

Hopefully, they wouldn't be the death of her.

Chapter 60

Myreen

It was the screams that woke her.

At first, they sounded so far away, Myreen thought they were a dream. She was so bone-deep tired and emotionally exhausted from the events of the past few days that she wanted to continue sleeping, even through the threat of a nightmare.

Something inside her triggered and her eyes snapped open.

The distant screams still sounded beyond the walls, punctuated by an echoing boom every now and then. Just outside her bedroom door, students were throwing their words at each other in haste, their feet scampering up and down the halls.

Her eyes found the clock, flashing in bright red numbers that it was just after midnight.

What the heck is going on?

She slid out of bed and hurried into her uniform—smart

clothing and all—before venturing out the door. The guards that had been assigned to watch her were strangely absent. She was briefly thrilled by the freedom it gave her, until a flock of harpy girls ran past her crying, looking scared out of their wits, before they disappeared into a room. In the common room, more students were openly weeping as they clung to each other, while others rushed out of their rooms still in their pajamas.

"Myreen!" Juliet's voice startled her as she was suddenly at her side.

"What's happening?" Myreen asked.

"I was going to ask you the same thing," Juliet said, looking over the mayhem before them. "You'd think the sky was falling or something."

"It's okay, they can't get through," Myreen overheard one of the dragon boys saying to the harpy girl he was attempting to soothe on one of the couches. It was Shawn, the guy Kol had sparred with that night he got injured, the night she healed him, the night she...

She blinked the memory away and went up to them. "What's going on out there? Who can't get through?"

The boy looked up at her. "Vampires. They're attacking the Dome."

"*What?*" Myreen gasped. An icy chill shot through her chest and rippled through her entire body.

She and Juliet exchanged panicked glances before sprinting out of the avian common room. The Grand Hall beyond was a zoo. Students stampeded through each other in a frenzy, some trying to escape the horrors of outside, and others trying to get outside to witness the attack for themselves.

Myreen and Juliet pushed through the hoard, hugging the

walls as a sort of shortcut. Finally, after being battered and bruised by countless shoulders and elbows, they made it through the main doors.

What she saw left her frozen in place.

Above their heads, white-faced wraiths rammed down on the Dome from the water that surrounded it, illuminated in flashes by the ultraviolet beams that blasted whenever they got too close. The beams burned the vampires even in water, but that didn't keep them from slamming into the thick glass in attempts to break it. Every now and then, some sort of projectile weapon fired at the glass from those hiding in the shadows.

A little voice inside Myreen's head tried to assure her that the glass couldn't be broken, not from the vampires diving at it. They were going to be fine. The morning sun would shine through the water and scare them away.

But every time the ultraviolet beams flashed, telltale spider veins in the glass caught the light, and they were spreading.

"Get out there!" General Dracul's voice barked across the campus. "Fend them off the best you can."

Myreen turned to see a fleet of the oldest mer students and graduates running toward the secret lake outlet to follow the general's orders. They were dressed in thick, water-resistant Kevlar smart tops, strapped with weapons that Myreen hadn't seen before.

Fear tightened every muscle in her body—fear that the glass would shatter, that everyone she cared for would drown in the flood or be slaughtered by the bloodthirsty monsters that waited outside.

"Miss Fairchild," the general's voice boomed as he approached.

“I need to be out there,” she declared, lifting her foot to follow the other mer.

“The hell you do,” he barked, planting a firm hand on her shoulder and keeping her from moving. “You’re the reason they’re here.”

She turned to face him, her fear turning into anger. “That’s exactly why I need to help. I won’t just stand idly by down here while people die for me out there.”

“Yes, you will. The future of all shifterkind depends on you staying safe from those monsters. You are duty-bound to let others make the sacrifices right now.”

“That’s bull—”

“Sir, let me take her out of the school.” The all-too familiar voice sliced through her heart with a bittersweet sting. Kol stepped into view, looking his father straight in the eye with all the confidence of the prince he was.

The corner of General Dracul’s lip twitched with slight amusement. He crossed his arms over his chest and looked down his nose at his son. “And why would I do that?”

“She’s not safe here,” Kol argued. “If they keep blasting at the glass, the Dome will give, and she’ll be a sitting duck. Sneaking her off campus is our best option.”

“How do you know they’re not waiting for her at the end of the subway?” Juliet snapped, fiery as ever.

“Indeed they are,” the general said. “Our soldiers are fighting them as we speak.”

Myreen’s heart thudded at that news. They really were trapped.

“But there’s another way out,” Kol intimated, looking only at Juliet as he spoke and avoiding eye contact with Myreen. “A secret tunnel along the subway line. For emergencies." He turned back to his father. "And this is an emergency."

The general shrugged. "Why should I trust you with such valuable cargo? You're clearly in love with the girl." He shook his head and made *tsk*ing sounds. "And I thought you knew better."

Myreen gasped at the general's accusation, her eyes fixed on Kol.

Kol looked down, then sheepishly turned vulnerable amber eyes on Myreen. She could see the truth of that statement inside their honeyed depths, and she didn't know how to feel about that.

"That's why I'm the perfect person for the job," Kol declared, meeting his father's eyes once more. "Because I'll do everything in my power to protect her."

Another boom shook the ground, deepening the general's frown and prickling the thick black hair on the back of Kol's neck. But neither of them broke from the staring contest they were having.

"Very well," the general sighed. "I'll send the Candida boy and a few others with you."

"No!" Myreen shouted, cutting into the discussion they were having about her life without her. "I'm not leaving."

Kol cast pleading eyes in her direction. "Myreen, please." He lifted a hand toward her.

She stepped backward. "I said no, Malkolm Dracul."

He looked at her for a moment, biting his lip as if debating something. "Well, you already hate me." Then he swooped down, picked her up around the waist, and threw her over his shoulder.

"Put me down this instant!" she yelled, slamming her fists

against his back as he carried her toward the main building.

"Let her go, Kol, or I'll be forced to unleash my fire on you," Juliet threatened, quick on his heels.

"I'm a dragon, I'll survive," Kol dismissed. "But you might burn your friend."

Juliet clenched her fists and pursed her lips, her face turning red.

Myreen didn't want to resort to it, but she wasn't going to let Kol take her away while everyone else suffered for her.

"Stop," she ordered with her siren voice.

Instantly, Kol stopped walking, standing in place just feet away from the main doors.

"Put me down." Even in her siren voice, she enunciated each word clearly, injecting the force of her will into every syllable.

Like the robot she always accused him of being, he set her down on her feet, a vacant look in the eyes she hated to love so much.

Before she knew what was happening, a hand struck her across the face, the force of it knocking her to the ground. Juliet tried to catch her, then clung to her protectively while Myreen tried to recover from the blow.

"How dare you use your siren powers on my son." The general towered over her, the shadow he cast darker than the murky waters outside the glass. The fury in his eyes was truly terrifying, and right now it was aimed at her. "Is that how you did it? Is that how you tricked him into falling in love with you?"

Behind him, Kol blinked hard several times and shook off the spell, horror and anger twisting his face as he saw what was happening.

He stormed toward his dad. "Father! What the—?"

"Attention Dome students and faculty," a smooth, dark voice spoke over the intercom. Though Myreen had only heard it once before, she knew without a doubt who it belonged to.

Draven.

Everyone under the Dome froze and looked off, giving their full attention to the words they heard.

"It is not our intention to kill you all tonight. We are here for one reason and one reason only. You have something that belongs to me, and I want it back. If you hand over Myreen Fairchild, the attack will cease, and we'll leave you in peace. For now. Refuse this request, and we'll slaughter each and every one of you. Is that something you want on your conscience, Myreen?"

The intercom turned off, and slowly all the faces of those around turned to her. Several students who'd been inside the main building flooded out the doors, filling the silent Dome with their whispers.

She could see the heads of Trish, Alessandra, and Joanna floating in the crowd, staring at her with fear in their eyes. Trish kept her mouth shut, and Alessandra's brows were creased in indecision.

It was Joanna who finally pushed through the crowd and spoke out against her. "What are we waiting for? Give her to them."

"Yeah, she's the one they want," a phoenix girl said.

"She's been nothing but trouble since she got here."

"She destroyed the greenhouse."

"She attacked Alessandra."

"No, she didn't," Alessandra defended.

Myreen had thought she was immune to the denigration of her fellow classmates by now, but seeing how quickly they were willing to sell her out stung like a sword to the belly.

"What is wrong with you people?" Kol put himself between the mob of frightened students and Myreen. "You would sacrifice an innocent girl for your own safety?"

"She's not innocent," someone called out.

"She's been in league with them from the start!" another shouted.

"You're all idiots!" Juliet roared, planting herself beside Kol. "Myreen is the sweetest person at this godforsaken school, and you've never given her a chance."

"A chance to what, turn on us?" Joanna retorted.

The general stepped forward. "Myreen stays and that's final. The simple fact is that her life is worth more than any of yours. She's the best chance we have against the vampires."

"Then let her go out there and fight them," someone yelled.

She wanted to. She looked up to the lake beyond the Dome and saw the mer battling the vampires. Some shot guns with special bullets that left trails of green all through the faces and arms of the vampires they hit. Some were the recipients of bullets fired by the vampires. Other shifters were locked in a morbid dance for survival, many of them losing and getting their throats bitten. All around the Dome, the water was stained with blood, flashing red every time the beams lit.

She wanted to go out there and fight. The prophecy said she was destined to end this war. She could go into the water and use all the skills she'd learned, all the techniques Oberon, Delphine and Ms. Heather had taught her.

She might be able to take out a few handfuls of vampires, if she got lucky. There was no way she could kill them all. Whatever the prophecy said, it couldn't have meant this moment. If she went out into the fight, she would ultimately lose, and many would still die. It would all be in vain.

Another boom rocked the Dome, and this time a long crack spiked through the outer layer of glass at the top. The crowd in front of her continued to argue. It was only a matter of time before the vampires got through and killed them all. As much as she hated to admit it, she cared very much for Kol's safety, maybe even more so than Juliet's. Surely more than her own.

There was only one course of action she could take.

Goodbye, friends.

As Kol, Juliet and the general had their backs turned to her while they yelled at the mob, she snuck around them as fast as she could, rushing toward the escape hatch that led into the lake. The last time she'd gone into this small dark room had been with Kendall. She let the memory of their last swim together fill her mind and distract her as she stripped down to her smart clothes and dropped into the water, surrendering to the transformation.

Her heart pounded a war cadence as she swam upward. One of the attacking vampires saw her and dove toward her, then stopped short, recognizing who she was. She sent a current through the water toward him nonetheless, blasting him away from her. Then she willed a sphere to form around her, a constantly spinning orb of pure current that would protect her should one of them get any ideas.

"Draven," she called out, manipulating the water to carry her voice. "I have accepted your terms. I will go with you, but first, you must send your vamps away, or the deal's off."

The pale bodies floated around her, waiting, the water still and silent as death.

At last, they began to ascend, swimming toward the surface with their weapons, letting the bodies of the mer they defeated sink into the depths.

She stayed in place, wanting to make sure that no vampire stayed behind. If Draven broke his word and sent them back, as she expected, she would fight to the death for her friends.

The water around the Dome was empty and dark. They really had gone.

Except for one.

A figure swam toward her from the shadows. She tensed from the top of her scalp to the tips of her toes, preparing to fight. As the murk cleared and the figure became clearer, she instantly recognized the face behind the diving mask.

"You made the right choice," Draven said. "It's time to come home, my child."

She swallowed, the water in her throat rendering the gesture useless. "How do I know you won't send your people back to the Dome once I'm gone?"

Draven waved his hands through the water. "You don't. But I give you my word—as the father who's been searching for you all your life—that I do not wish to kill your friends tonight. I have plans for them. Plans for you."

The loving father bit felt like a lie, like sickly-sweet sugar poured into the water she inhaled. She couldn't stand that she was the daughter of this monster, but she believed the rest. "Alright."

Even though his face was covered by the diving mask, she could sense his smile. "Now, come home." He put out a hand of welcome.

She took one last look down at the Dome. On the grass, Kol was being held back by students as he tried to get to the escape hatch to stop her. He looked up at her as she looked down at him, their eyes meeting for one last moment. His mouth shouted words she didn't hear, but his eyes begged her not to go, to turn around and go back inside.

She closed her eyes and turned away from him. Without any further hesitation, she took Draven's hand and let him guide her to the surface. She didn't know what awaited her up there, but at least Kol and Juliet—and all her classmates who were probably glad to be rid of her—would be safe.

So much for prophecies and fairytales.

ABOUT THE SHIFTER ACADEMY AUTHORS

This series is the brain child of 5 award-winning and *USA Today* best-selling paranormal romance and urban fantasy authors. For the Siren Prophecy Series, each character was brought to life by a different author. For the remainder of the ongoing Shifter Academy series, a new book will release every six weeks by one or more of the authors, as there are just too many stories to tell in this amazing shifter world. Engage more with the Shifter Academy world at: www.theShifterAcademy.com

Myreen was written by Tricia Barr. Follow Tricia's work here: www.tricia-barr.com

Oberon & Leif were written by Jesse Booth. Follow Jesse's work here: http://www.authorjessebooth.com

Kol was written by Joanna Reeder. Follow Joanna's work here: http://www.joannareeder.com

Kenzie was written by Angel Leya. Follow Angel's work here: http://www.angeleya.com

Juliet was written by Alessandra Jay. Follow Alessandra's work here: http://www.facebook.com/AuthorAlessandraJay/